W9-ATB-752

TAKE A MAGIC RIDE—

At the moment the first horse allowed the first human to mount and ride, a magical partnership began. Suddenly, previously unexplored lands were within reach, and the conquest of the unknown was carried forward at the gallop. Now let sixteen of today's finest fantasy writers spin such fast-paced tales of sorcery and splendor as:

"The Phantom Watch"—Betrayed by a wizard's spell she must turn to the fair's ghostly guardian to save her horses. But are even such splendid horses worth the price her savior demands in payment?

"Classical Horses"—Drawn by the beauty of a herd of Lippizaner horses, she volunteered to help the old woman care for them, little suspecting the magnitude of the task she was undertaking. . . .

"When Lightning Strikes"—It was rumored that the statue of the horse was a creation of magic. But it was not until her own life was threatened that she learned the truth about the power locked in stone. . . .

These are just a few of the thoroughbreds and their owners who make their homes in enchanted realms where the pastures are always green and both the herds and the human imagination can roam freely.

HORSE FANTASTIC

Other imagination-capturing anthologies from DAW Books:

CATFANTASTIC *Edited by Andre Norton and Martin H. Greenberg.* For cat lovers everywhere, a unique collection of fantastical cat tales, some set in the distant future on as yet unknown worlds, some set in our own world but not quite our own dimension, some recounting what happens when beings from the ancient past and creatures out of myth collide with modern-day felines.

CAT FANTASTIC II *Edited by Andre Norton and Martin H. Greenberg.* An all-new collection of fantasy's most original cat tales! Join such memorable cats as: Bomber, the ship's cat out for revenge on the German warship, *The Bismarck*; Graywhiskers, who ruled his kingdom with a weapon of his own creation; and Hermione, who protected her astronomer not from falling stars but from unexpected dangers lurking in his own home.

THE NIGHT FANTASTIC *Edited by Poul and Karen Anderson.* Let Poul Anderson, Ursula K. Le Guin, Isaac Asimov, Alan Dean Foster, Robert Silverberg, Fritz Leiber, and a host of other fantasy masters carry you away to magical realms where night becomes day as the waking world sleeps and sleeping worlds wake.

HORSE FANTASTIC

EDITED BY
MARTIN H. GREENBERG &
ROSALIND M. GREENBERG

DAW BOOKS, INC.
DONALD A. WOLLHEIM, FOUNDER
375 Hudson Street, New York, NY 10014

ELIZABETH R. WOLLHEIM
SHEILA E. GILBERT
PUBLISHERS

Introduction: Equus Fantasticus © 1991 by Jennifer Roberson.
Stolen Silver © 1991 by Mercedes Lackey.
Love at First Ride © 1991 by Mickey Zucker Reichert.
Dancer's Fire © 1991 by Josepha Sherman.
The Phantom Watch © 1991 by Charles Ingrid.
The Czechoslovakian Pigeon Farmer and The Pony that Wasn't a
Paint © 1991 by Mary Stanton.
Riding the Nightmare © 1991 by Jennifer Roberson.
When Lightning Strikes © 1991 by Lee Barwood.
Classical Horses © 1991 by Judith Tarr.
One Ten Three © 1991 by Barry N. Malzberg.
No Room for the Unicorn © 1991 by Laura Resnick.
The Horse Boy © 1991 by Mary Stanton.
The Power of Young Girls © 1991 by Constance Ash.
Malish © 1991 by Mike Resnick.
Wings © 1991 by Barbara Delaplace.
The Most Magical Thing About Rachel © 1991 by Nancy Springer.
Dream's Quarry © 1991 by Elizabeth Moon.
Silverdown's Gold © 1991 by Janny Wurts.

DAW Book Collectors No. 866.

First Printing, December 1991

1 2 3 4 5 6 7 8 9

DAW TRADEMARK REGISTERED
U.S. PAT. OFF. AND FOREIGN COUNTRIES
—MARCA REGISTRADA,
HECHO EN U.S.A.
PRINTED IN THE U.S.A.

To our two four-year-olds:
our daughter, Madeline Claire;
and our Trakehner mare, Allyce.

And to our friend, Nyla Naniot,
a fantastic horsewoman.

CONTENTS

INTRODUCTION: EQUUS FANTASTICUS

by Jennifer Roberson

There is magic in a horse. Just ask anyone who's had one.

We grow fat on horses. From childhood we are fed a specialized diet in the guise of stories, poems, and songs, condoning gluttony with the whip-slash of mane and tail, the toss of a flying forelock, the ringing beat of four sound hooves.

Who among us has not longed for a ride on Pegasus, testing wind and cloud; or gloried with Alexander in his beloved Bucephalus, for whom he named a city; or cried tears of joy as magnificent Secretariat made himself immortal in that incredible 31-length victory that won him the Triple Crown?

Horses are and have been everywhere. They abound in the pages of classic literature: Anna Sewell's *Black Beauty* and Mary O'Hara's *My Friend Flicka*, childhood staples both; Walter Farley's "Black Stallion" books, Steinbeck's *The Red Pony*, and Marguerite Henry's *Misty of Chincoteaque*. Even Edgar Allan Poe took his turn in the saddle with the chilling story "Metzengerstein," in which a conjured horse becomes the instrument of a dead enemy's revenge.

In folklore, horses play an invaluable part in the

legend, though often relegated merely to a means of transportation. To those of us insightful enough to comprehend that the horse part of the story was far more interesting and important than the people part, it was fascinating to wonder what Paul Revere's horse thought of his midnight ride, or the Headless Horseman's mount as he undertook his ghostly cross-country journey.

Horses also appear in music. The evocative country-and-western song "Ghostriders in the Sky" tantalized some of us with the image of ghost *horses* rather than the more mundane ghostly riders, and there are simple ballads of such singularly independent mounts as "The Strawberry Roan," a cowboy's lament about a bronc who refused to be ridden.

In some cases, horses are enshrined. Trigger, Roy Rogers' famous palomino, was stuffed and put on display after his death. Others join a cultural phenomenon, the trivia competition, as the subjects of questions such as: Who was Dale Evans' horse? (Buttermilk); Who was the sole survivor on the white man's side of Little Bighorn? (Comanche, a cavalry horse); To whom did actor Lee Marvin dedicate the Oscar awarded for his Best Supporting performance in *Cat Ballou?* (his horse, of course . . . which brings us to TV's *Mr. Ed*, a series about a talking horse.)

But to those of us particularly privileged to share a portion of our lives with living, breathing horses, such fictions pall. Well-versed in equine idiosyncrasies, we soon learn that stories, songs, and poems don't tell the half of it. Horses are beautiful, remarkable creatures, but they also have minds of their own. They are not dogs, to respond with unconditional love; nor are they ethereal, fey creatures.

Horses are contradictory: they are immense, solid creatures, such as the Clydesdales seen on the beer commercials, yet they are also incredibly fragile; witness horse racing's Thoroughbred, balancing thousands of pounds on four slender, delicate legs.

They come in a rainbow of colors: the golden palomino, the patchwork paint (and pinto), the spotted Appaloosa, the powdered-sugar red and blue roans, the dappled gray, the bay, the sorrel, the dun, the plain brown, the buckskin with black mane and tail, the uncommon true black and true white, even the colors hard to describe—the claybank and the *grulla*.

They are stallions, studs, mares, and geldings; when young they are fillies and colts; also, just to confuse matters further, weanlings, foals, and long-yearlings.

They are of breeds both large and small: Shetland and Welsh ponies; the scruffy Western mustang; elegant, aristocratic Arabs; skittish, born-to-run Thoroughbreds; powerful, compact Quarter Horses; the high-stepping, gaited Tennessee Walker and Saddlebred; the massive Percheron and Belgian—and Justin Morgan's horse.

Horses are perversely contrary: they are versatile and willing—but also stubborn and unyielding. They craftily pitch off an unwary rider onto his/her head—or stand over an injured cowboy for hours until help arrives. They find the lone tree on the prairie against which to scrape off a rider—and patiently wait out the toddler who stumbles under an equine belly.

A horse is terrified of fire, yet willingly turns aside a charging Brahma Bull. He adopts all manner of stallmates, including cats, goats, and chickens, then refuses to share a trailer with another of his own kind.

Horses are, in short, unique and oddly human—while retaining that unknown ingredient that makes them magical beings, animals far superior to others, even beloved dogs and cats, in so many different ways.

The Hollywood Western has died, replaced, critics claim, with the high-tech of science fiction, in which FTL spaceships take the place of outmoded horses as a means of transportation. In fact, some reviewers argued that *Star Wars* was actually a Western in SF disguise, pointing to Han Solo's *Millennium Falcon* as a modern/future incarnation of the cowboy's trusty steed.

This may be so. It may be that future generations will relegate horses to obscurity, mere anachronistic transporters: "Beam me up, John Wayne." But to those of us who grew up reading, riding, and breathing horses—or are simply fascinated by them—the dream remains reality for as long as we can create it.

STOLEN SILVER

by Mercedes Lackey

Silver stamped restively as another horse on the picket-line shifted and blundered into his hindquarters. Alberich clucked to quiet him and patted the stallion's neck; the beast swung his head about to blow softly into the young Captain's hair. Alberich smiled a little, thinking wistfully that the stallion was perhaps the only creature in the entire camp that felt anything like friendship for him.

And possibly the only creature that isn't waiting for me to fail.

Amazingly gentle for a stallion, Silver had caused no problems either in combat or here, on the picket-line. Which was just as well, for if he had, Alberich would have had him gelded or traded off for a more tractable mount, gift of the Voice of Vkandis Sunlord or no. Alberich had enough troubles without worrying about the behavior of his beast.

He wasn't sure where the graceful creature had come from; *Shin'a'in-bred*, they'd told him. Chosen for him out of a string of animals "liberated from the enemy." Which meant war-booty, from one of the constant conflicts along the borders. Silver hadn't come from one of the bandit nests, that was sure—the only beasts the bandits owned were as disreputable as their owners. Horses "liberated" from the bandits usually weren't worth keeping.

Silver probably came from Menmellith via Rethwellan; the King was rumored to have some kind of connection with the horse-breeding, bloodthirsty Shin'a'in nomads.

Whatever; when Alberich lost his faithful old Smoke a few weeks before, he hadn't expected to get anything better than the obstinate, intractable gelding he'd taken from its bandit-owner.

But fate ruled otherwise; the Voice chose to "honor" him with a superior replacement along with his commission, the letter that accompanied the paper pointing out that Silver was the perfect mount for a Captain of light cavalry. It was also another evidence of favoritism from above, with the implication that he had earned that favoritism outside of performance in the field. Not a gift that was likely to increase his popularity with some of the men under his command, and a beast that was going to make him pretty damned conspicuous in any encounter with the enemy.

Plus one that's an unlucky color. Those witchy-Heralds of Valdemar ride white horses, and the blue-eyed beasts may be witches, too, for all I know.

The horse nuzzled him again, showing as sweet a temper as any lady's mare. He scratched its nose, and it sighed with content; he wished _he_ could be as contented. Things had been bad enough before getting this commission. Now—

There was an uneasy, prickly sensation between his shoulder-blades as he went back to brushing his new mount down. He glanced over his shoulder, to intercept the glare of Leftenant Herdahl; the man dropped his gaze and brushed his horse's flank vigorously, but not quickly enough to prevent Alberich from seeing the hate and anger in the hot blue eyes.

The Voice had done Alberich no favors in rewarding him with the Captaincy and this prize mount, passing over Herdahl and Klaus, both his seniors in years of service, if not in experience. Neither of them had expected that *he* would be promoted over their heads; during the week's wait for word to come from Headquarters, they had saved their rivalry for each other.

Too bad they didn't murder each other, he thought resentfully, then suppressed the rest of the thought. It was said that some of the priests of Vkandis could pluck the thoughts from a man's head. It could have been thoughts like that one that had led to Herdahl's being passed over for promotion. But it could also be that this was a test, a way of flinging the ambitious young Leftenant Alberich into deep water, to see if he would survive the experience. If he did, well and good; he was of suitable material to continue to advance, perhaps even to the rank of Commander. If he did not—well, that was too bad. If his ambition undid him, then he wasn't fit enough for the post.

That was the way of things in the armies of Karse. You rose by watching your back, and (if the occasion arose) sticking careful knives into the backs of your less cautious fellows, and insuring other enemies took the punishment. All the while, the priests of the Sunlord, who were the ones who were truly in charge, watched and smiled and dispensed favors and punishments with the same dispassionate aloofness displayed by the One God.

But Alberich had given a good account of himself along the border, at the corner where Karse met Menmellith and the witch-nation Valdemar, in the campaign against the bandits there. He'd *earned* his rank, he told himself once again as Silver stamped and shifted his weight beneath the strokes of Alberich's brush. The spring sun burned down on his head, hotter than he expected without the breeze to cool him.

There was no reason to feel as if he'd cheated to get where he was. He'd led more successful sorties against the bandits in his first year in the field than the other two had achieved in their entire careers together. He'd cleared more territory than anyone of Leftenant rank ever had in that space of time—and when Captain Anberg had met with one too many arrows, the men had seemed willing that the Voice chose him over the other two candidates.

It had been the policy of late to permit the brigands to flourish, provided they confined their attentions to Valdemar and the Menmellith peasantry and left the inhabitants of Karse unmolested. A stupid policy, in Alberich's opinion; you couldn't trust bandits, that was the whole reason why they became bandits in the first place. If they could be trusted, they'd be in the army themselves, or in the Temple Guard, or even have turned mercenary. He'd seen the danger back when he was a youngster in the Academy, in his first tactics classes. He'd even said as much to one of his teachers—phrased as a question, of course—and had been ignored.

But as Alberich had predicted, there had been trouble from the brigands, once they began to multiply; problems that escalated past the point where they were useful. With complete disregard for the unwritten agreements between them and Karse, they struck everyone, and when they finally began attacking villages, the authorities deemed it time they were disposed of.

Alberich had just finished cavalry training as an officer when the troubles broke out; he'd spent most of his young life in the Karsite military schools. The ultimate authority was in the hands of the Voices, of course; the highest anyone not of the priesthood could expect to rise was to Commander. But officers were never taken from the ranks; many of the rank-and-file were conscripts, and although it was never openly stated, the

Voices did not trust their continued loyalty if they were given power.

Alberich, and many others like him, had been selected at the age of thirteen by a Voice sent every year, to search out young male-children, strong of body and quick of mind, to school into officers.

Alberich had both those qualities, developing expertise in many weapons with an ease that was the envy of his classmates, picking up his lessons in academic subjects with what seemed to be equal ease.

It wasn't ease; it was the fact that Alberich studied long and hard, knowing that there was no way for the bastard son of a tavern whore to advance in Karse except in the army. There was no place for him to go, no way to get into a trade, no hope for any but the most menial of jobs. The Voices didn't care about a man's parentage once he was chosen as an officer, they cared only about his abilities and whether or not he would use them in service to his God and country. It was a lonely life, though—his mother had loved and cared for him to the best of her abilities, and he'd had friends among the other children of similar circumstances. When he came to the Academy, he had no friends, and his mother was not permitted to contact him, lest she "distract him," or "contaminate his purity of purpose." Alberich had never seen her again, but both of them had known this was the only way for him to live a better life than she had.

Alberich had no illusions about the purity of the One God's priesthood. There were as many corrupt and venal priests as there were upright, and more fanatic than there were forgiving. He had seen plenty of the venal kind in the tavern; had hidden from one or two that had come seeking pleasures strictly forbidden by the One God's edicts. He had known they were coming, looking for him, and had managed to make himself scarce long before they arrived. Just as, somehow, he had known when the Voice was coming to look for young male children for the Academy, and had made certain he was noticed and questioned.

And that he had known which customers it was safe to cadge for a penny in return for running errands.

Or that he had known that drunk was going to try to set the stable afire.

Somehow. That was Alberich's secret. He knew things were going to happen. That was a witch-power, and forbidden by the Voices of the One God. If anyone knew he had it—

But he had also known, as surely as he had known all the rest, that he had to conceal the fact that he had this power, even before he knew the law against it.

He'd succeeded fairly well over the years, though it was getting harder and harder all the time. The power struggled inside him, wanting to break free, once or twice overwhelming him with visions so intense that for a moment he was blind and deaf to everything else. It was getting harder to concoct reasons for knowing things he had no business knowing, like the hiding places of the bandits they were chasing, the bolt-holes and escape routes. But it was harder still to ignore them, especially when subsequent visions showed him innocent people suffering because he didn't act on what he knew.

He brushed Silver's neck vigorously, the dust tickling his nose and making him want to sneeze—

—and between one brush-stroke and the next, he lost his sense of balance, went light-headed, and the dazzle that heralded a vision-to-come sparkled between his eyes and Silver's neck.

Not here! he thought desperately, clinging to Silver's mane and trying to pretend there was nothing wrong. *Not now, not with Herdahl watching—*

But the witch-power would not obey him, not this time.

A flash of blue light, blinding him. *The bandits he'd thought were south had slipped behind him, into the north, joining with two more packs of the curs, becoming a group large enough to take on his troops and give them an even fight. But first, they wanted a secure base. They were going to make Alberich meet them on ground of their choosing. Fortified ground.*

That this ground was already occupied was only a minor inconvenience . . . one that would soon be dealt with.

He fought free of the vision for a moment, clinging to Silver's shoulder like a drowning man, both hands full of the beast's silky mane, while the horse curved his head back and looked at him curiously. The big brown eyes flickered blue, briefly, like a half-hidden flash of lightning, reflecting—

—another burst of sapphire. *The bandits' target was a fortified village, a small one, built on the top of a hill, above the farm-fields. Ordinarily, these people would have no difficulty in holding off a score of bandits. But there were three times that number ranged against them, and a recent edict from the High Temple decreed that no one but the Temple Guard and the Army could possess anything but the simplest of weapons. Not three weeks ago, a detachment of priests and a Voice had come through here, divesting them of everything but knives, farm implements, and such simple bows and arrows as were suitable for waterfowl and small game. And while they were at it, a third of the able-bodied men had been conscripted for the regular Army.*

These people didn't have a chance.

The bandits drew closer, under the cover of a brush-filled ravine.

Alberich found himself on Silver's back, without knowing how he'd gotten there, without remembering that he'd flung saddle and bridle back on the beast.

No, not bridle; Silver still wore the hackamore he'd had on the picket-line. Alberich's bugle was in his hand; presumably he'd blown the muster, for his men were running toward him, buckling on swords and slinging quivers over their shoulders.

Blinding flash of cerulean—

The bandits attacked the village walls, overpowering the poor man who was trying to bar the gate against them, and swarming inside.

It hadn't happened yet, he knew that with the surety with which he knew his own name. It wasn't even going to happen in the next few moments. But it was going to happen *soon*—

They poured inside, cutting down anyone who resisted them, then throwing off what little restraint they had shown and launching into an orgy of looting and rapine. Alberich gagged as one of them grabbed a pregnant woman and with a single slash of his sword, murdered the child that ran to try and protect her, followed through to her—

The vision released him, and he found himself surrounded by dust and thunder, still on Silver's back—

—but leaning over the stallion's neck as now he led his troops up the road to the village of Sunsdale at full gallop. Hooves pounded the packed-earth of the road, making it impossible to hear or speak; the vibration thrummed into his bones as he shifted his weight with the stallion's turns. Silver ran easily, with no sign of distress, though all around him and behind him the other horses streamed saliva from the corners of their mouths, and their flanks ran with sweat and foam, as they strained to keep up.

The lack of a bit didn't seem to make any difference to the stallion; he answered to neck-rein and knee so readily he might have been anticipating Alberich's thoughts.

Alberich dismissed the uneasy feelings *that* prompted. Better not to think that he might have a second witch-power along with the first. He'd never shown any ability to control beasts by thought before. There was no reason to think he could now. The stallion was just superbly trained, that was all. And he had more important things to worry about.

They topped the crest of a hill; Sunsdale lay atop the next one, just as he had seen in his vision, and the brush-filled ravine beyond it.

There was no sign of trouble.

This time it's been a wild hare, he thought, disgusted at himself for allowing blind panic to overcome him. And for what? A daytime-nightmare? *Next time I'll probably see trolls under my bed*, he thought, just about to pull Silver up and bring the rest of his men to a halt—

When a flash of sunlight on metal betrayed the bandits' location.

He grabbed for the bugle dangling from his left wrist instead, and pulled his blade with the right; sounded the charge, and led the entire troop down the hill, an unstoppable torrent of hooves and steel, hitting the brigands' hidden line like an avalanche.

Sword in hand, Alberich limped wearily to another body sprawled amid the rocks and trampled weeds of the ravine, and thrust it through to make death certain. His sword felt heavy and unwieldy, his stomach churned, and there was a sour taste in his mouth. He didn't think he was going to lose control of himself, but he was glad he was almost at the end of the battle-line. He hated this part of the fighting—which wasn't fighting at all; it was nothing more than butchery.

But it was necessary. This scum was just as likely to be feigning death as to actually be dead. Other officers hadn't been that thorough and hadn't lived long enough to regret it.

Silver was being fed and watered along with the rest of the mounts by the youngsters of Sunsdale; the finest fodder and clearest spring water, and a round dozen young boys to brush and curry them clean. And the men were being fed and made much of by the older villagers. Gratitude had made them forgetful of the loss of their weapons and many of their men. Suddenly the army that had conscripted their relatives was no longer their adversary. Or else, since the troops had arrived out of nowhere like Vengeance of the Sunlord Himself, they assumed the One God had a hand in it, and it would be prudent to resign themselves to the sacrifice. And meanwhile, the instrument of their rescue probably ought to be well treated. . . .

Except for the Captain, who was doing a dirty job he refused to assign to anyone else.

Alberich made certain of two more corpses and looked dully around for more.

There weren't any, and he saw to his surprise that the sun was hardly more than a finger's breadth from the horizon. Shadows already filled the ravine, the evening breeze had picked up, and it was getting chilly. Last year's weeds tossed in the freshening wind as he gazed around at the long shadows cast by the scrubby trees. More time had passed than he thought—and if he didn't hurry, he was going to be late for SunDescending.

He scrambled over the slippery rocks of the ravine, cursing under his breath as his boots (meant for riding) skidded on the smooth, rounded boulders. The last thing he needed now was to be late for a Holy Service, especially this one. The priest here was bound to ask him for a Thanks-Prayer for the victory. If he was late, it would look as if he was arrogantly attributing the victory to his own abilities, and not the Hand of the Sunlord. And with an accusation like that hanging over his head, he'd be in danger not only of being deprived of his current rank, but of being demoted into the ranks, with no chance of promotion, a step up from stable-hand, but not a big one.

He fought his way over the edge, and half-ran, half-limped to the village gates, reaching them just as the sun touched the horizon. He put a little more speed into his weary, aching legs, and got to the edge of the crowd in the village square a scant breath before the priest began the First Chant.

He bowed his head with the others, and not until he raised his head at the end of it did he realize that the robes the priest wore were not black, but red. This was no mere village priest—this was a Voice!

He suppressed his start of surprise, and the shiver of fear that followed it. He didn't know what this village meant, or what had happened to require posting a Voice here, but there was little wonder now why they had submitted so tamely to the taking of their men and the confiscation of their weapons. No one sane would contradict a Voice.

The Voice held up his hand, and got instant silence; a silence so profound that the sounds of the horses on the picket-line came clearly over the walls. Horses stamped and whickered a little, and in the distance, a few lonely birds called, and the breeze rustled through the new leaves of the trees in the ravine. Alberich longed suddenly to be able to mount Silver and ride away from here, far away from the machinations of Voices and the omnipresent smell of death and blood. He yearned for somewhere clean, somewhere that he wouldn't have to guard his back from those he should be able to trust. . . .

"Today this village was saved from certain destruction," the Voice said, his words ringing out, but without passion, without any inflection whatsoever. "And for that, we offer Thanks-giving to Vkandis Sunlord, Most High, One God, to whom all things are known. The instrument of that salvation was Captain Alberich, who mustered his men in time to catch our attackers in the very act. It seems a miracle—"

During the speech, some of the men had been moving closer to Alberich, grouping themselves around him to bask in the admiration of the villagers.

Or so he thought. Until the Voice's tone hardened, and his next words proved their real intent.

"It *seems* a miracle—but it was not!" he thundered. "You were saved by the power of the One God, whose wrath destroyed the bandits, but Alberich betrayed the Sunlord by using the unholy powers of witchcraft! *Seize him!*"

The men grabbed him as he turned to run, throwing him to the ground and pinning him with superior numbers. He fought them anyway, struggling furiously, until someone brought the hilt of a knife down on the back of his head.

He didn't black out altogether, but he couldn't move or see; his eyes wouldn't focus, and a gray film obscured everything. He felt himself being dragged off by the arms—heaved into darkness—felt himself hitting a hard surface—heard the slamming of a door.

Then heard only confused murmurs as he lay in shadows, trying to regain his senses and his strength. Gradually his sight cleared, and he made out walls on all sides of him, close enough to touch. He raised his aching head cautiously, and made out the dim outline of an ill-fitting door. The floor, clearly, was dirt. And smelled unmistakably of birds.

They must have thrown him into some kind of shed, something that had once held chickens or pigeons. He was under no illusions that this meant his prison would be easy to escape; out here, the chicken-sheds were frequently built better than the houses, for chickens were more valuable than children.

Still, once darkness descended, it might be possible to get away. If he could overpower whatever guards the Voice had placed around him. If he could find a way out of the shed. . . .

If he could get past the Voice himself. There were stories that the Voices had other powers than plucking the thoughts from a man's head—stories that they commanded the services of demons tamed by the Sunlord—

While he lay there gathering his wits, another smell invaded the shed, overpowering even the stench of old bird-droppings. A sharp, thick smell . . . it took a moment for him to recognize it.

But when he did, he clawed his way up the wall he'd been thrown against, to stand wide-eyed in the darkness, nails digging into the wood behind him, heart pounding with stark terror.

Oil. They had poured oil around the foundations, splashed it up against the sides of the shed. And now he heard them out there, bringing piles of dry brush and wood to stack against the walls. The punishment for witchery was burning, and they were taking no chances; they were going to burn him now.

The noises outside stopped; the murmur of voices faded as his captors moved away.

Then the Voice called out, once—a set of three sharp, angry words—

And every crack and crevice in the building was

outlined in yellow and red, as the entire shed was engulfed in flames from outside.

Alberich cried out, and staggered away from the wall he'd been leaning against. The shed was bigger than he'd thought—but not big enough to protect him. The oil they'd spread so profligately made the flames burn hotter, and the wood of the shed was old, weathered, probably dry. Within moments, the very air scorched him; he hid his mouth in a fold of his shirt, but his lungs burned with every breath. His eyes streamed tears of pain as he turned, staggering, searching for an escape that didn't exist.

One of the walls burned through, showing the flames leaping from the wood and brush piled beyond it. He couldn't hear anything but the roar of the flames. At any moment now, the roof would cave in, burying him in burning debris.

:Look out!:

How he heard the warning—or how he knew to stagger back as far as he could without being incinerated on the spot—he did not know. But a heartbeat after that warning shout in his mind, a huge, silver-white shadow lofted through the hole in the burning wall, and landed beside him. It was still wearing his saddle and hackamore—

And it turned huge, impossibly *blue* eyes on him as he stood there gaping at it. It? No. *Him.*

:On!: the stallion snapped at him. *:The roof's about to go!:*

Whatever fear he had of the beast, he was more afraid of a death by burning. With hands that screamed with pain, he grabbed the saddle-bow and threw himself onto it. He hadn't even found the stirrups when the stallion turned on his hind feet.

There was a crack of collapsing wood, as fire engulfed them. Burning thatch fell before and behind them, sparks showering as the air was sucked into the blaze, hotter. . . .

But, amazingly, no fire licked at his flesh once he had mounted. . . .

Alberich sobbed with relief as the cool air surged into his lungs—the stallion's hooves hit the ground beyond the flames, and he gasped with pain as he was flung forward against the saddle-bow.

Then the real pain began, the torture of half-scorched skin, and the broken bones of his capture, jarred into agony by the stallion's headlong gallop into the night. The beast thundered toward the villagers, and they screamed and parted before it; soldiers and Voice alike were caught unawares, and not one of them raised a weapon in time to stop the flight.

:*Stay on,*: the stallion said grimly into his mind as the darkness was shattered by the red lightning of his own pain. :*Stay on, stay with me; we have a long way to go before we're safe. Stay with me.* . . . :

Safe where? he wanted to ask—but there was no way to ask around the pain. All he could do was to hang on, and hope he could do what the horse wanted.

An eternity later—as dawn rose as red as the flames that had nearly killed him—the stallion had slowed to a walk. Dawn was on their right, which meant that the stallion was heading north, across the border, into the witch-kingdom of Valdemar. Which only made sense, since what he'd thought was a horse had turned out to be one of the blue-eyed witch-beasts. . . .

None of it mattered. Now that the stallion had slowed to a walk, his pain had dulled, but he was exhausted and out of any energy to think or even feel with. What could the witches do to him, after all? Kill him? At the moment, that would be a kindness. . . .

The stallion stopped, and he looked up, trying to see through the film that had come over his vision. At first he thought he was seeing double; two white witch-beasts and two white-clad riders blocked the road. But then he realized that there *were* two of them, hastily dismounting, reaching for him.

He let himself slide down into their hands, hearing nothing he could understand, only a babble of strange syllables.

Then, in his mind—

:Can you hear me?:

:I—what?: he replied, without thinking.

:Taver says his name's Alberich,: came a second voice in his head. *:Alberich? Can you stay with us a little longer? We need to get you to a Healer. You're going into shock; fight it for us. Your Companion will help you if you let him.:*

His what? He shook his head; not in negation, in puzzlement. Where was he? All his life he'd heard that the witches of Valdemar were evil— but—

:And all our lives we've heard that nothing comes out of Karse but brigands and bad weather,: said the first voice, full of concern, but with an edge of humor to it. He shook his head again and peered up at the person supporting him on his right. A woman, with many laugh-lines etched around her generous mouth. She seemed to fit that first voice in his head, somehow. . . .

:So, which are you, Alberich?: she asked, as he fought to stay awake, feeling the presence of the stallion *(his Companion?)* like a steady shoulder to lean against, deep inside his soul. *:Brigand, or bad weather?:*

:Neither . . . I hope. . . .: he replied absently as he clung to consciousness as she'd asked.

:Good. I'd hate to think of a Companion Choosing a brigand to be a Herald,: she said, with her mouth

twitching a little, as if she was holding back a grin. :*And a thunderstorm in human guise would make uncomfortable company.*:

:*Choosing?*: he asked. :*What—what do you mean?*:

:*I mean that you're a Herald, my friend,*: she told him. :*Somehow your Companion managed to insinuate himself across the Border to get you, too. That's how Heralds of Valdemar are made; Companions Choose them—*: She looked up and away from him, and relief and satisfaction spread over her face at whatever it was she saw. :*—and the rest of it can wait. Aren's brought the Healer. Go ahead and let go, we'll take over from here.*:

He took her at her word and let the darkness take him. But her last words followed him down into the shadows, and instead of bringing the fear they *should* have given him, they brought him comfort and a peace he never expected.

:*It's a hell of a greeting, Herald Alberich, and a hell of a way to get here—but welcome to Valdemar, brother. Welcome. . . .*:

LOVE AT FIRST RIDE

by Mickey Zucker Reichert

Freshman Stephanie Jebbens shifted her backpack to her right shoulder, jerking her sandy ponytail free of the buckle. The winking red lights of the Conesville High School bus reflected eerie shadows against the forest of locust trees surrounding her father's pasture. Barbed wire sagged between rotting fence posts, strands and clumps of mane hair caught between the barbs. Beyond the autumn-brown weeds, six boarded horses stomped and twitched near the feeder, awaiting their evening hay. Stephanie sighed at the familiar, motley herd, rolling her dark eyes in frustration. *Horses, horses everywhere, but not a one for me.*

The glare of the lights disappeared. The bus roared away amid the pop and crackle of gravel against its tires.

Stephanie paced the line of the fence, identifying each horse from a distance by the color of its coat. Rory McKeon's dirty white Arabian swiped flies, nose to tail with the bulbous-headed bay the Smiths had rescued from the killer. The Steeles owned three horses: a palomino, a buckskin, and a shaggy black, none of which they rode often enough to keep tractable or mannered. The Popeman's muscled sorrel completed the group, a well-

26

conformed quarter horse that had raced in its second year.

Once, one other sorrel had walked among the herd. Meaning well, Stephanie's parents had bought her a gaunt, half-Arab mare scarcely larger than a pony. Now, she winced at the memory. It was all they could afford; she understood that. And the mare had fit in well with the scraggly band of boarders. *I get enough time on mediocre horses exercising these. Why would I want another?* Again, she sighed, her mind conjuring images of a massive warm-blood leaping a seven foot oxer, its skin taut over powerful hindquarters, knees gracefully bent, back arched. She painted herself into the image, hunched over its neck in a silver-garnished hunt seat. Then she searched desperately for a means and an answer. *There must be a way to make enough money to buy a show-ring jumper, even just a foal that I could train myself.* She had faced the dilemma too many times, and still it had no solution. The vision faded, beyond reach. *So long as my parents make me work the farm, I can't get a job. And without money, I'll never own a real horse.*

Stephanie kicked each fence post as she passed, sending down a shower of wood chips. The palomino whickered as she neared, and the bay trotted toward her for a handout. Then, a movement from the opposite side of the pasture caught her eyes. Some dark animal moved near the locusts, just beyond her field of vision.

Stephanie stared. *Too large for a fox or a deer.* Quickly, she recounted the six familiar horses. Then, too curious to continue, she let the backpack slide from her shoulder and ducked between the lowest two strands of barbed wire.

The bay greeted her with a friendly nudge.

"Quit it, Cody." Stephanie shoved the horse aside. As the buckskin and palomino closed in on her, she elbowed between them. "Come on. Bug off, you nags."

The bay prodded her arm with a fuzzy nose. The palomino nuzzled her pockets.

Whirling suddenly, Stephanie slapped the bay's muzzle.

The horse startled backward, sending the Arabian into a bucking run. The others followed, kicking and capering along the fence row.

Ignoring the herd's antics, Stephanie hurried toward the opposite end of the pasture where she had seen the unidentified animal. Distracted, she had lost track of its position, and now she wondered if she had seen it at all.

A breeze stirred through the multicolored leaves, sending a wash of oak, maple and locust to the ground. Green stubble peeked from beneath a blanket of hoof-crushed weeds. Stephanie stumbled over a gopher hole, tripped, and fell. Her hand sank into a pile of horse droppings.

"God damn it!" Stephanie lurched to her feet, flicking dung from her fingers, then wiping the residue against the weeds.

A hoof stepped into Stephanie's circle of vision. Startled, she looked up, tracing a shining black leg to a horse that could have walked out of her fondest reverie. It was love at first sight.

"Where? How?" Stephanie rose, staring at the perfect animal before her. It stood nearly seventeen hands, yet with none of the clumsy unsoundness that can accompany too much size. Its broad chest promised a tremendous lung capacity. Its croup sloped gently, its hindquarters as thick and defined as any quarter horse. Not a single white hair marred the sleek beauty of its black coat, shed to summer smoothness and shiny, as if recently oiled.

Stephanie gaped, unable to look away. *This can't be real. I'm dreaming. I have to be dreaming.*

She shook her head to dispel the image, but it remained, triangular ears cocked forward, head high. A breeze lifted the dark forelock, revealing wide, intelligent eyes. Autumn coolness spiraled through Stephanie, too real for dream. Suddenly, the horse broke into a trot, trumpeting its joy to the air, its long strides carrying it to the other horses in seconds.

Stephanie watched the sinews shift beneath glimmering fur, studied the fluid motions that made the other horses seem like awkward parodies. Then, the buckskin made an abrupt cut in front of the new black. The black shuddered back into a half rear, slender legs cleaving air, twisting like a human dancer in midair. As its forehooves touched ground, it took two strides, gathered itself, and leapt the fence with natural ease. Knees bent, back rounded, it cleared the five feet of wire cleanly.

"No!" Stephanie raced toward the horses. "Don't go. Please don't go away."

As if in answer, the black spun back without missing a stride. It bounded over the fence a second time, landing neatly inside the pasture. Then it went still. Its neck arched to a wide head, held proudly aloft. The forelegs remained in steady parallel, the hindlegs pulled back and slightly spread.

Stephanie's heart pounded. She wanted this horse more than anything in her life. Logic told her the animal had to belong to someone, yet, until she knew the owner, it was hers. *Pegasus*. Though unoriginal, the name fit for the moment. Not wanting to startle it, she approached slowly and with caution. "Pegasus. Come here, Pegasus."

The horse did not move. It kept its ears in her direction, revealing the position of its gaze.

As Stephanie drew up to it, she reached out a hand and touched a silky side.

The horse snorted, still unmoving.

The desire to climb aboard and ride caught Stephanie with sudden, violent urgency. To mount a strange horse bareback was stupid, yet Stephanie could think of nothing else. "Stand right there." Keeping one hand raised to steady the horse, she looked around for a boost. Finding a suitable rock, she rolled it to the black's side.

The horse remained in place. Only its ears moved, cocked backward to keep track of Stephanie's position.

Stephanie climbed onto the rock. Even as she reached for the beast, it took two strides forward, walking beyond her reach.

"Hold still!" Stepping down from the stone, she again rolled it to the horse's side and stood on it.

Once more, the animal moved away.

"Damn it!" Frustration gripped Stephanie. Trying to catch the horse off guard, she seized the withers and mane, jumping to mount without the rock. Her chest and upper abdomen struck the animal's back with enough force to drive air through her teeth. This time, the horse sprang forward.

"Whoa!" Unable to secure her seat, Stephanie tumbled to the weeds. The black raced off to join the herd, jet hooves drumming against the dirt.

Stephanie rose, brushing dirt from her jeans. The yearning to ride that horse seemed to swell through her, a necessity she could not banish. Yet chasing it around the field would accomplish nothing. Crossing the pasture, she ducked back through the wire, hefted her backpack and headed home. Her gaze locked on the black until distance blurred it to a distant spot, and it seemed to disappear.

The Jebbens' dirt driveway ended at an uneven square of concrete. Wooden stairs rose from it to a screened back porch. Wind snapped at sheets of plastic stapled to the framework to keep the winter gales and snow from the shingled floor. Work boots lay scattered across the porch, and a rickety table held a dish filled with table scraps for the barn cats. Stephanie Jebbens skirted the rain puddle that always collected in the sloping concrete and started up the stairs.

Stephanie's mother met her at the door, a house dress loose over her pudgy form, her short, dark hair speckled with dust. "How was your day, dear?"

Stephanie ignored the question. "Who's the new horse?"

The mother blinked, as if to rechannel the direction of her thoughts. "What new horse?"

The question seemed ludicrous to Stephanie. *Surely, even my horse-ignorant mother has to see how beautiful that creature is.* "The big black ..." She trailed off, realizing she had gotten so caught up in its beauty that she had forgotten to check its sex. "Warm-blood. Thoroughbred, I think."

"Black?" Mrs. Jebbens leaned against the frame, propping the screen door open with her knee. "You don't mean the Steele's Blackie, do you dear?"

"No, mom." Stephanie threw back her ponytail in exasperation. "I mean the new horse. It doesn't look anything like Blackie."

Mrs. Jebbens shook her head. "There is no new horse."

"Yes, there is. I saw it out in the pasture." Stephanie tossed her backpack to the cat's table.

"I don't know what you're talking about, Steph. There is no new horse."

"Yes, there is." Stephanie stomped her foot for emphasis, the sound hollow on the boards. "Come on, I'll show you." Turning, she headed back down the steps.

Mrs. Jebbens followed with obvious reluctance,

down the steps, across the driveway, and out onto the dirt truck path that led to the pasture. Impatient, Stephanie outdistanced her mother, drawing up to the barbed wire several paces in the lead. The six boarder horses grazed at stubble in the middle of the pasture. There was no sign of the black.

As Mrs. Jebbens came up beside her, Stephanie clambered up the metal gate for a full view of the field. It looked exactly as she had left it, a vast plain of dead leaves and dying weeds enclosed by barbed wire and the encroaching forest.

The black jumper was gone.

Three days passed without sight of the horse, and only Stephanie's mother's memory of being dragged to the pasture confirmed that it had not been a dream. Obsessed, Stephanie filled the margins of her school notes with sketches of horses: a huge, black stallion jumping cavaletti, a huge, black mare winning the Kentucky Derby, a huge, black gelding in a composed, Lipizzaner rear. Every day, she saved the apple from her lunch, and every day she wound up feeding it to Rory McKeon's white Arabian or the Steele's palomino.

By Saturday, Stephanie had to presume that the horse had escaped someone's barn, jumped into her father's pasture by accident, then returned to its home. Still, though she would surely never see the creature again, her hunger for it only grew. The jumper in her dreams darkened to black, and the image of its slender legs pounding across the pasture could not be banished.

On Saturday morning, Stephanie pitched flakes of hay over the wire and into the wooden feeder, lost in the reverie. The six boarders met the food with excited whickers. The chestnut guarded a central stake with laid-back ears, jerking its head or lifting its heels at any horse who came too close. A minor scuffle ensued as each animal claimed its own pile, then they settled into a calm pattern of eating. Stephanie stared out over their heads to the pasture beyond, seeking, as always, the Pegasus she believed she would never see again.

The black stood in the middle of the pasture, ignoring the hay.

"Oh, my God!" Stephanie clambered up and over the gate. Excitement goaded her to run to the horse, but common sense intervened. *I can't scare it. Please don't run away. Not this time.*

As she approached, Stephanie was again impressed by the refined head, the sloping shoulders, and the short back. Rather than enhance its beauty, her memories and drawings had fallen short, losing the perfection of its conformation. Now, she could see that the animal was male, presumably a stallion. If it had shown even a modicum of its beauty or talent as a yearling, gelding it seemed a wasteful shame. "Don't run away. Oh, God, please, don't run away." She rifled through her pockets, finding the apple she knew she had placed there. Removing it, she offered the fruit in her palm.

Still, the horse did not approach. It waited until she came right up to it and shoved the apple directly beneath its muzzle. Then, it took a dainty bite, chewing fully before reaching for another, so unlike the other horses who consistently drooled half-chewed chunks and foam over Stephanie's hand.

Stephanie stroked the silken head as it ate, fondling the forelock, desire for ownership a wildfire within her. "You're so beautiful," she whispered.

The horse took the last piece of apple in its lips, chewing quietly.

"Who are you? Where did you come from?"

"I'm Satan, Stephanie Jebbens." The voice sounded honey smooth and barely above a whisper. "And I come from hell."

Startled, Stephanie staggered backward, heart pounding, hand clutched to her throat. She glanced around for the source of the words, seeing nothing except the black horse, staring at her through wide brown eyes. "Who said that? Damn it, this isn't funny."

"I'm Satan, Stephanie Jebbens." The horse's lower lip twitched in time to the speech. "And there's nothing funny about that."

Okay, don't panic. This is a practical joke. There's a speaker hidden on this horse somewhere. Again, Stephanie patted the horse, feeling for lumps that might conceal hardware, running her fingers through the hollow of the ears. But the horse lacked even the normal leg chestnuts, cysts, and rain rot. It felt warm and very much alive. *This doesn't make sense. Even if one of my friends could afford a horse this magnificent, they'd never dare use it for a joke.* "I know. This is a dream. There's no other explanation."

The black stomped its forehoof. "Dreamers don't question. They accept the ludicrous as reality." The stallion thrust its head directly into Stephanie's face. Its breath reeked of a strange mixture: sweet apple and sulfur. "Are you finished with the nonsense? Are you ready to bargain?"

"Bargain?" Stephanie repeated, for lack of anything coherent to say. *This isn't happening. This isn't happening. This can't possibly be happening.* She backstepped.

"Bargain?" Satan mimicked. "Yes, bargain. What did you expect? That's what I do. Haven't you read the stories? Are you illiterate?"

"No," Stephanie answered defensively, fear, curiosity and doubt warring within her. "Look, I'm not buying this. You've got a speaker on you somewhere. Or someone's hiding around here."

"Oh, for the love of *me*." The horse rolled its eyes. "Whisper something in my ear."

"What?"

"Tell me to do something. Whisper in my ear. Either ear."

Stephanie approached again, more timidly. She ran a finger through the beast's right ear, then whispered into it. "Um, raise your right hoof." She stepped back.

The black hefted his right front hoof, plopping it onto Stephanie's knee. "Satisfied?"

Stephanie skittered away with a sharp gasp. "Oh, my God!" A muddy hoof print smeared her jeans.

"Would you please quit saying that? It's insulting."

"God! God! God! *God!*" Stephanie raised her hands, cringing behind her crossed index fingers.

The horse watched with mild curiosity. "What ... and please pardon the pun ... what the *hell* are you doing?" The words seemed less question and more an expression of exasperation. Obviously, he had seen the gesture a thousand times.

"Warding the devil away."

Satan gave a slobbery horse snort. "That crossed fingers jazz only works in vampire movies. Now, come on. Do we have a deal or not?"

"Not! I'm not making a bargain with the devil."

"Okay. Fine." The outline of the black horse went fuzzy, fading to distant gray. Even as it dispersed, it kept the conformation that had haunted Stephanie's hopes for years and her dreams for days, a glasslike impression of all that mattered to her. The more transparent it became, the more Stephanie felt as if it had seized her heart and taken her ability to love with it.

"Wait!" she screamed. "Wait!"

The horse disappeared.

Tears sprang to Stephanie's eyes, unbidden. She remembered all the books she had read on successful athletes. Every one had spoken of a determination and dedication that few people could understand. She recalled a weight lifter who had said on national television that if doctors invented a drug that would make him the world champion but kill him immediately after the event, he would take it without hesitation. The statement had sparked a flurry of articles and interviews. To her surprise, nearly every serious athlete had agreed. Then, she thought she had understood their drive. But now, given the chance herself, she had refused it.

"Wait," she said again, voice breathy with crying. The stallion filled her memory like a physical object. "At least explain the deal."

The same, deep voice boomed from nowhere. "You would own the horse for three years. In that time, we would win every show-ring jump contest you entered me into. Three years, no losses."

Stephanie could not help picturing the hearth in Ashley Connor's house, a study of dressage ribbons in blue, red, gold and white, tiny cups mounted on wooden bases, plaques, and pictures. All the girls in the popular clique owned beautiful, professionally-trained horses that had won contests since their days in 4-H. Ashley and her friends had even formed a group called Stardancers that performed before local rodeos and parades. Stephanie imagined her own bookshelves crammed full of blue ribbons and gold cups so numerous her parents used the extras as ashtrays. She imagined Ashley Connor gaping in awe and begging Stephanie to join the Stardancers. She imagined herself on the perfect, black stallion, weaving graceful patterns among the matched palominos and whites, not just one of the band, but its central focus.

Stephanie spoke toward the direction from which

she guessed the voice had come. "And when those three years are over? What happens?"

A pause followed. Then light flashed behind Stephanie, and she whirled to face Satan in the guise of the horse again. He spoke, his words incongruous with the gentle-featured animal. "I thought you claimed to be literate."

"I am," Stephanie shot back. "But I'm not agreeing to anything till I know what I'm agreeing to."

"I only make one deal. And I don't take American Express. If you win every show-ring competition you enter me in for the next three years, I get your soul."

A shiver suffused Stephanie. She shook back her ponytail and pulled her sweater more tightly around her. "And what happens to it then?"

"What happens to what?"

"My . . . soul."

Satan tossed his head. The wind caught his mane, sending it into a wild, glorious dance. "I'm not at liberty to discuss that."

Stephanie Jebbens opened her mouth to insist, then thought better of it. *It would get me nowhere. If he could discuss the afterlife, the people he talked to in the past would already have spread the word.* "What happens if I don't win?"

"If you lose even one contest, the deal is broken. Your soul is free, and you owe me nothing."

"I need time to think things over."

The edges of Satan's wide mouth curled downward beneath the velvety nose. Stephanie had never seen a horse frown before. "Well, hurry up, then. There're a hundred other young women out there who would take my offer in a second."

Two or three dozen at Conesville alone. Stephanie had to agree. Again, she studied the black stallion, seeking flaws that did not exist. There had never been a horse like this one before, nor would there ever be again. *At least, not for me if I refuse the offer*.

"Come on," Satan said. He dropped to his fore knees, like a camel, to help her mount.

Stephanie hesitated.

"Come on. One ride costs you nothing."

Now Stephanie came forward, trembling with excitement. Gingerly, she approached from the left, flinging her right leg over the animal's spine.

Satan rose, his movement smooth as water. He took three walking steps. "Ready?"

Stephanie wound her hands in his mane. "Ready," she said, not at all certain that she was.

Muscles shifted warmly along Stephanie's legs. Then, the black leapt into a gallop with all the power of a volcano exploding. Despite its strength, the opening charge came with an agility that allowed Stephanie to adjust easily to the change. Then, the slender legs were pumping in a gentle rhythm, sleek head forward, mane striping Stephanie's face and fingers like ink.

Stephanie felt as if she were flying. The wind sang around her, tugging her clothes and hair behind until they seemed weightless, leaving her a natural freedom beyond life and eternity. She saw no sign of the other horses, nor did she miss them. The pasture seemed to disappear, replaced by a single, narrow strip of world: the running horse and Stephanie Jebbens.

The fence loomed suddenly before them, its highest strand looking impossibly high, its barbs monstrous. Fear gripped Stephanie. *Not bareback! I can't jump that thing bareback*. She twisted her hands farther into the mane, pressing forward in a jump position, knowing she no longer had a choice.

Stephanie felt a fluid shift, as the horse's focus flowed to the hindquarters, then the effortless impulsion as its forelegs folded into position and its heels left the ground. It soared with a calm confidence, like a bird used to split second banks and glides in midair. The moment seemed to last forever, the cool touch of breeze surrounding her, the freedom from earthly concerns or supports, the driving vitality of the arrow-sleek creature beneath her. Then the forelegs grazed ground, rising immediately into the flying run she hoped would never end.

Yet end it did. After an hour that passed like a heartbeat, Satan drew to a graceful halt and dropped to his knees to let Stephanie dismount.

Reluctantly, Stephanie lowered herself to the ground. She stared at the animal, still feeling its power surging through her, and the need to own it became a grasping, desperate necessity. "Stay," she said. "Don't go."

"We have a deal, then," Satan said, his voice a whisper that scarcely grazed the wind.

Stephanie Jebbens recalled every Satan bargaining story she had ever heard: *The Devil and Daniel Webster*, *The Devil and the Fiddler*, and others whose titles she could not recall. In every case, the bargainer had rescued his soul through a loophole. *There're a thousand ways to win a competition and ten thousand ways to lose it. All I have to do is see to it that we lose one contest.* "Yes," she said, as softly. "We have a deal."

That night, an aunt the Jebbens' scarcely knew passed away, leaving Stephanie a black stallion called Satan's Promise, along with his trailer, show tack, and garb that fit her like a glove. It was the same horse; there could be no mistaking it. Yet, it pawed and pranced like any other, munched hay, nuzzled for carrots, and never again spoke to Stephanie. Still, horse and rider launched into a show-ring jump team that seemed unstoppable as well as unbeatable, sweeping the local fairs and shows in the first year of competition.

One by one, ribbons, photos, and trophies replaced the books on Stephanie's shelves. She joined the Stardancers. Boys who would never have glanced in her direction now joked with her and stole her from her partners at dances. Girls who used to giggle as they passed her, began inviting her to share jokes and seats in the cafeteria. And, every day after school, Satan's Promise greeted her with a romp and a whinny, a beacon in a pasture of dross, making the motley boarders appear smaller and duller and shaggier than ever.

As the third year got underway, Stephanie removed the last novel from her case, replacing it with a winning plaque carved to the shape of a horse. She sat cross-legged on the floor of her room, studying the glittering array of metal and plastic like a queen surveying a conquest. She had not forgotten the bargain. In fact, rising fear made it seem to ache within her, churning ideas with a steady desperation. As she rode to her myriad victories, she had watched lesser rider's techniques, analyzing and memorizing for the day when she would have to lower herself to them. *Horse and rider are a team. Satan's Promise may not make mistakes, but he can't keep me from making them.* Until now, they had ridden as a perfect team, blended to a single entity. Surely, her change would catch him by surprise.

Stephanie rose, wondering how Satan would react when he realized he had been tricked again. Would he try to claim her soul anyway? Her blood ran cold. Then she gained solace from the remembrance that in all the stories she had ever read the devil was forced to keep his promise and leave empty-handed. And what would happen to Satan's Promise? Would the horse get ill and die? Would it simply disappear? In any case, she knew that once the deal was broken, she would no longer own the creature that had become the sole focus of her life for the last two years. *So I have to time this right.*

Soon enough, Stephanie knew she would compete in the ASPCA Championship. *And only a fool would risk losing a horse like Satan's Promise until after the Olympics.* Now, she frowned. By waiting until after the Games, she would leave herself only a month to escape her bargain. *Three weeks with three weekends to show.* Few horses could handle three weekends in a row, and fewer owners were cruel enough to try. *So much the better. If Satan's Promise loses because he's tired, I don't even need to make a mistake. In the meantime, I've got eight tries.* A chill spiraled through her. *And I can't afford to fail.*

Months later, Stephanie stared at the Olympic gold medal dangling from the center of the bookcase in its place of ultimate honor. More than a week had passed since she had taken it, yet she never tired of gawking at it or displaying it for anyone who would look. Nor did she grow bored of telling the story: the long water in and out that required Satan's Promise to fly, the tight angle turns and jumps that tried the finest horses in equine history, and the garish horizontal crossed rails that spooked her nearest competitor, knocking his performance from silver to bronze. And her own accomplishment did not go unlauded. *I was far more than a passenger. Without a competent rider with strength of position and balance, the best horse in the world is useless.*

Mrs. Jebbens' voice wafted up the staircase. "Stephanie? Stephanie, are you getting ready, honey?" Apparently, she addressed her next words to Stephanie's father. "I hope she's not sick. She's usually up early on the day of a meet."

"I don't feel good, mom," Stephanie lied, rolling

beneath the blankets until the pillow dislodged and the covers rode up over her head. She smiled at the simple brilliance of her plan. She had paid her entry fee to three separate events, which meant she had entered those contests. *Contests I must lose by default.*

Mrs. Jebbens' footfalls clumped up the stairs. Stephanie's door edged open. "Steph? Are you all right?"

"Just a little stomach ache. Probably the excitement."

Mrs. Jebbens approached the bed, glancing over the awards before stopping before Stephanie. She placed a plump hand on Stephanie's forehead. "No fever. Why don't you just rest?"

"But I'll miss the contests," Stephanie protested feebly.

"Just as well." Mrs. Jebbens planted a kiss on her daughter's forehead. "You need some time off. And so does Satan's Promise." She replaced the pillow. "Now, is there anything I can get—"

The shrill of the telephone interrupted the question. Mrs. Jebbens whirled and trotted down the steps to answer it.

Stephanie sat up, again examining the Olympic gold from a distance.

Shortly, her mother called up the stairs. "There's a tornado watch. You're not missing anything. Turns out your competition was canceled.

Canceled. Stephanie felt as if the walls of the room had closed in on her. Breathing became an effort. *No event, no entry, and no loss.* Suddenly, the next few weekends trebled in significance. *There's more than one way to trick a demon.* And Stephanie knew she would have to find something foolproof. And soon.

The following Saturday, Stephanie awakened early. In her excitement, she "accidentally" groomed, wrapped, and loaded the Steele's Blackie. But when she arrived at the show grounds, the horse that backed from the trailer was Satan's Promise, looking sleeker in natural coat than Blackie had after hours of attention. Fear clutched Stephanie to the edge of nausea. The day passed in a blur. She kept no conscious memory of the events, but the two blue ribbons spoke volumes.

That night, Stephanie could not rest. Barraged by strings of frustrated thought, she tossed and rolled helplessly, sleep a distant fixation. At length, she arose, padding down the stairs to the finished recreation room in the basement. She did not bother with the lights. Moonlight shining through the casement windows shed enough to reveal the familiar, ratty couches and chairs, the television, and her father's racks of hunting guns. She knew he kept the 12-gauge shotgun at the top loaded to handle raccoons and foxes in the chicken coop. Seizing it gingerly, she lowered it from the rack, slipped into the root cellar, up the stairs, and out the lower door. She pulled on a pair of mud-caked work boots set to dry on the concrete walk beneath the porch.

A night breeze ruffled her hair like a friend, tossing strands into her face. The stars shone bright in a sky lit by the waxing moon. Clutching the shotgun, Stephanie ran toward the pasture, the overlarge boots clumping and slapping on the path. Arriving at the gate, she looked for Satan's Promise.

The six boarder horses greeted her with whinnies. Darkness dulled them to blotches of gray, but even night's pitch could not have disguised the perfect silhouette of the jumper. Satan's Promise was gone.

"No!" Stephanie flung the gun to the ground, clutching the cold steel of the cattle gate. Metal clanged against metal as the shotgun tumbled, sending a tremor of impact through the gate.

"No! God, no!" Repeatedly, she slammed her fist against the bars, feeling rust flake free beneath her fingers. Grabbing up the gun, she returned to the house, replaced the 12-gauge, and went back to bed.

And could not sleep.

Satan's Promise did not return. He was not there to greet Stephanie after school on Monday. He was not there when Stephanie threw out the morning and evening hay. And when she slipped out at night with the shotgun, Satan's Promise was not there.

Saturday morning, Stephanie awakened from a dream of clouds and cherubs to a room crammed full of trophies and ribbons. Moonlight gleamed from a panorama of blue and gold on the bookshelves, a monument to three years of fulfilled promises. Yet now those same victories that had elevated Stephanie Jebbens from quiet high school freshman to Olympic gold medalist seemed hollow. *I've got so much to live for. What good are awards and applause if I'm dead?* A shiver racked her, so intense and sudden that it ached through her muscles. *I've got to stop thinking like this. The devil is evil. He can't win. I've got the world and God on my side. Besides, Satan's Promise has run away. I can't take first place if I can't find him.*

The digital clock read 4:45 a.m. Stephanie tossed aside the cover sheet, dressed hurriedly, and ran outside. A dark shape grazing near the trailer dashed all hope that she might lose because she had no horse to ride. Satan's Promise had returned.

Quickly, Stephanie ducked back into the house. Taking the 12-gauge from its familiar slot, she dashed outside. The horse glanced up as she aimed, its nostrils wide and red. It whickered a greeting.

Stephanie's finger tightened on the trigger.

And nothing happened.

Stephanie's heart seemed to pound as loudly as the gunshot she had expected. In the darkness, she explored the trigger area with her fingers, careful to keep the barrel pointed toward the horse. The mechanism had bent, presumably when it had struck the pasture gate. *I don't believe this.*

Satan's Promise returned to grazing on the lawn. Mr. Jebbens' voice wafted from the upstairs bedroom window. "You up already, Steph?"

Stephanie glanced up to the dark blotch of her father's head, outlined against the cloudless sky, and hoped he could not see as well from the opposite direction. She hesitated long enough to respond in her normal speaking voice. "It's just me. Promise is back."

"All right. Good." Mr. Jebbens' head retreated.

Stephanie let out a pent up breath she had not realized she had been holding. *Maybe I could just tell them about this devil horse. They could help me get rid of him.* But she knew the thought was folly. *No one would believe the story. Especially now. They'd think I cracked under the strain. They'd make me miss the contest today. Then Satan would see the events got canceled, and I'd lose my last chance at freedom.* She rushed the gun back to its place on the rack and started preparing her horse methodically.

Stephanie Jebbens perched atop her stallion, awaiting her turn in the show-jump ring. She had entered both of the open jumping contests, and the number "2" kept running through her mind in swirling dioramas. *Two chances to lose. Two chances at life.*

The crowd applauded the previous rider. Then the voice announced her approach over the loudspeaker. "Olympic winner, Stephanie Jebbens, riding Satan's Promise." A hearty cheer rose from the audience, but Stephanie heard none of it. Her ears buzzed as her horse surged forward in a time gaining start, gliding toward a red and white striped vertical. Clearing it effortlessly, Satan raced toward a figure eight spread fence.

Now's my chance. Stephanie signaled the jump early, nearly tearing on the reins. Satan's Promise answered, missing his take-off and surging into the leap too soon. For the first time, she felt him stiffen, struggling to reach the final fence. He seemed to hover in the air forever. Then, he came down, twisting his hindlegs, but not far enough. The tip of a hoof struck the last bar, rattling it. *Time penalty. Now I'm sure to lose.* Stephanie's hopes soared. She felt suddenly free, able to enjoy the smooth rises and falls of the horse for the first time since winning had become a familiar certainty.

Stephanie Jebbens and Satan's Promise left the ring to a thunder of applause. Sweat slicked the black's back, and foam rose on his chest.

He's nervous. I've got him now. Stephanie fairly beamed as her time came up on the board, and the penalty brought the total to three minutes and five. Ten seconds *under* the next best time. Stephanie's smile wilted. She became suddenly, fanatically interested in the competition. One by one, she watched as every following horse touched or knocked down the same post Satan's Promise had hit. And Stephanie Jebbens took the event, with five seconds and little dignity to spare.

Desperation nearly suffocated Stephanie. She scarcely heard her win announced, did not notice the sea of congratulations, and even the horse show crowds seemed to disappear. The world narrowed to Stephanie Jebbens and her wonder horse and her single last chance to save her soul. *It's hopeless.*

The time to Stephanie's final event seemed to

drag into a tormenting eternity. The other contestants brushed and curried, making last minute adjustments to their tack, or studying the sequence of separate fences, combinations and turns. Some paced out stride lengths. Others eyeballed the distances, mentally converting angles and distances.

Stephanie stood in silence, looking and feeling like a lamb before the slaughter. Even the start of the competition did not rouse her from her trance. Dispassionately, she watched the two jumpers ahead of her, noted without judgment that each one scored a penalizing rub and finished with a barely adequate time. *He's not taking any chances. He'll be alert for me to urge or delay takeoffs.* She rode out into the ring. And, as Satan's first hoof touched the packed earth, an idea came in a rush. *There's one sure-fire way to lose this contest.* The dizziness disappeared, leaving Stephanie almost painfully alert. *Those other two have already finished, so he can't just have everyone get disqualified.* She felt flushed with the joy of certain victory. *Take this, Satan. My soul is mine again!*

Satan's Promise seemed to take no notice of the change. He made a perfect launch over a five foot triple bar, his gait even and unhurried. Stephanie waited until the horse was in the air, attentive to its own equilibrium, and its role in a winning team. Then, with the same calm, stable attitude that had won her gold medal, Stephanie sprang from the horse's back, aware that a fall meant instant disqualification.

Stephanie felt Satan's Promise go rigid as she left his back, heard him whinny in wild frustration. She struck the ground hard enough to bruise her side, the pain disappearing beneath a stormy rush of triumph. *I'm free! I've bested the devil, and now my soul is safe!* She rolled from habit, wanting to scream her excitement to the world, thinking of the dances she would attend, the boy she would marry, the life filled with more winning horses, more ribbons, more glory. *I'm free.* She tensed to rise amidst the audience's collective gasp.

Stephanie saw a flash of black. A familiar voice lanced into her head: *You're still mine, Stephanie Jebbens.* Then a hoof crashed down on her, sheering between the helmet and the collar of her shirt. Agony flashed through her neck. She felt a sickening crack. The next breath would not come, and she spiraled into a permanent oblivion.

Megan Towncrest dropped her broom and rushed to the rail in the moment before the dense silence erupted into screams. Her mind registered the scene in an instant: an Olympic gold medalist only a year older than herself, her head at an angle that denied life. Above the corpse, a black horse more beautiful than any she had seen in reverie or reality stared, as if waiting for its rider to rise and climb back into the saddle. *Loyal as well as talented and beautiful. I'd sell my soul for a horse like that.*

For Megan Towncrest, it was love at first sight.

DANCER'S FIRE

by Josepha Sherman

The moon was still up when I arrived at the race-track; exercise riders—successful ones, at any rate—don't get many chances to sleep late. I don't know what whim made me turn left instead of right, so that instead of passing through the paddock into the familiar bustle of the waking back-stretch and its long rows of barns full of yawning, whinnying horses I found myself in the great mass of the grandstand, silent and still clean in these hours before opening. I wandered down to the rail and looked out over the low, dark rectangles of the tote boards to the sweep of the track. Union Downs is a big course, second only to the majestic mile and a half of Belmont, and the wide rings of dirt and turf encircling the grassy infield and its geese-filled lake looked like something out of an older, more mysterious age.

I couldn't stand here staring like an idiot. I had a job to do, horses to work. Besides, if I stayed here much longer, some security guard was going to come along and ask me embarrassing questions. It had been a long time since I'd been stupid enough to so much as smoke a joint, but some people had equally long memories.

A flicker of movement startled me: a horse was on the track. My first thought was that it had to be an escapee from one of the barns; horses have people beat all hollow when it comes to being escape artists. I was all set to go back to one of the barns and spread the word—

But then moonlight blazed full on a bright bay coat, and I froze.

That was Dancer's Fire down there, sleek as a greyhound. Oh, I could recite all her statistics without having to stop and think: three-year-old bay filly by Dancer's Pride out of Laura's Secret—classic Northern Dancer and Secretariat blood-lines—ten for ten in her races, winner of the filly Triple Crown this spring. Cold statistics didn't tell it all though: the unbreakable will to race, to win, the fierce spirit within the delicate frame that could never be less than the best. I had been her exercise rider, and honored, too; Dancer's Fire moved quick and smooth as living flame. And if that double dose of Nasrullah blood back a few generations in her pedigree gave her a fiery temperament, too, well, a few bites were a small price to pay to handle greatness. She never bit me hard, anyhow, and had a way of suddenly sticking her soft muzzle against my neck and giving me the barest swipe with her tongue as though saying she was sorry. . . .

That was Dancer's Fire down there, no mistaking it, from the odd little jagged blaze on her fore-head to the three elegant white stockings on her slender legs. A picture to warm a horse fan's heart. Only one trouble with it:

Dancer's Fire was dead.

She had died in the middle of her last race a month ago, a never-should-have-been-run match race against Proud Trumpet, the three-year-old colt sensation, right here at Union Downs. Match races are usually won by the horse that takes the lead from the start, but those two horses had surged down the backstretch like one, ears pinned, necks outstretched, every muscle straining, churning, driving for the wire—

And just before that wire, the filly's heart had broken. Massive arterial hemorrhaging, the vets had called it, which is their fancy way of saying fatal heart attack. Dancer's Fire was dead, and like everyone else in the business, I had done my share of mourning this past month, tried my best to ignore that one empty stall, and gone on with life.

So what was she doing here now? As I watched, aching at the sight of her, Dancer's Fire paced nervously back and forth, stopping to anxiously paw the ground, her bright coat washy with sweat, then raised her proud head, searching for—

For what? What could a dead racehorse, or a racehorse ghost, or whatever I was seeing, possibly want? I'd been clean too long to be hallucinating now, though there were supposed to be such things as drug flashbacks. And yet . . .

"Dancer?" I asked, very softly.

I swear she heard me. Her ears pricked, and for a long moment she stared right at me. Then Dancer's Fire turned smoothly, trotted down the backstretch . . . and vanished.

Well, it wasn't the sort of thing you talked about, not if you wanted to keep your job, not if you didn't want a new reputation as a crazy. I did my work that morning, which was primarily to ride amiable Pleasant Lad a brisk five furlongs, and was glad it *was* old Laddie. A four-year-old brown gelding, lop-eared and homely like his daddy, he's quick enough (when he wants to be) to have actually set a couple of track records, but he's as calm and unshockable as an old cow, which was pretty much what I wanted just then. As he worked his lazy way down the track, blowing hard to make me think he was trying his best, I tried to put what I'd seen earlier down to a trick of the moonlight. The reality of warm, smelly, friendly horse under me helped.

That day, the should-have-been winner of the first race stumbled just short of the finish, almost as though he'd been cut off by another horse that wasn't there. I told myself he was only a cheap claimer, after all, probably sore-legged; that he'd stumbled pretty much where Dancer's Fire had died had nothing to do with it.

Nerves tight, I forced myself back to the track that night, this time with Hank, one of the security guards, at my side. Sure enough, Dancer's Fire was there, pacing anxiously before the grandstand.

"There!" I yelped. "Do you see that?"

Hank blinked, then shone his flashlight down on the track. Dancer's Fire glinted in its light, bright as a living horse, but the man only shrugged. "Nothing down there."

"You mean you don't see—" I caught myself in mid-cry. "Ah, never mind. I thought I saw someone down on the track. Must have been mistaken."

I slunk away, feeling more scared than when Zack's Pride, a thousand pounds of thoroughly loony stallion, had charged me.

A ghost horse only I could see. Maybe *I* was the loony this time. Maybe my past was catching up with me, scrambling my brains years after I'd gone clean. Maybe . . .

The next day, the should-have-been winner of the fourth race, a two-year-old filly who had been leading the other babies by an easy four lengths, suddenly shied halfway across the 'track at nothing. Well she *was* only a baby, after all; everyone knew two-year-olds sometimes did crazy things. Besides, if there were, by some wild, ridiculous, impossible chance, a ghostly racer on the track, wouldn't *every* horse have sensed it? I mean, didn't all the stories say animals Saw Things?

Maybe they did. For all I knew, good old unflappable Laddie could see the ghost of every horse since Eclipse. That didn't mean he'd turn one lazy hair about it. Maybe only *some* horses were scared of spooks. Even spooks trying to race with them.

If there were such things. If I wasn't quietly going over the edge, or—

Ah, hell. There wasn't anyone I could tell about this; my job might be secure right now, I was a good enough rider for that, but I couldn't afford having anyone start bringing up the bad old days. I finally went and looked up past RACING FORMS, dating from the day after that deadly match race. There wasn't anything really dramatic in them, nothing to make me yell for help. And yet ... almost every day there had been one race in which a sure winner didn't. There'd be a note that this horse had run out—bolted to the outer rail—or that horse had shied, like that silly two-year-old. There was even one race where the almost-winner had suddenly reared. They'd said he'd tried to jump a shadow, horses will do that sometimes, but I ... well, I called myself a hundred kinds of idiot, but the memory of Dancer's Fire prancing nervously in the moonlight wouldn't leave me alone.

And at last, even though I really didn't want to do it, I went back to the track at night.

She was there, Dancer's Fire, pacing about and searching restlessly by the waning moonlight, the very image of a nervous, unhappy horse ... I couldn't stand it. Without stopping to think, I slipped down to the track, and called her name, very softly so no one would hear me.

She heard. She trotted up to me, looking so thoroughly real, so thoroughly alive I could almost forget the painful memories of a month ago. But her hoofs made no sound, and her dark mane was ruffled by a wind that wasn't there. A ghost horse.

But how could I be afraid of her? Dead or alive, this was still Dancer's Fire, and in her fierce eyes was that look of total trust a horse so rarely holds for anyone human, and a terrible fear she'd never known while alive. Dancer knew something was wrong, knew she wasn't supposed to be here, and she was crying out to me in her silent equine way to help her, but—

"I'm sorry," I whispered painfully. "I don't know what you want."

No? As I watched her resume her frustrated, head-tossing pacing, radiating that bewildered terror, an idea slipped into my head. What if. . . ?

"Oh, no," I said aloud. "That's ridiculous."

Was it? In life she'd always been driven by that unshakable will to win. Why should she have changed now?

"Hell, horse, you're going to get me in a *lot* of trouble."

But what else could I do? No one else could help her—no one else could even see her! Watching her miserable pacing, sensing her pain and fright, I knew I had to take the chance.

"Wait till tomorrow night, Dancer," I begged her. "Just wait till tomorrow night."

If I'd let myself stop to think about it, I probably would have turned myself in to the loony squad. This really was a crazy idea, without the slightest guarantee it would work. I had a good job, good horses to ride for a trainer I respected. I'd almost certainly be throwing all that away, and with my background, I'd probably have to leave town, head out to another track and start all over. God, crazy wasn't the half of it.

But how could I possibly leave Dancer's Fire like that? With a shock, I realized she had been more than just another horse, more even than an equine superstar. Animal or no, she'd been a friend. And you just didn't leave a friend trapped in what looked like an endless loop of fear.

Things probably would have gone differently if Proud Trumpet had still been here. Security was always superstar-tight around his barn; likely I would have gotten arrested the moment I approached the stall. But Proud Trumpet's trainer had shipped him back out to Santa Anita right after that tragic match race.

Pleasant Lad was a different story. I won't say security was lax at our barn; it wasn't. But ... well, Laddie, for all his speed, was Laddie. No one was going to steal a lazy, homely, unflashy gelding.

No one was stealing him now, just borrowing him a little. I wanted a horse who wasn't going to have hysterics on me. Laddie, bless his lazy soul, never even blinked when I snapped a lead rope onto his halter and bound up his hoofs with rags so they wouldn't clop. Together, his tack tucked under my arm, we stole out of the dark stall in the middle of the night, me on the lookout for guards' flashlights, sure I was going to feel a hard hand on my shoulder with every step, him going along as placidly as a stable pony, stopping only now and again to yawn.

We reached the track, and the moon (waning but still bright enough) obligingly came out from behind a cloud. Dancer's Fire was waiting for us. Pleasant Lad took one look and stopped dead, ears shooting up in sheer equine astonishment.

"You see her, too," I whispered, feeling a rush of relief wash over me. "Hallelujah."

Laddie, as I've said, was Laddie. He took one deep sniff at Dancer's Fire, presumably picking up no scent of horse, then seemed to shrug and accept the situation. Refusing to let myself think about what I was doing, I took the rags off his hoofs and tacked him up, then vaulted up onto his back and started slowly down the track. Was Dancer's Fire bound to the one spot where she had died? No. As I'd hoped, she had the freedom of the whole track, and followed us silently.

As I've said, Union Downs is a big course, which means that a mile and a quarter race starts just at the end of the first turn. It seemed to take all night to get there, me jogging Pleasant Lad to warm him up (if he was puzzled by the whole business, at least he moved out with, for him, good grace), Dancer's Fire cantering smoothly at our side. Of course there was no starting gate in place, but I hoped that wouldn't matter. What the hell, we didn't have anything else right either, not Proud Trumpet, not jockeys or outriders or anything that would make this the exact copy of the match race. For all I knew, none of this would make a difference, except that I would be out of a job.

"What the hell," I repeated aloud to the two horses—one snorting, one eerily silent—"let's try it."

I yelled in Laddie's ear. Startled, he took off like a shot, and Dancer's Fire went with him.

I had expected her to pass us in a flash. After all, even assuming she would run like a normal, earthbound horse, with no jockey or tack burdening her she was carrying over a hundred pounds lighter weight. All I'd hoped to do was give her the illusion of one last winning race. But for whatever ghostly reason, Dancer's Fire was replaying her final start, just as though the stands were full of screaming fans, just as though it were Proud Trumpet with Corson up, not Pleasant Lad with a fool of an exercise rider aboard. She ran neck and neck with Laddie, her lovely head outstretched, nostrils wide, dark eyes wild with their usual fire.

And Laddie, good old Laddie—maybe he was overcome by the weirdness of it all, maybe he felt something of Dancer's Fire's urgency, but this once in his life he needed no prodding, this once he ran with all his strength and will. I crouched low over the straining neck, burying my face in his tossing mane, feeling the bunch and release of powerful muscles under me, hearing the thunder of his hoofs (his hoofs alone) as we swept through the far turn and down into the long straightaway towards the finish line. The three-eighths pole went by in a striped blur, and the little clock all exercise riders carry in their minds screamed that we were surely shooting for some kind of weird track record.

Then all at once Dancer's Fire seemed to stumble, all at once I realized we were at the spot where she had died and knew she would replay that final scene, die and die again—

"No!" Struggling with Laddie to slow him down, I shouted over the rush of wind at the filly, "Damn you, no! You never surrendered to anyone or anything in your life— You can't give up now! I won't let you give up!"

It was a stupid thing to yell, as though she were a human to understand me, or even a living horse. But in my voice just then was what was in my heart: all the rage and love and anguish for her, for every brave, beautiful animal that ever died racing its heart out. And maybe she caught the pain behind my words, maybe she felt that surge of raw, despairing love, because all at once Dancer's Fire seemed to blaze with strength. I saw the merest shadow of a horse sink to the track, but she—oh, she swept past mortal Laddie as though he were a stable pony, she flew on, and she was suddenly herself and more, she was Ruffian, Twilight Tear, Black Gold, all those doomed, brave, wonderful horses, and I could only shout, my sight blurring, "Yes, oh yes, you beautiful things, run!" and she was a horse of flame and air so radiant the breath caught in my throat—

But just as suddenly she was only her own lovely self. It was Dancer's Fire, her proud head high, her tail a shining banner, who surged past the finish line alone, winner of her final, finest race.

In the next moment she had vanished into the darkness. I let poor, puzzled Pleasant Lad finish his race, then eased him up. Springing to the track on feet that seemed too wobbly to hold me up, I started to walk him the lonely, weary way back, stroking his sweaty neck and murmuring to him, thinking that though the wild run didn't seem to have done him any harm, he'd need a lot of hot-walking before he'd cooled enough to be put safely back in his stall. I'd pretty much ruined his training schedule for him, which wasn't going to endear me to trainer or owner.

I stopped short, Laddie (reverting to his old lazy self) stopping with me without a fuss. There was a commotion in the grandstand, the sharp stabs of flashlights piercing the night. They couldn't very well have missed our midnight race.

"There goes my job," I told Laddie. "It was worth it."

God, if only I could be sure I was right! If only I could know it hadn't all been in vain!

Then a soft muzzle brushed my neck—and it wasn't Laddie's, I was looking straight at him. A warm tongue took the barest swipe at my skin in a way that only one horse ever had.

Dancer's Fire.

But when I turned to look, she was gone free, and only empty, tranquil racetrack met my eyes.

THE PHANTOM WATCH

by Charles Ingrid

"**Y**e've been cheated, all right," burly Thom said, as he thumped down a tankard of ale. "But ye've no proof, and without proof, ye can't go to the wards or th' court. All that's left at the King's Fair is half truths, if any. The watch in't what it used to be."

Amry watched a lip of foam curl over the rim and slop onto the planken table, where it bubbled into a wet stain. The innkeep absentmindedly wiped the stain dry with his apron before lowering his bulk onto the bench, shrewdly watching her companion, her brother-in-law.

"Then there's naught can be done," Magray answered. "He's forced us to sell to him. We're to show him the horses the last candlemark before dusk." He drowned the sorrow of his words in his tankard. "I've been to the courts anyway."

"And?"

"And they turned me away. Wouldn't even give me a hearing. Says if Naliff wants to buy diseased stock and take them away, we should be thankful for the deal." He licked at foam clinging to his mustache. "I curse the day I ever heard of the King's Fair!"

Amry felt as though she'd fallen off horseback and had had the wind knocked out of her. Her stomach and lungs clenched to breathe. "We can't

give up! Magray, you stood for Ilsa's love, though
the whole family were against you at first. Stand
now! We can't sell."

"There's no choice to it, lass. Sold or they'll
butcher our stock in the morning. That wizard has
the fair officials thinking the horses are diseased,
and they'll be slaughtered, and that'll be the end
of it."

Beyond Thom's thick shoulders and Magray's
bent ones, she could see her reflection in a battered war shield hanging behind the bar. She listened to their quiet words as they talked in the
near deserted inn, and as her eyes met her reflection's, Amry's face flushed. Then she pushed her
hair from her forehead in a defiant gesture. It was
as good as words. Don't let them get away with
it, she told herself silently.

Her gaze flicked back as Thom growled, "Don't
be a fool, Magray. Nay, man ... he's coveted that
stallion and mares of yers the minute ye marched
'em through the stockyard gates. He and his foul
sorcery could care less about ye, as long as he has
th' beasts."

"We don't sell our stallions, or cut them either,"
Amry said. "We've got to have time to prove what
Naliff's done. Magic like his isn't allowed."

"Not allowed, no, but," and the innkeep gave a
heavy shrug. "Lass, ye're young and innocent yet.
Knowin' what Naliff's done and provin' it are two
entirely different things. Ye've no witnesses but
me t' say yer stock was healthy when ye brought
'em through—he'll have bribed ever'one else. And
I'm nay witness th' court will allow, seein' as howt
affects me as well. I'm to be fined for stablin' yer
poxy herd ... and anyone with riding beasts
warned away from here for th' next ten-day. Else
why d' ye think the Half Helm stands empty this
afternoon, eh? We'll weather it. Th' Helm has a

fine reputation. We're here, fair or no, th' year around."

"But we can't quit now."

Magray looked at her from under bats' wings of brows. "Do you suggest we follow the wizard, then, and find ourselves turned into boils, too? No, we'll go home. We've other stock, though the stud's a bit young, and we'll start over again. It won't be the first time a greedy man's tried to ruin us—and failed." His faded gray eyes met Amry's intense blue ones. "Come on, lass. I'll take you around the fair. It'll be your first and last chance to see it. Besides, I promised Ilsa presents."

She stood firm. Her voice rang out. "The only way to fight magic is with magic!"

As Magray unfolded his lanky height, Thom put back his head in laughter. "Why, then, girl, ye might as well go to th' phantom half helm, for all the help ye'll find against Naliff."

"A phantom watch?"

Thom stood up and took Amry's cool hand in his big, warm paw, and led her outside. They blinked for a moment. In the last glinting rays of the afternoon, he pointed at the swinging sign over the inn. "Me grandma named this inn after him."

She saw only a half helm boldly painted under the name, in flaking gray paint. Then, as she squinted, she thought she saw the ghostly outlines, faded by weather and time, of a face. "A ghost?"

"A half helm," he asserted. "Once a real man, though full of mystery. The only honest man at th' King's Fair." The innkeeper led her back inside the shadowed taproom. "A man o' tragedy, as the story goes."

Magray folded his arms. "I've had enough of tragedy."

"Let me hear, please," Amry begged. She sat

down on a stool and hugged her knees under her chin. Her own family history was proud of its survival, and she never tired of hearing that story.

"He'd been wronged by a woman, me grandma said. He'd come from noble blood, that much was obvious, and had loved and been wronged by her. So he drifted to the King's Fair in search of her, and here he stayed. He started the watch, to protect fairgoers and strays. He was a big man, brawny and 'andsome, but he'd no heart left for love. He helped any who came to 'im and died in his tracks when he got old, still makin' the rounds." Thom's voice lowered dramatically. "He never found his woman nor the peace he sought neither. 'Tis said he still makes his rounds. That's why, on the full moon, I allus leave a glass on th' table when I shut th' taproom down fer the night. Me grandma done it, and me dad and now me. Sometimes th' beer's there in th' morning, flat and soured—but sometimes, it's been drained to th' bottom and th' glass turned upsidedown on th' bar."

Magray brayed, startling Amry, breaking the silence which had brought cat hair prickles to the back of her neck. He took her hand and squeezed it. "A good ghost story, that, Master Thom."

Thom laughed, too, and shook his head. He wagged a finger. "Never you mind, Magray. I leave a glass like I said, and draw me own conclusions. Go do your business, see the fair, and think better of us."

But as Amry left, she turned and looked over her shoulder to her image which stood like a tall, untried yearling in the corner of the room, and something unsaid passed through their gaze. Do something! the other seemed to urge her. Amry swallowed tightly and followed her brother-in-law out the door.

*   *   *

Magray made a face at her. "Couldn't you have worn something more . . . fetching?"

She pointed a finger at him. "You want to hamper Ilsa with skirts and fine dresses, that's her business. But I wear what I want, and when I work with my horses, I wear trousers!"

Magray's brows fluttered. "It wouldn't hurt to sweeten the wizard with a little honey."

She entered the stock pen and Hammer came to her, his proud neck crested, despite the boils and hives which stood out through his fiery coat. His ribs showed and his hooves were fraying as though brittle. All this in two days . . . whatever the wizard had struck them with. She caught her breath and stroked the stallion. He put his muzzle down to her ear, making chuffing sounds as if he spoke with her.

Amry looked up at Magray. "I know," she answered the horse. "He hears, but he doesn't listen." She took a comb from the pack hanging on the corral railing and began delicately to groom the beast. The herbs she'd put into their drinking buckets seemed to have quelled the fierce itching of earlier, but she'd no magic potion to heal them. Nor had she any doubt Naliff probably did.

This trip had been a testing for both her and her brother-in-law. Magray was probably still aware of the uneasy acceptance he'd had into the family. He'd horse sense enough, though no sense for the horses of Dahar, despite marrying Ilsa. Her sister should have told him all, Amry thought, and leaned into the brush. Hammer grunted and leaned back.

Magray picked up a second brush and took the gray mare Daharma, Hammer's favorite.

As for Amry, her testing had been as trainer, to show their stock and develop new interest in it, beyond the borders of their own countryside. The family had been hesitant about letting her go and this disaster was all her fault. She laced her fingers into Hammer's mane. "How can I undo all this?"

Magray responded as if the question was for him. "Sell the horses."

Hammer turned his head. With a thoughtful look on his sculpted face, he lifted a hoof and planted it firmly, but lightly, on Magray's booted foot.

The lanky man yelped. "Get him off, Amry."

She hid her smile against the chestnut's flank. "Be careful what you say, Magray. He's thinking of shifting his weight."

The stallion's hide rippled with muscles.

"All right, all right. I'll think of something. But you hold your sass when Naliff's here. In this part of the world, a woman holds her tongue."

"All right. But see if you can sell the mares only. Hammer stays with me." Magray came from another part of the world, Amry thought, one she never wished to visit. Hammer moved his hoof as Amry scratched his chin with the brush. The horse made a contented sound.

The mares flung up their heads and moved away from the railing as a man approached, Daharma leaving Magray with a handful of pewter mane. Hammer stood his ground, nostrils flaring.

Naliff put his hands upon the top bar carefully. He dressed in blacks and russets, rings flashing on every finger, sidelocks curled, and his dark eyes drinking in the beauty of their horses. Amry abhorred him.

"The illness has not sapped their spirit," the wizard said to Magray. "We may have a deal yet. Can you show me their paces?"

Her brother-in-law flashed her a warning look as he stepped through the bars and joined the man. Amry put up her brush, and stood, one hand lightly on Hammer's withers.

"First of all, noble sir, the horses were healthy when we brought them from Dahar."

Naliff licked his lips. "I don't doubt that. There is always hazard when traveling from one region to another. It's a wonder your own health hasn't suffered from the change in diet and water. If we can deal quickly, I might be able to help you. Or the courts will force you to put down your stock, to keep the illness from spreading." He looked about. "Who's riding?"

"I am," said Amry. She grasped a hank of Hammer's mane and vaulted up bareback. She tried to ignore the greedy eyes drinking up the sight of her.

The stallion did everything she asked of him, as she knew he would, their lines melded into one fluid being with one thought and one rhythm. The mares paced close so that she could slide onto their backs as well, and she showed off each of their skills, a mare for ladies' riding, a battle mount, a hunter for jumping terrain, a cutting horse for stock, a pleasure horse for the sheer joy of riding.

But always she came back to Hammer, her pride and joy, his body moving with power and grace. When she slipped finally from his back, sweat darkened his coat and his nostrils were cupped wide for air, their delicate inner lining wine-dark. He lipped at her sleeve.

Magray and the wizard spoke closely, in voices she could not hear. Naliff looked up once, hungrily, at her, and then quickly back to her brother-in-law. Then he took his leave. Magray looked after him. He turned reluctantly to Amry as she approached.

"What happened?"

"We haven't much choice, Amry. If he doesn't take the horses, he'll force the issue with the courts to have them destroyed."

"I know that! What happened?"

"He'll take them all. If I sell your services as well. So I did."

"What?" Her face went hot. "You did what?"

"It's a common practice here. Don't worry. You can slip off later—I'll come get you. It's our only way of getting out of here."

"What about Hammer?"

"He'll take him only if you can keep him in hand. Otherwise, he's to be gelded and broken. You did a fine job with him . . . too fine. The wizard knows he'll only perform like that for you. If you refuse to come along, he'll leave the horse to be put down."

She leaned against the rails in cold shock. "We don't sell our stallions," she protested feebly. "We don't geld them or sell them."

"I know that," Magray said impatiently. "And I think it's stupid. Any breeder will tell you that gelding can improve some horses."

"These are horses of Dahar. And you know nothing if you don't know that!" She could never leave Hammer. Magray had sold them both into slavery, unwitting of what he did. Amry pushed angrily through the bars. Hammer made a whicker as if punctuating her statement.

Magray caught her elbow. "Where there's life, there's hope. We can work it out."

She paused. She scuffed her boots in the dust, reminding herself that this was her sister's husband, new to the family and new to Dahar. "All right," she said. "We'll find a way."

"Good." He smiled tentatively. "Let's see the fair while there's time."

Amry went with him, boiling inside. If she was to have justice, she'd have to find it herself, she knew. Magray had only worsened things. He'd had no right to sell her services as well, although she knew she'd go, just to stay with her horses, hoping to find a way to free them. But there had to be another way.

The fair was as wondrous as she'd always heard. The scent of charcoal fires and exotic spices sizzling in pans over them filled the dusk with smoky mystery. The booths spilled over with every sort of treasure she could ever dream. Colors dazzled her until she squeezed her eyes tightly shut, remembering only the lush green valleys of her home else she would be blinded to their beauty once she left the fair. She opened them with a sharp cry as she stumbled into the corner of a booth, fetched up against it, and grabbed for her knee.

"Well, beauty," a hoarse voice observed. "You'd see more of the fair if you kept your eyes open."

Amry scrubbed out the angry sting of her shin, then turned about. If the booth had been as flimsy as some of them, she'd have brought it crashing down. But no, this booth was built like a rock—and just as hard, she thought ruefully, as Magray halted, waiting for her. The sign hanging over proclaimed for those who could read, "Four generations at the King's Fair" and below it, the tools of the leatherwork trade were engraved.

She felt drawn. The richness of tanned leather filled her nostrils. She smiled at the woman enthroned beyond, her lap filled with a chamois blouse, her nimble fingers in the process of sewing beads to it.

Magray flexed impatiently. "Amry?"

"A minute, please."

He looked at the ground as fairgoers brushed past him. "I'll be a stall or two down," he said, and left abruptly.

The leatherworker woman looked at Amry. The elder woman's complexion was as finely drawn as the leather she worked, and her silver hair was pulled tightly back into a bun at the nape of her neck.

Amry said, "You must know all the tales of the fair."

"Ask me your questions and I'll give you my answers. I've no time for dancing around, beauty."

"The ghost of the night watch."

The woman put a silencing finger over her shocked expression. "Best not to mention *him* at night. Come in, girl, and look, if you please," the woman added, her voice rich with the accent of another country. "You are a girl, are you not?"

Amry flushed. She still wore leather trousers and boots, and a big sleeved shirt under her beaded vest, but for the riding and training she did, it was practical. And, even here at the fair, she'd been recognized as undeniably female. Nimble fingers she could not catch were forever pinching her bottom. Despite the trousers, the cascade of honey-colored hair she left waving free about her face and shoulders when she wasn't riding gave her away. She pointed up at the sign. "Is that true? Four generations?"

"Indeed it is. Five, now, though my son is out gambling or wenching somewhere tonight."

Amry offered the leathermaker her hand. "I'm Amry."

The hardened and callused hand of the other grasped hers. "Hist, beauty. Don't be so quick to give away your true name. There's magic in it, you know. Call me Fahren."

With a catch in her breath, scarcely able to believe her luck in the other's superstition, Amry sat down on a stool opposite Fahren. "Tell me," she said. There seemed no other solution. "Tell me about the Silver Helm."

The woman tilted her head, then sighed a little. "Not my goods, but the ghost that brought you."

Fahren crossed her wrists over the chamois blouse in her lap. She smiled faintly. The signboard creaked as it swung back and forth in a light breeze. "Tell me your story."

And so Amry did, from the wintery morning when the family had decided, against strict tradition, to make the long journey to send the horses to the fair. To participate in the exhibitions of horsemanship, to demonstrate their bloodstock, sleek, fine, fast and proud mounts. Not for sale, these, but to show the buyers at the King's Fair what they had bred, and to take orders for the future. From those days to the long ride, and then the disastrous morning (was it only yesterday?) that the wizard Nallif had cast eyes on the stallion Hammer and attempted to buy him. Amry's gentle rebuff seemed to have angered the wizard. With the dawn had come livestock inspectors and the accusation of disease-ridden animals.

Amry's lips thinned as she told the tale, and she tossed her head, so that her mane of hair fanned over the back of her shoulders as she described the boils that affected the tender lips of her horses, and the splitting hooves, and the other symptoms Naliff had devised.

"Diseased," Fahren repeated, the only interruption she made, until Amry finished the tale with the ghost story told by Master Thom. She did not tell of Magray's disgraceful bargain.

Silence fell. Amry stirred then, wondering briefly that they had not been interrupted, despite the growing crowd of evening shoppers and revelers. A man stopped then, picked up a vest and, after a quick negotiation with Fahren, took away his purchase.

Fahren sat down with a swirl of skirts. "This is bad," she said. "All things pass through the King's Fair sooner or later, even evil. There is little you can do to stop Naliff now, though if we had time, we could trap him in his own devices."

"I thought of going to the phantom for justice." Fahren shuddered.

"Then you *have* heard of him."

"He passes by each moonlit night, but few can see him unless they're looking. As for finding him, he has a way of finding those looking for him. But a tale that Master Thom spins to sell ale is not necessarily a tale of what happened." Fahren took a deep breath as if to ease her hoarse throat. "There are two sides to every story. The man Thom describes as a paladin was an embittered man. He was kind to all he met, but a deep and festering darkness grew in his heart as the one he hoped most to meet never came. As he grew old, he despaired and turned to dark gods to continue the search."

"Dark gods?"

"It is rumored he gave his soul to Thorn."

Was it only Amry's imagination that all over the fair grounds, lanterns dimmed and candles guttered as Fahren uttered the name? She held back a shiver. "So that one gave him the power to walk after death."

"Another side of the tale. It's said those who've met him, particularly young ladies, have sorrowed of the meeting. Our phantom asks a heavy toll of those he would aid."

Amry made a sign against the dreaded visage of Thorn. Turning to him would be an even greater evil than letting the greedy Naliff have her horses.

Fahren sighed, "So, beauty, you must decide. The loss is great, but I think your family would mourn your loss even more." She stroked Amry's hand. "Let it be."

Magray called down the isleway, "Come on. We've more to see."

As Amry turned to go, Fahren grasped her hand tightly, fearfully. "Remember what I've said," she pleaded. "Think of me if you need a friend. The phantom watch is not for the likes of you!"

Amry felt the cold, hard touch of the leatherworker's hand long after Magray marched her down the lanes and amidst the booths.

After the fair wore out Magray and they both returned to the Half Helm, Amry lay awake staring at the ceiling. As she tried to claim the inner peace of sleep, she thought of her great-grandmother and what she would have done. Lindala had come to Dahar, fallen in love and married, but a vengeful shadow from her past followed. This lord ruined Lindala and her husband Marford, taking away all their steadings but the valley lands to which they again fled. Unable to pursue them further, the lord sent a curse after their sons as well.

As was her birthright, Lindala had taken a breeding pair of horses, defying the angry lord. And then she had started over, stripped of Marford's heritage as well as her own, and they built a new one together. No, Lindala had not been a quitter. Nor had she accepted as her lot the curse on her sons, and the secret of her mother's magic was one buried deep within the family.

As for Amry, she had no magic but her heritage with which to fight the wizard Naliff. Magray's bargain was no deal she intended to honor. Amry bit her lip. She slipped out from under the covers and went to her pack where she found papers Ilsa had prepared if Magray had not passed his testing. It had been Ilsa's decision, though Amry did not regret it. The man had heard but had not listened to the history of the family and what they had worked so hard to build and protect. She dressed and left her room. The sheaf of papers she slipped under her brother-in-law's door. Then Amry took a tavern lantern and went to the stock pens outside the fair, where her diseased horses stood in the moonlight, awaiting their doom.

Hammer threw up his head and sniffed, then came trotting to the fence, his dark red hide dappled black by night. He whuffled her empty hand. The mares followed cautiously: Fawn, Rosebud, skittish Daharma, fleet Empress and, lastly, stubborn Dancer. Amry felt a sudden warmth flood her eyes, and her vision of them blurred. In the moonlight, she saw no blemishes, no fever blisters, no haggard ribs or lackluster hides. Sure of his triumph, Naliff had already turned his fraudulent magics elsewhere, it seemed.

Hammer nibbled at the cuff of her shirt. She pulled on his long forelock. "No," she whispered. "You're right. We'll not be laid low again by the whims of a mad man." She shivered as Hammer snorted. "I thought of him, as well."

She left the pungent familiarity of the stock pens for the outer boundaries of the fair. Even at night, the grounds shone like a gem, a little dimmed, the gaiety slightly muffled. The fair never slept. She picked an out of the way corner, its grass lightly trampled, the sticklike tree a lone sentinel, and sat down, waiting. Her lantern cast an aura against the night.

Amry had slept. Her cricked neck jerked her back awake, and, for a moment, she dropped her hand to the inside calf of her boot, feeling for her dagger. She cursed herself for nine-tenths of a fool, even isolated as she was.

A coldness that was not natural washed over her. Darker than shadow, an apparition stood over her. A faraway lantern reflected silverly off his half helm. Amry's tongue clove to the roof of her mouth as she looked up at him, and the phantom stared down at her.

"A bit of a girl like you shouldn't be out this late at night," the paladin ward said, and his voice was thinly human. "I stayed to watch over you, but it's time you should be off."

"Thank you, sir."

The apparition wavered. He had been handsome once, square-jawed and broad of forehead. She couldn't see the color of his eyes, for he had no real color left to him, none but that of the silver helm he wore. He seemed to remember something as he leaned on a shod fighting staff. "How is it you see me?"

"I was looking for you."

Embers came to life in the death-stilled eyes. "Why? Have you work for me?"

"I do." She scrambled to her feet.

His form became more solid. "What do you wish?"

"Justice."

The being laughed dryly. "There is fair-law and fair-court. That's where you'll find justice, among the living. Those who look for me have other ... desires."

His gaze had heated. It swept over her. She remembered Fahren's warning and shivered. "It's justice I want and the court won't give it to me. I have no proof of the foul sorcery done."

The man tilted his head up a little, as if gauging the moonlight. He balanced his weighted stave in his hands. "There'll be a price to pay."

"For my family's honor, I'll pay it."

His eyes met her gaze. "It's not my price, but Thorn's," he warned.

"I know. But Magray's given up and I've no one else to turn to."

"Then tell me your story."

In halting words, Amry told the phantom of

Naliff's greed and fraud. It seemed to her that the phantom grew heated as she talked, gaining substance with every word, and taking on her own anger. When she'd finished, there was silence.

Then, "And you wish his death."

"No! But I want him to admit his deceit and I want my horses back."

"And who will take them from the fair?"

Amry's breath fluttered in her throat a second at the implication. She got out, "Magray will be strong enough for that. He'll take them back."

The ward twirled his stave, then nodded abruptly. "It's done, then. You wait here for me. I'll have your justice my way." He left, in a wind of bitter cold and righteous heat.

Amry staggered back, her heart pounding with what she'd done. The tree caught her up, bracing her retreat. She thought a moment of running and then realized the futility of it—and that she had given her word. She closed her eyes in fear. Scant moments later, a figure loomed in the dark. Amry quailed, thinking her end had come so quickly.

"There you are! You're white as a ghost."

Amry looked up, as Fahren caught her wrists, and the elder woman looked keenly at her. "What are you doing here? Your brother came by the booth, saying you were missing. He was half mad." She caught her breath. "You've seen the phantom, haven't you? My beauty, what have you done?"

Amry laughed wildly. "I've gone for justice to the only one who can give it to me."

"No." Fahren tried to warm her cold hands between her callused palms. "Where is he?"

"Just gone."

"Then we have a while. Listen to me closely, for you must stand for yourself until I come back with a priestess—"

"That's how I knew to come to you." Amry stared with sudden realization. "And why no one interrupted us at the booth."

Fahren made a face. "Do you think we would abandon the king or the King's Fair to Thorn?" Fine lines creased in her face. "Will you be all right while I go get help?"

"I'll try. What can we do?"

"I'm not sure. The Silver Helm has been gone so long, no one remembers his name—our records were sketchy then. By the time we knew of his phantom existence, he'd been dead for thirty some years, and his name all but lost, and it's been decades since then. He could be Alfred, or Brethed or Roston or any of a half dozen other common names. This I do know: he was a just man in life, and the shackles Thorn put on him are thin ones that he could break easily enough, if he wished."

A sharpness pierced Amry's thoughts at her words. It was Hammer's trumpet, from the stock pens, calling her. She straightened and withdrew her hands from Fahren's. "What will happen to me when he returns?"

"He'll ask you three questions. There's a chance, a slight one, that he will let you free. If not . . . the lucky ones die, Amry." Fahren swallowed tightly.

"Then I'll have to live until you get back."

Leaning forward, the priestess leatherworker kissed her forehead lightly in blessing. "I'll be back as soon as I can."

Her lantern, low on oil, spluttered out as Fahren left. Amry toed it aside, saying to herself, "There're two sides to every story."

She went to the stock pen and freed Hammer. The stud paced by her side, her touch on him feather-light. He stood with her as she sat down under the stick tree, to watch for the phantom, waiting for her fate to return. She told him of the deal she'd made, better she thought, than Magray's.

The stallion did not seem to agree and if any had watched, they would have thought the two deep in conversation.

He came just after her eyes had grown heavy, and she thought she might have to sleep again. Hammer stomped in warning as bitter cold swept over her again. The ward put a hand out to help her. The touch of him was like breaking the ice off a water bucket on a winter's morn.

He drew away at her flinch.

"It's done," the ghostly fair-ward announced. "Naliff is a vain and greedy man, with a liking for wine. He drank overly much and found the wrong man to boast to. The judge, an honest man, will meet him at the stock pens in the morning. Naliff, like his liquor, can't hold his magic. The deception is over. Your horses will be returned to your family at daybreak."

How simple, she thought. *Magray should have thought of it*. Aloud, she said, "And what of me?"

The phantom seemed hesitant, weighing his staff in his hands once more. He looked down at her. "It is not in me to take what is not mine or even *his*. I'll ask three questions of you ... if the answers please me, you're free to go. If not," the glowing eyes looked over the stallion. "Even he cannot carry you away from me."

Amry tried to moisten her lips. Hammer nudged her, giving her the strength to do what she had determined. "I agree. But Fahren tells me that Thorn cannot hold you, if you decide to quit your bargain with him. You had a reputation for being a good man."

The phantom made a hollow sound. "So good that no one remembers my name. I've been dead these many years, but one day, flesh of her flesh will come to the fair, and then I'll have my vengeance." He smiled and Amry saw the glow of fair lanterns through his parted lips as he grew transparent. "You may be too young to answer what I have to ask."

Amry flexed her shoulders, wondering if she had time. "Then ask away."

"Why would a woman say she loved a man and then leave him?"

She stood a moment. She knew nothing of love but that she felt for her family and her horses. The ghost misjudged her silence and grated, "If you wait for moonlight to pass, or dawn to come, you wait in vain. They've no power over me. I'll be here until I've collected my price."

Hammer snorted defiance. The ward ignored him.

Amry tilted her head, answering, "I was only thinking! The question you asked has no right or wrong answer without knowing the man or woman. If you were just and kind and loved her—"

"With all my heart and soul!" the phantom declared.

"Then I would say, she left for love."

He snorted then, in disbelief. "Love?"

"Yes. She loved you so much that she felt the only way to save you was to leave you."

The ward considered that a moment. Moonlight glimmered off his helm. From the tightening of his ghostly lips, Amry knew she hadn't pleased him with her answer. She shifted. "The second question?"

"Why did she never return to me?"

Amry looked across the empty meadow to the boundaries of the fair, and saw no one to save her but herself and the stallion at her back. She cleared her throat. "Perhaps she found another to love, and he loved her back, and she settled for that, knowing she could never return to you."

The outlines of his hands blurred as they tightened about the staff. He swiped its tip viciously at the ground. "Then she played me falsely, after all."

"If that is what you wish to think. And the third question?"

"Are you that eager to be lost to Thorn?"

"No."

His amber eyes glittered. "Then tell me—what is my name?"

Amry felt as though she clung precariously to a bolting horse, and wrapped her fingers tightly about the side seams of her trousers. "Before I answer that . . . may I tell you a story? A story about my family?"

His lip lifted in a sneer. "Why would I be wanting to hear that?"

"Because my first two answers didn't please you, but if you knew about my family—you might think differently."

The phantom stared at her, then dipped his head. "I'll listen."

"My great-grandmother built our heritage. She'd been betrothed, but a wicked lord drove her away from his son. She went, under great protest, but she couldn't do anything else because the lord even threatened his own son's life. And she fled to Dahar, where we make our home."

"Where she no doubt met your great-grandfather and began a dynasty."

Amry smiled faintly. "Something like that. Only, the wicked lord was inflamed with jealousy and vengeance. He did his best to ruin them. Trading rights, land charter, lordship, all he took away or ruined by deceit. But my great-grandparents made their own life and survived. A curse was laid on the sons of their line, and my great-grandmother worked a magic to protect them—" Amry reached out and stroked Hammer's jaw line. "Today, the horses of Dahar are like no other in the world. We treat with kings and lords again, and carry our heads with pride."

"Which fairy tale no doubt colored your answers to my questions."

Amry unclenched a hand and grasped her fate instead. "No tale, phantom ... there are two sides to every story, and the tale you just heard was your own. The answer to your last question is the name of the lordling my great-grand-mother fled to protect, Sir Roston. I am the child of Lindala."

Gouts of flame spouted from the being's eye sockets. "Vengeance is mine!" the phantom wailed. Hammer reared in protest, protecting her, and in the gory light, a man's shadowy form could be seen within his stallion's outline, son of the son of the son of the mother. Amry gasped with fright as the two squared off, phantom and horse. Hammer struck. His hoof rang off the silver helm. Sparks shot into the velvet night.

Holding onto his stave as though it were his salvation, the phantom fell to his knees. "Lindala— her son and her daughter—I see her in your faces."

"You believe?" Magray had not been able to.

The phantom doubled over. A sound came out then that she recognized. Hammer came to earth as Amry kneeled close. The long-dead man sobbed.

She reached out to touch him. "I'm sorry, lord," she murmured. "But all things come to the King's Fair sooner or later ... even the truth."

When Fahren hurried back to the spindly tree at the fairground's edge, a robed noviate panting at her heels, she found both the dawn and Amry waiting for her, chestnut stallion at her side. She clasped the girl in a grateful hug. "We're in time!"

Amry smiled, a bittersweet expression. "In time to take this pile of ash, all that's left of a poor soul who's finally escaped Thorn's hold. Take it, he asked, to the garden of Light ... and pray for him." And she pointed at the final remains of the phantom watch, an empty silver helm toppled to the side.

THE CZECHOSLOVAKIAN PIGEON FARMER AND THE PONY THAT WASN'T A PAINT

by Mary Stanton

The ad showed up in the "Livestock For Sale" section of the *Byron County Farm Weekly*.

PAINT PONY FOR SALE: To good home only. Papers. Good confirmation. $850. Call 546-8237.

When Hank came in for supper, irritable from the slow, dull work of discing the north forty, Maureen brandished the newspaper in front of him, dragging the bottom edge through the tuna casserole.

"Eight hundred and fifty dollars!" said Maureen. "For a registered Paint!"

'Hulluva lot for a damn pony,' said Hank. He drained his beer, wiped his mouth carefully with his napkin, and reached across the supper table to swtich the television to a rerun of *Family Feud*.

"Of course it's too much for a pony. It's a ridiculous price for a pony. But it isn't a pony!"

"What?"

"Look. The people that placed the ad didn't even spell 'conformation' right." She rustled the *Farm Weekly* disdainfully. "Bunch of amateurs. 'Confirmation' indeed. No, I'll bet you anything that this 'Paint pony' is a horse. Fourteen hands at least, or maybe bigger. I mean, what kind of

81

fool would ask that kind of money for a pony? And the papers—see, it says right here, 'papers'—whoever heard of a registered Paint pony? Now, a registered Paint horse is a different matter."

"Paints are spotted, right?"

"Right. This is a bargain. This is the kind of deal that only comes along once in a lifetime. I'm going to call these people right now, before somebody else figures out what's going on and gets there first."

"Look," said Hank. "The buckskin mare's not been dead a week. Why don't you wait to buy a new horse. Look around a bit."

"You *promised*," said Maureen, summoning ready tears, "you promised I could have a new horse. And I've always, always wanted a Paint. It's a wonderful, wonderful breed. They make fantastic riding horses."

"The ad says, 'pony,' " Hank pointed out.

"The ad also says eight hundred and fifty dollars," said Maureen.

She sailed through the kitchen like a heron after bass in the stock pond, dived for the phone, and made the call.

"Hello? Pliz?" said a distant voice.

"Hello," said Maureen in carefully modulated, brightly cheerful tones. "This is Maureen Reddick. I'm calling about that ad for the pony you had in the newspaper."

"Yah!" said the voice, more enthusiastically. "Is *gut* pony. Needs *gut* home."

"Oh, we have that," promised Maureen. "A fine airy box stall, and a little paddock outside of it. We own a farm, you see. Sir, I just have one question," What *was* that accent? Czechoslovakian, probably. And the voice was fairly androgynous—maybe it wasn't a "sir," but a "ma'am." "This—ah—"she laughed a little, "*pony* you've got. How big is it? How tall?"

"Beeg?" said the voice in a puzzled way, "How beeg you want?"

"Oh, fifteen hands, at least," said Maureen firmly. "I couldn't be bothered to look at anything smaller. I'm just not in the market for a small pony, you understand."

"Thees pony iss, I theenk, maybe feefteen hands."

Bingo! "Great!" said Maureen, "If you can tell us where you live, we'll be over right away."

"Hah!" said Maureen gleefully, after she had dragged the resisting Hank into the pickup truck, and they were gunning down the road. "That poor guy—at least, I *think* it was a guy—didn't even speak English well, much less know a pony from a horse. I'm telling you, sweetie, this is a *deal*."

"Left on Slocum Road?" asked Hank, bored.

"Right, I mean yes, left. He said there's a sign in front of the house, and a blue Chevy in the driveway."

"What does it say on the sign, Maureen? I mean, there're signs and signs." He shifted down with an exasperated roar of the engine. "Keep out?" he suggested. "No trespassers? Beware of . . ."

"People who shoot birds will be shot," said Maureen.

"Hah?"

"Look, there's the blue car. And there's the sign. It says, 'People who shoot birds will be shot.' "

Hank switched off the ignition and gazed rather thoughtfully at the sign. It had been painted with firm strokes of a wide brush, the kind that's normally used to paint a fence. The house itself was dilapidated; windows sported boards instead of glass, and the freshest paint by 20 years appeared on the peeling sign and nowhere else. Pigeons swooped gracefully out of a tiny shed attached to the one car garage.

"My Christ," said Hank. "Passenger pigeons."

"I thought they were extinct."

"Not quite, I guess. That's unbelievable. Passenger pigeons!"

"The place is tidy, at least," said Maureen doubtfully.

Hank agreed this was true. The gravel drive had been carefully swept free of leaves, the grass was trimmed, and the boards on the windows, although undeniably boards, and not glass, had been neatly lined up with one another.

"Hai!"

Maureen jumped.

A stocky, thickset old man stumped out from behind the shed. He was carrying an armful of timothy hay. Maureen, to her astonishment, noticed that it must have been hand-scythed, for the long and slender reeds lay neatly parallel to one another in the old man's arms.

"Um, we called about the horse, I mean pony," said Maureen.

"Yess!" The old man seemed overjoyed to see them. His white mustache, rimmed with yellow, trembled with delight. "Sheeba, iss. Sheeba iss *gut* pony. She need *gut* home."

"Why're you selling?" asked Hank, craftily.

"Oh," the old man shrugged, a massive, self-deprecating shrug, "I don' unnerstan' thees pony. I got no use for thees pony. I got pigeons for passenger," he waved vaguely at the circling birds, "I don' need pony no more."

"Passenger pigeons," said Hank. "Those are passenger pigeons, and I thought whatever of those birds were left were in zoos. How did you. . . ?"

"Pigeons for passengers," said the old man firmly. "Come, I show you pony. Follow, pliz."

They followed the old farmer to the back of the shed. A trim paddock formed a U at the rear entrance, and the old man rattled the paddock gate. "Shheba!" he shouted. "SheeBA!"

Maureen fixed her gaze expectantly on the open back door of the shed.

Hank nudged her. "Down there," he said, "closer to the ground."

One of the smallest ponies Maureen ever seen tripped out of the shed. Perfectly shaped, the pony was glossy black, with a diamondlike sheen to its hooves.

"That's not a horse" said Maureen, "that's a pony!"

"Feefteen leetle tiny hands," muttered Hank.

"Iss *pony*," said the farmer.

"And it's not even a Paint!" wailed Maureen.

"It *iss*," said the farmer. "Iss Paint pony. You see? You can do anythink weeth thees pony." The old man grasped the pony by the forelegs and hauled it up on his chest. The pony blinked patiently at Hank and Maureen over the old man's shoulder. "Anythink!" The farmer dropped the pony's foreleg with a thump, skipped around to the hindquarters, and pulled the hind feet skyward. "See!" he crowed in triumph, "eef I unnerstan' thees pony, I kip!"

"Keep," said Maureen involuntarily, "you mean *keep* it. Gosh, it's really a little love, Hank. And so pretty."

"Yas! And thees pony's confirmation ..." The old man formed a circle with his thumb and forefinger and beamed.

"*Confor* ..." muttered Maureen, "Oh, never mind. Hank, he's right about the conformation. The hocks are clean, the pasterns are sloped properly, and the general, all around shape is pretty good." She spoke up, in the firm belief that the farmer would understand English if it was at the proper pitch. "Eight hundred and fifty dollars is too much," she said. "This pony is worth maybe—two hundred dollars."

"Two hun ..." roared the farmer. "No! Is *gut*

pony. Has *gut* confirmation. The bast! In the old country, thees pony *chip* at eight hundred feefty dollars."

"Cheap, huh," said Maureen. "Well, let me tell *you*, mister, that in this *new* country, the United States of America, two hundred dollars is a damn good price."

"Actually," said the pony, "I can confirm that, Lazlo. Given the current rate of exchange between Ph'aaint and this planet, it's a fair price. And as for you, ma'am," the pony turned courteously to Maureen, "I can confirm that you're right about my color. I am not a Paint, that is, a spotted horse, but a Ph'aaint. As you can see, we Ph'aaints do have excellent confirmation abilities, perhaps the best in the galaxy, if you are not offended by my immodesty."

"I tell you," the old man shouted in exasperation, "I no unnerstan' thees pony!"

"Pigeons for passengers," said Hank faintly. He looked up at the circling birds, and for an icy moment, thought he saw tiny booted feet peeking from the pin feathers.

"Hank," said Maureen, "Hank. I want to go home. NOW."

"Paint," said Hank, looking at the pony, who gave him a genial wink.

"Hank!"

They raced for the pickup. Hank jammed the key into the ignition. They tore down the drive and swerved a frantic left turn onto the road.

"Hai" shouted Lazlo the pigeon farmer after the receding truck. "You no like thees pony? You no like pony, you wanna see my randy rooster?"

Maureen pressed her knees together and shrieked, "Drive, Hank, drive!"

RIDING THE NIGHTMARE

by Jennifer Roberson

Clayt Simmons worked at getting his gloved right hand through the snug handle of the bareback rigging. The rosin squeaked as he yanked on his fingers with his free hand, pulling the palm through to curve itself around the suitcase-style handle.

—heard the squeal of leather, the advice and comments of cowboys, the slamming of the chute gate—

Already Clayt could feel the tightness in his chest and belly, but tried to ignore it. Tried to think only of the horse he had to ride for eight seconds.

—the grunt of the mare beneath him, the roaring fog in which he had survived for eight seconds and more. The crowd, as always, was a blur; the rodeo announcer's voice a reverberating rumble in the coliseum—

If he stayed aboard until the buzzer and somehow managed, simultaneously, to show off his riding skill, he might win a dollar or two. And the good Lord knew he needed it. Needed it *badly*, what with bank loans due on his father's ranch. Ranchers were as bad off as the farmers.

—felt the leather of his glove, the painful tightness

*of the rigging handle; heard the chinging spur-song
as he set rowels against the mare's shoulders—*

Abruptly, Clayt frowned. He wasn't *on* a mare.
He was on a gelding, a big splotchy dun-and-white
gelding named Evil-Eye. Not a mare. Not a black,
angry mare—

"Hey, cowboy, you still with us?"

He twitched, jerked unceremoniously out of his
reverie. Clayt looked up from the gelding, blinking, frowning, still a bit disoriented. Cowboys
lined the chute he inhabited. Some helped. Some
watched the action in the arena. One or two stared
at him as if he'd lost his mind.

He wasn't so sure he hadn't, what with taking
a walkabout while getting set on the big old
splotchy bronc. It disturbed him. He knew better.
A cowboy losing his concentration in the rodeo
arena generally lived to regret it. Profoundly and
painfully.

The animal shifted beneath him, quivering with
pent-up excitement and anticipation. Old Evil-Eye
clearly knew what was happening and what was
expected of him. Clayt was too smart to label any
horse "stupid." A cowboy might be completely
dedicated to riding a bronc no matter what the
horse did to dissuade him of it, but the bronc was
every bit as dedicated to shedding the rider on
his back. It was an even match of will, strategy,
strength, and skill.

Most of all, for man or animal, it was the *challenge*. Pure and simple.

—heard her angry scream—

Clayt bit down on his lip. Already chapped, it
broke; he tasted the salt-copper tang of blood. It
hurt, but the pain helped. It sharpened his wits
and made him recall that more was riding on this
bronc than just a rookie cowboy trying to win a
few bucks and a reputation. He *needed* the win.
More than the champions and other top riders did,

who flew from rodeo to rodeo aboard private jets or commercial airliners. More than the hometown boys riding for a lark, showing off their manhood to fathers and mothers and girlfriends.

The horse's back was bony and uncomfortable, but foam rubber padding tucked into his jeans helped a little. Clayt shifted carefully on big Evil-Eye, edging his way up toward the rawhide bare-back rigging so he could reach forward with booted feet to set the spurs in front of the gelding's shoulders, almost on his chest. If Clayt missed setting those spurs the first jump out of the chute, he'd be disqualified.

He couldn't afford that. He couldn't afford the fifty-dollar entry fee, either, but riding the horse was better than riding the fence. Besides, it was what he did. His *job*, as much as selling shoes or tending bar was for others. It was all he *could* do, to help his father pay the bank.

Clayt heard his name blurted out of the PA system, reduced to familiar-sounding syllables he couldn't, in that moment, quite fit together into something identifiable. But it didn't really matter. He knew what it meant.

Time to go to work. Time to roll the dice.

He sucked in a gut-deep breath and nodded to the gateman. The lever whanged up and Clayt heard Evil-Eye's grunt of surprise as the chuteman yanked on the flank strap, locking sheepskin-padded belt around loins.

Free of snug confinement, the splotchy dun-and-white gelding exploded into the arena.

Electric lights bled into banks of glowing blobs. Watching faces smeared into a montage of flesh on flesh on flesh, with staring eyes and gaping mouths, emitting nothing more than *noise*. The announcer's accompanying commentary was a dim, nagging underscore to the equine violence between Clayt's legs.

Eight seconds became an eternity.

Evil-Eye was a powerful, experienced bronc who had no patience for rookie cowboys. He humped and spun and bucked, each thrust jarring Clayt's vertebrae together until he thought his spine was little more than stale, crusty oatmeal. Breath wheezed out of his chest and stayed out, taunting him with its absence.

The gelding was grunting. So was Clayt, trying to suck in air. And then it didn't matter any more because he was sailing toward Evil-Eye's ears.

And beyond, as his hand came loose of the handle.

In a tangle of arms and legs and sore pride, Clayt dug a hole in the dirt.

Damn. Damn. *Damn.*

He picked himself up, spat grit, retrieved his fallen hat. Heard the announcer asking the crowd to give the hard-luck cowboy a hand. Hated the commiserating applause as he walked toward the railing in disgust. Hated himself for hating it; what else could the crowd do? It was *his* job to ride the horse, theirs to applaud his efforts, no matter what the outcome.

Except he hadn't done his job.

He slapped the dusty hat against his leg. "*Damn.*"

Other cowboys squatted in a row of wide-brimmed hats and bent boots against the railing. Clayt, finished riding until he drew his second mount for a later performance, hunched down at the end of the line and stared glumly at the chutes.

"Tough luck," someone said. "Old Evil-Eye is a rough son. You did all right."

It was something. "All right" did not put prize money in his pockets, but the comment pleased Clayt anyway. He was brand new on the rodeo circuit, and there was an unspoken, unacknowledged apprenticeship a rookie was required to serve before being admitted to the loosely-organized brotherhood of men who rode horses and bulls, tied calves, or roped and wrestled steers in order to make a living.

Clayt knew he was more than "all right" in the small ranch arenas of West Texas. But the huge indoor rodeos of the Professional Rodeo Cowboys Association were a far cry from what he was used to.

This was the Big Time. This was Money, if he won. And to do that, he had to ride the bronc to the buzzer with as much skill and showmanship as he had in him. However much that *was*; God knew he hadn't shown much aboard Evil-Eye.

"Damn," he said again, very quietly, as the worm of shame and regret twisted deep in his belly.

—heard the crashing and smashing and angry squealing—

And abruptly, Clayt knew it was real. *Real* real, not a dream or walkabout, but happening that very moment in Chute 4, close by, where a horse reared in the chute, front legs flailing, beating wood, scraping white paint off boards to show the bone-gray, naked underbelly.

Like the others, he looked. Like the others, his sensitized ears picked out the curses and orders from the chute crew as men tried to settle the animal. And, like the others, he saw the cowboy on the angry bronc—at least as much as he could: a low-set gray hat and beneath it a white, staring face, masklike in apprehension.

Clayt didn't blame the cowboy for being afraid. A chute-fighter was the worst kind of bronc to draw because it was easy for the horse to go down while confined, to break flailing legs and smash head into wooden walls.

But more than that, Clayt knew, it was easy for the horse to ram a rider into the slats and corners

of the snug wooden chute; crushing spine, snapping arms, mashing legs and feet, cracking ribs
and pelvis.

The cowboy squatting at his right shook his
head. "That mare is about the meanest I ever
seen," he said. His tone was matter-of-fact, but
Clayt heard a tinge of admiration for such determined hostility. "If she can't kill you in the chute,
she does a tap-dance on you in the arena."

Clayt didn't take his eyes off the chute-fighting
mare. He couldn't. Because, somehow, he knew
her. *Knew* her, in some bizarre, uncanny way. Not
quite déjà vu, because he'd never seen her before.

Nonetheless, he knew her. And the realization
shook him.

He felt queasy. Cold. Sweaty, all at once and all
over, like he'd been jerked awake from the depths
of a too-vivid, unsettling dream.

—heard the crashing in the chute—

Forcibly, over the noise, he made himself ask,
"You've ridden her, then?"

The cowboy laughed, pushing a toothpick around
in his mouth with his tongue. "Ain't *nobody* rode
that witch. She's damn near a renegade."

The black mare screamed again, singing a song
Clayt recognized from his dreams. From the things
he called his walkabouts. Sweat stung his armpits.

The gate to Chute 4 crashed open, freeing the
mare from her prison. But the cowboy did not
accompany her. Numbly, Clayt saw he lay crumpled in the chute, unmoving, while the mare held
sovereignty in the arena.

Still hunkered down in the dirt, Clayt watched
the mare cast a rolling eye over the row of men
against the rail. Her direction abruptly shifted,
altering from a straightaway run down the center
of the arena to a sweeping charge of every man
squatting in the dirt.

Cowboys scattered, hurdling the railing into the

front-row seats; ducking striking hooves; running
for the chutes and relative safety. The dance was
not unknown, but almost uniformly reserved for
the bulls. It was not a thing generally associated
with Bareback or Saddle Bronc Riding.

But Clayt had no more time to ponder it,
because he was the only man still in range and
the mare was coming at him.

No. Not at him. *For* him, as if she'd picked him
out.

He heard rasping breath and snapping teeth,
bared in a vicious equine grin. Black ears were
pinned back into nothingness, making her head
look skinned. Dark eyes were fixed solely on him,
on *him*—

He leapt for the upper rail. Grasped it, swung
over, hung there, stiffly balanced; jerked his head
around to watch her go by.

And noticed, for the first time, there were no
pick-up men in the arena. Ordinarily, two mounted
men chased loose horses out of the arena into the
holding pens, but this time there were none. The
mare had the place to herself.

She made a circuit of the arena as if searching
for new prey. The announcer was having a field
day with it, telling the audience how the mare had
never been ridden and probably never would be,
the classic Horse Who Can't Be Rode.

"Nightmare," the announcer boomed into the
arena. "That's Nightmare, in the flesh."

Clayt, still clinging to the railing, watched as
the mare, ragged black tail aslash, went through
the alley gate at a gallop, heading at last for the
holding pens behind the coliseum.

Slowly, he jumped down into the dirt. Made his
way thoughtfully out of the arena through the
alley, and to the portable pens. Where she waited.

For him.

*   *   *

Her black coat was dull, ragged, fuzzy from winter. Mane and tail were snarled and matted. Eyes were half-closed, sleepy-lidded, barely reflecting the illumination from sodium lights that flooded pens and stock with a weak, pinkish light, like fresh blood cut with water.

Her very isolation bespoke a resounding lack of sociability. She was not alone in the pen, being confined with other broncs, but she stood in a corner, patently ignoring the other horses who milled around, snuffling in the dirt, lipping listlessly at dinner remains. She did none of it, the mare, holding solitary court.

Black nostrils flared slightly, sucking in the smells of the pen, the arena, the world, and for an odd, uncanny moment, Clayt saw it and smelled it through *her* senses.

Steps faltered. Stopped entirely. Frozen, he let the smells wash over him. Tasted the flavors in the air: urine, manure, sweat, weariness.

"Penned up," he said raggedly, "by wood, wire, steel . . . trapped by piles of shit and puddles of piss . . . surrounded by stupid bastards who don't understand what they've got—"

He broke it off as the mare turned her head. Her eyes, now fully alert, focused on him. *Saw* him. Took note of who he was with grave deliberation.

She made her way to the pen rails almost delicately, but with a resounding determination. Clayt saw she wasn't really very big for a rodeo bronc. But he'd seen her in the arena and knew full well she was capable of power as impressive as that used by Evil-Eye, tipping off a rookie cowboy. Or flinging off an experienced champion.

Ten feet and a set of metal rails separated man from mare. Clayt knew it wasn't enough.

"Mare," he said. "Black mare."

She watched him from eyes that gave back no light at all.

"Hey, mare . . . black mare . . . *Nightmare*—"

She did not so much as flick an ear.

Clayt approached the pen. Not because he wanted to; because he *had* to. If he didn't, she won. And he couldn't let a horse win. Not at something like this. Something so primal and compelling.

Broncs, Clayt knew quite well, were neither friendly nor pettable animals, prized for feral instincts rather than docility. Having worked closely with animals all his life, he held no idealized opinion of horses. He knew they could be meantempered and sly and dangerous whenever they damn well felt like it.

And yet he went forward to the pen, to the mare, who watched him with dead dark eyes more alert than any he'd ever seen, even in dogs. In men.

"Black mare," Clayt crooned.

She put out her head, nostrils flaring as she sucked in his scent. Her ears were forward, not pinned back, and the tangled forelock fell between her ears to dangle from her face. For one incongruous moment the angry mare of the arena resembled nothing so much as a curious filly.

He was not stupid. He did not offer her his fingers like John the Baptist's head on a silver platter. He moved his hand to within a few inches of the rail, and waited.

Dark eyes inspected it. Lips wrinkled as she opened her mouth, baring strong teeth; he whipped his hand away as she lunged.

The mare snorted. Squealed. Stomped one hoof as if in disappointment. Clayt could not help but wonder if she were cursing him even as he cursed her.

"Wicked little witch, aren't you?" he asked. "You'd just love to take a hunk of hide out of me."

"It's nothing personal," said a voice from behind. "She'll go after anyone who gets in her way."

Clayt jerked around, oddly embarrassed to be

caught with the mare, and saw the stock contractor approaching. He knew Buck Talbot by reputation only, and by the excellent stock he owned. All the Professional Rodeo Cowboys Association rodeos wanted Talbot because his stock was guaranteed to put on a show. Active broncs and bulls resulted in more competitors and higher paychecks, if riders managed to stay aboard.

Talbot limped a little. A lot of rodeo men did, after years of the punishing sport. In his day, Talbot had been one of the best of the roughstock riders before turning to stock contracting.

He was big and wrinkled, like old leather left too long in the sun. Brown-eyed, gray-haired, somewhere in his fifties, looking older, aging richly like good bourbon. "You better be praying you don't draw her tomorrow. She's nasty through and through."

Clayt looked from Talbot to the mare. "I saw her tonight. She almost had me for dinner, and I wasn't even on her back."

Talbot's right cheek was distended by tobacco. He shifted it, leaned, spat. "You'd best be glad you weren't. That cowboy she jammed up in the chute has a busted pelvis and six cracked ribs."

Something quivered inside of Clayt. Something deep and cold. Something *elemental*, whispering of things far out of his ken. It took all he had not to show it to Talbot.

Clayt swallowed. Smiled stiffly. "Still, if someone was lucky enough to ride her to the buzzer, he'd have a lot of money in his pocket."

Talbot worked his chaw, studying Clayt speculatively. His tone was blandly casual. "You reckon you're the cowboy to do it?"

Cowboys generally were not the bragging type, particularly around men like Buck Talbot. Clayt was no exception, having nothing to brag about. So he just smiled again in the way his grandma

called sweet and boyish, natural as grass is
green, rolled a shoulder, hooked thumbs into his
beltloops.

"I reckon I'd like to *try*," he said, "but that don't
mean I'd accomplish it."

Talbot's answering smile was slow, but warm.
"I saw you on Evil-Eye. He's a tough old son to
ride, if you don't know him. You did all right. Give
yourself time to learn the stock on the circuit, and
you'll be picking up day-money here and there."

Clayt looked back at the black mare. She stood
by the rails, watching him; watching *him*, not Talbot, with dead dark eyes and something akin to
recognition.

He licked his lips. "If I could ride *her*, I'd get
day-money here."

"Don't bet on it." Talbot shook his head as Clayt
jerked his head around to stare at him. "No, boy,
I'm not saying you're no good. What I'm saying
is, *no* one's ridden her yet." He leaned, spat, thrust
a scarred chin in the mare's direction. "I got her
off a rancher in Colorado . . . said she just turned
up in his pasture one day. He put ads in all the
papers and asked around, but no one ever claimed
her. Then he found out why: no one could stay
aboard her. So he sold her to me dirt cheap, figur-
ing I'd get some use out of her." The contractor
shrugged. "I didn't think she'd really do much
under the best in the business—she ain't too big—
but she had the last laugh." He looked from the
mare to Clayt. "She's killed two men, boy. You
know that, don't you?"

Clayt nearly gaped. "*Killed*—"

A nod of the hat. "Two weeks apart. They came
off her just out of the chute and didn't get away
quick enough." Talbot's mouth jerked in quick
sympathy. "She stomped 'em good."

Clayt knew rodeo was dangerous, but only rarely deadly. Bull riders faced goring each time they

boarded one of the beasts; some of them had been ripped wide open by lethal horns. Bronc riders broke bones or got their heads kicked occasionally, but he couldn't recall even five cowboys dying in the arena since the sport turned professional.

Certainly not two weeks apart. Nor thanks to the same horse.

Clayt looked at Talbot. "But you didn't chow her," he said.

Talbot swore and spat. "Hell, boy, she's just a horse . . . and no horse I ever heard of is capable of premeditated murder." He shook his head. "Those two men fell under her hooves, which is easy enough to do coming off a bronc. I've done it myself." He grinned crookedly, tapping a finger against his scarred chin. "She's a tough little witch, but nothing more than that."

Clayt looked at the mare. "Maybe," he said. "Maybe."

Talbot's tone hardened. "She's a *bronc*, cowboy. There to be ridden. You draw her, you do your damn best to ride her, hear? Give the folks a show . . ." Abruptly, the smile was back; he slapped Clayt's back. "Ride her to the buzzer, cowboy, and put some money in your pocket. Show us the man is tougher than the mare."

Talbot was walking away before his words were finished. Clayt watched him go. Then swung back to look at the mare.

"But *is* he?" he asked. "Or is *she*?"

Clayt slept out in his pickup truck, parked on the arena grounds. He didn't have money for a motel room, but even then he wanted to be alone. He might have spent a few hours in the bars or hitting the cowboy parties, but held back. He didn't feel like hitting the bars, and as for the parties—well, he didn't think he'd earned the right yet. His PRCA permit was only a week old.

In the cab of his truck, snugged up in his bedroll, Clayt dreamed. Like a dog fruitlessly chasing rabbits, feet twitched and eyelids jumped. The dream circled him like a wary wolf at a winter campsite, evaluating the most effective direction from which to come. Then it slipped through his barriers and crept in relentlessly, noiselessly, spilling fear and pain into his sleep.

—*the arena, atop a roaring engine of hatred and brutality. It was no horse he rode, but something nameless, something ageless and formless, shaped of ancient hatreds and hunger. His body, locked onto the animal, was flung from side to side like a rag doll, free arm flailing in the air. His right hand was trapped in the rigging handle, numb from the battering.*

He spurred. He dug, driving steel rowels deep into black flesh, trying to lance the boil of hostility, to let out the river of virulence. But the pain only seemed to intensify the power she flung at him. He was helpless. He was afraid—

Clayt awoke with a jerk, banging his knee on the gear shift lever jutting out of the floorboards. Hot, cold, sweaty, sick; he bit deeply into his lip to fight back the bile that threatened to spew out of his mouth. His entire body ached with a bone-deep pain that had nothing to do with the brief ride on Evil-Eye. It was the pain of failure and fear.

He had ridden the black mare in his dream, and she had won.

Decisively.

She stood on the far side of the holding pen, half-hidden behind the other horses, but he knew she was as aware of him as he of her. He was certain of it. That certainty sent a prickle up his backbone that began at the base of his spine and ended in his hair, like a fingertip of ice. He shivered head to toe once, suppressed a second involuntary wave, forced himself to approach the pen railing.

"—*Nightmare,*" *the announcer said. "That's Nightmare, in the flesh—*"

A roan gelding wandered too close to her. Clayt, stunned by the speed of her reflexes, saw her lash out a back hoof and smash it against the roan's left knee. Rendered instantly lame, he squealed and lunged, limping, away from snapping teeth as she pursued him into a cluster of other broncs. They milled in confusion, shaking heads and snorting, giving way to the little mare.

"Enough," Clayt said sharply. "It isn't that roan you want ... it's me." He took a step closer. "Well, here I am. Let him be, mare. I'm *here.*"

She turned. Looked. Stood very still.

"Yeah," Clayt said, "me. What are you waiting for?"

She was not one for prevarication. With a delicacy that belied the power of her small-boned frame and the ragged, unkempt appearance, the mare crossed the pen to the rails and thrust her head through. It very nearly put her lips in his shirt pocket.

Clayt wavered, but held his ground. He trusted his own reflexes as well as he trusted hers, if trust were the proper word. He stood, even as she did, and waited.

Dark eyes gleamed. Lips dug at fabric, seeking the contents of his pocket, which was empty. Life on a ranch precluded men from carrying treats, since none of the stock was a pet, even if she *had* been the sort of animal Clayt wanted to pamper.

Which she wasn't. Merely one he wanted to *ride.*

"I drew you," he told her, "this morning. But I

expect you know that. I expect you knew it from the very first."

Lips dug, shoving insistently, threatening fabric and the flesh beneath.

"Come tonight," he said, "I'm supposed to climb aboard your back and try to last through eight seconds of hell . . . *and* however long it takes me to get out of your way once I've hit the dirt."

The mare stopped lipping his shirt. She did not withdraw her head. She stood there with her muzzle pressed against his chest directly over his heart, and looked him dead in the eye.

"That's right," he whispered gently. "You and me, mare. And one of us has to lose."

She exhaled. Hot breath set his buttons afire.

Clayt smiled, slow and sweet and boyish. "But you knew that already."

Dead dark eyes didn't blink.

When he climbed down on the mare in the chute, Clayt nearly climbed off again. She was penned in, confined, *imprisoned* in the narrow chute, and he was astonished at the magnitude of her anger. He could feel it even through the hide covering bones and muscles and viscera. Her body, her *being*, tingled with it, like static electricity, only much more powerful.

Certainly more deadly.

"Jesus Christ," he whispered.

One of the cowboys working the chute smiled. "She packs a powerful wallop, cowboy. Be ready for her."

Clayt drew in a deep breath and carefully worked his gloved right hand into the rigging handle. He didn't want to upset her with any sudden movements. He could sense the fury building within, licking through her body. She trembled with its strength, barely suppressing it.

Carefully he edged closer to the rigging. With

his free hand, Clayt reached out and touched her neck. "Mare," he crooned, "black mare."

She stilled instantly. He felt her sudden quietude, her comprehension of *who* straddled her back. Boots braced his weight against the boards, not yet settling against her shoulders. She was closely confined, but not so tightly she couldn't move.

With calm deliberation, the mare turned her head as far as she was able and rolled a single opaque eye in his direction. She saw him, she *knew* him, and understood his need.

At least as well as her own.

"Eight seconds," Clayt muttered. "Only eight—"

A familiar voice intruded. Buck Talbot, climbing up the chute. "You ready?"

Clayt's mouth was dry. "Not yet. Almost."

Talbot's seamed face was not cruel, nor was his tone. "These people paid their money, cowboy . . . and I got a show to run."

Clayt nodded. Slowly he settled himself on the mare's back. Felt the power of hatred so tightly leashed, so carefully controlled—

—heard the squeal of leather, the advice and comments of cowboys . . . the grunt of the horse beneath him . . . the roaring fog in which he must live for eight long, too long seconds—

She knew him. She wanted him.

—heard the chinging of the spur-song—

She was lying in wait for *him*.

Jesus— But Clayt broke it off. Wet dry lips. Worked his feet forward, taking care not to touch her with his spurs. He knew she didn't require them in order to perform, but rules were rules, even in rodeo. And without them, he'd have felt like a quarterback lacking his helmet.

"Easy," he crooned, "easy, girl . . . easy mare . . . it's me . . . old Clayt . . . you know me."

Too well.

Slowly, he reached forward with his spurs, and set them, so very gently, against taut, quivering flesh.

Petitioning, in silence, as so many cowboys did: *Only eight seconds . . . just eight . . . it's all I ask, I promise . . .*

"You ready?" Talbot asked.

Clayt crossed himself. He wasn't Catholic. He did it just to be sure. To be *safe*—

Clayt expelled it through the desert of throat and mouth. "Outside!"

The gate lever whanged up. Clayt felt the beast gather itself, and then it was loosed into the arena, freed of its confinement, and he knew the true definition of fear did not exist in his or any other lexicon.

He didn't know if he marked her out. He didn't even know if he was still aboard her. Only that he was caught up in a maelstrom of such unrelenting and magnificent rage and hatred and ferocity that its magnitude reduced to utter insignificance his desire to last the ride.

All he wanted now was to *survive*.

He tasted blood from a bitten lip. Smelled it in his nostrils. Heard the blurred, formless voice of the announcer, talking the audience through his ride. And he hated him for it; hated *them* for it, every one of them, for presuming to share anything of his ride aboard the mare, who was more than merely bronc. More than even equine.

He sensed it. Raw. Primal. Elemental in its purity. It tested the waters carefully, putting out a toe. Considered a moment. Then, satisfied, it slithered out of darkness into daylight.

Bringing the nightmare with it.

—torn free of the mare. His brief flight was painless, his landing of a considerably different nature. He lay sprawled on his back, sucking air and staring

*at lights. Over his head hung suspended a succubus
dressed in horsehair.*

*Dead, dark eyes. The lining of rage-reddened nostrils. Hot, steaming breath, bathing his face, crisping
the matter of his eyes, turning his hair to ash.*

*And hooves, deadly hooves, preparing to slash into
him, to tear flesh, shred muscle, smash bones—*

"It's not *real!*" Clayt shouted. "It's only a dream—
only a *dream*—"

And so it was, for one insubstantial moment,
long enough for Clayt to grin his relief. And then
reality broke like a dropped wineglass, spilling
over into nightmare.

His grip was gone, torn out of the bareback
rigging. He was coming off. He didn't know how
long he had stayed aboard—one second? two seconds? three?—or if the buzzer had ever sounded.
He knew only that if he came off, she would kill
him.

Like how many men before him?

The mare screamed. Clayt opened his mouth to
scream back.

But didn't. Couldn't. He was sprawled facedown
in the dirt with a mouthful of it, and found he
could not move.

He couldn't even *look*.

Silence struck him first, battering his ears. The
cavernous arena was a tomb, lacking all sound.
All sound; not even the cry of a vendor or the blatting of a disgruntled steer. All Clayt could hear
was the too-rapid, too-heavy thumping of his
heart.

Were they waiting for her to finish him?

No. She'd have done it already.

Clayt hitched himself up on his elbows. Spat
dirt, wiped face, pushed up to squat on knees.

And saw the mare.

She lay in a tumbled heap, neck bent, as if a
wire had snared legs in mid-leap and jerked her

down, like in old Hollywood movies, before the
wire was outlawed. She didn't move. Didn't
breathe.

Clayt knelt there next to her, empty of all the
emotions he might have expected to feel; feeling
nothing but an anguish and grief born of something far outside his ken.

"Nightmare," he crooned, in the noisy silence of
the tomb.

And swore, looking into her dead dark eye, that
the mare heard him. Saw him. *Marked* him, even
as the life passed from her.

Buck Talbot put the envelope into Clayt's hand.
"You won day-money," he said. "You rode her to
the buzzer, and beyond." He paused, speaking
more gently. "You won, Clayt. You beat the black-
hearted witch at her own game."

"Did I?" Clayt asked dully. "I thought all I did
was kill a horse."

Talbot leaned, spat, shook his head. "Hell, boy,
she was after your hide. That backflip she tried
was meant to kill. But you came off, and she misjudged." He shrugged. "It happens. And I can't say
I'm sorry to lose her; I'd sooner have a horse dead
any day than a man."

Clayt held up the envelope. "You sure you don't
want some of this as compensation?"

The stock contractor gave him a friendly shove.
"Go home, cowboy . . . or wherever it is you're
bound. Maybe a bar . . . maybe a shiny little girl."
He grinned around the lump of tobacco. "Enjoy
it, Clayt. The first win never comes easy, and you
earned it."

Clayt didn't think so. But he put the envelope
away in his shirt pocket, thanked the man, went
away to his truck, shining dully in artificial light.

He opened the door to his side, hearing the
familiar squeak. But he didn't climb in at once.

Instead, he tipped his head back and looked up at the stars. "I didn't mean to kill her," he said. "I just wanted to *ride* her."

Then he climbed into his truck, turned the engine over, drove away into the darkness.

Clayt drove on automatic pilot, thankful his reflexes were good. He was out of the city and into the countryside, headlights painting the dark highway in twin stripes of illumination. Few cars were on the road.

Blood money, that's what it was. It would help his father, but that wouldn't wash the taint free. He'd spend his life recalling the singleminded determination and ferocity of the mare, the feral instincts that resurrected the reality of the Old West and injected some badly needed fresh blood into the New, where rich cowboys rode helicopters and poor ones sold off sections of land to meet the mortgage payment. Where proud men like his father had to grit teeth and ask the bank for a loan, when grandfathers before them had home-steaded the land.

Anachronism, Clayt reflected, having heard the word applied to cowboys in a TV special. A man out of place. *Behind* his time, instead of ahead of it. So many of them were.

The whine of the radio irritated him. Clayt turned it off, preferring silence. But silence was not what he heard.

He heard the squeal of leather. The advice and comments of cowboys. The slamming of the chute gate, the grunt of the horse beneath him, the roar-ing fog in which he had to live for eight seconds or more. The crowd, as always, was a blur. The announcer's voice a rumble.

He felt the leather of his glove and the painful tightness of the rigging handle. Heard the ringing spur-song as he set rowels against black shoulders.

And he heard her angry scream.

"I didn't mean it!" he shouted. "I didn't mean to do it!"

Knowing the Nightmare didn't care.

The light was lurid—blue and red—splashing in endless repetition against the sheer cliff wall. The static crackle of the Highway Patrol radio shredded the silence. One trooper made notations on his clipboard. The other talked quietly with the tow-truck driver, then turned back to watch the ambulance pull away. No lights. No siren. No urgency.

He walked slowly back to his partner. "What is it they say—only the good die young? Well, I don't know how good he was, but he damn-sure was young. Nineteen, according to the license."

The other continued writing. "Didn't smell any alcohol. Drugs, maybe, you think?"

"Maybe. Let the coroner figure it out." The first trooper flipped aside shattered glass with one foot. "No skid marks. No indication he even *tried* to brake before he hit the wall."

"Maybe he just drove smack into it. Lost control." The other clicked his pen closed. "Well, I'm done. The rest can wait till morning."

Idly, they watched the tow-truck driver inspecting the pickup prior to hooking up.

"Hey," the man said, "this guy hit a horse?"

It put frowns on both their faces. "No evidence of it, and we checked thoroughly all around the truck. Why?"

The driver gestured. "Clear as day, if you look. Here—in the bed."

Both troopers went over to the unblemished back of the pickup, peering into the open, boxlike bed. And saw, clear as day, a mosaic of bloody hoofprints shining wetly in the light.

WHEN LIGHTNING STRIKES

by Lee Barwood

The air conditioner hummed noisily, a new note in its vibrating song that promised trouble. Reesa stirred uneasily, remembering sweltering streets and a stifling train, hoping the cool air wouldn't quit till she could buy a new unit. Cool kept the sanctuary of her home unbreached, her memories at bay.

But somehow she knew she wouldn't be that lucky. The unit was secondhand when she'd bought it; at the time it was all she could afford. She'd known since summer started it was time for a new one. Why she'd stalled she didn't know; she lived alone and had the money. She wasn't rich, but her job was good, her bills were paid, and there was money in the bank—and she could have forestalled this.

Forestalled the memories.

Heat brought them all back; summer heat, sweltering nights, airless rooms radiating summer's oppression. Even winter heat, rooms filled with too many bodies and too little air with a heating system run amok and windows thrown wide in the desperate search for air, could send her back years in the blink of an eye. Then she'd be nervous and unsettled for days.

Because in the heat she remembered the promise she'd made, and broken. Even though it wasn't her fault, although it was a child's unkeepable promise and as an adult she knew its futility, she still felt guilty. She'd fled the city as soon as she could afford to, taking an apartment far away from where she'd once lived, though she still worked in Manhattan. Someday, she knew, she'd have to go back to face things.

The promise.

And the memory. Of hoofbeats. Hoofbeats in the night, drumming on hot pavement, echoing in the courtyard, filling the darkness with the sound of flight. Of escape. Of freedom.

She had her freedom now, but the hoofbeats that echoed in her memory when the night was hot and the windows were wide reminded her that the creature that had saved her not once, but twice, only one short of the magical three times— if her memory could be believed, that is—was still trapped in stone, still bound in captivity that could only lead to utter destruction.

She forced the thoughts away and was just beginning to breathe easier when the air conditioner chugged alarmingly and died. The flow of cool air stopped abruptly; in its wake the apartment rapidly grew stuffy. The temperature had hit one hundred for the third day in a row, even on the Island, and with the humidity that had risen from the ocean to settle everywhere like a thick, fuggy blanket, the night wouldn't cool much beyond eighty. In the city, streets and buildings would radiate stored heat from the day and even open windows wouldn't bring much relief.

Just like the old days.

Her window had overlooked the courtyard, she remembered unwillingly; there was never a breeze, although she could hear things. Oh, yes, she could hear very well, particularly the hoofbeats that echoed on hard pavement as they left the courtyard, leaping the wrought iron gate and heading for the cooler, greener streets of the park. There had been four of the buildings on a small city block, linked by alleys gated and fenced in wrought iron and sharing the central courtyard with peonies and roses and a fountain in the middle. On the other side of the street was the park, which had stopped being a nice place to go before Reesa entered her teens.

Her mother had died there, mugged on the way home from work. Her purse was empty and she'd died, literally, for nothing. It was that night everything had turned bitter. Or was it? It was so impossible that all these years later Reesa still couldn't trust what she thought were memories—etched crystal clear in her mind, but so patently impossible that the adult Reesa had serious doubts about her mental well-being as a child. As an adult, too, if she still couldn't let it go—

She realized where her thoughts were heading, snapped her book closed, and got up. It was still early, still light. If she went now, P. C. Richards or somebody would be open, and maybe she could get the new air conditioner tonight.

Not have to go through all this again.

She pulled her hair back into a ponytail, thrust her feet into Reeboks, and, grabbing her purse, left the rapidly warming apartment.

When she got to the store, she was lucky; despite the heat wave, they had the unit she needed, and loaded it into her car. Reesa breathed a sigh of relief as she handed over her credit card. It would be a challenge to get it upstairs, but there was a dolly in the garage, and she could install it herself. She'd put in the old one years ago.

On impulse, she stopped at the stationery store next door. Feeling unaccountably lucky, she bought a lottery ticket—something she seldom did.

"Be a good week to win," the clerk said. "A real biggie this week."

"Is it?" she said, fishing out a dollar. "Good. I could use a biggie."

And whistling, she got back into her car and drove home.

The apartment was cool again at last, and she slept; but her dreams were troubled. She saw again the old apartment, the courtyard with its huge pink and red peonies and roses of all colors.

And in the center, the fountain—the focus of her life as a child. The fountain with the statue of the horse.

Reesa had loved horses with all her heart. She had put a real live horse at the top of every Christmas list; collected china, ceramic, glass, and even plastic horses with a determination bordering on mania; read every horse book she could get her hands on, stretching the patience of the local librarian; and driven her parents crazy with periodic recitations of the lineage of the Thoroughbred as a breed ("Byerly Turk, Godolphin Barb, Darley Arabian") till they were ready to scream.

But they lived in a Queens apartment; the Kellys were far from rich, and Reesa was one of four children (three older brothers), so money was tight. A horse was a pipe dream, despite the fact that she knew a person could buy a horse cheap at Pony Penning Day on Chincoteague; hadn't Marguerite Henry said so in her books? She saved her allowance, made bridles and hackamores from string and yarn, and drew horses on scrap paper, notebooks, and even textbooks till her teachers reprimanded her (while secretly commending her skill).

Then one cold December night, a snowy Christmas Eve when a horse had appeared yet once more at the top of her Christmas list, Reesa's mother had taken her downstairs to the courtyard behind the building.

"Reesa," she'd begun patiently, settling them both on the seats around the outside of the fountain, "you know your daddy and I haven't much money."

Reesa had nodded, shoulders slumping; she knew what was coming next.

"We can't afford to get you a horse, honey. Even if we could, we couldn't keep him here, and stabling costs money. So does feed, and all the other things a horse needs."

Reesa nodded reluctantly. She knew these things. She'd read about taking care of horses. "There's my allowance," she offered bravely.

"It's not enough, honey," Inez Kelly said. "We just don't have enough to get you a horse. Not now, and not next year, and not the year after. You'll have to wait till you're grown up, or till you have a job of your own." Her voice was kind but firm.

Reesa had started to cry; silently she sat in the snowy courtyard with tears rolling down her cold cheeks. She couldn't help it. She wanted a horse so much; it was all she dreamed of, talked about, hoped for.

"Reesa." Her mother's voice broke through her misery. "There was a reason I brought you down here tonight."

Reesa only sniffed. What could her mother possibly tell her that she would care about, after telling her she couldn't ever have a horse till she was grown? Might as well have said forever. Her biggest brother Lennie had only just gotten his working papers, and he was ages older than Reesa.

"Don't you want to hear what I have to say?"

Reesa shook her head.

"Not even if it's magic?"

Reesa looked up. She might not believe in Santa Claus any more—she'd known since she was six that Santa, if he were real, could have brought her a horse any time so he must not be real—but she did believe in magic.

"What magic?" she asked reluctantly.

"The magic of the horse in the fountain."

Reesa loved the horse in the fountain. He was big and strong, with a barrel chest and a tossing mane, flashing eyes and dancing hoofs. Percheron or Clydesdale, Reesa had thought, maybe even Shire, with just enough Arabian introduced into the bloodline to make his lines finer and his speed and intelligence greater. She knew his every inch, from hoofs and fetlocks to eartips and the flow of his magnificent tail, from powerful shoulders to broad flanks. He was magic for her, of course— with or without the fountain spray that made him glisten in the sun—and always had been, from the time she was old enough to know what he was; but magic for other people? For grownups? In spite of herself she was interested.

"What magic?" she asked, after careful consideration. "You aren't making fun of me, are you?"

"No, Reesa, I'm not," her mother said softly. "He really is magic. He was when he was sculpted. Would you like to hear his story?"

Reesa nodded.

"When we first moved into this building," her mother said, "before even Lennie was born, an old man used to come sometimes to look at the fountain. He'd sit here, and stare at the horse, and sometimes his eyes would fill up with tears. One day I asked him why.

" 'I sculpted him,' he told me. 'I carved the marble that stands there, and I could never do that horse justice. He saved my daughter's life.' He sighed, and wiped away a tear. 'Even after all this time,' he said, 'I still come here to tell him how grateful I am, and how much I miss him.' "

Reesa had been fascinated despite herself. "He saved her life?"

"Oh, yes," her mother said. "See the plaque there?" She pointed, and Reesa saw for the first time a bronze plaque with engraving on it. She read it: "In memory of Hero, with love and gratitude for my daughter's life." Inez put an arm around Reesa. "She'd been out riding, the man told me; it was a hot day, and his daughter had stopped to rest under a big oak tree. A storm blew up, and she decided to stay under the tree to wait it out."

"But it's dangerous to stay under a tree in a thunderstorm," Reesa had said, remembering what she'd been taught, and her mother nodded in approval.

"That's right, it is," she'd agreed. "But I guess she forgot. Only Hero didn't; he pushed and prodded at her till she got up to look for safer shelter. Only just then," Reesa's mother said, "lightning struck. It hit the tree, and broke off a huge branch. It fell just exactly where the sculptor's daughter had been sitting."

"Was she hurt?" Reesa demanded.

"No," her mother said. "She wasn't even scratched; it was a miracle the lightning didn't strike her directly. But Hero was killed; the branch hit him. And when she told her father what happened, he decided Hero should have a memorial." She looked up at the statue. "So he made him one."

Reesa was torn between horror at Hero's untimely death and fierce pride in his actual heroism. "How did his statue end up here?" she demanded at last, unable to think of any other questions.

"I'm not sure, to tell you the truth," Inez said. "The man never said. I'd already asked him more than I had a right to, and didn't dare ask anything else." She thought a moment. "Maybe they lived here once."

Reesa said nothing, staring at the horse she'd come to think of as her friend. The courtyard was where she came to read, to study, just to sit and think; since it was walled and gated, it was safer than the park across the street (although that would change all too soon). Finally she said, "But where's the magic?"

"The magic is," her mother told her slowly, "that since Hero died young, if you love him enough, and you wish hard enough, maybe you can bring him back to finish his normal lifespan."

"You mean for real?" Reesa asked, unable to decide if she should believe or not. It was close enough to what she wanted to believe.

Inez was staring at the statue now, not looking at Reesa. "Why not?" she said softly. "Stranger things have happened. . . ." Her voice trailed off. It was a moment before she spoke again. "He'd live only at night, in the moonlight; you'd never see him, but you'd hear his hoofbeats on the pavement."

Reesa sighed. If she could bring such a wonderful horse back to life, she would; but such an abstract instead of the live horse she wanted for herself was not the Christmas gift she'd hoped for.

They'd gone back up to the apartment at last, Reesa shivering from the cold, glad for once that the heat was excessive in her top floor room.

But later that night it got stifling. Reesa opened her window—a frequent occurrence in winter in their building, where sometimes the apartment was hot, sometimes cold, depending on the price of heating oil and the whim of the super and/or landlord. And on how troublesome the tenants had been.

She went back to bed, still unhappy she wouldn't get a horse.

But she did love Hero. She always had. She thought again about his bravery, and shed a tear when she thought of how he had died to save his mistress. It wasn't fair, she thought, that he should have died for being so smart, so brave.

And just then, when instead of thinking like other children on Christmas Eve and listening for the sound of an impossible sleigh, Reesa contemplated the nature of heroism, she heard them.

Hoofbeats in the courtyard. The hoofbeats of a big horse, walking on slate, then picking up speed, hoofs clattering on stone walkways as the animal circled the fountain. Reesa sat up in disbelief, then ran to her window, where she looked out, desperate to see something—anything.

But there were only shadows in the courtyard, although she heard the horse circle the fountain one last time, then go down one of the alleys and pause. Just for a moment.

Then the sound resumed on the far side of the wrought iron gate, as if the horse had jumped the fence.

She lay awake for a long time, listening, but she didn't hear him come back.

In the morning, when she looked out, the fountain was as it had been the night before. Hero was in his place, and there was no sign of hoofprints—although fresh snow had fallen during the night and his tracks would have been covered anyway.

In time she forgot about it, dismissing it as a dream because she never found any proof that Hero had actually left his place in the fountain and gone wandering.

But that summer, she heard the hoofbeats more often.

She came to accept it as fact, that Hero went out to run free at night, and she didn't even mind the heat of that summer because it meant leaving the windows open to listen for the sounds of hoofbeats in the night.

But she went on wanting a horse, and trying to

think of ways a girl her age could make enough money to buy and keep one.

The adult Reesa woke the next morning to a smoothly running air conditioner, weeping for a dead horse bound in marble and a little girl who never got her dream. But angry at herself for such weakness, she brushed away her tears and went to stand in a pounding cold shower, then dressed and tore off to work to get away from her own thoughts.

She came home that night tired from the heat and her troubled sleep the night before, and turned up the cold control on the air conditioner, determined to ward off any repeats. When the bedroom was downright chilly, she climbed into bed.

But the memories refused to be denied, and she dreamed again.

This time it was worse. She was a child again, a little older; she'd gotten permission to stay at a friend's house overnight for a slumber party—an attached row house about three blocks away. As if it were all happening again, she felt the heat in the house that hot summer night, the scratchy rug beneath her elbows as she lay on the floor in her friend's room playing a game.

Suddenly, she never had known quite how it started, she was in the midst of an argument. The others accused her of cheating, and Reesa never, ever cheated. Furious, she collected her things, then stormed out into the warm darkness, evading her friend's parents.

She started to walk home alone. She knew the way perfectly well, and even though it was dark she wasn't afraid. Her parents always told her to be careful, and that she was never to be out alone after dark, but she was too angry to wait—and too ashamed of the others' accusation of cheating even to tell her parents about it. Never mind that it wasn't true.

She'd gone a block before she realized there were footsteps behind her, footsteps echoing her own in the semi-quiet street. She started to walk faster, heard the other steps speed up to match her own. She began to be afraid, but before she could break into a run a voice behind her said, "Hey, can I ask you some directions?"

Reesa hesitated. She was still afraid, but the question was reasonable. And the hesitation cost her her chance to escape, because before she realized it, she was seized from behind—and suddenly there were three of them, young and tough and terrifying. She opened her mouth to scream, but one of them covered it with his hand—and she bit down, hard. When he let go, cursing, she screamed anyway.

And heard hoofbeats.

It was like watching slow motion. There was a dapple of moonlight and shadow in the middle of the street, and then suddenly, impossibly, Hero was upon her attackers, teeth and hoofs flashing in a fury of stone made flesh. The youths holding Reesa dropped her and fled, crying out in pain and fear as the giant horse pursued them.

But one of them, carrying a heavy stick, suddenly turned as he ran and took a swipe at Hero. Reesa heard the crack as wood connected—with stone?—and with a scream of equine rage Hero reached out a long neck and seized his assailant by the collar. He shook the youth as a terrier shakes a rat, then dropped him limp to the ground.

By then the other two were gone, out of sight down an alley. Reesa, limp herself, knelt on the sidewalk, trembling. Hero turned and came toward her, shaking his head repeatedly as if it hurt; then he gently nudged her to her feet and stood by her side as she clung to him for support.

After a moment she was able to look at his head, and was shocked to see a long dark trickle down one side. Blood! And there was no sign of his right ear—

Reesa let go of the horse and looked down the street toward where he'd dropped the youth. The body lay perfectly still in the middle of the sidewalk, but something near it caught the lamplight.

Hesitantly Reesa walked close enough to see what it was.

A marble ear. . . .

Reverently she bent and picked it up, then gathered her belongings at Hero's gentle urging.

"I'm sorry," she told him, tears starting. "If you hadn't come to help me you'd never have been hurt. That's not how it's supposed to be." She knelt, gravely, the way she'd read knights swearing sacred oaths did. "I swear, Hero, I'll find a way to make you better some day. I'll get you out of here and make you real again, all the time. I swear it with all my heart."

The horse nudged her once again, and she walked home in his company unafraid. When they reached the front of the building, he left her, trotting off to leap the gate into the alley.

She went upstairs, the marble ear hidden safely in her bag, and said nothing of her ordeal when her mother opened the door.

In the morning the radio said that a body had been found two blocks away, just a short time after she'd gotten home. Her mother was horrified, and promptly forbade her once more ever to go out at night alone again. Reesa only nodded; she had her own reasons to regret her rashness.

But within her, something sang: Hero was alive! He could and did leave the fountain, he could live as a real horse. And someday, she swore again to herself, she'd find a way to take him away from the courtyard, let him live again. The way he was meant to live, with room to run and pastures to graze in and a snug barn for shelter from storms and snow.

Reesa woke in tears again in the morning, remembering the dream. Muttering, "I'm too old for this," she stumbled through her morning routine of coffee, shower, and dressing, then headed out into the relentless heat for another day's work.

Yet one more night the dreams came. This time was worst of all: it was the night her mother died. Inez Kelly was walking home from the subway station rather than spend the money for bus fare. She'd evidently cut through the park—something she seldom did—and never made it home. Reesa and her brothers were waiting supper, reluctant to eat without her, and their father, just home himself, was pacing the floor. "Surely she just stopped at the store," he muttered for about the third time, and then he shrugged into his jacket. "Kids, stay here and eat your dinner. I'll meet your mother; we'll be back in a few minutes." He was gone before any of them could say anything.

But when Dennis Kelly returned it was hours later. He was white and shaking, and a cop was with him.

"We'll do everything we can to find them, Mr. Kelly," the cop was saying for what must have been the hundredth time. "We'll call you as soon as we know anything."

"But why would they kill her?" Kelly asked, bewildered. "She didn't even have any money. Why did they kill her?"

"Is Mom dead?" asked Lennie disbelievingly. Dennis Kelly did not answer; the cop looked at

Lennie, then at Roy and Gus and Reesa, and his eyes went wide with sympathy.

Reesa couldn't cry at first. She was too angry, too miserable. Then she thought that if she'd told her mother about her own trouble on the way home that night from the slumber party—that night three years ago—maybe she would have been more careful. She decided that it was her fault her mother had died, just as it had been her fault that Hero was hurt.

And then she did something even more stupid than she had the night of the slumber party. After the relatives and friends who had come to offer sympathy left, after she and her brothers were supposed to be in bed, she got dressed and went out to get them—the ones who did this to her mother.

She'd begged for and gotten karate lessons after the slumber party incident; remembering the body that had been found, her parents had agreed. She'd gotten good, and she'd gotten cocky.

And now she thought she'd give them what they deserved.

She must have gone mad with grief, the adult part of her mind thought in the dream, even as her thirteen-year-old self went out in search of certain disaster.

She found them, all right, or others like them. But they saw her before she saw them, and before she knew it she was seized and helpless, just like the last time. She fought to the best of her ability, but there were too many of them and they were all much bigger than she was. And they made it plain they were going to enjoy hurting her. She screamed when one of them seized her hair to pull her head back, and then stared with wide, terrified eyes as a knife blade flashed in her face. One carried a gun; when he hit the side of her head with it, the night blazed with red pain.

She didn't even hear the hoofbeats till Hero's shrill cry of fury demanded their attention.

Before she could call out to warn him off, he'd attacked; there were five this time, though, not three, and they were considerably tougher than the last gang. Teeth and hoofs and a body the size of a small car were a distinct advantage, however, and the damage Hero inflicted before the gang could manage a defense was substantial. Reesa fought free from the man holding her and used what karate skills she could to level him, then cried out, "Hero, go!"

But just then there was the crack of the gun. Hero screamed again, this time in pain, and Reesa ran to the downed man holding the gun. She kicked it out of his hand before he could fire again, and then she kicked him again and again until he didn't move.

But once again, the damage was done. Hero stood on three legs, his left foreleg dangling uselessly and streaming blood. Reesa, her berserker rage gone now and only grief left, wept as she led the horse back toward the courtyard. at a slow hobble. She murmured soothing nonsense to him all the way, and paid no attention to the sirens in the distance.

But Hero couldn't leap the gate; she had to break the lock to let him in, and coax him back to his place on the fountain. She stayed there for a long time, crying.

Her brothers found her there in the morning, sound asleep, tearstreaks on her face and blood on her hands. The horse statue was missing its left front hoof, and Reesa never explained what happened to anyone. The hoofbeats she heard after that were a crippled, pitiful cadence, plodding around the courtyard; they never leapt the gate again. Reesa learned to sleep with her radio on, then added headphones; finally she got a job and moved out to her own apartment where her first purchase was an air conditioner.

So that she could shut out the sounds of the summer nights.

And the memories.

When Reesa woke Saturday morning she felt groggy and dull. It seemed to take forever to get going, and she couldn't get the dream out of her mind. She went out to do her laundry and the week's shopping, but moved so slowly that it was late in the day before she was through. She stopped off on the way home for takeout food, and bought a bottle of aspirins for good measure; she felt so draggy she thought she must be sick. But she dreaded trying to sleep again, so she made one last stop around the corner from home and picked up some movies from the video rental place.

Occasionally she sat up late and treated herself to a movie marathon; she hadn't done it for a long time, and decided after the first two that the third movie required popcorn. She shut the machine down and left the television on while she went to pop it.

When she came back into the room, the numbers were being drawn for the weekly lottery. Reesa had never paid much attention before, but for some reason this time she scrambled for a pencil and wrote down the numbers.

She checked them against her ticket, feeling slightly foolish. But when the first number matched, and then the second, she began to feel nervous. Third number ... fourth ... fifth. It was impossible.

The sixth number matched; the jackpot was twenty-one million dollars.

That night, when she finally got to sleep, ticket safely under her pillow, Reesa dreamed again. But it was a very strange dream indeed.

She was in an old, grand house surrounded by trees and acres of grass; parts of it were shabby, but parts were beautiful, and she knew somehow that she'd done a lot of work to bring the beauty back. She walked down a long hallway, and came to a large hothouse room. She opened the door and went in, and sat at the edge of a fountain. It was Hero's fountain, and he stood there, whole and beautiful again, just like the parts of the house she had worked on. The bronze plate on the base of the fountain shone with fresh polish, and Reesa read the inscription. It said, "Old promises can be kept."

And when she woke in the morning it all seemed like a dream.

But the ticket numbers still matched.

She filed her lottery claim and started house-hunting—for a big old place in need of restoration, with a hothouse room big enough to hold an old fountain. She hired an agent to get the fountain for her, and a restoration firm to repair the damages she knew there'd be.

She was sick when she saw what was left of poor Hero. The buildings she'd grown up in were so far gone that they'd been boarded up and condemned. Addicts and derelicts roamed the halls, and slept in the courtyard where roses and peonies once bloomed; vandals had done terrible things to the marble horse that used to dominate Reesa's dreams.

But the restoration company she hired was good, and when finally the hothouse room in her new-old house and the fountain were ready for one another, she was pleased and impressed.

She found herself wandering the hallways, just as in her dream; now that she no longer needed to work, she spent most of her time in restoration or in caring for the exotic flowers that once more filled the old hothouse.

And she spent the now-winter nights wanting to throw the windows wide, half afraid and half eager to hear hoofbeats in the darkness. But nothing happened; weeks passed into months, and soon it was summer again.

Reesa had always wanted to start her own business, but never had the money or the nerve. Now she found she had both, and what she chose centered naturally enough in the hothouse: she raised her exotic flowers for sale. She spent most of her time there, in Hero's restored company, and worked on potting and propagating, forcing and maintenance while the fountain's spray gave the room its required humidity. She studied books and journals about her newly chosen field, sitting on the bench of the fountain for hours at a time, on soft cushions she'd ordered to fit, while soft music played on the stereo she'd installed.

And she came to sit in the hothouse every time there was a thunderstorm, fascinated by the dance of lightning through the panes of glass overhead.

One sultry summer night she sat on the edge of the fountain to watch what promised to be a spectacular storm. She remembered the story her mother had told her of Hero, and looked up at his marble form. "At least you're safe indoors now, Hero, and nothing can touch you again," she whispered, and settled down to listen to the soft sounds of the fountain playing in its pool and the beginning patter of rain on the glass roof.

The rainsounds were soothing, and before she knew it Reesa was dozing on the cushioned bench. But suddenly there was a brilliant flash, followed immediately by a resounding roar that shook not only the panes of glass in the hothouse but the very house itself. Reesa jerked awake in time to see a huge treetop come closer and closer, its trunk shredding along the path the lightning had traveled.

She cried out in terror and ducked as the limb shattered the roof; shards of glass flew everywhere.

She looked up to find that Hero's statue had once again saved her life; a great pane had come flying toward her only to be blocked by the marble horse. But the animal standing before her was still stone, and Reesa shook her head; surely, she thought, three times ought to be the charm.

When she stopped shaking, she got up to leave.

But another flash turned the night sky white with brilliance; then the house plunged into total darkness as the lights went out. The thunder came at the same time, deafening Reesa; the very ground under her feet shook.

She stood still for a moment, waiting for her vision to adjust and hoping the lights would come back on. When they didn't, she edged cautiously toward where she thought the door ought to be.

But she came up against something solid.

Something solid, and warm, and very large. Something that whickered at her, and lipped her hair with gusty affection.

"Hero?" she whispered, not daring to believe. She reached out a cautious hand and found warm, short-haired skin beneath it. Her hand ran along a well-remembered back, up a muscular, thick-maned neck and found a head. A large head, Percheron or Clydesdale, maybe, or even Shire, with just enough Arabian blood to make the lines finer. . . .

The lights came back on then, and Reesa began to cry. Hero stood there, dappled moonlight and shadow, but alive—and when she turned to look at the fountain, there was only water, playing into an unadorned pool. . . .

CLASSICAL HORSES

by Judith Tarr

I.

The yard was full of Lipizzans.

I'd been driving by, missing my old mare and thinking maybe it was time to find another horse, and I'd slowed because I always do, going along any row of fence with horses behind it, and there they were. Not the usual bays and chestnuts and occasional gray, but a herd of little thick white horses that weren't—but couldn't be—but were.

They weren't the Vienna School. They came from somewhere in Florida, Janna told me afterward, and they'd been doing something at the armory, and they needed a place to board for the night. I didn't know Janna then. I wouldn't have stopped, either, just gone down to a crawl and stared, except for the two horses in the paddock. It wasn't that they were wild with all the running and clattering. It was that they were quiet. A chestnut and a gray, not big, just about Morgan-sized, and maybe Morgan-built, too, but finer in the leg and shorter in the back than most I'd seen—and of course you don't see a gray Morgan. But as upheaded as any Morgan you'd want to look at, with a good arch to their necks, and ears pricked sharply forward, watching the show.

I pulled over without even thinking about it. I

remember wondering that it was odd, me staring at two perfectly nice but perfectly normal horses, with all those white stallions taking turns around the yard and being walked into the barn. The gray would be white when he was older, there was that. He had a bright eye, but calm. When one of the Lipps circled past his fence, his head came up higher and he stamped. Then he lifted himself up, smooth and sweet as you please, and held for a long breathless while. He was, I couldn't help but notice, a stallion.

The chestnut watched him with what I could have sworn was amusement. His ears flicked back and then forward. His muscles bunched. He soared up, even smoother than the gray, and lashed back hard enough to take the head off anyone who might have dared to stand behind him.

Levade, capriole. Then they were quiet again, head to tail, rubbing one another's withers like any old plow horses.

I got out of the car. No one looked at me or even seemed to have noticed the demonstration in the paddock. I wandered toward the fence. The chestnut spared me a glance. The gray was too busy having his neck rubbed. I didn't try to lure them over. I leaned against the post and watched the stallions, but with a corner of an eye for the ones in the paddock.

There was an old surrey on the other side, with a tarp half draped over it, half folded back. Someone sat in the seat. She was old, how old I couldn't tell; just that she was over sixty, and probably over seventy, and maybe eighty, too. It didn't keep her from sitting perfectly straight, or from looking at me with eyes as young as her face was old, large in their big round sockets, and a quite beautiful shade of gray. She didn't smile. If she had, I might have ducked and left.

As it was, I took my time, but after a while I went over. "Hello," I said.

She nodded.

I supposed I knew who she was. I'd heard about a woman who had a farm out this way. She was ninety, people said, if she was a day, and she still drove her own horses. Had even been riding them up till a little while ago, when she broke her hip— not riding, either, but falling down in her house like any other very old lady. She had a cane beside her, with a brass horse's head.

"Nice horses," I said, cocking my head at the two in the paddock.

She nodded again. I wondered if she could talk. She didn't look as if she'd had a stroke, and no one had said anything about her being mute.

"Not often you see two stallions in a paddock together," I went on.

"They've always been together."

Her voice was quiet and a little thin, but it wasn't the old-lady voice I might have expected. She had an interesting accent. European, more or less.

"Brothers?" I asked.

"Twins."

I stared at them. They did look a lot alike, except for the color: bright copper chestnut, almost gold, and dapple gray, with the mane and tail already silver.

"That's rare," I said.

"Very."

I stuck out a hand, a little late, and introduced myself. Her hand was thin and knobby, but she had a respectable grip. "You're Mrs. Tiffney, of course."

She laughed, which was surprising. She sounded impossibly young. "Of course! I'm the only antique human on the farm." She kept on smiling at me. "My yard is full of Lipizzans, and you notice my two ponies?"

"Big ponies," I said. "If they're that. Morgans?"

"No," she said. She didn't tell me what they were. I didn't, at that point, ask. Someone was standing behind me. Janna, I knew later. She wanted to know what to do about someone named Ragweed, who was in heat, and Florence had categorically refused to move her Warmblood for any silly circus horse, and the show manager wanted to know if he could use the shavings in the new barn, but she wasn't sure what to charge him for them, if she let him have them at all, since no one had told her if there was going to be a delivery this week.

It went on like that. I found myself dumping feed in nervous boarders' bins and helping Janna pitch hay to the horses that had been put out to pasture for the night. There were people around—this was a big barn, and the guests had plenty of grooms of their own—but one way and another I seemed to have been adopted. Or to have adopted the place.

"Do you always take in strangers?" I asked Janna. It was late by then. We were up in the office, drinking coffee from the urn and feeling fairly comfortable. Feeding horses together can do that to people. She'd sent the kids home, and the grooms were gone to their hotel or bedded down in the barn. Even Mrs. Tiffney had gone to the house that stood on the hill behind the barns.

Janna yawned till her jaw cracked. She didn't apologize. She was comfortable people, about my age and about my size, with the no-nonsense air that stable managers either learn early or give up and become bitchy instead. "We take in strays," she said. "Plenty of cats. Too damn many dogs. Horses, as often as not. People, not that often. People are a bad lot."

"Maybe I am, too," I said.

"Mrs. Tiffney likes you," said Janna.

"Just like that?"

Janna shrugged. "She's good at judging animals."

"People-type animals, too?"

Janna didn't answer. She poured more coffee instead, first for me, then for herself. "Do you ride?" she asked.

"Not since the winter. I had a mare up at Meadow Farm; Arab. Did dressage with her. She got twisted intestine. Had to put her down." It still hurt to say that.

Janna was horse people. She understood. "Looking for another?"

"Starting to."

"None for sale here right now," she said. "But some of the boarders take leases. There's always someone wanting a horse ridden. If you want to try one of them, take a lesson. . . ."

I tried one, and then another. I took a lesson. I took two. Pretty soon I was a regular, though I didn't settle on any particular horse. The ones that came up weren't quite what I was looking for, and the ones I might have been interested in weren't for sale or lease, but I had plenty of chances to ride them.

What I was mostly interested in was just being there. Someone had put up a sampler in the tackroom: "Peaceable Kingdom." Tacky and sentimental, but it fit. There were always dogs around and cats underfoot. Janna gave most of the lessons, but she had a couple of older kids to help with the beginners. I didn't do any teaching. I did enough of that every day, down in the trenches.

There were thirty horses in the two barns, minus the one-night stand of Lipizzans. The farm owned a few ponies and a couple of school horses, and Mrs. Tiffney's pair of stallions, who had a corner of the old barn to themselves. They weren't kept for stud, weren't anything registered that anyone knew of. They were just Mrs. Tiffney's horses, the red and the gray—Zan and Bali. She drove them as a team, pulling a surrey in the summer and a sleigh in the winter. Janna rode them every day if she could. Bali was a pretty decent jumper. Zan was happier as a dressage horse, though he'd jump if Janna asked; and I'd seen what he could do in the way of caprioles. Bali was the quiet one, though that wasn't saying he was gentle—he had plenty of spirit. Zan was the one you had to watch. He'd snake his head out if you walked by his stall, and get titchy if he thought you owed him a carrot or a bit of apple. Bali was more likely to charm it out of you. Zan expected it, or else.

I got friendly with most of the horses, even Florence's precious Warmblood, but those two had brought me in first, and I always had a soft spot for them. They seemed to know who I was, too, and Bali started to nicker when I came, though I thought that was more for his daily apple than for me. If Mrs. Tiffney was there, I'd help her and Janna harness them up for her to take her drive around the pastures and down the road, or sit with her while she watched Janna ride one or the other of them. The day she asked me if I'd like to ride Bali—Janna was saddling Zan then—I should have been prepared, and in a way I was, but I was surprised. I had my saddle, I was wearing my boots; I'd been riding Sam for his owner, who was jetsetting in Atlantic City. But people didn't just ride Mrs. Tiffney's horses.

I said so. She laughed at me. "No, they don't. Unless I tell them to. Go and saddle Bali. He'll be much happier to be with his brother."

He was that. I felt as if I was all over his back— first-ride nerves, I always get them in front of the owner. But he had lovely gaits, and he seemed determined to show me all of them. Fourteen. I'd counted once at Meadow Farm, when I watched the riding master. Walk: collected, working, medium, extended. Trot: ditto. Canter: ditto. And then, because Mrs. Tiffney told me to do it, and because Janna was there to set my legs where they belonged and to guide my hands, the two gaits almost no one ever gets to ride: passage, the graceful, elevated, slow-motion trot; and piaffe, "Spanish trot" that in Vienna they do between the pillars, not an inch forward, but all that power and impulsion concentrated in one place, in perfect control, to the touch of the leg and the support of the hand and the will of the rider that by then is perfectly melded with that of the horse.

I dropped down and hugged Bali till he snorted. I was grinning like an idiot. Janna was grinning, too. I could have sworn even Zan was, flirting his tail at his brother as he went by.

Mrs. Tiffney smiled. She looked quite as satisfied as Bali did when I pulled back to look at him, though I thought he might be laughing, too. And told myself to stop anthropomorphizing, but how often does anyone get to ride a high-school horse?

II.

Not long after that, Mrs. Tiffney taught me to drive. I'd never learned that, had always been out riding when chances came up. It was easier than riding in some ways. Harder in others, with two horses to think of, and turning axes, and all those bits and pieces of harness.

We didn't talk much through all of this. The horses were enough. Sometimes I mentioned something that had happened at school, or said I'd have to leave early to have dinner with a friend, or mentioned that I was thinking of going back to grad school.

"In what?" she asked me.

"Classics, probably," I said. "I've got the Masters in it, but all I teach is Latin. I'd like to get my Greek back before I lose it. And teach in college. High school's a war zone, most of the time. You can't really teach. Mostly you just play policeman and hope most of your classes can read."

"Surely," she said, "if they can take Latin, they can read English?"

She sounded properly shocked. I laughed sourly. "You'd think so, wouldn't you? But we're egalitarian at Jonathan Small. Anyone who wants anything can take it. Can't be elitist, now, can we? Though I finally got them to give me a remedial Latin class—remedial reading, for kids who can't read English. It does work. And it keeps them from going nuts in a regular class."

"Democracy," said Mrs. Tiffney, "was never intended for everyone."

I couldn't help it. I laughed. I couldn't stop. When I finally did manage to suck in a breath, she was watching me patiently. She didn't look offended. She didn't say anything further, either, except to ask me to turn around and put the team into a trot.

When we'd cooled the horses and cleaned the harness—she insisted on doing it herself, no matter what anyone said—she invited me to the house. I almost refused. I'm shy about things like that, and I had classes in the morning. But maybe I had amends to make. I shouldn't have laughed at her.

From the outside it was nothing in particular. A big white frame house with pillars in front: New England Neoclassical. Janna had the upstairs rear, which I'd seen already, steep twisty staircases and rooms with interesting ceilings, dipping and swooping at the roof's whim, and a fireplace that worked.

Downstairs was much the same, but the ceilings were halfway to the sky, rimmed with ornate moldings, and there seemed to be a fireplace in every room, even the kitchen. There were books everywhere, on shelves to the ceiling, on revolving shelves beside the big comfortable chairs, between bookends on tables and mantelpieces. And in through the books there were wonderful things: a bust of a Roman senator, a medieval triptych of angels and saints around a Madonna and child, an African mask, a Greek krater, a bronze horse that must have been Greek, too, and hanging from the ceiling, so surprising that I laughed, a papier-maché pterodactyl with carefully painted-in silvery-gray fur.

Mrs. Tiffney wasn't going to let me help her with the cups and cookies, but she didn't try too hard to stop me. She did insist that I get comfortable in the living room while she waited for the water to boil. I wandered where she pointed, past the den and the library I'd already seen, to the front room with its wide windows and its Oriental carpet. It was full of books as all the other rooms were, and its fireplace was marble, cream-pale in the light from the tall windows. There was a painting over it, an odd one, perfectly round, with what must have been hundreds of figures in concentric circles.

When I came closer I saw that it wasn't a painting, precisely. More of a bas-relief, with a rim that must have been gold leaf, and inside it a rim of beautiful blue shading to green and gray and white, sea-colors, and in the center a field of stars—I picked out the gold dots of constellations, Orion and the Dipper, and the moon in silver phases—and between them more people than I

could begin to count, doing more things than a
glance could take in. They had a classical look,
neoclassical more probably, not quite elaborate
enough to be baroque, not quite off-center enough
to be medieval.

I found my finger creeping up to touch, to see if
it was really real. I shoved my hand in the pocket
of my jacket.

A kettle shrieked in the kitchen. I almost bolted
toward it. Hating to leave that wonderful thing,
but glad to escape the temptation to touch it.

"Did you know," I said to Mrs. Tiffney as she
filled the teapot, "that you have the shield of
Achilles in your living room?"

She didn't look at me oddly. Just smiled. "Yes,"
she said. "I thought you'd recognize it."

I picked up the tray before she could do it, and
carried it back through the rooms. The shield—
yes, it was a shield, or meant to be one, clearly
and, now that I noticed, rather markedly convex—
glowed at me while Mrs. Tiffney poured tea and I
ate cookies. I don't remember what the cookies
tasted like. They were good, I suppose. I was
counting circles. There was the city at peace, yes.
And the city at war. The wedding and the battle.
The trial, the ambush. The field and the vineyard.
The cattle and the lions. The sheep and the shep-
herds. The dancing floor and the dancers.

"Someone," I said, "made himself a masterpiece."

Mrs. Tiffney nodded. She was still smiling, sip-
ping tea, looking sometimes at me and sometimes
at the marvel over her mantel.

"People argue," I said. "Over how it really was
supposed to be. Your artist went for the simplest
way out—the circles."

"Sometimes simplest is best," Mrs. Tiffney said.

I nodded. The cattle were gold, I noticed, with
a patina that made them look like real animals,
and their horns looked like tin, or something else

grayish-silvery. Base metal, probably, gilded or foiled over. Whoever this artist was, whenever he worked—I was almost ready to say seventeenth century, or very good twentieth with a very large budget—he knew his Homer. Loved him, to do every detail, wrinkles of snarls on the lions' muzzles, curls of hair on the bulls' foreheads, bright red flashes of blood where the lions had struck.

"This should be in a museum," I said.

Mrs. Tiffney didn't frown, but her smile was gone. "I suppose it should. But I'm selfish. I think it's happier here, where people live, and can touch it if they want to, and it can know the air and the light."

Pure heresy, of course. A wonder like this should have the best protection money could buy, controlled climate, controlled access, everything and anything to preserve it for the ages.

But it was beautiful up there in this living room, with late daylight on it and a bit of breeze blowing through. I got up without thinking and went over to it, and touched it. The figures were cool, raised so that I could have seen them without eyes, and they wove and flowed around one another, a long undulating line that came back to where it began.

I wasn't breathing. I drew a breath in slowly. "I've never," I said, "seen a thing like this. Or anything that came close to it."

"There's only one like it in the world," Mrs. Tiffney said. She bent forward to fill my cup again. I sat back down, took another cookie.

"And you say you don't believe in democracy," I said. "If keeping this out of a museum isn't democratic, then what is?"

"This is simple sense, and giving a masterpiece the setting it loves best." She sipped delicately from the little china cup. "It's been in my family for a very long time. When it first came to us, we promised its maker that we would care for it as he asked us to do, never to hide it away and never to sell it, or to give it except as a gift to one who could love it as he loved it. It was the eldest daughter's dowry, when such things were done. Now I'm the last," she said, "and it goes to no daughter after me."

I was still wrapped up in the wonder of the thing, or I would never have said what came into my head. "Janna says you have daughters. Two of them. And granddaughters."

"Stepdaughters," she said. She didn't seem offended. "I was my husband's second wife. We had a son, but he died early, and he had no children. My husband's children were never quite sure what to make of me. Now that I'm old, you see, I'm permitted to be eccentric. But when I was younger, with children who resented their father's marrying again so soon after their mother died, I was simply too odd for words. All my antiquities, and my books, and that dreadful garish thing that I *would* hang in the parlor—"

"It's not garish!"

She laughed. "It's hardly in the most contemporary of taste; especially when contemporary was Art Deco. And pockets full of coins of the Caesars, and gowns out of the *Très Riches Heures*, and once, as a favor to a friend, a mummy in the basement: oh, I was odd. Alarmingly so. The mummy went back home with as many of her treasures as we could find. I, unfortunately, lacked the grace to do the same."

"So you are Greek," I said.

She nodded.

"The artist—he was, too?"

"Yes," she said, "very. He wouldn't sign his work. He said that it would speak for itself."

"It does," I said, looking at it again, as if I could begin to help myself. "Oh, it does."

III.

That was in the early spring. In late spring, just after lilac time, I came to ride Bali—those days, I was riding him almost every day, or driving them both with Mrs. Tiffney—and found the place deserted except for one of the stablehands. She was new and a bit shy, just waved and kept on with the stall she was cleaning.

The stallions were both in their stalls. Usually they were out at this time of day. I wondered if they'd come up lame, or got sick. Zan didn't whip his head out the way he usually did and snap his teeth in my face. Bali didn't nicker, though he came to the door when I opened it. His eyes were clear. So was his nose. He didn't limp as I brought him out. But he wasn't himself. He didn't throw his head around on the crossties, he didn't flag his tail, he didn't grab for the back of my shirt the way he'd taken to, to see me jump. He just stood there, letting me groom him.

I looked in Zan's stall. Zan looked back at me. Nothing wrong with him, either, that I could see or feel. Except that the spirit had gone out of him. He actually looked old. So did Bali, who was still young enough to be more a dapple than a gray.

"You look as if you lost a friend," I said.

Zan's ears went flat. Bali grabbed the right crosstie in his teeth and shook it, hard.

I had a little sense left. I remembered to get him back in his stall before I bolted.

Mrs. Tiffney was in the hospital. She'd had another fall, and maybe a heart attack. They weren't sure yet. I wouldn't have got that much out of anybody if Janna hadn't driven in as I came haring out of the barn. She looked as worn as the horses did, as if she hadn't slept in a week.

"Last night," she said when I'd dragged her up

to the office and got coffee into her. "I was down-stairs borrowing some milk, or she'd have gone on lying there till God knows when. The ambulance took forever to come. Then she wanted the para-medics to carry her up to her own bed. I thought she'd have another heart attack, fighting them when they took her out."

I gulped coffee. It was just barely warm. My throat hurt. "Is she going to be all right?"

Janna shrugged. "They don't know yet. The har-pies came in this morning—her daughters, I mean. Aileen isn't so bad, but Celia . . ." She rubbed her eyes. They must have felt as if they were full of sand. "Celia has been trying for years to make her mother live somewhere, as she puts it, 'appro-priate.' A nursing home, she means. She's old enough for one herself, if you ask me."

"Maybe she thinks she's doing what's best," I said.

"I'm sure she is," said Janna. "What's best for Celia. She'd love to have this place. She'd sell it for a golf course, probably. Or condos. Horses are a big waste of money, she says. So's that great big house up there on the hill, with just two women living in it."

"And kids," I said, "in the summer, when you have camp."

"Not enough profit in that." Janna put down her half-empty cup. "She married a stockbroker, but Mrs. Tiffney always said Celia did the thinking for the pair of them, in and out of the office. If she'd been born forty years later, *she'd* have been the broker, and she probably wouldn't have married at all."

It still wouldn't have done Mrs. Tiffney any good, I thought, after I'd bullied Janna into bed and done what needed doing in the barn and driven slowly home. Mrs. Tiffney's horses didn't look any brighter when I looked in on them, just before I left, though, Bali let his nose rest in my palm for a minute. Thanking me, I imagined, for understanding. Just being a horse, actually, with a human he'd adopted into his personal herd.

Mrs. Tiffney wasn't allowed visitors, except for immediate family. In Janna's opinion, and I admit in mine, the hospital would have done better to bar the family and let in the friends. Aileen did answer Janna's calls, which was more than Celia would do; so we knew that Mrs. Tiffney hadn't broken her hip again but she had had a heart attack, and she was supposed to stay very, very quiet. She'd been asking after her horses. Janna was able to pass on some of the news, though Aileen wasn't horse people; she didn't understand half of what Janna told her, and she probably mixed up the rest.

I actually saw her with her sister, a few days after Mrs. Tiffney went to the hospital. They'd come to the house, they said, to get a few things their mother needed. I think Celia was checking out the property. They were a bit of a surprise. The slim blade of a woman in the Chanel suit turned out to be Aileen. Celia was the plump matronly lady in sensible brogues. She knew about horses and asked sharp questions about the barn's expenses. Aileen looked a little green at the dirt and the smell. She didn't touch anything, and she walked very carefully, watching where she put her feet.

I was walking Bali down after a ride. He was still a bit off, but he'd been willing enough to work. If he'd been human, I'd have said he was drowning his sorrows. I brought him out of the ring for some of the good grass along the fence, and there was Aileen, stubbing out a cigarette and looking a little alarmed at the huge animal coming toward her. Little Bali, not quite fifteen hands, kept on coming, though I did my best to encour-

age him with a patch of clover. He had his sights
set on another one a precise foot from Aileen's
right shoe. She backed away.

"I'm sorry," I said. "He's got a mind of his
own."

"He always did," said Aileen. She eyed him. He
flopped his ears at a fly and took another mouthful
of clover. "You must be Laura—Ms. Michaels, that
is. My mother has told me about you."

For some reason I wanted to cry. "Has she?
She's talking, then?"

"She's very frail, but she's quite lucid. All she
can talk about, most days, is her horses, and that
dreadful platter of hers. You've seen it, she says.
Isn't it gaudy?"

"I think it's quite beautiful," I said a bit stiffly—
jerkily, too. Bali had thrown up his head on the
other end of the leadrope, near knocking me off
my feet, and attacked a fly on his flank. For an
instant I thought he was going after Aileen. So did
she: she beat a rapid retreat.

But she didn't run away completely. She seemed
to come to a decision. "Mother has asked to see
you. Celia said no, but I think you should go."

I stood flatfooted. Bali was cropping grass again,
not a care in the world. "Why?" was all I could
think to ask.

"You ride her horses," said Aileen.

IV.

Mrs. Tiffney looked even frailer than Aileen had
warned me she would, white face and white hair
against the white sheet, and tubes and wires and
machines all doing their inscrutable business while
she simply tried to stay alive. I'd been not-think-
ing, up till then. I'd been expecting that this
would go away, she'd come back, everything
would be the way it was before.

Looking at her, I knew she wasn't coming back. She might go to a nursing home first, for a little while, but not for long. The life was ebbing out of her even while I stood there.

She'd been asleep, I thought, till her eyes opened. They were still the same, bigger than ever in her shrunken face. Her smile made me almost forget all the rest of it. She reached out her arms to me. I hugged her, being very careful with her tubes and wires, and her brittle bones in the midst of them.

Aileen had come in with me. When I glanced back to where she'd been, she was gone.

"Aileen was always tactful," Mrs. Tiffney said. "Brave, even, if she saw a way to get by Celia."

Her voice was an old-lady voice as it never had been before, thin and reedy. But no quaver in it.

"And how are my horses?" she asked me.

I had fifteen minutes, the nurse at the desk had told me. I spent them telling her what she most wanted to know. I babbled, maybe, to get it all in. She didn't seem to mind.

"And my ponies?" she asked. "My Xanthos and Balios?"

I'd been saving them for last. I started a little at their names. No one had told me that was what they were. Then I smiled. Of course the woman who had Achilles' shield—as genius had imagined it, long after Achilles was dead—would name her horses after Achilles' horses. She'd had a pair like them, Janna had told me, for as long as anyone had known her. Maybe it was part of the family tradition, like the shield on the wall.

"They're well," I answered her, once I remembered to stop maundering and talk. "They miss you. I had Bali out this morning; Janna and I did a pas-de-deux. We walked them past the surrey after, and they both stopped. I swear, they were asking where you were."

"You haven't told them?"

She sounded so severe, and so stern, that I stared at her.

She closed her eyes. The lids looked as thin as parchment. "No. Of course you wouldn't know. And they'd have heard people talking."

"We've been pretty quiet," I said. And when she opened her eyes and fixed them on me: "We did talk about it while we put the horses out. We'll tell them properly if you like."

"It would be a courtesy," she said, still severely. Then, with a glint: "However silly you may feel."

I didn't know about feeling silly. I talked to my cats at home. I talked to the horses when I rode them or brushed them. "I'll tell them," I said.

She shut her eyes again. I stood up. I was past my fifteen minutes. The nurse would be coming in to chase me out, unless I got myself out first. But when I started to draw back, she reached and caught my hand. I hadn't known there was so much strength in her.

"Look after my horses," she said. "Whatever happens, look after them. Promise me."

I'm not proud to admit that the first thing I thought of was how much it would cost to keep two horses. And the second was that Celia might have something to say about that. The third was something like a proper thought. "I'll do my best," I said.

"You'll do it," she said. "Promise!"

Her machines were starting to jerk and flicker. "I promise," I said, to calm her down mostly. But meaning it.

"And the shield," she said. "That, too. They go together, the horses and the shield. When I die—"

"You're not going to die."

She ignored me. "When I die, they choose to whom they go. It will be you, I think. The horses have chosen you already."

"But—"

"Look to Xanthos. Balios is the sweet one, the one who loves more easily, who gives himself first and without reservation. Xanthos is as wise as he is wicked. He was silenced long ago, and never spoke again, but his wits are as sharp as they ever were."

I opened my mouth. Closed it. She'd gone out of her head. She was dreaming old dreams, taking the name for the thing, and making her very real if by no means ordinary horses into horses out of a story. I'd done it myself when I was younger: little rafter-hipped cranky-tempered Katisha was the Prophet's own chosen mare, because she was a bay with one white foot and a star. But that hadn't made her the first of the Khamsa, any more than Mrs. Tiffney's wishing made her horses Achilles' horses. Or her shield—her neoclassical masterpiece—Achilles' shield.

They were treasures enough by themselves. I almost said so. But she was holding so tight, and looking so urgent, that I just nodded.

She nodded back. "The first moonlit night after I die, make sure you're at the barn. Watch the horses. Do whatever they ask you to do."

What could I do, except nod?

She let me go so suddenly that I gasped. But she was still breathing. "Remember," she said, no more than a whisper.

Then the nurse came charging in, took a look at the monitors, and ordered me out. The last I saw of Mrs. Tiffney was the nurse's white back and Mrs. Tiffney's white face, and her eyes on me, willing me to remember.

V.

She died two days later, early in the morning of a gray and rainy day. She went in her sleep, Janna told me, and she went without pain. When I saw her laid out in the casket—and how Celia could think the shield was gaudy and reckon peach satin and mahogany with brass fittings tasteful, I would never understand—she was smiling. The funeral parlor was so full of flowers I could barely breathe, and so full of people I couldn't move, though it tended to flow toward the casket and then away into clumps on the edges. I recognized people from the barn, wide-eyed, white-faced kids with their parents, older ones alone or with friends, looking intensely uncomfortable but very determined, and the boarders in a cluster near the door. They all looked odd and half-complete in suits and dresses, without horses beside them or peering over their shoulders.

I said a proper few words to Celia, who didn't seem to recognize me, and to Aileen, who did. Celia didn't look as triumphant as I suspected she felt. Her mother had been such a trial to her for so long, and now the trial was over. She'd get the property and the estate—she'd have to share with Aileen, of course, and there'd be bequests, but she'd hardly care for that. She'd administer it all, if she had anything to say about it.

"She lived a full life," a woman said behind me in the syrupy voice some people reserve for funerals. "She died happy. Doesn't she look wonderful, Celia?"

There was a knot in my throat, so thick and so solid that I couldn't swallow. I said something to somebody—it might have been Janna, who didn't look wonderful, either—and got out of there.

The horses were real. They didn't make empty noises, or drown me in flowers. Bali stood still while I cried in his mane, and when I wrapped my arms around his neck, he wrapped his neck around me.

Finally I pulled back. He had an infection, or something in the new hay had got to him: his eyes were streaming. So, when I turned around, were Zan's. I sniffled hard and got a cloth for them and a tissue for me, and wiped us all dry. "All right," I said. "So you're crying, too. Horses don't cry. You've got an allergy. What is it, mold in the hay?"

Bali bit me. Not hard enough to do damage, but hard enough to hurt. I was so shocked that I didn't even whack his nose; just stood there. And he shouldered past me. He didn't have a halter on. I'd come in to the stall to get him, forgotten the halter on its hook, and started bawling. I grabbed for him. He kept on going.

Zan arched his neck, oh so delicately, and bared his long yellow teeth, and slid the bar on his door. I lunged. He was out, not moving fast at all, just fast enough to stay out of my reach.

I snatched halters on the way by. Zan pirouetted in the aisle and plucked them both out of my hands, and gave me a look that said as clear as if he'd spoken, "Not those, stupid." Then he spun again and waited.

I heard Mrs. Tiffney's voice. I was imagining it, of course. *Watch the horses. Do whatever they ask you to do.*

They certainly weren't acting like normal stallions on the loose. Bali was waiting, up past Zan, with his most melting expression. Zan—there was no other word for it—glared. His opinion of my intelligence, never very high to begin with, was dropping fast.

And it was dark, but there was a moon, a white half-moon in a field of stars like the ones in the center of the shield. Which was resting against the barn wall, just outside the door to the yard. And where the surrey used to stand was something else. I told myself it was the moon that made the old-fashioned black carriage look like something ages older and much smaller, and not black at all. Not in the least. That was gold, glimmering in the light from the aisle. And gold on the harness that lay on the ground beside it.

"But," I said, "I don't know *how* to yoke up a chariot."

Zan snorted at me. Bali was kinder. He went up to the pole that rested on the ground and positioned himself just so, and cocked an ear. After a minute Zan did the same, but his ears were flat in disgust. If he was choosing me, whatever that meant, he wasn't going to make it easy.

The harness wasn't that hard to figure out, once I'd had a good look at it. Or as good as moonlight and aislelight would give me. The yoke, of course, instead of collars. The bridles were familiar enough, and the reins. I ran those the way they seemed to want to run. The horses were patient, even Zan.

When they were harnessed, I stood back. I don't know what I was thinking. Nothing, by then. Except maybe that this wasn't happening. Something in the combination of moonlight and barn light made the horses shine. Bali, of course, with his silver mane and tail and his pewter coat. But Zan, too, a light that seemed to grow the longer I stood there, not silver but gold, lambent in the dark.

"Immortal horses," I said. "Bright gifts the gods gave to Peleus, and he to his son, and his son—" I broke off. "But the gods are dead!"

Zan shook his head in the bridle, baring his teeth at me. Bali watched me quietly. His ear slanted back. *Get in the chariot,* he meant. And how I knew that, I didn't want to know. No more than how I knew to pick up the shield—heavy as all heaven, but lighter than I'd expected, even so— and hang it where it best seemed to fit, by the left side of the chariot. I picked up the reins. They weren't any different from driving the surrey, though I was standing up in a vehicle that seemed no heavier than an eggshell, and no better sprung than one either, for all its pretty gilding. I didn't pretend that I was telling the horses where to go. They started at a walk, maneuvering carefully out of the yard where I'd seen Lipizzans, so long ago it seemed now, though it wasn't even nine months. Hardly long enough to carry a baby to term.

They took the way I'd driven so often, down the road a bit and into the woods. The moon didn't quite reach through the new leaves, but the horses were shining, silver and red-gold, bright enough to light the woods around them. The track was clear and smooth. They stretched into a trot.

The wind was soft in my face. It was a warm night, the first after a week of damp and rain, and everything smelled green, with sweetness that was apple blossoms, growing stronger as we went on. By the time we came out into the orchard, my lungs were full of it.

The trees were all in bloom, and the moon made them shine as bright almost as Bali's coat. He was cantering now, he and his brother, and the chariot rocked and rattled. I wrapped the reins around the post that seemed made for just that, and concentrated on hanging on. If I'd had any sense at all I would have hauled the horses down to a walk, turned them around and made them go back home. But all the strangeness had caught up with me. My head was full of moon and night and apple blossoms, and old, old stories, and the shield-rim under my left hand and the chariot's side under my right, and the horses running ahead of me, the chestnut, the gray, Xanthos, Balios, who couldn't be, who couldn't begin to be, but who surely were.

And I'd inherited them. I'd had the letter this morning, in her firm clear hand, with a date on it that made me start: the day after I'd first seen the shield. The shield was mine, if the horses chose me; and they were mine, too, and the wherewithal to keep and house them. That was how she put it. Tonight, in the way the moon's light fell, I knew that Janna had an inheritance, too; that Celia would be very surprised when the will was read. Oh, she'd have a handsome sum, and she'd grow richer than she'd been to begin with, once she'd invested it. And Aileen had a sum as large, which she wouldn't manage a tenth as well, unless she handed it over to Celia. But the land was Janna's, and the barn, and the horses, and the house, and everything that went with them, except Xanthos and Balios and the shield that a god had made to protect a legend in battle.

The moon had made a seer of me. I'd wake up in the morning with a headache and a sour stomach, and maybe a little regret for the dream I'd lost in waking.

It didn't feel like a dream, for all its strangeness. The night air was real, and the branch that whipped my face as the horses turned, mounting the hill. From the top of it, over the orchard that surrounded it, you could see for miles, down to the river on one side and over the ridges on the other, rolling outward in circles, with towns in the hollows, and fields full of cows, and the Riccis' vineyard with its rows of vines on poles; and maybe, through a gap in the last ridge, a glimmer that was the ocean. Here was higher than the hill Mrs. Tiffney's house stood on: it lay just below, with the barns beyond it. In the daytime you could see the rings and the hunt course, and the riders going through their paces like a dance.

Tonight the orchard was like a field of snow, and the hills were dark with once in a while a glimmer of light, and where Mrs. Tiffney's house stood, a shadow with a light at the top of it.

Janna, home where she belonged, alone in the quiet rooms.

I found I couldn't care that she might be checking the barn, and she'd find the lights on and Mrs. Tiffney's horses missing. Or maybe she wouldn't. Maybe it was all dark and quiet, the doors shut, the horses asleep, everything asleep but me, and the horses who had brought me here. I got down from the chariot and went to their heads, smoothing Bali's forelock, venturing—carefully—to stroke Zan's neck. He allowed it. I slid my hand to the poll, round the ear, down past the plate of the cheek. He didn't nip or pull away. I touched the velvet of his nose. He blew into my palm. His eyes were bright. Immortal eyes. "How do you stand it?" I asked him. "Bound to mortal flesh that withers and dies, and you never age a day? How many have you loved, and however long they lived, in the end, all too soon, they died?"

He didn't speak. He'd been able to, once. I saw it in his eyes. Dust and clamor and a terrible roil of war, the charioteer cut down, the loved one—loved more than the master, for the master owned them, but the charioteer belonged to them, Patroklos who was never strong enough to fight his prince's battle—and the bitterness after, the prince taking vengeance, and the stallion speaking, foretelling the master's death. He'd grieved for the prince, too, and the prince's son in his time, and his son's son, and how it had come to daughters instead of sons—that he wasn't telling me. It was enough that it had been.

Bali rested his nose on my shoulder. Zan nipped lightly, very lightly, at my palm. Claiming me. The wind blew over us. West wind.

I laughed, up there on the hilltop, with the wind in my hair. Little no-name no-pedigree horses: by west wind out of storm wind, or maybe she had been a Harpy, like Celia and her sister. I belonged to them now. And a gaudy great platter that owned me as much as they did.

I'd cry again in a little while. I'd lost a friend; I owed her grief. But she'd be glad that I could laugh, who'd known exactly what she was doing when she filled her yard with Lipizzans and lured me in, and snared me for her stallions.

I leaned on Xanthos' shoulder, and Balios leaned lightly on mine. They were shining still, and brighter than the moon, but they were warm to the touch, real and solid horses. We stood there, the three of us, mortal I and immortal they, and watched the moon go down.

ONE TEN THREE

by Barry N. Malzberg

I am in the paddock inspecting the horses and thinking as one tends to do increasingly at this stage of life of time's winged chariot drawing near even though these are the flat races at Ozone Park, Queens, when the filly being escorted through and around the small tunnels of grass and dirt looks at me and says distinctly, I am a lock in this race. I would not turn me down. At eight to one I am a distinct overlay.

This communication is stunning; it is a shock. It is a voice within my head and yet outside my head if you follow what I am saying. Turning my head to the right, then to the left, inclining it toward the seat of purpose so to speak I note that none of the denizens of paddock observers seem to have shared this insight. Camped in their customary oblivion they are looking at figures, making notes on the entries, engaging in deep discussion with one another or with themselves, etc. The usual paddock business in short.

I am speaking to you, the filly says. She lifts her head and looks at me with powerful, soulful eyes. This is a direct communication within the confines of a relationship. I tell you, I cannot lose this. You had better get down on me. It is five minutes to post.

The name of this filly, one of eight in a maiden

153

special weights in Man's Fate. I should make this part of the exposition clear, also that this is the name of a famous book by Andre Malraux who is a Frenchman not connected to the Dreyfus case, a work of philosophy of some significance published around the time of World War II. Also that the field is still within the paddock, circling and taking the air five minutes until post because this is deep, foul winter at South Ozone Park in Queens, gray and eight degrees at first post and it is agreed that exposure of jockeys to elements for the customary duration of the ten minute parade to the post would be most cruel. Also, the jockeys are participants in a union not available at this time to horses. That is all the exposition that is necessary in this context except to add that my name is Fred and that it has not been my history to have had conversations with horses, much less self-announced and prospective winners.

That's what you say, Fred, Man's Fate says to me. The fact is that you have had conversations with horses for most of your adult life. The difference is that this is the first time that a horse has responded to *you*. Man's Fate gave a little whinny at this final confidence or perhaps the word is whicker and said, Take it or leave it, Fred. All your life you have been looking for a tip and now when you have one you search for qualification.

Man's Fate became a popular post-existentialist text in upper level college philosophy courses during the 1960s. I know this, too, it is remarkable the detritus of information which can accumulate to one through decades of assiduous following of the horses. Noting that the bearer of that name is a chestnut filly with a noseband and red blinkers, that she in addition has a shadow roll and rear *and* front bandages, a normally bad sign, I shrug, tip my head in what I take to be a courteous gesture, turn from the paddock and its spare, cold-stricken onlookers and make my way through the sinister aspect of this unpleasant racetrack to the enclosure of the lower grandstand. Careful study of the *Racing Form*, a copyrighted publication of the well-loved Annenberg family informs me that Man's Fate worked out in one ten three over five and a half furlongs Wednesday past and has not previously experimented with blinkers. A three-year-old by Sinatra out of Keep the Faith whose sire was Never Bend, the filly has had only one previous race, much earlier this year at Thistledown where she finished eighth in a ten horse field, beaten by multiples of lengths at a distance of four furlongs, maiden special weights. There are no other figures accompanying the one ten three and the name of the trainer, W.L. Mariposa, is unknown to me as is that of the owner which is the same. The jockey is Stevens, an undistinguished journeyman, riding two pounds overweight at 116. One ten three is an outstanding workout for six furlongs but something less than distinguished for five and a half and Man's Fate finished her four furlong gambol in March, my calculations assure me, in something in excess of 54 seconds.

This is not encouraging, I say aloud on the line. These are not quantifying signs.

The man in front of me says, Could you not stick your paper in my ear? You are reshaping my ear-lobe unpleasantly.

I am sorry, I say, readjusting the Racing Form. It is still not encouraging.

That is for sure, the man with the rearranged ear says, rubbing it thoughtfully. It is not encouragement which brings us out here. One might say it is the reverse. He stares earnestly at the program in his right hand. But in that case, he says, why bet the race?

This is a powerful and intelligent question which

accompanies me all the way in the brief line to
the window, having no answer of distinction, I bet
twenty dollars on the filly to win, twenty dollars
to place and forty to show, all of this with the dim
feeling that it is not my senses which have departed so much as my capital. Nonetheless, the ticket
which is pushed over the counter to me, has the
reassuring heft and feel of a prayerbook, some
kind of Talmudic investiture slammed out of cold
steel to my purchase. In the old days a bet such
as this would have required several tickets of pink,
gray, and green hue, but we are living in the sullen and apocalyptic nineties now, the era of Off
Track Betting and computerized simulcasting
equipment and have sacrificed colors and varying
denominations as well as most of our convictions.
We older followers of the horse, that is to say. I
have no idea whether this is true of those who
have entered the arena after new totalizer equipment and off track betting. There is very little
communication amongst the generations—even
less than there is between the man and the
horse—and I am perfectly happy to leave it that
way.

I ascend the escalator to the brittle and crumbling spaces of the upper grandstand. Aqueduct
will be closed soon, the rumors say, Belmont will
become an all-year track and Aqueduct will
become an extension of what I grew up calling
Idlewild Airport. Where Kelso's hoofs grazed,
stewards will wink and anti-terrorist patrols will
run their careful radium. In the meantime, in
these exhausted days of the millennium and my
own career, I continue to bet and now, it would
appear, converse lately with horses. I return to my
seat which has been occupied by folded shards of
newspaper during this customary expedition to
the paddock and also by the right hand of my

companion and sometime wife Henrietta who has had her own problems with the late millennium.

You took your time, she said. It's one minute to post.

Well, I know that, I say. A horse was talking to me in the paddock. It wouldn't have been polite to leave.

Henrietta takes this with the same stolidity and lack of fundamental expression which has characterized our relationship from the first and shrugs. Did you bet? she says.

Yes, I did. I got down in time.

You bet the horse that spoke to you, I suppose.

Well, yes, I say. That didn't seem unreasonable. She said that she was ready to win.

And you trusted her.

Well, I say, apologetically at that, a horse never spoke to me before. It was kind of a new thing. So I thought I'd take a chance. You want to know which one?

No, Henrietta says, why don't you keep it a secret for luck? She looks at her own *Form* spread out on her lap. I am glad I decided to pass this race. Even by maiden special late winter standards, these are a bunch of cats and dogs. One ten three for *five* furlongs. That's milk horse time.

I think you mean five and a half, I say.

Henrietta looks at the form, runs her pencil to a figure. Okay, she says. Five and a half, right. Not that this makes any difference.

Meanwhile, as this affectionate and gently marital conversation has ensued, the horses have approached and been loaded into the starting gate far across what will some day be tarmac. The fog and gloom of this part of the country at this time of the year obscure any natural view of these proceedings, but the closed circuit televisions, several hundred of them, provide the view in color. Man's Fate is somewhere in the middle, the four horse, being loaded willingly enough. I put my hand into the pocket with the ticket, squeeze it for luck. A last flash of the odds board brings the filly down to six to one. Perhaps I am not the only person with whom she has had conversations.

We will have to do something to invigorate our marriage, Henrietta says. I was reading this article in REDBOOK about bringing the sparkle back. We are doing too many of the same things at the same time.

I think they'll break any second, I say.

You have to constantly find new activities and shared interests, Henrietta says. I don't think we've had a new interest in seventeen years.

The doors of the starting gate are open, the bell stopping all wagers sounds, and the fillies lurch into motion. Man's Fate is somewhere in the middle of the pack.

I was never that interested in horses, Henrietta says. Dog shows, maybe, and movie stars. I wanted to get a degree in art history when I started college. It's a funny way from there to here.

Watch the screen, I say.

You watch it, Henrietta says. I am considering basic facets of my life.

The race goes on. Having already demonstrated impatience with expository material and its necessity, I will simply point out that Man's Fate, hanging on the outside all the way, finally gets to the center of the track at the stretch turn and then begins to canter unpleasantly, losing her action. Soon enough she is bearing out and sometime shortly after that the horses have crossed the finish line, carrying away my eighty dollars and the first metaphysical experience I have had since I looked deep into Henrietta's eyes some years ago and realized that I had forgotten her maiden name and the circumstances under which we met.

There is a dull growling in the upper grandstand, neither sonorous nor menacing but post-autumnal in its sourness and elisionary aspect. There simply are not many in attendance in South Ozone Park on bleak Wednesdays in January and those who have come have exhausted most of their energy simply by making that appearance. I guess I will go downstairs, I say.

Did you lose? Henrietta says. You don't seem very enthusiastic. I guess that you did not make this one.

That would be a fair assumption, I say. Civility must rule. Passion comes and mostly goes but civility is the last ghost at the reception.

I would not have expected otherwise, I say. Still, it was an interesting experience.

You see, even if they speak to you they give you wrong information. You have a credulous face, Fred. Everyone can lie to you.

I suppose so, I say. I heave upright, give Henrietta an absent caress on the shoulder that if extended to its logical conclusion might not have been so tender and amble away, take the down escalator, emerge at the ground level, ease my way through the few stragglers waiting for the race to become official so that they can get on the payout line. I walk on the concrete lawn some day to be a point of debarkation and walk to the rail where the unsaddled Man's Fate, snorting through her shadow roll, is being escorted by a groom up the track. She gives me a contemptuous look. The look is purely contemptuous. One does not need to anthropomorphize to understand that glare. Bad conditions, she says. I got shuffled back.

You weren't shuffled back, I say. You weren't impeded. They have the monitors all over now, nothing gets by me like in the old days. You broke late, fell back, bore out. I am shouting somewhat uncontrollably, I fear. Three old men look at me with some interest and then scurry away. You have no excuses, I say.

Man's Fate shakes off her escort, rears merrily, drops to her knees and snorts, then commences a lazy gallop. I have to scuttle to keep up with her. All right, she says, bearing in somewhat to the rail. All right, I lied to you a little. I had no idea at all whether I was going to win or not. But I thought it would be an interesting experiment.

Interesting experiment? To lose me eighty dollars?

What do dollars mean to a horse? Man's Fate says. The groom curses, runs after her, she shakes her reins and canters away. I don't care about your idiot quantifications. I wanted to talk to one of you, that was all. I always thought it would be interesting and so I did, that's all. It's like interspecies communication.

Communication? I lost eighty dollars! You made a fool of me!

Man's Fate shakes her head gaily, dances by the groom, reverses field, moves up the track again. Sauntering counterclockwise, she begins to move to very good speed, favoring her left foreleg only slightly now.

You made a fool of yourself, she says. I was only the medium for your stupidity. What do you want of a horse, anyway? You think this is an easy job?

The filly is now in a full gallop, showing no effects of her loss, no indication of heat in her left foreleg. This is serious business, I realize. She is really running.

She runs all around the track, a mile and an eighth. I clock her in one forty six and two which is outstanding time. For the six furlongs bringing her to the top of the stretch, she is by my own figures exactly one ten three, race horse time indeed.

She done it for spite. The whole thing for what? Animal liberation?

Henrietta is silent all the way home. The horse-laugh fills the spaces in my head. No sign of the eighty in the wallet, though. The exchange of eighty for a horselaugh is a definite clue that I am moving down in class.

NO ROOM FOR THE UNICORN

by Laura Resnick

I *wanted* the unicorn to come along, despite what some have said. My father Lamech, may he rest in peace, never liked the unicorn, this is true, but then he was not a man who was widely known for his tolerant views. Before I was married, he would bang his shepherd's staff on my head if I even *looked* at the pretty Hittite girls on the other side of the valley. This taught me to be more lenient when my son Ham brought home a girl who didn't keep kosher. In any case, Lamech gave up the ghost long before I built the ark, so it's not as if his opinion on the subject was of great concern to me then, what with the end of the world bearing down on us, and all.

No, as far as I was concerned, the unicorn was welcome.

In case you didn't know, by the way, there was only one unicorn. Some have said that unicorns were as numerous in those days as the cedars of Lebanon, as the lilies of the field, as the children of Adam, but that's a lot of *hazarai*. There was only the one.

He lived near us in the land of Nod, east of Eden. At least, we always *figured* the unicorn was a he, but who can tell for sure? Like I said, there was only one, and he wasn't built precisely like a stallion *or* a mare, if you take my meaning.

There were giants in the earth in those days, as well as a unicorn. Those were the days of heroes and men of great renown: Methuselah, Seth, Adam, Jared, Enoch. Men lived for centuries, and they took as many wives as they pleased. Everyone spoke one language, so travel wasn't such a hassle. Interest rates were low, and a father could afford decent weddings for all his daughters, so long as he didn't have too many. Yes, times were good. But then a few bad apples had to go and spoil it for everyone.

In these heathen times, you might think it strange that I took Yahweh at his word the first time he told me he was going to make it rain for forty days and forty nights, but we were used to the strange and magical powers that ruled our lives then. Yahweh's awesome miracles were a daily occurrence for us, so commonplace that we often scarcely noticed them—and perhaps that was one of the things that made him really mad. He told me that mankind was irredeemable, and that he would destroy the world and start anew.

His instructions were very specific. I was to take my wife, my children, and their spouses on board an ark of my own construction, and we would stay aboard until the rain was over and the sun had dried up the land. As for the animals, I was supposed to find one pair, a male and a female, of every species. He was very clear on this point: *two* of every kind.

Well, it was a tall order, especially considering that Yahweh didn't give me a whole lot of time to accomplish all this—not that I'm criticizing. But I was a shepherd, not a naval architect. I mean, I had never even *seen* a boat, much less learned how to build one. So, after watching me struggle futilely for a few days, Yahweh heaved a sigh that shook the pillars of the earth and told me how to do it.

"This is how to make it, Noah," He said to me. "Make an ark of resinous wood, then caulk it with pitch inside and out. The length of the ark is to be three hundred cubits, its breadth fifty cubits, and its height thirty cubits." Of course, He went into more detail, but I'm an old man now and can't quite remember. I was an old man even *then*, in fact—six hundred years old, to be frank. So, I'm sure you can see how all of this was a bit of a strain.

I had to send some of my family out after these pairs of animals, since not all of them were cooperative. My wife was furious, because Yahweh had said we must bring the *un*clean animals, as well as the clean. Believe me, given a choice in the matter, I'd have left the rats and puff adders behind and taken the unicorn along. I mean, how would *you* like to spend more than forty days in a boat with cobras, hyenas, spiders, hippos, bullfrogs, jackals, vultures, and lions while the world is coming to an end?

The unicorn appeared one day while I was working on the ark. He was a pretty smart animal, and he obviously knew something big was afoot. He was beautiful, too, despite that silly single horn sticking out of his forehead, the horn about which my father had always made such obscene comments.

The unicorn was white, a pure, glistening, undefiled color, whiter than goat's milk. He was big, though not as big as some have said, his back being about as high as a man's shoulder. His pale hooves were slightly mottled, like mother-of-pearl or fine marble from the north, and his eyes were as blue as the sky over Eden, the land from which he had come with our forefathers. His mane was long and wavy, as shiny and soft as a maiden's.

Speaking of maidens, I've heard a lot of strange stories about unicorns and virgins. It's complete fabrication. Maidens had nothing to do with the unicorn, and he reacted no differently to them than to the rest of us. There was, however, a widow named Zipporah who ... Well, it was a long time ago, so why stir it up again?

And as for grinding up the horn of the unicorn to make a potion which would render men more potent—even if such a thing had occurred to us, do you seriously imagine the beast would have let us catch him and cut off his horn? As I've said, he was not stupid.

I suppose he was so smart because he had lived so long. My grandfather Methuselah told me that the unicorn had been around long before his own birth, and when you consider that Methuselah was nine hundred years old when he told me this, it's pretty impressive. The unicorn never aged, though. I figure he was more than a thousand years old when the flood came, but he looked fit and muscular, his coat shiny and sleek, his legs sturdy and strong, his eyes alert, his gait quick, his movements agile. If I could have asked the unicorn one single question, it would have been how he kept in such good shape. At six hundred, I was really starting to show my age.

I suppose that if the unicorn could have asked me one question, it would have been what was I doing building an ark in the middle of terra firma.

He was dying of curiosity, I could see that. He was usually very independent and elusive, but once I started building the ark, he started hanging around all of the time. Meanwhile, the animals began lining up two by two. Some were brought by my children, others came on their own, apparently having been warned by Yahweh about the catastrophe to come. He had created them after all, so there was no reason He couldn't speak to them.

One day it finally occurred to me that I had

never seen another unicorn. This worried me, since it had never before dawned on me that I might have to leave the unicorn behind. But Yahweh had said *two* of each species, and He had said it several times.

"You'd better go find a lady unicorn," I said to the unicorn.

He stared at me, his blue eyes sparkling with curiosity, his round nostrils quivering. He sniffed the edge of the ark.

"Go already," I ordered. "Find a mate to bring on board with you."

Well, the dumb beast just poked some reeds with his horn and kept standing around. In an effort to make him leave, I threw a flagon at him. He dodged it and pranced around playfully, thinking this was a new game, though I was an old man and had not played with him for several hundred years. I threw a few more things at him and shouted a little. When he finally realized it wasn't a game, he moped and looked hurt, letting his head hang down and his horn scratch the dirt. You could make the unicorn happy, sad, or curious, but you could never make him do what you wanted him to do.

Since he obviously wasn't going to find a mate himself, and since the flood was getting closer every day, I decided to send my son Japheth out to find a lady unicorn. No one had any idea where to look, and it seemed kind of hopeless, but he tried anyhow. He's a good boy, if only he would get a haircut now and then.

Japheth searched in the west, since that's where the unicorn had come from. He could only go so far, though, since Eden, if it even still existed, was forbidden to men. And under the circumstances, he thought it best not to try Yahweh's patience.

By the time Japheth returned to us, his quest having proved unsuccessful, the sky was darkening with thunderclouds such as no man has ever seen since. A wind came up which tore saplings out of the ground by their very roots, knocked down our simple shepherd's tents, and stripped the wool from our sheep as they clung precariously to the rocky hills.

Despite all of this, I managed to get Yahweh's attention for a few minutes, for my heart was heavy about the unicorn. We had failed to find his mate, but couldn't Yahweh permit us to take him aboard anyhow? The Lord God didn't exactly answer my prayer, He only repeated what He had been saying every day: there must be *two* of each species, a male and a female, of fowls after their kind, and of cattle after their kind, of every creeping thing that creepeth upon the earth, and so on.

As the storm swelled above our heads, as the end of the world drew near, as the sky thundered with Yahweh's rage, we loaded the ark. There were green alligators, long-necked geese, ivory-toothed elephants, venomous serpents, furry-legged spiders, slinking panthers, roes and hinds, monkeys and leopards, wolves and bears. Every kind of creature came aboard the ark, save one—the loveliest of all.

The unicorn pranced excitedly around the ark as we loaded it. Of all the beasts, he was the only one who knew something monumental was afoot, yet the others lumbered aboard dumbly, guaranteed of Yahweh's protection, while the unicorn vainly awaited his turn beneath the angry sky. In the end, perhaps realizing we meant to leave him behind, he stopped prancing and merely watched, his pale eyes growing opaque, his head lowering, his fur growing dull for the first time in a thousand years as the fierce wind coated everything with sand and dust.

The rain started to fall just as we loaded the last of the food supplies into the ark. My family all rushed on board and took their places, and I followed them. There was a moment when, ignoring my wife's urgent plea to remain safely on board, I went back for the unicorn. But as I made to help him aboard, the air around us filled with the echoing crash of Yahweh's wrath, the sky opened up, and a bolt of lightning scorched the earth around us.

I had been taught that God was imponderable and unknowable. For whatever reason, He intended for the unicorn to remain behind, to perish in the flood, to disappear forever from the face of the earth. And so I left him there to die.

The unicorn was not angry at my desertion, since anger was not in his nature. He remained near the ark that night as the terrible downpour carried away everything we had owned in the old life and flooded the valley in which we had lived.

By morning, the water had risen high enough to move the ark, and we began floating away from the world's past. According to Yahweh, the future would not begin until the waters withdrew and subsided. This would be a strange time of waiting for us, while He washed the earth clean and destroyed what was, in order to make room for what would be.

I looked out the small window which I had made with Yahweh's patient instruction. The unicorn had found high ground during the night, and he stood there without moving, watching us as we floated away. He was drenched and bedraggled, and he held his foreleg up slightly, as if he had hurt it in the climb to safety. He looked wistful and lonely, but unafraid; fear was not in his nature, either.

Did he blame me, I wondered? Did he know we would never again return to the land of Nod? Did he know that Yahweh had chosen to destroy him in the infancy of the world, never to be seen again, only to be spoken of as a vague, improbable myth?

The unicorn never moved as we disappeared, floating away amidst the relentless downpour, the crash of thunder, and the swirling waters of the flood. I wondered how long he remained in that spot, and whether his death came fast or slow, whether he drowned in a few minutes or lingered for days on some rocky peak, injured, hungry, and cold.

You probably know most of the rest of the story; it rained for forty straight days. We weren't idle, though. Do you have any idea how much food all those animals consumed, and how much mess they made as a consequence? And trying to keep the lions away from the lambs, and the leopards away from the harts, and the mice away from the elephants, and the asps away from *everybody* was no small task either. We filled up our spare time, when we had it, with backgammon and mah-jong. And, of course, we prayed, not wanting Yahweh to forget that He intended to spare us.

The rain finally stopped, and, as Yahweh had instructed, we sent a dove out to reconnoiter. To tell the truth, it was a pretty grim time. Every living thing on the face of the earth was wiped out, people, animals, creeping things, and birds. Everything with the least breath of life in its nostrils, everything on dry land, just like the stories say—all dead. Only those of us who had entered the ark survived.

Little by little, the waters ebbed, though it took longer than any of us had really planned on. Finally, on the seventeenth day of the seventh month, the ark came to rest on Mount Ararat. We were able to get out and stretch our legs, though it was a couple of more months before the waters subsided enough for us to get on with our lives.

I built an altar, but I didn't make any sacrifices,

contrary to what you've heard. What was I going to sacrifice? There were only two of every species of animal, and I'd gone to too much trouble saving them to sacrifice them now. I guess Yahweh saw the logic in that, because He made a covenant with me anyhow, and we were blessed with the rainbow and the promise that nothing like this would *ever* happen to us again.

I'm ancient now, set in my ways and stubborn about my habits. This is a new world, and I cannot get comfortable in it. Although Yahweh has been kind to me, there is no place for me here. Soon I will give up the ghost, like Lamech and Methuselah, and like their fathers before them, which is why I set this down.

For you who will never see a unicorn, I wanted the truth to be known. And know this, too. If I questioned Yahweh's compassion in leaving the unicorn behind, to die in the flood which destroyed the old world before the new world was created, I understand His wisdom now.

Those were different times, back before the flood. Men heard God when He whispered in their ears, and heeded His warnings. We lived as giants, surrounded by Yahweh's magic and miracles.

The unicorn, curious, lonely, or perhaps scenting his destiny—who can say for sure?—followed our forefathers out of Eden. He danced around us in the land of Nod, a beautiful, immortal creature, incapable of anger, fear, or treachery. Perhaps he was fit for the world we knew then, but he was unfit for the world which followed. For in this new world with no place for giants, there is no room for the unicorn.

THE HORSE BOY

by Mary Stanton

I

When Bakar the horse boy ducked into the Muck-master's hut after supper, the old man leapt from his pallet in the corner and clouted him on the ear.

"*That's* for missing your dinner when I told you to be here at sunset. You were spending more time than you should with that horse, weren't you? Leaving your other chores for me to do!"

It wasn't a hard slap, more of a buffet, delivered with the heel of the old man's hand and aimed at Bakar's jaw rather than the tender ear itself. But Bakar, unprepared for the blow, blinked back tears.

"Sit down," the Muckmaster grumbled. "Here. I brought you a peach. I had some bread, too, but they caught me and I had to empty my sleeve. The peach is sweet and hardly bruised at all. It's from the Queen's own garden. A cull, can you believe it?" The old man's muddy brown eyes slid sideways and he grinned. "The cook let me take it from the waste bin. Eat! Eat!

Bakar crouched in the straw that carpeted the hut and bit into the peach. He doubted the story about the cook. Juice flooded his mouth, a sweet perfume. He sniffed back tears.

"Don't tell me that clip on the ear hurt, you lazy boy. You deserve that and more for being late. With that scruffy mare, were you?"

"I was exercising Tierza. She is a little weak in the hindquarters, and if I build her up, they will not . . . they will not . . ." Bakar bit his lip hard.

"Tcha! That mare! She will end up to feed the pigs, that one!"

"She will not," said Bakar, with passion.

The Muckmaster shuffled through the straw and fussed with the oil lamp in the corner. It was something of danger with the straw about, but he was very proud of it, having talked the Third Housekeeper (he said) out of it. Where the precious oil came from to light it, Bakar didn't know and didn't ask.

Bakar finished the peach and tossed the pit out the open door.

"Tcha!" The Muckmaster awkwardly leapt after it, his left leg dragging, and brought it back, dropping it carefully into the skin pouch he wore about his waist on a leather string. He patted the pouch. "Waste! We'll find a place to plant it and perhaps we will have our own peaches and I won't have to borrow from the cook. *Now*," he scowled fiercely, "now you will help me clean up this place. While you were messing about with this mare, you expected me to do your chores for you? This place is no better than a pig. . . ." he stopped, working his lips, avoiding a glance at Bakar's skinny forearm. The wounds from the boars in the pig pit had healed now, but flesh would never fill the crescent-shaped scars and they gleamed whitely in the lamp light. "So," he said in a gentler voice, "you keep the Queen's mare as clean as Allah's feet, but not our house. And you miss supper so that the meat will never rise on those skinny bones of yours. What else did you do that you were so late?"

"I soaked Tierza's hooves with olive oil," Bakar said. "And I had to leave the cloth wrapped around her feet for a while. They will shine now, when the sun hits them, and perhaps Nimit the Stablemaster will choose her for the Queen to ride."

"The smallest, scrubbiest mare in the stable! Psh! You do what you do for nothing. For less than nothing. I've told you that before. As for Nimit," he paused, and stroked his beard. Bakar noticed that his hand trembled a little. "You stay away from Nimit."

"I am not afraid of Nimit," said Bakar, which wasn't true.

"Who's afraid of Nimit?" The Muckmaster's hand went to his twisted leg. "He is stupid, that one, that is all. Shake out those bed coverings now and get the little rake. I want you to sweep the floor."

Bakar slid from his haunches to his backside and yawned, "I did it this morning, while you were mucking out stalls. Thank you for the peach."

"Huh. Then we'll sleep, now. There's work that waits in the morning."

Bakar sighed, went to his pallet, and curled into the muslin coverings. The old man smoothed the cloth around his shoulders and patted his arm, "Did you piss?"

Bakar sighed, went outside to the clay bowl to relieve himself and came back to his bed. Sometimes in the night when the bad dreams came, he wet himself before he could wake up and get away from the jeering faces hanging over the boar pit. The grunts of the pigs would fill his ears with a terrible low screaming. And the old man would insist that he wash when he couldn't hold his water—coverings, pallet, floor, and worst of all, himself. Bakar settled into bed and yawned once more. Across the room, the Muckmaster carefully blew out the lamp and settled himself with a satisfied groan.

"Ha! There's extra straw in my mattress!"

Bakar smiled in the dark.

"So, I won't send you back to your thieving friends after all."

Bakar remembered Marek, and the stump where his hand had been after they caught him stealing in the bazaar. The red blood had pumped like a fountain in the Queen's Court, and Bakar had run ducking through the crowd; he had not seen Marek again. The Muckmaster must have caught his thought, for he said, "If you didn't spend so much time with that Tierza, that mud-colored mare, there would be new friends to make in the Royal Stable. Why do you do it? The Third Privy Cleaner wouldn't even ride that mare. Just a miserable gift from some saint-forsaken northern tribe, that one is. I'll bet you a fistful of coppers the Queen hasn't laid eyes on that mare since she came."

"Then the Queen's stupid," said Bakar.

The Muckmaster sat straight up in bed, his white hair faintly luminous in the moonlight from the doorway. "Bakar! Do you want the pigs to get the rest of you? There'd be a reason this time—not just for a Court gentlemen's sport. It may not even be a pig pit they throw you into. Not for treason. That's red-hot pokers, that is, and Nimit himself would take pleasure in the job. Nimit took the flesh from Hakkim's back with his whip four days ago because he left a twist of wet straw in the lead stallion's stall. Nimit called *that*, something, yes, 'disrespect for the Royal Person.'"

"Nimit had lost at the game of shells in the market that morning," said Bakar. "He's a piece of camel dung, anyway."

"Camel piss," said the Muckmaster.

"Toad turds," giggled Bakar.

The old man sighed.

"Nimit knows nothing about horses," said Bakar. "Gambling, maybe, but not horses. Take, oh, Tierza, for example. She's three times the horse of some he chooses for the Queen to ride. And what place is she assigned? The very last stall in the barn, in the shadows, so that no one can see how fine she is."

"That mare," said the Muckmaster. "She isn't noticed by the other horses, much less by the Stablemaster, or the Queen herself. You've seen her turned out for exercises with the other mares. When they aren't ignoring her completely, she's getting kicked and bitten. If her own herd doesn't respect her, why should anyone else?" He paused, then said gently, "Do not place your love and faith in animals, my boy, or in people, either. That mare may go the way of others like her. You know. You know."

Bakar knew. Not worthy. Put down. And thrown into the pit. That gentle mare, fed to the boars!

"She has Royal blood. You can see it in her eyes."

"You can't see it in her coat! You have a lot to learn about horses, boy, if you think they, too, don't know the difference between a commoner and a Royal."

Bakar snorted.

"This is true. She has obviously failed the Test, and the tribe that gave her as tribute to the Queen had already passed her off as unworthy."

"What Test?"

"Allah tests both man and horse in this life, Bakar, so that both may have the chance to enter heaven when they die. Now, some men he blesses more than others, with cleverness for example, or the gift of a silver tongue. Allah's test for me, say, would be something like, 'How many peaches will you find in the waste bin, Muckmaster mine?'' So the more peaches I gather, the better man I will be in the good Lord's sight. Others, such as you, Bakar, he tests in that pit. . . ."

"Then there must be a test for Tierza, too," said Bakar.

"I said that, didn't I? And she has failed it."

"You don't know that!"

"Do you know the Test of the Horse, Bakar? It is a terrible thing that these tribes do in the name of Allah. But the horse that passes the Test is a worthy horse indeed, and when the chosen one passes from this life to the next, it is to the Courts of the One Hundred and Five, where Equus the Horse God reigns through the will of Allah. Where the rivers run crystal sweet, the trees are tents of shade, and all of heaven is grass."

"And the Test?"

"Each year, when the time arrives for the mares and stallions to be bred, the desert chieftains herd them to a place—a valley say, or a canyon, where there is no water, only heat. Where there is no grass, only sand and rock. And they are left there, the horses, for three full days and nights, under the sun."

Bakar thought of the pig pit. It had been so hot, his sweat had dried instantly in the air.

"The horses are left there, Bakar, and their tongues swell with thirst. Their heads hang to their knees in hunger. They wait, as horses will, with only an occasional cry.

"And the fourth day, before sunrise, the chieftains gather. They line the horses up at the mouth of the canyon, or valley, where a river lies beyond. The horses scream at the scent of water, and as the first finger of the sun pokes over the desert, their masters let down the gate.

"The horses leap and race to the river. And as they run, one by one their masters call their names. Hola! they cry. Stop!

"Those horses that halt and choose their masters over their thirst are the mares and stallions that pass the Test. And they are chosen, Bakar, for breeding, for war, for all the glory that man can give them. And at the end of their worthy lives, they pass to the Courts, and to the palace of Equus and his band of the Chosen."

"Tierza can pass this Test," said Bakar.

"And I would like two strong legs! Tierza would knock over the Vizier himself to reach a bowl of grain the moment after she'd eaten."

But Bakar was asleep. And as he slept, he dreamed.

He dreamed that the moon shone down on Baghdad in a silver arc that fell outside their door. And he dreamed that he rose from his pallet and walked with the moon puddled at his feet. He dreamed that he walked, walked, walked, as a horse will walk, with a light, four-beat step, and that the scent of flowers from the Queen's gardens rose about him like a mist. A sweet call came from the moon. The arc hardened to a bridge. He walked up the silvery bridge, leaving the spires and minarets of the city far below him.

The silver bridge wound into misty clouds and ended at a pale white gate. Bakar breathed in roses. He reached out one scarred hand and pushed the gate open, then passed through to an oasis.

It was an oasis of a kind he had never seen before, had only heard about in the Muckmaster's tales of heaven: a field of grass, deep green, starred with flowers the colors of jewels at the Queen's throat; a river wound through the silken green, a diamond serpentine; the water rippled over shiny black stones with the sound of crystal bells.

There, at the river's edge, drinking from its

waters, stood the most beautiful mare Bakar had
ever seen.

She was the color of the great gold seal on the
palace gates, a gold that rivaled the Sun's heart.
Her eyes were a clear ruby, touched with gentle-
ness and sorrow. She raised her head from the
river and looked at Bakar.

Welcome, horse boy.

Bakar blinked. Her voice was sweet inside his
head. He fell to his knees, as when he and the
Muckmaster prayed six times each day.

"Your Majesty," he whispered.

*I am Jehanna, breedmistress to our Lord Equus.
Dreamspeaker to the chosen mares in the Courts of
The One Hundred and Five.* The scent of roses was
very strong. *Get up, Bakar, and follow me.*

She flicked her tail and it cascaded over her
hindquarters like a fall of silk. Bakar rose and followed her through the springy grass. They walked
beside the river as it looped and circled the green
field.

The river looped again, and then again, and they
came to the crest of a valley. The valley's slopes
were covered with broad-leaved trees. Under the
trees were mares, a hundred of them or more—
their coats a brilliant rainbow in the sun. Their
hides gleamed chestnut, gold, silver, white, and a
black as deep as the depths of evening. Bakar
looked, and looked again. Each coat was different.
Each mare a deeper or a lighter shade than the
one before, but none were the color of a puddle in
a dry river, the color of Tierza, the color of mud.

*The mares of Equus, Bakar. Each of the Blesséd
mares has passed the Test, Bakar. Neither faith nor
love is easy.* Jehanna looked at him. Her ruby eyes
glowed more brightly than the sun, the scent of
roses was strong, and Bakar saw all the world
jewel-toned.

Bakar . . .

Her scent swept over him,
Bakar . . .
He reached up to touch her silky mane . . .
"Bakar!"

He woke, suddenly, in his own bed, and the Muckmaster was there, waving a flower from the Queen's garden under his nose.

"Where did you get that!" he demanded. "You're a foolish old man and one of these days you aren't going to be able to talk yourself out of a whipping."

"Dust bin!" said the Muckmaster gleefully. He waved the flower under his nose, then turned and placed it carefully in a clay cup on the shelf with the lamp. "Only slightly bruised! A cull, can you believe it?"

"And the cook said you could have it."

"The cook? No. Not the cook. The Second Undergardener himself. Bakar, you slept late. The breakfast barrack is closed. If you don't hurry, you'll be late for morning feed in the stable."

Bakar leapt to his feet, washed hastily, and ran to the stable. He liked to be there first, before the sun rose, when the stables were alive only with the sounds of the horses stamping lightly in their stalls. He raced into the great building, the marble center aisle cool and sweating slightly against his bare feet. A few of the horse boys were already there, feeding and watering their charges. Bakar went past the row of gold-trimmed marble stalls that housed the Royal favorites. He passed El Hakimer, the lead stallion, who was as white as milk. He went past the three royal mares, one sat-in-black, one cedar-brown, one dappled like the morning dawn. He trotted by the cedar-faced stalls that were next, the stalls where the outer members of the Royal household kept their mounts, and finally, to the very back of the great barn where a few stuccoed stalls had been built as quarters for those horses the Queen had been given in tribute, whose quality was poor, whose coats were the dun of the desert, or the dusty gray of rocks, or the color of a river bottom, like Tierza.

Bakar's heart stopped, then thumped against his chest like a giant fist. A piece of black silk had been tied to the latch of Tierza's stall.

Tierza looked expectantly over the edge of her box, her brown eyes meeting his own.

"Tcha, tcha," said Bakar, and Tierza whickered in response. Black silk. The sign of the Royal Horse Physician. A judgment. A sentence, that Tierza was a cull, to be thrown out like the peach pits. Bakar picked up the two skin buckets that sat outside Tierza's door and went out the back to the granary. The Grainkeeper, a withered scrap of a man with a filthy turban, wielded a stingy scoop. The portions of grain tended to be larger for firstcomers, and Bakar joined the line of waiting horse boys, shaking with rage and fear. He would barter something, or offer to play at shells for his clay supper cup if the ration was short today. But the Grainkeeper was only mildly surly, and Tierza's grain bucket was filled just short of the top.

Bakar rinsed out the water bucket and filled it from the trough. Balancing the buckets carefully, he made his way back to Tierza's stall.

Tierza laid her head on the edge of her half door and looked at him.

Bakar set the buckets down and looked back.

Tierza had the dish-shaped muzzle of the true desert breeds and the slender, elegant feet and ankles of her kind. But her ears were larger than beauty allowed and her muzzle was more coarse than fine. Although she was standing quietly, Bakar knew that she dished slightly when she moved, a flaw that could not be improved by feed or exercise.

Worst of all was her color: the dull dun of a river bottom after an infrequent rain.

"You would look as fine as any of Equus' mares in a tasseled bridle," said Bakar.

Tierza pawed at the dirt floor.

"With gold tassels. And a silk saddle cloth. And reins of flowers. You'd be fit for the Queen herself."

Tierza snorted.

Bakar blinked back tears. He was no fool.

"The Queen will never ride you, Tierza. Your coat is not the black of a night without the moon, nor is it as white as the brood mare's milk." He leaned forward and whispered urgently in her ear.

"But you can pass the Test. That only a few can pass. The bravest. The best. I know you would pass the Test. And if you did, Tierza, if you did— the Queen holds courage above the color of your coat, or your ugly ears."

Leaving the feed and water outside the stall, Bakar slipped inside. He ran his hands over the mare's hindquarters, feeling the lump of flesh from a kick she'd gotten in the turnout area the day before, tracing the almost-healed scar from a bite on her withers. Unlike the scars on his own body, this would fill the flesh and eventually be gone.

Tierza raised her head suddenly, ears pricked forward. Bakar listened; the heavy slap of a sandal sounded in the marble aisle.

"Pig Boy!" Nimit's heavy face thrust forward over the half door. His eyebrows were oddly peaked and deep brackets grooved the flesh on either side of his mouth, so that he looked, always, saturnine and scowling. He was very tall. Rumor had it that he had been one of the Queen's Assassins before he had done something so terrible that he had to be retired to the post of Stablemaster.

"This mare's been culled," said Nimit in deep satisfaction as he fingered the black silk.

"When is it to be, your Excellency?"

Nimit reached out, grabbed Bakar's neck, and pulled him over the top of the half door. He opened his hand and Bakar tumbled to the aisle.

"What business is it of yours, Pig Boy?"

"None, your Excellency," said Bakar humbly.

"That's right. The Ax-man comes three days from now, not that it's any of your business, right, Pig Boy?"

"Yes, your Excellency."

Nimit peered into the stall. Tierza was backed into a corner, ears flattened.

Nimit spat. "This ugly piece of shit! And you, too," he grinned. "You watch it, Pig Boy, or the Ax-man may come for you."

The slap of his sandals pounded in Bakar's ears long after he had gone.

He would do it. He would give her one last chance.

He would give Tierza a chance to pass the Test.

On the fourth day, he would place the water and feed bucket at the very front of the stable, right before the stall of El Hakimer the stallion. When he called her, if she failed, she'd fail in front of the others, and it wouldn't matter, not with the Ax-man waiting.

And if she succeeded . . . he thought of the green meadows and the river, of the glory that would be hers, out of all the horses in the stable.

He gave the scar on her withers a light, dismissive blow; he shut his ears to her plaintive whinny when he left without giving her food or water.

II

"There was no manure in Tierza's stall today, and very little piss, either," said the Muckmaster on the second day. "The black silk hangs from her door, but she is still a member of the Royal Herd. Her head is hanging down almost to her knees. I'm surprised at you for not noticing. You spend most of your time in her stall."

"I know," said Bakar. He pulled a cleaning rag from the shelf and wiped imaginary dust from the lamp.

"You know?" The old man settled himself cross-legged in the straw and produced two peaches from his sleeve. He tossed one to Bakar and bit into the other. "You know and have done nothing?"

Bakar ate the peach. He spit the pit out and handed it to the old man to put into his pouch. The Muckmaster looked into Bakar's eyes. His own widened in sudden shock. The peach pit rolled into the straw, forgotten.

"Aaaaah! Aieeee!" He rocked back and forth on his heels as if he were praying. "You will be whipped until the flesh lies away from your bones! To starve the Queen's mare! To take water from her in the heat!" Tears rolled in the gullies of his cheeks, like stones in a river bed. "Nimit will kill you," he whispered. "Oh, Bakar. My boy. You will die for this."

III

The third day had been fiercely hot, the sun beating on the streets of Baghdad like a great bronze fist, the heat so dry that the sweat was sucked off Bakar in an instant, leaving no cooling breath behind.

Tierza's tongue showed purple-gray and patchy between her lips. Her brown eyes filmed with a sickly yellow and her fine-drawn head sunk almost to her knees.

"Tcha, tcha, tcha," Bakar smoothed her ears and neck with his hand. "Tomorrow, mare, it will be over."

He ached to bring her water. Just a sip, no more, to take the dreadful color from her tongue. Her coat was dry and staring under his hand.

"Allah tests both man and horse," the Muckmaster had told him. There was a reason, wasn't there? For her patchy tongue and despairing look?

When Bakar returned to the hut, the Muckmaster ignored him, turning his back to the boy, his face to the wall, refusing to speak as he had the day past.

IV

Bakar slept and woke, slept and woke, and he dreamed no dreams of heaven. And long before the sun had any thought of rising over the desert's rim, he was back in the Royal Stable, slipping past the Third Watch to sit at Tierza's feet.

She breathed now with a rasping sigh, and her tongue was gray and swollen.

The prayer call would signal dawn, but Bakar watched the night with straining eyes anyway. He had hidden Tierza's daily ration of grain in a chest of saddle cloths in the robing room, and he got it now, filling the bucket half full so that the grain wouldn't hit her starving belly like a blow. He filled the water bucket to the very top, then crept down the marble aisle to the marble entrance to the Stable, where El Hakimer stood in the predawn dark. The stallion snorted fiercely at his approach.

"She will pass the Test," he said to the stallion, "and you will beg to give her foals."

Bakar listened for the dawn. Slowly, the eastern sky began to lighten to a fresh faint dun, the color of Tierza's coat.

The Muezzin's cry greeted the sun. The fourth day had begun. Bakar took off down the aisle to Tierza's stall as if he'd started a race. He heard her kicking as he ran. Bakar skidded to a halt outside her stall, ignoring the burn of the marble on his feet. Reaching for the latch, he threw his weight behind the door to open it.

"Pig Boy!"

Nimit: striding down the marble aisle, his black whip curled around his bare chest, dagger slapping against his leather loin cloth. Tierza quieted suddenly; Bakar heard her chesty breaths.

Bakar thought: Nimit will not look at her. He never does. He will walk past—spit in my direction, perhaps—but he will not look at her. I will wait until he goes and then I will let her out.

Bakar thought: If I am the only one to see—how will the Queen know if she has passed the Test? Who would believe me?

Bakar looked down at his forearms, braced against the stable door. The scars gleamed against his skin.

He pushed the door open.

Tierza burst past him in a flaming rush of speed, hooves striking sparks from the floor. Her hindquarters bunched under her coat and she screamed at the smell of water.

"You little bastard!" Nimit shouted. He leapt out of the way as Tierza swept past him.

Bakar followed her, dodging the sudden tongue of Nimit's whip.

"Tierza!" shouted Bakar like the desert masters, "Tierza, hola!"

One ear flicked back. The mare ran on. Then, from out of nowhere, the bent figure of the Muckmaster loomed in front of her. She swerved, narrowly missing the old man, and screamed again.

"Tierza! Tiieeerrzzaa! STOP!" Bakar's throat went raw.

She stopped. Suddenly. And stood, just out of reach of the water-filled buckets, her flanks shuddering in and out.

Bakar ran toward her, his heart high and singing, Nimit raging unheeded at his heels. He reached her, patted her flanks, whispered in her ear. The mare mumbled at his palm and rolled her eyes in appeal.

"Come now, come now," Bakar whispered. "Drink, drink."

She walked forward, stood at the bucket, and looked at him.

"Yes, Tierza, drink."

She bent her muzzle to the bucket and drank.

Some part of Bakar had been waiting for Nimit's whip, but when it came, the pain was so fierce and unexpected that he screamed.

Nimit said nothing. Flat black eyes narrowed, lip caught between his teeth, he raised the whip again.

"Master Nimit, wait!" The Muckmaster sidled forward, thrusting Bakar behind him with one skinny arm. "This foolish, miserable boy. He almost ruined my Test!"

"Out of my way, dungscraper. This piece of trash let this horse run me down. Let her out of the stall right in my path. I'll lay his backbone open to the air."

The Muckmaster whirled and clouted Bakar on the ear. "Stupid!" he screamed. "*I* was the one to get the Queen's reward! And you thought you'd steal it from me, eh? I took you in when you were just a street boy. Look at the gratitude I get." He turned and bowed low to Nimit, his forehead nearly touching the floor. "Look, I ask you, Stablemaster, how this boy steals from me. He knew today was the day that the mare Tierza was to pass or fail the Test. I was to come and tempt her with the water. I was the one to call her name, and see if she halted to my bidding. And *I* was the one to get the Queen's reward."

"This little bastard has put this bag of bones to

the Test?" Nimit roared with laughter. "Then the Ax-man will take care of him, too!" He cracked the whip in the air.

"On his own? All by himself? You are making a joke, your Excellency. Of course he didn't. He would never dare. I was the one who was to get the reward. I was the one who was asked to do this thing."

Nimit lowered the whip and his face darkened. "If there are any rewards to be had, dungscraper, they are mine."

The Muckmaster cringed and bowed. Bakar held tightly to Tierza's mane.

"So, what is this reward?" asked Nimit.

"Why, rubies, your honor." The Muckmaster jiggled the pouch at his rawhide belt. "One—small one—for me. To give the mare the Test. And more, perhaps, if she passed."

Nimit grinned. "And where is this ruby?"

The Muckmaster held up the pouch and smoothed it over a small bulge.

Peach pits! thought Bakar. Oh, Allah!

"Give it to me." Nimit stretched his hand out.

"Oh, but now it is all ruined, your honor. All because of this miserable boy."

Nimit grunted. "This is cock dung. If this mare were to be Tested, I would know about it. Who told you to give the Test? Where did this ruby come from?"

The Muckmaster grinned and bowed, rubbing his hands together. "You know Aziel? The Second Handmaiden to the Dresser of the Queen? The one with breasts like ..." the Muckmaster drew a poetic line in the air. "She gave me this ruby—a small one, and deeply flawed, to be sure—but a ruby nonetheless."

"Why?"

"Well, why indeed? I was near the Queen's Garden. For you must know that I walk there of an evening to pick up any dead or dying flowers that may impede the path of our Queen on her walks . . ."

Watch it, Bakar thought.

". . . and Aziel called to me. At first I thought, dare I say it? That she had in mind to give an old man some sport . . ."

Nimit growled menacingly.

". . . but of course, when the Second Handmaiden to the Dresser of the Queen calls one, one dare not disobey."

The Muckmaster stretched up and in a low voice said into Nimit's ear, "She said that the Dresser to the Queen had told her, Aziel, that the Queen had a fancy to see which of the horses in her stable would pass the Test of Allah."

"And why did Her Majesty not tell me of this wish?" asked Nimit, his voice deceptively soft.

"Why, Her Gracious Majesty would never place the Royal Stablemaster in danger, would she? Oh, no, your Excellency, you are far too valuable a servant, and I—what am I?—nothing—and if I Tested these horses—in secret, you understand— why, no one need know if one of them failed. For such a failure would not reflect at all well on The Royal Stablemaster, and if it were public, then something would have to be done to save the Queen from embarrassment. And—to be frank with you, your Excellency, not even the ruby itself would have tempted me to do this thing, for many of these horses—yes, El Hakimer himself—are used to the soft palace life, and who knows if they would stop at the sound of your voice when you called, NOT" said the Muckmaster, backing hastily away from Nimit's upraised fist, "because of you, your Excellency, all the world knows how good a horseman you are, but does all the world know what's in the mind of the horse?"

"I will see this ruby, old man, because I think

you are as full of dung as a camel on the second day of a caravan."

"It is *my* ruby, your Excellency," said the Muckmaster with a degree of dignity.

"You will give me the ruby, and we will say no more about it, old man. Not to Aziel or the Third from the Fifteenth Dresser to her Royal Highness, or whatever, but because I don't believe you."

The muckmaster bowed again. Bakar looked into Tierza's dark brown eyes. The Muckmaster laughed lightly. "Shall we game for it? I understand your Excellency is a master of the game of shells." With an improbably quick movement, he took three walnut shells from his pouch and moved them enticingly around the marble floor.

Nimit scratched his thick black beard.

"My own poor talent is nothing as to yours, Excellency. At least, not from the tales I hear in the bazaar," said the Muckmaster. "Here. Sit."

Nimit crouched opposite the Muckmaster. "All right," he said. "I will play for this ruby." He made a grab for the middle shell, but the Muckmaster whipped it deftly from under his thick fingers. Nimit scowled, "No! I will play the boy here."

Bakar couldn't be certain, but he thought the old man paled.

"The boy? What possible sport could there be in gaming with a boy? Now I, your Excellency, have long wanted to test my skills . . ."

"Shut up!" Nimit pushed the old man back, and he went sprawling. Bakar leapt forward, his hand at the small knife he carried in his tunic. Nimit grinned, and reached for the knife in his scabbard.

"Oh, all right!" said the Muckmaster from his place on the floor. He got up, fussily brushed off his clothes, and gave Bakar a shove. "Test your skill, test your skill." Bakar looked up and the old man smiled a terrible smile, full of grief.

"I tell you what, your Excellency," said the
Muckmaster, his voice high and thin, "You shall
play, oh, let's say for a peach pit. For I do believe
that I have left the ruby tucked in a safe place,
away from this thieving boy."

Nimit glanced up. He was half in shadow, half
in the sunshine that was pouring through the open
stable door. Bakar noticed that the horse boys,
arriving to do morning chores, had gathered in a
silent huddle near the stall of the Royal stallion.
The whites of Nimit's eyes gleamed.

"We will play for the ruby, old man. If the boy
loses, it is mine. If the boy wins," he shrugged,
teeth yellow in his dark beard, "why, I am an hon-
orable man, and you shall keep the ruby."

Bakar squatted on the marble, the walnut shells
before him. He moved the shells deftly. Feeling
the weight of an object under the one with a nick
out of the shell, he tipped quickly and looked as
it fell back against the marble.

Peach pit.

He glanced quickly at the Muckmaster, then
back to the shell. His hands moved as fast as he
could make them, but he could hear the slight
drag of the peach pit across the floor.

"Stop!" Nimit said. He reached over and picked
up the center shell.

Tierza snorted.

The space beneath the shell was empty.

Bakar moved the shells again, fingers flying.

Tierza snorted a time.

Nimit picked up the shell on Bakar's left.

Empty space beneath.

Nimit bared his teeth in a grin. His hand went
to his whip, then back to his knee.

Bakar worked the shells once more. The peach
pit was in the center shell; he could feel its weight
against the floor. He dropped his hands and sat

back on his haunches. Suddenly, the stallion El Hakimer gave a glad cry, as if in welcome. A scent of wild roses came to Bakar, and a crystalline chime of water over rock.

Nimit reached out to the shell on Bakar's right. Teirza snorted a third time.

Nimit took up the center shell.

Beneath it lay a small ruby glowing as red as the gold mare's eye in Bakar's dream.

The Muckmaster turned a breath into a cough. The horse boys crowded around. Nimit picked up the ruby and tucked it into his turban. "So, Muckmaster, it was no lie."

"No," the Muckmaster cleared his voice, and said more strongly, "I do not lie, Excellency."

"You will tell Aziel the mare Tierza passed the Test," said Nimit. "I will take the black silk from her stall myself. There may be more such rubies."

"The mare Tierza is one horse who passed the Test, yes," said the Muckmaster, his eyes on the floor where the ruby had been, "but will all the mares in the stable pass this test—as soft as they are with the good life you have given them?"

"Hm," said Nimit.

"Perhaps I should tell Aziel, the Second Handmaiden to the Dresser of the Queen that this mare, Tierza, just in from the desert, has passed the Test, but only because you, Nimit, called her. And since her Royal Majesty has made it clear that she does not wish her best Stablemaster to be at risk, perhaps it will end there."

"You be sure it does," said Nimit. He turned to the gaping horse boys. "What are you camel dung looking at! Get back to work. And you, Pig Boy— take this mare to her stall." He tapped his turban and grinned at the Muckmaster. "No more of these Tests, dungscraper."

The Muckmaster shook his head, and Nimit went away.

Bakar began to lead Tierza back to her stall. The Muckmaster gripped his arm and said in an urgent voice, "Bakar! That ruby! From the peach pit!"

"Yes, old man?"

"That other peach pit. The one that rolled on the floor. You make sure and find it tonight when we get home. And perhaps I should dig up the ones I planted to turn into trees!"

"Yes, Muckmaster," said Bakar, and kissed him.

THE POWER OF YOUNG GIRLS

by Constance Ash

Roxanne slapped the jumping bat's leather handle against her white stretch jeans. "I want to stay here. Whenever I begin to have friends, you drag me away to a new neighborhood."

Simone blew cigarette smoke out of the fine flute of her nose. Her shoulders shifted slightly inside the nacreous silk kimono embroidered with birds, coral wing feathers outstretched, gift of Larry Wing, her lover. The skin of her smooth, tan throat was as luminous as the pearly silk. "You more resemble those in Biden School's Equine Club and the Uptown Riding Academy classes."

Roxanne tossed her long, crinkled hair, which rebelled against bows and combs, still de rigueur in riding class. Her head sat upon a slender neck rising out of the crumpled tie-neck white linen blouse worn under a long, beige jacket trimmed in brown suede. Her skin was espresso, much darker than Simone's cafe-au-lait. "I also resemble the kids here, too, though I don't go to District 13 like everybody else. Some of the kids treat me like a real person, instead of the dressy Parisian mannequin I am at Biden. I refuse to move again!"

"It will be years before you're self-supporting. You will never be able to pass for white, so you are not free to refuse. You will shower, you will put on clean clothes while I dress. You will go with me to see this loft," Simone stated.

Simone's voice was a contralto. Her English moved to the francophone cadences of the tragic island where she'd been born, and the Brooklyn community of Haitian diaspora to which Grandmere Josephine transplanted Simone during her childhood. She had lived in Josephine's flat until Roxanne began kindergarten.

Thereafter, Simone had moved the two of them several times, and there'd been as many schools, until Roxanne turned thirteen. Then she was enrolled at Biden, a private school in the City. The long morning and afternoon commute, Simone's determination that Roxanne excel academically, if not socially, had not effectively fenced her off from the neighborhoods where they'd lived.

"You are preparing for real life, which only begins after University." She stubbed out her cigarette. "Your friends here? Most of them will be pregnant, on drugs and peddling their asses on the street before the next school year comes around. Their ambitions amount to dealing drugs to finance playing at music biz."

Roxanne said, "Do you believe the Biden kids don't use drugs, don't have sex, and don't want to be on MTV? Half of them have parents who've already done it!"

Simone didn't flinch. "'Nevertheless, those who go to Biden have the opportunity to correct their mistakes. The gang you hang out with here don't. We are moving."

After their first move, Simone changed their last name to keep Roxanne's grandmother and father from finding them.

Simone told Roxanne that her father's name was Prosper. Prosper had been a driver in a limousine company servicing Swift, Carver, and Choam when Simone met him. Before Roxanne's birth, Prosper had become ridden by the horse, heroin.

Roxanne never saw her grandmother Josephine after the first move, heard from her, or about her. When the rare hours of her privacy fell within days auspicious for her, she searched for Josephine in the fat Brooklyn telephone directory. But her grandmother was called by one and all, including Simone, as "MaMa Josephine." There was no last name, no matter how diligently she went down the long columns, that rose up to her. But her memories of Josephine came into sharp focus during this concentrated scanning, so something was achieved after all.

She heard drums beating and bells ringing, smelled cigars and rum. She saw warm, powdered bosoms runneled with sweat, bare-chested, slender dark men, waving arms together in a communal exaltation defiant of the grave.

Except for those memories Roxanne would have believed she'd been born dead. Moving again meant moving so far away from her beginnings that the chance of recovering them dwindled to nail paring of a dying moon.

Simone was ashamed of Grandmere Josephine because she was dark—darker than Roxanne, wore Caribbean colors, and honored the *loas*. That was why Roxanne wore neutral, classic clothes and attended a private school where Roxanne was separated from her background by an education as demanding as it was progressive. That was why there were ballet, tennis, and golf lessons to keep Roxanne so occupied she would be allowed free time only if she gave up riding. As Simone knew very well, giving up riding was out of the question for her daughter.

Only with the horses living first in her imagination, and those others in her riding classes, did Roxanne feel as if she lived. When she gave herself to horses, she was free of Simone's constant surveillance. Surveillance was surely putting her spirit into a coffin.

When May turns into June, even cruel, crumbling New York has perfect weather. The sun shines in a blue sky clear of acid brown smog. The air is warmly sensual, with low humidity. Light breezes spangle leafy shadows over the cracked sidewalks, and change the prison-cement canyons into a landscape of magnificent vitality.

Outside Simone's brownstone, the Avenue was blocked off for the Memorial Day street fair.

The very air shimmied and shook from the percussive rhythms of samba, salsa, merengue, reggae, calypso, and the other bands making American music out of countless African traditions. People were together in all colors of the human rainbow, celebrating their survival of another winter.

Boisterous dancers, wearing sequined, feathered costumes in dazzling mango orange, avocado green, and bougainvillea red, shared bottles of beer and rum, beckoned one and all to join in the arm waving, hip shaking, ass waggling celebration.

Blinking lights advertised gambling in the basement of the Italian Catholic Church of the Resurrection. St. Patrick's Cathedral offered Black Velvets, three parts Guiness Ale and two parts champagne, a drink beloved at Irish track meets. The precinct's Policeman's Athletic Association sold raffle tickets on a red Acura.

Greasy delicacies popped on grills, blending flavors from every continent into the voluptuous tang of the Caribbean, crossroads of the world since the fifteenth century.

Simone wore her armor of high Creole hauteur, impervious to the carnival atmosphere that penetrated as deep as the F train's cavernous dungeon of a station. Trinidadians played steel pans on the platform amid a swirl of full-skirted girls and bare-calved boys.

Simone led them to the uptown track. Roxanne said, "MaMa, we could have saved time by meeting in the City after my lesson. I'm wasting this beautiful Saturday afternoon underground when I need to thaw out in the sun like everyone else."

Simone touched the hollows behind Roxanne's ears, and the one in her throat, with the wand of her silver Chanel perfume travel bottle. Chanel was no competition for the frigid, winter subway reek that lingered until the hot, wet summer fetor crawled down in July.

Her mother's fingers were long, impeccably groomed, the nails bare of polish. "You are not like everyone else. You are my child. After you see the loft, I'm taking you to McCready & Schrieber's, so they can measure your feet for two pairs of Italian, custom made boots. You do agree that bootmakers deserve the respect of clean feet?"

"Yes, MaMa, you are right as always."

A slight smile sketched itself on Simone's mouth. "Those are the most beautiful words in the English language."

Roxanne's obedience received rewards. This time it was an expenditure for her riding outfit. Her good grades had gotten her Florian, a big chestnut gelding who was a competition class jumper. Going to the same parties as the kids from school got her excused from her mother's professional social engagements. Participating in competition classes got her more time at the Academy, and excused from golf.

The unvoiced consequence of disobedience was Simone leaving her. She had abandoned both mother and father of her child. Parents dumped kids all the time, even those who went to Biden.

But using horses in Simone's manner of using

things exacted a high price. She felt herself becoming as cold as her mother.

This morning she had to admit she'd hurt Florian. She was impatient. She wanted that soaring, flying moment when, after good warm-up and meticulously picked-up rhythm, they accelerated through time, leaving it all together as they took one obstacle after another without fault.

She didn't go over him as carefully as she should before warm-up exercises. It was such a beautiful day she pushed too fast through the warm-ups, and then over the first jumps. Florian's balance was off, so was hers. When she put him to the four-foot chicken coop jump, wider at the bottom than the top, they landed wrong and Florian came up lame.

Once, when she was very young and Simone escorted her to all her classes, her mother asked, "All this carrying of manure, combing and brushing and rubbing, does this make you a better rider?" These classes in mucking and grooming ate deeply into Simone's time, which was expensive.

"Of course, MaMa! The horses know me better, and I know them better, which allows me to know whether my pony's sick or not."

"I can see you are telling the truth, Roxanne. Anything that encourages you to be a rider is yours, even my time."

Even then Roxanne knew Simone allowed Roxanne to ride because horses were a hobby that removed her daughter far away from ruined, rural Haiti and Brooklyn, and thereby, removed Simone, too.

She aimed herself at competitive show jumping. It allowed her to manage Simone. International show events were centers where finance and prestige met. It was an attribute of her daughter that Simone could talk about at dinner parties when conversation turned to offspring.

But for Roxanne, horses were more important judges than Simone. Horses judged her by her behavior with them, what she had in her, what came out in their partnership. They did not notice the color of her skin.

After giving the loft agent a check, and the phone number of her lawyer, Simone took them to Mezzo Giorno on Spring Street. They sat at one of the restaurant's sidewalk tables.

"The bathrooms in that loft, MaMa, are older than the two of us put together. The floors squeak and splinter. The walls look like a valley in Africa bombed with DDT to wipe out tsetse flies."

Simone's tongue flicked cappuchino froth from the center of her full, lower lip. They sat at a table without an umbrella. She turned up her face, like a golden flower, to the sun. In such a moment Roxanne could not help but be in love with her mother. Simone possessed the seductive power of Ezili, the *loa* of female attraction.

"That's the vision of the artist removing herself to an upstate place, now that she's getting old. The place is sound. She, and the artists who first moved here, renovated the building and put it up to code. Paint, new floors, and bathrooms are small problems a reputable renovation gang, failed artists supporting themselves, can correct in a short time, even in New York," Simone said.

"I like it here. I'm two subway stops away from Swift, Carver, and Choam." She was also closer to Roxanne during the hours she was home alone.

At SC&C Simone was number one member of the international investment division's team. Her CEO trusted her with all his secrets. Unlike the rest of his division, she was both female and mulatta. With those two strikes against her, she'd never be able to unseat him. Additionally, she being exotically elegant, he enjoyed looking at her in the same way he enjoyed the other expensive objects ornamenting his life. In return for the security Simone gave his career he sprinkled her with a few points out of his own share in every rainmaker deal they brought to SC&C. Now she was a Vice President.

He discreetly boasted that Simone was his end runner. "French is her first language, English her second, and her third is computers. She speaks finance with a French inflection in German and Japanese. She crunches numbers more creatively than all of the before-mentioned. As lagniappe, she's beautiful. She taught me that word, 'lagniappe.' It means the extra, unexpected bonus." One of her extra, expected bonuses, was her excellent assistance in keeping the Equal Opportunists off SC&C's back.

Head house slave, was how Roxanne saw Simone's position. The esteem in which her CEO held her mother was the same in which her ancestors were held by their white masters in the days before Haiti's slave revolution. And the children sired upon them, neither white nor black, were brought up to be the same, always, to serve.

As portions of American finance burned out at the end of the eighties, and further conflagrations followed in the nineties, Simone's CEO, and his corporate body, prospered. He believed his foresight, bringing Simone out of SC&C's back office building, across the street and up to his floor, had been among his wisest moves.

Simone had financed her pregnancy, and later, college, as a permanent temporary in SC&C's word processing pool. By the time she graduated she was working for the head of the computer systems division. While in systems her outside interest was German.

In those days her lover's residence was Munich, but during the seventies he spent most of his time in New York. When she was moved to the investment division, Simone's interest turned to Japanese. Larry Wing appeared in the eighties, an American Japanese who brokered art between Pacific money and New York dealers.

"This neighborhood will do nicely while you finish at Biden and go on to the Sorbonne. You'll spend less time on the subway, too. An Italian Catholic Church and its School hold the center of real estate here. St. Anthony's won't be selling out to developers. The Italians watch the playground, so drug dealers can't take over."

Simone uncrossed her legs, while a trio of college boys with letter sweatshirts draped over their shoulders hotly watched.

"Roxanne," she said, "it is not me they are watching, it is *us*. Now, a taxi to McCready & Schrieber's for your boots."

That evening Simone opened a bottle of her favorite Châteauneuf-du-Pape wine and a fresh pack of Gitanes. She stood before the speakerphone like a muscle-sculptor psyching herself for heavy lifting. The lap top was open to her phone directory. She took her gold plated, inscribed calculator, provided at Christmas by one of the SS&C's electronics suppliers, out of its slip case. Before midnight contracts arrived by fax, hard copy to be messengered to her at SC&C on Monday. Renovation on the loft had begun.

They spent their last day in the Brooklyn brownstone before the New York school year, which continued through June, was over. As with all their other moves, Simone was adamant that nothing come with them from the old place except their clothes, personal treasures, and the electronic gear. She scrutinized all of it with the thoroughness of a CIA agent, before their things were packed and sent off to Manhattan.

"Why must we get rid of everything, Simone?

Why all this vacuuming and sweeping and disinfecting? I'm old enough to be told."

Only her mother's silent mouth and cold eyes answered her.

"What are you afraid of, MaMa?"

"I am afraid of nothing but my daughter becoming a horse instead of the rider."

"What kind of answer is that? I'm not your fucking *zombie*, a slave made of the living dead, who moves only at your will."

"Don't you ever use that word again!"

Simone slapped her hard across the mouth with the hand wearing a thick gold band projecting a smoky yellow topaz in the bezel.

Roxanne fell against the packing carton enclosing the refrigerator. Her fingers flew to her mouth. There was blood. Simone hadn't struck her in years. She felt so cold that she put on a sweater.

After Simone put the tissues that staunched the bleeding into the garbage, Roxanne helped her carry the garbage, boxes of rejected possessions, the old furniture, and empty vacuum cleaner bags to a rented truck.

"It's a good thing all that horse exercise has made you strong, Roxanne. It would be impossible to manage without you."

That was Simone's apology.

Simone drove it to an abandoned area in the Bronx where they dumped it.

Their actions were swift, practiced. Everything was soaked with lighter fuel. Simone set it afire. They took off. Simone loved being at the wheel the way Roxanne loved the jumping ring. Middle-Eastern taxi drivers, whose driver training consisted of tanks, had nothing on her.

She turned in the rental. A car service picked them up. They stayed up all night unpacking in the Manhattan loft, its bright, shining, renovation thoroughly complete. A decorator arrived in the morning with the new furniture.

Later in the week Roxanne got called out of computer graphics class to an administrator telephone. Beepers were not allowed at Biden.

Roxanne nearly hyperventilated. "You're leaving me all alone for a whole weekend?

"I'm sorry to give you such short notice. You'll be safe without me in our new place. It's so sudden, this flying to Los Angeles. I'm running home to pack. You know, of course, you can bring someone home from school to stay with you."

"Yes, MaMa." Not bloody likely, getting a chance like this to be alone for so many hours, Roxanne thought.

The party everyone in her class, who'd been invited, looked forward to all week was drinking their host's parents' liquor cabinet dry. It was Summer Solstice, one of the most powerful nights of the year. It was an auspicious time to go looking for her past.

After school she put on a ripped Sepultura t-shirt advertising a speed metal band from Brazil and their album, *Schizophrenia*, and a ripped pair of lace leggings. She leapt barefoot through the huge, empty space that was the loft's living room, drunk with the pleasure of privacy.

She opened the concealing panels over their ballet barre and mirror, which made the space appear even more enormous. The Georgia O'Keeffe reflected in the mirror was their "spot" when she and Simone did ballet exercises together before bed. Jane Fonda was Simone's ideal of the American business woman, but her ideal as Woman was Audrey Hepburn, who had started as a ballerina.

Roxanne popped a *Vodou Adjae* CD on the loft system and potted it to the max. The loft was soundproofed.

She turned on the A/C fans and the smoke inhalers, which keep the odor of Simone's Gitanes and Chanel under control.

Her own bedroom had built-in cedarwood closets and fixtures, white furniture and carpets, all draped in ice blue satin and lace, the decorator's idea. In there Roxanne dropped a second *Vodou Adjae* on her own CD player, caught it up with the cut running in the living room.

She unfastened the security gates and threw up her triple-paned window all the way. Palmate shadows from the ailanthus trees growing in the courtyard outside sashayed into the room. The sunlight filtered through the leaves made everything warmer. The courtyard was a meeting place for street cats and loft pets. The sharp odor of their piss markings made her room feel less like a viewing room in an expensive mortuary.

Simone approved of CDs and cassettes, as she approved of designer boutiques and riding. Roxanne's collection of CDs and cassettes were neatly shelved, title spines turned outward, easy for Simone to police. The music her mother saw was scores from ballets, top forty pop singers, and some stupid sixties rock and roll.

The music Roxanne listened to was kept at school, in her Walkman, or carried in her backpack, along with her books about African religions and music. She'd brought home an eclectic mix, not knowing what she'd want. She'd targeted on *Vodou* right away.

The green light flickered up and down the towers of Babylon, glimmered through the plastic jewel boxes of music that she traded at school from kids whose parents worked in the music business, were ethnomusicologists, artists, musicians and journalists, or bought from Harry in the Times Square subway station. It came from Africa, the Caribbean, Mexico, Brazil. All of it was rooted in Africa. It was recorded in Europe, Canada, Japan, and the United States.

Her mother used her money to get her daughter, descended from African slaves into the boss world. But she didn't see that the music that sustained the slave world had penetrated into the hearts and souls of the boss white world.

Grandmere Josephine filled her house with many altars. Josephine was a *mambo*, the female leader of a *hunfor*, where the *loas* were called to ride the celebrants.

The drums and voices of *Vodou Adjae* sounded like what she remembered of ceremonies in MaMa Josephine's Brooklyn *hunfor*.

Roxanne built her altar around the Mac II ci in the living room. In vodou, as in the other African religions transported to the New World in slaver ships, the *loas* were associated with Catholic saints. When a *loa* was called down, the human host was mounted and became the *loa*'s horse. But this was the good old USA. She could ride herself.

The African powers in the New World survived in syncretic religions. There was always room for something new.

The only power she had over Simone came from the horse, so Horse was her allied spirit. Horse's santo was the swiftest, the strongest, the most beautiful and the most free. He was the Black. The only bond he accepted was love. He embodied most perfectly the spiritual ideal of Horse.

His santo's portrait was a page she carefully tore out long ago from the Brooklyn Library's picture book of THE BLACK STALLION by Walter Farley. It was the first action in her life that Roxanne remembered clearly from the days when her mother still hit her when she was bad.

Josephine saw her do it. She laughed, and helped her smuggle it out of the library. She promised never to tell on her to Simone. They laminated it. "The Big Negro Horse gives you spirit. Simone hits you too much. But she loves you, like I love you both."

Roxanne had managed to keep it secret from Simone all these years. She clipped it to the copy stand, over the latest conversion sheet of yen, deutchemarks, and dollars US. Her mother didn't like Roxanne studying Spanish instead of Japanese or German. "Why not at least Italian? With Spanish you could run factories in Latin America. But you'd still find Japanese necessary to get into finance."

On either side of the big screen she put a Cuban Coiba cigar and an unopened bottle of Havana Club rum. She'd gotten them both from a girl in her computer graphics class whose mother, an ethnomusicologist, was more often on a field trip than in New York.

She lined up her horses on the computer desk's extension leaf. They were tributes to Simone's power in the world. But, as they had been bought for Simone's daughter, she shared in that power.

She took them out in the order that they'd been received.

The fragile blue dream of a horse had been blown out of a Venetian glass pipe during Simone's first business trip taken with her CEO. It was his gift to the child left without her mother for the first time. That month Roxanne had suffered nightmares in which Simone never came back. But during the day she was happy. The sitter let her wear what she wanted, and, within reason, eat and sleep as she liked.

The German had given her a Frankish champion's charger carved out of wood from the Black Forest. A bronze cast of Northern Dancer was a souvenir from Miami's race track and a Florida real estate developer around briefly between the Munich banker and Larry Wing. Larry's contribution was a terra cotta reproduction of a general's mount from Japan's sixteenth century, bought at the Metropolitan Museum's gift shop.

She turned on the Mac. Almost instantly she heard the short musical phrase that signaled she could begin. It read the disk holding all the images she'd scanned this last year in computer graphics class.

She clicked the mouse. Roxanne reasoned there was so much blood spilled every day that the spirit powers no longer felt honored by such an offering. Electricity: that was the blood of New York, upstreaming the entire world's information. Computer systems, they hoovered electricity.

"Legba, you are first called, for you are first of the first, the remover of barriers." Click. "You open the way between flesh and spirit." Click.

An old Negro man in rags appeared in the seventeen-inch screen. He stood on the Brooklyn Bridge spanning the dirty green water between Manhattan and Brooklyn.

An auspicious choice, she thought. That was surely the crossroads between her past and her present.

The cigarette between his broken teeth was scavenged off the street. He carried a garbage bag full of cans and bottles, and leaned on a crutch.

"Legba, here is a true Havana cigar for you, and Havana rum, very rare, very expensive in New York. Help me remember. Help me to go back."

Roxanne lit the Coiba and left it to smoke. She filled a crystal double shot glass with the Havana Club. She popped the repeat button on both CD players to keep *Vodou Adjae* going and raced back to the Mac. The music made her want to dance. But she had to keep the mouse moving or else the screen saver would replace Legba before he'd savored his cigar.

Roxanne picked up the cigar and inhaled it,

sipped from the shot glass to show the *Mystère*, in his guise as a homeless old Negro man that she, in her expensive surroundings, felt friendly confederation.

Delicately, she tamped out the cigar. "PaPa Legba, there is more from where this tribute comes." Then she allowed the Screen Saver fish to come up.

She danced, while waiting to learn where she should move next.

She pulled down a street grid of Brooklyn and opened three windows. Legba stayed in the upper corner. She, wearing her formal riding outfit, was there, mounted on Florian. The Bridge was in another window.

The loft was full of male and female voices rising in gorgeous harmony over the solid drum bottom. "Legba, 'Guato' e! Oh qui-a ou ye!"

Roxanne studied the screen, opening and closing windows, making smaller, larger, merging images. She brightened and darkened colors, substituted others. She got rid of the grid. The Bridge was now on the near edge of the screen. She and Florian were over it, on the other side. She needed more room. Legba slipped back to Ville-au-Camps, where the *loas* live.

She rubbed her eyes. It was dark in the loft. She hadn't noticed night come down. Click. The fish spawned through the blue water, pulsing gold, blue, and red.

This was good. She was approaching that state, whether at the keyboard or in the ring, where something happened. There was no one to tell her that she should stop now. It was a naked feeling, as though her classes and her mother were clothes that cut her off from herself.

Click. Keyboard. Click. Click. Keyboard.

Instead of wearing the traditional, muted colors of the show ring, she was in red and white.

Click. There were no streets, no bridges. In front of Florian's hooves water lapped. In the distance was a white ship. She stood at the rim of Agwé's power, with no idea of how Florian had taken her there. Brooklyn was behind her. And she didn't know how to backtrack, other than starting all over.

Click. Pull down. There was Legba. He was laughing. "You asked me to open the way for you to go back! Is Florian afraid of wet feet?"

She lit the cigar again, blew out the smoke. "Follow the ship. Don't forget the rum," Legba advised. Click.

A wave, big as the chicken coop jump, rose out of the water and hung without breaking. An azure blue fish with gold fins could be seen inside the wave as if it were in an aquarium.

Florian snorted and tossed his head. "We can take that one any day," he told her. He backed the length that gave him his best approach stride. He gathered, powered with his quarters, and went up and over. They were cantering after the distant ship, over the water.

Endless waves unfurled and currents ribboned beneath them. Florian was a hunter, the quarry the white ship. She lit the cigar to balance the smoke from the white ship, and rum slopped over the double shot glass as if were at sea.

Florian wasn't tiring, but Roxanne's bottom, back and neck, as well as her eyes, were. The fish swam.

She got out of the chair and drifted on the tides of the music to the *loas*. They were getting plenty to eat out of the Mac. The kitchen area was partially walled in wavy glass blocks. The light over the sink was burning. Roxanne gobbled the leftover Chinese in the refrigerator. She'd started off for Brooklyn to find Josephine. But she and Florian had accelerated out of time and left it behind.

Click. A range of hills rose out of the water, mountain range after mountain range tumbled with white mist. Haiti. The white ship was behind them, beneath was the great Bay of Gonaïves.

Click. They rode over a rich land. Wild ducks browsed and alligators lazed in the sun.

Click. Sugar cane and plantains, avocado, mango, cashew, cotton, coconut, calabash tree, gourd vines, yams, rice and kaffir. All of it grew wild, free for anyone hungry, thirsty, without clothes. This was the Cul-de-Sac Plain. It was foolish for the people to risk their lives for the humiliation of living in the concrete prisons of New York when they had this.

Click.

Roxanne reached out her hand for a mango, hesitated. There were, after all, so few growing for so many people. She had only to pick up the telephone and call for a dozen, if she wanted mango.

Click. Keyboard. A raffish skeleton in a top hat, smirking, filled up the screen. He zoomed to a leafless tree. *Zombie* shuffled in a dance around a gibbet. The upside-down body was blistered with pus-filled burns. His testicles were stuffed in his mouth. Underneath, where the *Zombie* danced, was soaked in blood from his macheted throat, and the bullets that had torn him open.

"The Cul-de-Sac Plain, my sweet black bride. All are mine in the end. So, have you no cigar, no rum for Baron Samedi?"

Roxanne pulled Florian's head up so he didn't eat what was growing on the grave at his hooves.

"I honor the Baron and his family. But I see no spade, pick, and hoe. The keeper of the cemetery is known by his tools."

His laugh squished through the blood running between his teeth. "I have new tools, for I always keep up with the world. Here they are—electrodes, DDT, an M-16. You've contributed generously to the first tool of these times, but I remain fond of the old ways as well. A Cuban cigar and rum, if you please. These scratching on the Plain can't scratch up the best."

"I am looking for MaMa Josephine. She's my grandmere. She lives in Brooklyn now. You can't tell me anything."

"Oh, but the Baron can. She ran away from here, taking the girl that was to be my bride with her. I had been promised her by the *bocor* of Josephine's *hunfor*. Through the man Simone married, the *bocor* found them both. But he only was able to give me Josephine. He had no control over Simone, and all she'd acquired. Whenever he gets close to Simone, she disappears. But you came of your own will, a most acceptable substitute, with your bride gifts of Simone's money, her electricity, your expensive cigars, and rum."

"The rum was given to me, a gift to me, Baron, not to you."

"Would you give some to your poor Grandmere? Here is Josephine to greet you."

One of the shuffling *Zombie* detached itself from the corpse dance. Florian reared. Roxanne brought him down, turned him in with a tight bit.

The *Zombie* carried a hoe wrong-way around, the pole skittering over the barren ground. "The Black, Roxanne. You ride, you are not the ridden. Simone promised to get you away." The *Zombie* struck out with the hoe, stinging Florian on his favored fetlock.

He reared again, to escape the pain. Roxanne clung to his neck like a tick, her Italian-booted feet pointed to his tail.

She was the Rider.

Click. Click. Click. Keyboard. Click.

Florian came down, his tail sweeping around like the storm cloud settling upon the mountain range point called Le Selle, the Saddle. They were in full-out gallop. The hard scrabble paths through hacked, burned, and slashed forest never touched his hooves, where only women's feet, not even mules, could go.

Click. Click.

Over Le Selle a window opened in the colliding clouds. Within a lightning tree stood Chango, *loa* of storm and war. "Wearing my colors, red and white, was fine strategy, daughter of my bride, Simone. You've gone back, my child. Now it's forward to war against the Baron's favored weapons."

Roxanne lit the cigar and poured the rum. She was practiced enough that the fish didn't show up.

"Can the Plain ever be what it was?"

"Haiti has had wars and revolutions one after another. The Baron has kept up with the world in his own domain. It is time for me to keep up within mine. Wars must be different than they used to be. War has always meant destruction. You must learn the war of creation, production, and redemption. Listen to Simone, my bride of electricity. She can give you the knowledge and the power that can begin the huge deployment of power, strategy, and tactics to correct this ruin."

Click.

Replace and save. Exit.

Shut off the CD. Take a shower. It was Saturday morning already. She couldn't wait to ride Florian.

Monday night, when Simone was jet-lagged to the max, Roxanne hit her with everything she had.

"MaMa, was Grandmere Josephine kidnapped and killed by a *bocor* who worked with both hands before we moved the first time? And you and I are still hunted for Baron Samedi?"

Simone's tired face shut down with the finality of a coffin lid. Then, slowly, by degrees, it opened.

"I smell cigars and rum. Is there any left for me?"

Simone didn't go to work the next day, and Roxanne didn't go to school. They took the subway to Brooklyn, to the house where Josephine used to live.

MALISH

by Mike Resnick

His name was Malicious, and you can look it up in the *American Racing Manual*: from ages 2 to 4, he won 5 of his 46 starts, had seven different owners, and never changed hands for more than $800.

His method of running was simple and to the point: he was usually last out of the gate, last on the backstretch, last around the far turn, and last at the finish wire.

He didn't have a nickname back then, either. Exterminator may have been Old Bones, and Man o' War was Big Red, and of course Equipoise was the Chocolate Soldier, but Malicious was just plain Malicious.

Turns out he was pretty well-named, after all.

It was at Santa Anita in February of 1935—and *this* you can't look up in the *Racing Manual*, or the *Daily Racing Form Chart Book*, or any of the other usual sources, so you're just going to have to take my word for it—and Malicious was being rubbed down by Chancey McGregor, who had once been a jockey until he got too heavy, and had latched on as a groom because he didn't know anything but the racetrack. Chancey had been trying to supplement his income by betting on the races, but he was no better at picking horses than at riding them—he had a passion for claimers who were moving up in class, which any tout will tell you is a quick way to go broke—and old Chancey, he was getting mighty desperate, and on this particular morning he stopped rubbing Malicious and put him in his stall, and then started trading low whispers with a gnarly little man who had just appeared in the shed row with no visitor's pass or anything, and after a couple of minutes they shook hands and the gnarly little man pricked Chancey's thumb with something sharp and then held it onto a piece of paper.

Well, Chancey started winning big that very afternoon, and the next day he hit a 200-to-1 shot, and the day after that he knocked down a $768.40 daily double. And because he was a good-hearted man, he spread his money around, made a lot of girls happy, at least temporarily, and even started bringing sugar cubes to the barn with him every morning. Old Malicious, he just loved those sugar cubes, and because he was just a horse, he decided that he loved Chancey McGregor, too.

Then one hot July day that summer—Malicious had now lost 14 in a row since he upset a cheap field back in October the previous year—Chancey was rubbing him down at Hollywood Park, adjusting the bandages on his forelegs, and suddenly the gnarly little man appeared inside the stall.

"It's time," he whispered to Chancey.

Chancey dropped his sponge onto the straw that covered the floor of the stall and just kind of backed away, his eyes so wide they looked like they were going to pop out of his head.

"But it's only July," he said in a real shaky voice.

"A deal's a deal," said the gnarly man.

"But I was supposed to have two years!" whimpered Chancey.

"You've been betting at five tracks with your bookie," said the gnarly man with a grin. "You've had two years' worth of winning, and now I've come to claim what's mine."

Chancey backed away from the gnarly man, putting Malicious between them. The little man advanced toward him, and Malicious, who sensed that his source of sugar cubes was in trouble, lashed out with a forefoot and caught the gnarly little man right in the middle of the forehead. It was a blow that would have killed most normal men, but as you've probably guessed by now, this wasn't any normal man in the stall with Malicious and Chancey, and he just sat down hard.

"You can't keep away from me forever, Chancey McGregor," he hissed, pointing a skinny finger at the groom. "I'll get you for this." He turned to Malicious. "I'll get you *both* for this, horse, and you can count on it!"

And with that, there was a puff of smoke, and suddenly the gnarly little man was gone.

Well, the gnarly little man, being who he was, didn't have to wait long to catch up with Chancey. He found him cavorting with fast gamblers and loose women two nights later, and off he took him, and that was the end of Chancey McGregor.

But Malicious was another story. Three times the gnarly little man tried to approach Malicious in his stall, and three times Malicious kicked him clear out into the aisle, and finally the gnarly little man decided to change his tactics, and what he did was to wait for Malicious on the far turn with a great big stick in his hand. Being who he was, he made sure that nobody in the grandstand or the clubhouse could see him, but it wouldn't have been a proper vengeance if Malicious couldn't see him, so he made a little adjustment, and just as Malicious hit the far turn, trailing by his usual 20 lengths, up popped the gnarly little man, swinging the stick for all he was worth.

"I got you now, horse!" he screamed—but Mali-

cious took off like the devil was after him, which
was exactly the case, and won the race by seven
lengths.

As he was being led to the winner's circle, Malicious looked off to his left, and there was the
gnarly little man, glaring at him.

"I'll be waiting for you next time, horse," he
promised, and sure enough, he was.

And Malicious won *that* race by nine lengths.

And the gnarly little man kept waiting, and
Malicious kept moving into high gear every time
he hit the far turn, and before long the crowds fell
in love with him, and Joe Hernandez, who called
just about every race ever run in California,
became famous for crying ". . . and here comes
Malish!"

Santa Anita started selling Malish t-shirts 30
years before t-shirts became popular, and Hollywood Park sold Malish coffee mugs, and every
time old Malish won, he made the national news.
At the end of his seventh year, he even led the
Rose Bowl parade in Pasadena. (Don't take *my*
word for it; there was a photo of it in *Time*.)

By the time he turned eight years old, Malish
started slowing down, and the only thing that kept
him safe was that the gnarly little man was slowing down, too, and one day he came to Malish's
stall, and this time he looked more tired than
angry, and Malish just stared at him without kicking or biting.

"Horse," said the gnarly little man, "you got
more gumption than most people I know, and I'm
here to declare a truce. What do you say to that?"

Malish whinnied, and the gnarly little man
tossed him a couple of sugar cubes, and that was
the last Malish ever did see of him.

He lost his next eleven races, and then they
retired him, and the California crowd fell in love
with Seabiscuit, and that was that.

Except that here and there, now and then, you can still find a couple of railbirds from the old days who will tell you about old Malish, the horse who ran like Satan himself was chasing him down the homestretch.

That's the story. There really was a Malicious, and he used to take off on the far turn like nobody's business, and it's all pretty much the truth, except for the parts that aren't, and they're pretty minor parts at that.

Like I said, you can look it up.

WINGS

by Barbara Delaplace

It was a dark and stormy night when Mrs. Henrietta Greenwood found the baby pegasus huddled under one of her rose bushes.

True, that's a clichéd sort of opening (except for the pegasus part), but then Mrs. Greenwood was the sort of woman that was spoken of in chichés.

Her house was a standard model clapboard bungalow, with the usual selection of shrubs and flowers (including the aforementioned roses) decorating the front yard. Inside, the furniture was the well-worn sort one would expect to find in the home of an aging widow, and there was a popcorn-stitch afghan draped over the sofa. She collected sets of decorative salt and pepper shakers—the kind that could be bought at the dime store, not the antique variety. She had a small white poodle named, perhaps inevitably, "Snowflake." And the neighborhood kids loved teasing it into paroxysms of yapping rage, and delighted in snickering at her when she came out of the house to tell them to stop. The neighborhood parents regarded her as slightly dotty but harmless, and nothing out of the ordinary had ever happened to her.

Until the business with the pegasus.

She'd gone to bed early, because the gusty wind and pouring rain had prevented her from taking her regular evening walk with Snowflake. And besides, she liked being snuggled under the comforter as she listened to the wind blow through her opened bedroom window, with the little dog curled up in the angle behind her knees for company. It didn't ease her loneliness completely, of course, for she still missed her husband even though she probably should have been used to it after ten years of widowhood. But it helped.

And it was during a lull in the wind that she heard the odd noise just outside her window. Oh, not the sort of noise that sends a chill down the back of a woman living alone as she wonders if she really *did* lock the back door before going to bed, but rather a soft whicker. Snowflake heard it, too; she could see his head raised, ears pricked, as he turned toward the window. So she got out of bed to look, shivering as another chilly breeze whirled into the room. "It's certainly no night for anything to be outside in this weather," she told the dog as she peered out the window. (Yes, she talked to her little Snowflake all the time. That should hardly surprise you.) But she couldn't see anything, peer as she might, and she decided it must have been some night animal passing by, perhaps a raccoon.

"Nothing exciting, little boy," she said as she climbed back under the covers. But Snowflake kept looking at the window with alert interest. A moment later he got to his feet and gave a brief "Whuff!" Mrs. Greenwood still couldn't hear anything herself, but when Snowflake jumped off the bed, trotted over to the window, and stood up on his hind legs to look over the sill, she decided there really must be something outside after all. She got out of bed again and was pulling on her flannel bathrobe when she heard another whicker, this one definitely sounding forlorn. There was nothing for it but to hunt up the flashlight, which she did, muttering as she pawed through the dresser drawer, "I really must tidy this up one of these days, little boy."

Snowflake wasn't listening, of course; a dog can only concentrate on one thing at a time, and he was busy looking out the window. Mrs. Greenwood joined him there and began aiming the flashlight at the greenery just outside. She couldn't be sure—the shrubs kept tossing in the wind, obscuring her view—but she thought she saw something small and furry and very wet under her favorite American Beauty rose. And it gave another lonely whimper.

Being a gentle woman who loved animals, Mrs. Greenwood couldn't just leave the poor whatever-it-was there. So she went out to the kitchen, slid her bare feet into clammy rubber boots, draped a raincoat around her like a cape, and opened the back door just in time to get a fresh gale of cold rainy wind in her face. "Damnation!" she cursed as she began her solitary trudge around the corner of the house, the flashlight beam bobbing before her. (Snowflake, being a sensible dog, had decided to stay inside to defend the house against strangers.)

But her grumbling died away when she got a good look at the pathetic little bundle under the rosebush. With increasing surprise, she made out a long slender muzzle, a large dark eye turned suspiciously upon her, and a bedraggled ruffle of mane.

"Why, it's a foal, little boy!" she exclaimed, forgetting Snowflake was back at the ranch on guard duty.

The foal stared at her, and Mrs. Greenwood looked back at the foal. She freely admitted she didn't know much about horses. She was far more familiar with the stray cats, dogs, and baby birds that somehow seemed to know they'd find a warm bed and a meal or two at her home. But even to her inexpert eye, it was obvious this little fellow was different. For one thing, it was much smaller than she remembered colts being. For another, there were those tiny wings sprouting from—

Wings?

Mrs. Greenwood blinked a couple of times. This was ridiculous. She only needed those glasses for reading; otherwise her vision was fine. But there they were, quite plainly visible in the flashlight's glow: pale-spotted feathers laid neatly along the foal's dark wet back. She stared again, until the cold drops trickling down her neck reminded her it was the middle of the night, the rain was coming down harder than ever, and she'd better do something about getting the two of them inside where it was warm.

The foal obviously regarded her motives as questionable, for it wobbled to its feet as she moved closer. Though it was hardly the time and place for formal courtesy, Mrs. Greenwood went through the getting-to-know-you ritual humans used with all animals including, it now seemed, baby pegasi. (She decided on the spot that "pegasuses" was simply too awkward.) It sniffed delicately at her hand, then regarded her gravely. Taking that as permission, she gathered up the little creature in her arms and staggered back around the corner. Fortunately, the latch hadn't caught properly, and a kick was enough to open the door. Snowflake was waiting and escorted them inside, courteously resigned to hosting yet another temporary visitor.

Dripping a trail of rainwater behind her, she carried the foal into the bathroom, where the rubber-backed rug would provide solid footing for those tiny black hooves, and where she could get both of them dried. The foal tossed its—no, *his* head, she saw upon closer inspection—and gave foal-sized snorts of mistrust when she first draped last week's bath towel around him. But after a moment, he settled down and seemed to enjoy the brisk rubdown she gave him. Then she gave herself an equally vigorous rubdown with a second towel, and tossed both into the hamper, before settling back on her knees to inspect her new charge in proper light.

As she watched, he extended his wings to dry them in the warm air. She could see the feathers were slightly darker than his mahogany-red coat and splashed with copper-gold spots.

A winged horse. Nothing like this had ever happened to her. In fact, nothing at all had ever happened to her. She realized he was looking back at her, and she didn't need the mirror to remind her what he'd see: a lonely old woman with graying hair and an aging figure. An ordinary woman whose dreams had all aged away, too.

Well, she might be ordinary, but she had some extraordinary problems now. What did you feed a winged foal? "Nothing tonight, I'm afraid," she told him. "I used up the last of the milk at supper. I'll have to get something for you first thing in the morning." And where was she going to put him? The garden shed, she decided, once she cleared a space for a stall. "But for now, I think you'll do just fine in the basement, won't he, little boy?" Snowflake yawned, reminding Mrs. Greenwood that it was now *very* late and she was tired.

She took a couple of old blankets from the wall cupboard, then turned to coax the colt into following her. "Well, now, what am I going to call you? You have to have a name. How about Star, for the starry spots on your wings? Come along, Star." He followed her out of the bathroom and down the hall, but when they came to the basement stairs even a non-equestrienne like Mrs. Greenwood could see they were too much for a tired little horse, even a winged one, and she picked him up and carried him downstairs.

The basement was warm and dry, and she spread the blankets into a bed. "Now, Star, you just settle down and get some rest." And somewhat to her surprise the foal did just that, curling up on the blankets and closing his eyes. She quietly climbed the stairs and went to bed herself, Snowflake a warm ball as usual against the back of her knees. For some reason, she no longer felt quite so lonely.

The next morning was sunny and mild, much more in keeping with spring than last night's storm. Accompanied by Snowflake, and still in her dressing gown and slippers, Mrs. Greenwood turned Star loose in the large back garden. He skittered across the dewy grass, tossing up his heels now and then. She smiled at his antics and went inside to get dressed.

She was just gathering up her purse and shopping bag (wondering, as she did so, whether canned baby milk would work as well for baby horses as it did for baby people) when she heard Snowflake's eager bark from the yard. She stepped outside and saw the poodle scampering—with a most uncharacteristic loss of dignity—at the side of the foal as he trotted about the yard. "Well, I'm glad you two are getting along," she said as she locked the back door. The garden fence was high and sturdy, and she decided that the animals could stay outside while she went shopping. As she left, the two began to sort out the rules for a game of I'll-chase-you-and-then-you-can-chase-me, and she realized that Snowflake hadn't been this bouncy and full of life since he was a puppy.

The town Mrs. Greenwood lived in was a pretty small place, so it didn't take long for her to reach the so-called "business center," which was really just the part of town where the bank, drugstore, dry cleaner's, hardware, and grocery stores were located. She entered Drindle's Drugstore and headed to the Baby Supplies section. Mr. Drindle noticed immediately, being an inquisitive man. And since he was in a first-rate occupation to know a lot about folks' more personal affairs, he was also an unfailing source of local gossip.

"So, Mrs. Greenwood! In the family way?" He laughed heartily as she dropped her purchases on the counter; he always enjoyed his own jokes.

"Oh, no, nothing like that, Mr. Drindle." She watched as he rang up the cans of baby formula and the nursing bottle and nipples. "I've just got another stray on my hands, and he's so young I don't think he's weaned yet."

"Those nipples are awfully big for a puppy or kitten, you know."

"Well, now, you won't believe it, but this one's a colt."

"A colt! Where ever did you find *that*?" he boomed. "Somebody didn't just leave him in a basket at your door with a note saying 'Please look after my little Seabiscuit,' did they?" More laughter.

"No, I found him under one of my rose bushes. I just haven't *any* idea how he got there." Actually, she had her suspicions—*birds* migrated this time of year, so why not? But she wasn't going to say anything to Telephone-telegraph-tell-a-Drindle or he'd have the town ready to cart her off to the State Home for the Confused. To say nothing of every representative of the media within three states showing up in her front yard.

"He must have somehow strayed off one of the ranches during the storm, that's all."

"That does seem like the most likely explanation."

"Well, what are you going to do with him? You're hardly set up to handle a horse, even with that backyard of yours. I'll bet you're going to use part of your garden shed as a stall, aren't you?"

Damnation! Does the man know everything? "Well, yes, that's where I thought I'd put him for a while."

"And you can't just feed him baby formula, you know. You'll need those supplements the vet uses when she has a mare who rejects her foal. I'll ask Dr. Bowen for some when she comes in to pick up her prescription refill. Her ulcer's bothering her again, you know," he added in a confidential tone. "And I'll bring it by myself. You want to make sure he's getting all his vitamins and things."

"Why, thank you, Mr. Drindle."

Curse you, Mr. Drindle.

Mrs. Greenwood felt an understandable reluctance to let anyone else see Star. "I certainly do want to make sure he's eating all the right things." She could only hope news of some juicy scandal would pop up and divert him before Dr. Bowen arrived for her medicine.

She made her escape as soon as gracefully possible, and headed home. When she opened the gate into the backyard, she couldn't help but chuckle: Star was stretched out flat on his side in the sunshine, and Snowflake was curled up against his belly with his head resting on the foal's flank. She left them snoozing while she went into the kitchen to warm up some formula for what she assumed must be a very hungry young foal.

Star was indeed very hungry and eagerly drank from the baby bottle; in fact, he took a second bottle and part of a third before subsiding back onto the grass with a contented sigh. Mrs. Greenwood sighed with satisfaction as well, and went about the job of clearing space in the garden shed for a makeshift stall.

She'd just gotten to the stage of wondering if she really *could* fit more than one object in the same space—the cultivator and lawn mower, for instance—when Snowflake exploded into a volley of barking. That outburst was closely followed by a knock at the garden gate. Brushing off her dusty hands, she went up the path to see who was there, accompanied by a furiously yapping poodle. (Snowflake took his guard duties seriously.)

"Shush now, Snowflake!" With any luck, it'd only be the paperboy and she could tell him she'd meet him at the front door with the money.

But luck was in short supply today. It was Mr. Drindle, smiling and holding a paper bag. Her heart sank as she pictured TV crews wading through her rose bushes.

"Here they are, Mrs. Greenwood, just as promised!"

Well, what can't be cured must be endured, she thought to herself. Mentally squaring her shoulders, she put on a welcoming smile and opened the gate. "Thank you, Mr. Drindle. It's good of you to come by. *Do* be quiet, Snowflake!" The poodle redoubled his barking as the druggist stepped through the gate.

"No trouble at all, Mrs. Greenwood, no trouble at all!" He looked down at the angry dog. "I left Sally to run the store for a bit. Thought I'd like to see your new horse myself, you know."

Yes, she certainly did know. Considering the possible attractions of moving to Dismal Seepage, Alberta, where at least there'd be some privacy, she led her unwelcome guest into the garden. Snowflake followed at his heels, still barking. Star, who had been drowsing in the broken shade of the grape trellis until alerted by the dog's warning, was now sitting up and watching their approach with cautious interest.

"My, but he's small," said Mr. Drindle, half his attention on the noisy poodle, who was only inches from his ankle.

"I thought so, too, but I really don't know much about horses," said Mrs. Greenwood. Or pegasi. Well, the wings were folded and not terribly obvious.

"You're awfully young to stray away from your mom, little fellow. What did you do, fly away?" he laughed. The laughter seemed to infuriate Snowflake further, and he began to snarl at Mr. Drindle. The druggist began to edge back up the path toward the gate.

"With *those* wings? Why, they're nowhere *near* big enough.'" Mrs. Greenwood was about to continue, when she realized he was looking at her with mild surprise. "Surely you noticed. They're small, I know, but ..." Her voice trailed off uncertainly.

"You enjoy your little jokes, eh, Mrs. Greenwood?" His attention still wasn't really focused on her but rather on Snowflake, who seemed to be seriously considering taking things beyond the verbal to the physical.

"But I'm *not* joking. Look at his shoulders!"

"Of course, Mrs. Greenwood. You're absolutely right, he has fine shoulders." Mr. Drindle's retreat toward the gate was gaining momentum.

"But that's not what I said! He has *wings!*" Was the man *blind?*

Another couple of feet and he was able to grab the latch on the gate. "Whatever you say, Mrs. Greenwood. Don't bother, I'll let myself out. Bye!" And Mr. Drindle was through the gate with surprising speed for someone of his bulk. Snowflake gave a couple of admonishing growls to the closed gate, then turned and looked at his mistress with complete satisfaction written on his furry face.

After that, she didn't invite anyone to her home. And the rumor started going around the small community that maybe Mrs. Greenwood had been living alone too long and was getting a little confused. The neighborhood kids started snickering at her when they passed her on the street or in the grocery store. The neighborhood parents began watching her with grave faces and exchanged concerned looks when they thought she wouldn't notice. But she noticed the looks and held her head high. *I'm not dotty!* she reminded herself. *Just because I can see the wings and they can't doesn't mean I'm losing it.* But another part of her whispered, *Maybe you are. How come you're the only one who can see them?*

Meanwhile, Star fed heartily on augmented baby formula and grew like a spring weed. Star and Snowflake continued to romp together, and Mrs. Greenwood found herself laughing more than she had in ages at their silly antics. Sometimes she joined in—the animals were delighted to have something else to chase—and on those nights she always seemed to sleep well, without the familiar ache of loneliness. She found herself awakening the following mornings completely refreshed and at peace. She realized that for a long time she'd faced each day as something to be lived through, with a safe, ordinary routine to keep her mind and body occupied; now she looked forward to each new morning.

Star's wings grew apace with the rest of him, the flight feathers lengthening almost visibly each day. He began to exercise them just like any fledgling, and his wingbeats gradually became stronger and more rapid, raising currents of air about him. At first they were gentle little zephyrs that barely stirred the grasses; then they became sturdy breezes that scattered dry leaves; and at last they burgeoned to drafts that whirled the leaves around his head.

Not that the sight of Star exercising his wings was a dignified one. Mrs. Greenwood chuckled at the sight of the little horse snorting as he teetered on hoof-tips, wings beating frantically while Snow-flake barked encouragement.

And the day he actually flew for the first time . . . well, it certainly didn't start out with celestial music playing as he soared majestically skyward.

He'd been getting enough lift to get a couple of inches off the ground for several days. But this particular day he seemed unusually excited, and as soon as Snowflake and Mrs. Greenwood appeared (at the dressing-gown-and-slippers stage of the early morning) and she let him out of his stall, he cantered into the garden, head tossing. He stretched each wing, one after the other, as he always did; the stall in the garden shed was roomy enough for a little pegasus but not for his wings as well.

And then he spread his wings and gave a leap off the ground—and he flew. Clumsily, with his legs awkward and dangling, and with much wavering of altitude and direction—but he was *flying!*

Or rather, he was until his legs met up with a rhododendron. That proved too much, and he floundered into the bush in a flurry of wings and scattering blossoms. Mrs. Greenwood burst out laughing as his head emerged from what had been her prized Buckingham, a cluster of dark green leaves and rose-colored flowers draped over one ear like the last word in spring hats. Snowflake looked on, his poodle's mustaches bristling with dignified restraint, as she chortled while helping Star untangle hooves and wings and legs from the bush.

Once back on four feet, Star again spread his wings and flew. This time he stayed airborne for almost half a minute before touching down—only to miss his footing and collapse in a most inelegant heap. He gathered his legs and his dignity together, and stood up to try again. Mrs. Greenwood thought she could almost read the determination on his face.

And *this* time he not only managed to stay in the air for an entire minute, he also managed to land without collapsing in a heap. She cheered, and Snowflake forgot his reserve and barked excitedly as he ran in circles around the colt. Star danced along the grass before them, triumphant. And Mrs. Greenwood decided she didn't want to trade places with anyone in the world at this moment, regardless of the snickers and whispers. For some reason, she could see something that they couldn't, and she felt the richer for it.

Star divided the next few days between longer and longer bouts of flight, and resting between those bouts. Mrs. Greenwood suddenly realized that sometime soon he would leave the nest like any other fledgling, to make his own way in the world. She wouldn't be able to stop him, or protect him. The realization didn't make it any easier to bear.

And one night—not a dark and stormy one this time, but a night brightly lit by the full moon—it happened. She was roused from a deep sleep by Star's eager whinnying. She was just about to roll over and go back to sleep (for he did sometimes neigh at night) when there came a reply to his whinny—a deeper, richer version.

And it came from the sky.

Snowflake was already up on his hind legs at the window, but Mrs. Greenwood knew she'd have to go outside, and go she did. She stepped off the porch and looked down the garden to the shed. She couldn't be certain, because the grape trellis and apple trees were blocking her view, but she thought she saw a dark shape hovering over it. She hurried down the path, then stopped with a gasp. There, circling gracefully above her little garden shed, was a creature that belonged in myth: a magnificent winged horse, a fully-grown pegasus, moonlight-maned, dark-bodied, wings dappled with silvery spots.

Star whinnied again from his stall, and the pegasus answered. Mrs. Greenwood reached out a reluctant hand to open the door, and he rushed past her and with a sweep of his wings leapt into the sky.

The pegasus had to be Star's mother, for they fluttered about one another, nuzzling and whickering and caressing each other with brushes of their wings. Mrs. Greenwood felt her heart swell with warmth as she watched the reunion between dam and colt. And she knew—*knew*—that the whisperers were wrong. She wasn't losing it! She had never felt more vividly alive and aware than she did right now.

In their delight the two winged horses, the great and the small, whirled and swooped in the moonlit air. And a feather, perhaps loosened in the joyful violence, perhaps ready to fall because it was almost time for molt anyway, fell from a wing and spiraled to earth. It landed at Mrs. Greenwood's feet, and she picked it up without thinking as she watched the two gradually climb higher and higher, until they were lost in the night sky.

* * *

The little pegasus never came back, of course. And when the neighborhood parents asked her where he had gone, and she told them, "He flew away," (she figured there was no point in breaking a lifetime habit of telling the truth at this late date) that brought the conversation to a premature end. Folks still exchanged grave looks about her and whispered amongst themselves. The neighborhood kids still snickered. After a while she became resigned to it.

But on her dressing table she kept the fallen feather, brown spangled with gold, and remembered that sometimes extraordinary things *do* happen to ordinary people.

And on stormy nights when the wind whipped through her open window, she sometimes lay awake and listened, just in case. And Snowflake, who knew the truth of things, listened with her.

THE MOST MAGICAL THING ABOUT RACHEL

by Nancy Springer

> The sorrel horse of sunset
> And the silver horse of dawn,
> Neither of them is mine.
> The black horse of the north wind,
> The blood bay of the south,
> Neither of them is mine.
>
> The stallion of the high sky
> And the great brown mare of earth,
> Neither of them is mine;
> But the spotted horse with wild white eyes,
> Him I ride to paradise,
> To paradise.
>
> —Rachel's song

"The most magical thing about horses," Wilsy would gush to the parents, "is the way they give people back to themselves." I always snorted and shook flies off my head at this point, but nobody paid attention to me. They had to listen to Mrs. Wilson while she burbled on: "As Winston Churchill said, there is something about the outside of a horse that is good for the inside of a man." She always gave a little speech on the first night of each summer's eight weeks of Horseback Riding for the Handicapped. And I always stood there, a placid wall-eyed pinto gelding, saddled, sedate and patiently waiting, thinking, *Give me a break. Horses are not about people and their pathetic insides. Horses are about wind and sky and mares in heat and the great herd always galloping somewhere. Magical—what does she know of magic? What does any human know of the sun mare with her wings of flame, of the moon stallion's cold changing eye, of the black mane blowing behind the stars? Give humans back to themselves, indeed. Who is going to give horses back to themselves?*

Nevertheless, every year when they put a child on me, I plodded around the ring tamely. And every year the children started off wobbly in body or mind or both, and always over the course of the summer weeks their heads came up as if they were foals growing—for all of which I cared nothing, yet I did it all. The sun mother plodded through her daily rounds, and so could I. There was a sense in me of a fate working itself out, of a time coming, a debt being built which some season would be repaid.

Yet when that summer came, the moon stallion did not neigh and break free from his tether. The sun mother did not leap from her course and dash off to search for her missing colt, the one who eternally wanders beyond the edge of the world. It all started very quietly.

"The most magical thing about horses," Wilsy invoked as usual. She liked that word, magic, and used it in her farm name: Magic Acres. Every horse on the place had "Magic" plastered onto its so-called name. "This is Magic Make a Cake," she introduced me, and she helped this year's assigned rider up the mounting ramp and onto my back.

It was a young woman, the only adult in the handicapped riding class, and at once I scented her thoughts: about justice and poetry and sex. It startled me that she, one of the wobblies, was thinking about these primal things, but why shouldn't she? A wobbly wants to live, too. I smelled her thinking about sex, I felt her looking at some of the male humans and sizing them up and imagining the ecstatic act with them, and I could tell by something wistful in the tilt of her body that she had never done it. Because her head lolled sideward and her shoulders hunched, because her hands wavered in air and her spindly legs pitched her in all directions as she walked, no one had ever wanted her. Or not the way she wished to be wanted. Dreaming fool.

Wilsy was holding forth. "As Winston Churchill said, there's something about the outside of a horse—"

"It wasn't Churchill," muttered the young woman on my back. "It wasn't Abe Lincoln either."

"—that's good for the inside of a man."

"It was some other sexist God-given gung-homocentric."

"Rachel?" Mrs. Wilson turned toward me and my rider. "You said something?"

"I said I'm not a man."

Wilsy blinked but recovered rapidly. "Well, of course Churchill meant everyone. He knew how good horseback riding would be for all of us." She clapped her hands. "C'mon, everybody! Into the ring!"

The women walking with Rachel were curious about her and asked her questions they would never have asked a child: What is your handicap? Cerebral Palsy. Oh, that's too bad. Do you have to use a wheelchair? No. Crutches? No. Leg braces? No. Well it could be worse, then. Can you live by yourself? No. Why not? I fall a lot. Do you have a job? No. Why not?

"Try to find a job when you look like you're drunk all the time," Rachel said.

She would have made a good front-of-the-herd mare. There was bite to her, and kick. They didn't like it—I had noticed Wilsy and her friends expected the wobblies to be sweet and grateful. They started talking to each other past this Rachel person as if she wasn't there, and she started talking to me.

"It's the damn truth," she told the back of my head. "You're cute when you're a kid, you're a poster child, but once you grow up, forget it. No life for you. No job, no lover, no kinks, no lambada, no fun. Handicapped people are supposed to be thinking about other things, like nuns." I swiveled my ears, listening to her, and she smoothed my mane with one of her wobbly hands. "No free pony rides, either. So how long you been doing this, horse?"

Too plodding long.

"What did she say your name was? Cake Mix? That's no fair. Just because you've got spots." She was quite serious. I liked that. "Just because you remind her of a marble cake, no dignity for you. When color is the most superficial thing about a person. A horse, I mean. Tell you what. Just between you and me, let's find you another name."

Fine by me.

"You let me know when I say the right one, okay?"

Sure. Whatever.

"Okay. Possibilities: Colorado, like the river. Desperado. Chippewa Condor. Chippewa Wings."

I flung up my head and started to tremble, for in the poetry of her searching voice I felt a mystic sort of mastery, I felt her power. It was as if—I had never thought about it before, because horses change names whenever they change owners, we are like slaves that way—but now I sensed that there indeed was an innate name for me, a true name from the wide fields beyond the stars, the great grasslands I had run before my birth; perhaps I had even chosen it myself! And forgotten it since—but if this Rachel woman found it, I would remember, and everything would change.

I stood like some general's bronze horse scenting battle, with my legs stiff, my neck crested, my ears pricked so high their tips nearly touched, quivering—we could stand still now, for we had been lined up with the others in the center of the ring, we were supposed to be doing exercises, but no one wanted to tell Rachel what to do, and she continued to stroke my mane and say names to me.

"Medicine Hat," she said. "Cochise. Sun Dancer, Rain Dancer, Ghost Dancer. Shaman."

Shaman.

SHAMAN.

The name shot through me like the touch of a cattle prod. I reared up. Those hands of hers were useless for grasping with, yet somehow she did not fall off—the fire of the name had fused us into oneness. She was the lightning, I was the storm. She was the passenger, I the psychopomp who would take her to the spirit realm.

I knew what I had to do. I went mad. Wilsy was rushing toward me to grab my reins, afraid I would throw my rider, and I leapt from a standing start into a gallop, with bared teeth and flattened ears I charged her, roaring a horse's roar deep in my chest. She squealed and sidestepped—I knocked her down with my shoulder, racing past her, and I did not bother to jump the ring's fence—I went through it, splintering the rails like so many straws. People screamed. Through the commotion I heard Wilsy piping thinly, like a bird, "Stop! Cake, what do you think you're doing?" Her voice had no power over me at all. I bucked my way across the pasture, tail flying. Somewhere far behind me Wilsy wailed, "Oh, my God, what's the matter with him? He's always been such a good horse." On my back Rachel was gasping and giggling. I neighed the way my god might neigh some day when she wants to end the world, I nickered a horse laugh and reared again so that both of us looked upward, toward where the stallion of the high sky reared over us all with his white mane floating on the smooth blue arch of his neck.

"Cake, no!" Wilsy and her gang caught up to us, as I meant they should. I charged her again. My mouth was foaming and my white weird eyes were ablaze with pale fire, I could feel it, but she stood her ground, shouting, trying to turn me— Wilsy is brave, I'll give her that. I flattened her, but managed not to step on her, and she got up still shouting. "My God, I think he's rabid. Hang on, Rachel! Sam!" That was her husband. "Samuel, get the gun! Quick!"

"Shaman," Rachel whispered to me, "get out of here, they're going to shoot you!"

I knew it, and instead of running in crazed hightail circles any longer I stopped where I was and sank gently to the ground. Rachel snatched her legs up in time to keep them from being caught and crushed under me, then sat where she was, still on my back, as I shivered and groaned and laid my head down. I felt weak and in pain—it was not all my idea, what was happening; it was the fate in me taking charge of my body. "Shaman," Rachel breathed to me, "it will be all right, I promise you," and she stayed with me. I heard frightened children crying somewhere, and I sensed how a mob of humans ringed me like a stake fence, but one else wanted to come near me. Only Rachel touched me, straddling me and stroking my neck till the moment when Sam ran up and shot me between the eyes.

"Oh!" Rachel exclaimed from my back. "Oh! Oh, I *see!* They are all more than one color, like you."

I could see now, too. My spirit had carried her spirit up through the seven levels of cloud and loud bells and blinding light, and now they all awaited us, the great ones, particolored, as she had said. The stallion of night and the north wind was shining pure black, but starred all over with flecks of snowflake white. Dawn was a roan filly, pearl gray mottled with pink. Sunset was a yellow dun streaked with red. Earth was a gentle shaggy mare, brown with pinto markings, oceans, not unlike mine. There were many others: sky, south wind, the colts of all the skittish breezes, dappled moon, sun mother—I could not look at the sun mother, she blazed too bright. Her mane and tail stood up like feathers and streamed like fire. And while two colors or more were in the others, all colors seemed to be in her.

I understood much, but not the purpose of the journey. What did these great ones require from Rachel? On my back her body was taut as that of a wild filly being tamed. Through the quivering of her knees against my shoulders I could feel her excitement, her fear.

"Rachel," a voice of fire spoke, "you have done well to bring Shaman back to me."

It must be hard for you humans with your weak senses to understand how a horse can hear such things. You know only the surface of all that is, but a horse, even a broomtail bronc, can see the ghosts of ancestors in the air, can know by a prickling in the nostrils how a thundercloud has the soul of a predator, can hear a rider's thoughts through the reins, can smell in the night the thin pale manes of the stars. The sun mother's voice was palomino flame hanging in stardark, but I heard it burning in my bones.

She said, "You have done nobly, Rachel. Now do this: Bring my colt back to me." Yearning blazed hot in the words. She said, "Shaman will take you to the place where the world stops and the far fields start. Dream of my son as you travel, and name him, and call him by name so that he will come to you. Find him, my daughter.''

Rachel said, "Am I your daughter?" Then I knew even more than before that there was magic in Rachel; she, too, could hear words of fire! But I did not yet know the most magical thing about Rachel.

She spoke on; her voice shook, but she raised it boldly. She said, "If I am your daughter, why am I a wobbly weakling of a human sitting on a spotted horse? Do not tell me to go questing for your son on Shaman's back. I want four strong legs of my own to run on. I want to gallop over oceans and clouds and mountains and never be tired and never fall down again. I want to be strong, and I want for once to be beautiful."

There was a long silence, and the sun mother's fire darkened, as if this was a thing that could cause trouble. Yet her voice when she finally spoke burned as gentle as a lover's warm gaze. "Very well," she said. "You will be like me, and beautiful. Get off Shaman."

Rachel looked down. Seven levels of sky yawned below her. And she sensed, rightly, that she did not know how to tread those cloud-meadows as I did. It took hooves to run with the blue stallion.

"You must get down if I am to change you," sun mother said. "You will not fall, I promise you."

But Wilsy was not there to help her, or anyone with hands to steady her wobbly body as she got down off my back. She had to do it alone, and I could feel her shaking with effort and fear as she tried to make her wayward arms and legs obey her. I stood foursquare and rock-steady on my footing of ether while with her awkward fingers Rachel clutched my mane, slipping herself down my shoulder. But then a spasm of her arm jerked her hand away from me, she lost her grip, she screamed. Panicked, I lunged to help her—

Sun mother was quicker, and true to her word. Before Rachel's feet touched the ether through which they would have plunged, they were no longer bony weakling human feet but strong hard hooves. She stood in horse form beside me, and she was indeed very beautiful, with a body rounded and shapely and the shining chestnut color of a deer in summer, all except her face, which blazed entirely white. Her tail was full, dark and long, her mane tawny, fine and so long it hung down off her neck over one shoulder to her fetlocks. Out of her white blaze, half hidden by the long spirals of her fawn-colored forelock, her eyes gazed, huge and dreaming, the gray-blue color of violets in twilight.

She moved a few short paces, trying her hooves, dancing them. She flung up her comely head and neighed. "When I have found him," that neigh cried, "my reward will be this: I shall be his bride."

The fiery voice of the sun mother replied, "That is why I have called you daughter. Go now."

"Willingly."

She ran across the wide tallgrass honey-colored fields of paradise. She ran across the black plains between the stars, and leapt from prong to prong of the horseshoe moon, and whipped the sky's white mountaintops with her mane and tail, ecstatic from the running, the leaping. Her legs wandered in all directions as she ran, for she was still Rachel and would always be; nothing, not even the power of the sun mother, could change that. She still wobbled—but now her wavering leaps were a sweet thing to see, like the curveting of a foal yet unborn in the meadows of heaven. She never fell. This is the difference between four legs and two, there is not so dire a need of balance.

She could be Rachel, and yet be winsome and strong and full of joy.

I did not stay behind to converse with my gods, but ran by her side, for I was in love with her.

When we reached the earthly mountaintops at the edge of the world her hooves rang on the stone as she leapt from peak to peak. "Chosen One," sang the ringing of her hooves, calling. "Sun Runner, Star Son, Milord, my Prince, come to me."

I was in love with her, but she was in love already with her dream of him.

We reached the ocean at the edge of the world and ran on top of the waves. The wind from beyond the world lifted her long fine fawn-colored mane until it rippled and swelled like the ocean. "Prince of Passion," the billowing of her mane sang. "Crown Colt, Glory Horse, True Quest, Light in the West, come to me."

Very well, I thought, very well. Her dream of him would not match the truth should we ever find him. It could not possibly. No such horse could be.

We reached the huge heavy fall of water over the edge of the world into the chasm, the abyss, of beyond. The depth of the abyss frightened me as seven levels of high sky had not. I hung back, but Rachel leapt onward, and I had to follow. She flung herself into a black void, and the void supported her as she galloped down past a world's worth of thundering water. The salt spray of that water stung her nostrils so that they flared and shone red with her blood, and her blood sang, "Fire in the West, Skyfire, Sunfire, Far Star, Wandering One, come to me."

Constantly I ran by her side, but I did not speak to her of my love. How could I? She would give me only pity. I was a gelding.

Her very breath sang to the stallion of her

dreams, "Wandering Spark, Flame in the Dark, Comet, Dark Comet—"

He came to her, streaking across the black void he came, and he was all her dreams wished him to be, and more.

His mane of soft white fire made a crown of glory for his princely head. His white-fire tail streamed vast behind him. Except for mane and tail he was utter black, yet shone so that he seemed bright, white. His eyes were deep as night, glimmering as if with starglow. The blessing of his father the moon lay like a cloak of light on his great shoulders. His jewel-black hooves were winged with light.

She stood motionless at the sight of him, and I knew how her breath stopped, I could scent her terror and hope and delight. I knew all thoughts of her errand had flown out of her. Nothing was left but exaltation.

He came before her dancing on those winged hooves. He arched his white-fire crest and breathed on her the holy heat of his nostrils. I heard no words in that message. There was no need. The comet-curve of her neck answered his, the white blaze of her forehead answered him, her mane mingled with his, the meeting of their heads and necks formed a shape like a heart. Into the vastness beyond the world they went away together, and I stood on nothingness and watched them go.

Then I went back to the mountains at the edge of the world and waited for her. I knew there were other things I could have done: I could have gone back to the wide fields of sky and spent the rest of my spirit life talking with my gods, learning the secrets of all their mysteries. Or, if I wished to cling to my sadness, I could have gone back to haunt the earthly fields of Magic Acres, where in a muddy pasture my body lay buried. But I did neither. Though I felt frozen with defeat, my heart would not let me go away. On the stony top of the tallest mountain I took my place, I lay watchful on the keel of my chest, put my nose to my fore-knees and waited.

I waited for a long time. The sun mother ran her course again and again. Seasons passed.

It was her colt, Dark Comet, that starfire wan-derer, who brought Rachel back to me. Across the sorrel dapplings of the sunset I saw her coming with him out of infinitude. I lifted my head, and found I had become part of the stone of the moun-taintop—I crackled like thunder as I got to my feet, and boulders fell down. Like a monument on four pillars of stone I stood there, and they came before me as if before an altar or a throne.

"It is your choice," the stallion of her dream said to Rachel. Like his mother's, his voice was made of fire, but his was passionfire. It could burn, but he controlled it for her sake. He loved her the way a stallion loves a young mare running in the wind.

Rachel spoke to him, or perhaps to me, naming her choices, and her voice was made of the breath in her warm wide nostrils. "If you come back with me, the world will end," she said.

"It will burn up like dry grass." The words were simple and white-fire true—I knew to my stone bones that they were true. The flying of a comet in the sky of the world is an omen of doom. We shamans know that the world will end when a comet flies into the embrace of the sun.

"Yet I will do it if you command me to," he said. "But if you do not, then someone must tell my mother of the danger, what I have become, so that she understands I may not see her again."

Rachel went on, "If I stay with you, then our foal will become like you, another eternal wan-derer in the cold."

"Yes. And you will grieve as my mother grieves."

"I will grieve anyway because I must leave you." Now her voice was a young mare's cry of despair. "I cannot leave you. How can I leave you?"

"Ask Shaman," he said.

"What am I to do, all my life without you?"

"Ask Shaman."

"Shaman," she begged, and the moment my name left the poet-fire of her mind, I was myself again, a spotted horse standing on a mountaintop waiting for her. I neighed with gladness—I should not have done it when she was so wretched, but I could not help it, I was so filled with joy to be with her, and I could not keep from stretching out my neck to nuzzle her.

"Shaman will be with you, all your life without me. If you wish it so. You must choose, beloved." Dark Comet's voice had gone very low, barely a glimmer, very gentle.

Rachel hid the white blaze of her face against the slope of my shoulder. She could not say it, but this was her choice. The foal. The world. And me, though it could scarcely be said that she loved me.

"You are very brave," Dark Comet breathed to her. "Good-bye, my love." And he was gone, a white teardrop of fire flying across the void to the far darkness where he would endlessly wander. Rachel trembled against me, not lifting her head to see him go. Her trembling increased, her arms hugged my neck, her hands tangled in my mane— she was a frail human woman again, crying on my shoulder.

"Shaman," she wept.

I am here. I would always be there, always be hers.

"Shaman, it was beautiful, so beautiful. Can you understand?"

Yes. I could, for in a way I loved him, too.

She wept a while longer, then lifted her head,

and I knelt before her. I got down on the stone so that she could climb onto me for the long journey back.

Sun mother was a spotted horse made partly of fiery anger, partly of black despair.

"I want my colt!" Her wrath roared out in flames ten miles long. "Let the world end, what do I care?"

She did not, in fact, burn up the earth, though the people who lived on it remembered for years afterward the scorching drought of that summer. But the fire of her fury sent her pantheon running in terror, drove Rachel and me away from her so that we reeled in pain across the seventh level of clouds. Long whips of flame pursued us. I smelled my own singed hair and squealed in fear. Rachel cried out, "Don't! You're burning me. Don't kill me! The baby—I'm carrying his baby!"

"You! And you are but a useless human!"

Now I was angry, enraged for Rachel's sake, and I lashed my tail so that its angry whistling shouted back at the sun mother, "Rachel is the bravest and most magical of humans."

"Be her cuckold, then, Shaman, as you are so fond of her!" Sun mother lunged at us, and her leaps carry far; before I could do more than whinny in terror her great wing of fire had closed over me. For a moment I thought I was dead a second time. Pain took me apart. But it did not kill me. I felt a great change—everything about me rotated on a new axis, my limbs took on a different angle to my body, my head no longer nodded in front but sat squatly atop me, my back grew short and useless for carrying—Rachel slid off me, screaming, falling. Her fumbling hands caught at my mane, or rather my hair, and hung on for just a moment—it was enough. I turned, I caught her in my arms. We fell together.

We fell slowly back to earth. I was, after all, yet Shaman, just as she was always Rachel. I am the psychopomp; I have power to die, and travel to the spirit world, and come back alive. And I had power to bring Rachel back with me.

I have said she did not love me. But during that journey she held tightly to me, and we talked, and I think she began to love me a little.

"Where am I to go?" she asked me. "What am I to do?"

"Home," I told her. "The people, your mother, the others, they will be glad to see you back. Your body has been lying all this time in a hospital bed. They will make glad shoutings when it opens its eyes and speaks to them."

"But I cannot bear it. After I have run across the ocean and between the stars, to go back to a place where there is nothing for me, no life's work, no lover, not even a home of my own—"

"I will be there with you," I told her, "if you let me."

Erect, clutching one another, we drifted down through the lowest level of sky, spiraling like maple wings. I held Rachel by the waist. She kept her hands on my shoulders, but pulled back her head to look at me. Her smile was wry.

I said, "Am I a very strange looking man?"

"You are a particolored man." Her gaze wandered over me. "Your hair is like your mane used to be, part dark and part light. Your face is part brown, part white. So are your shoulders. And your eyes are pale." Her smile softened. "You are different. But so am I."

"Still pinto," I remarked, and then I knew what she had maybe not yet thought of. Clothing covered me, the ballooning trousers of a clown, but I did not have to look. I knew.

She saw my face change. "What is it?" she asked.

"Nothing."

"Shaman, tell me what is wrong."

I had to turn my eyes away. "Still a pinto and still a gelding," I told her. "I am no threat to your memories of Dark Comet, my lady."

She was silent, but she put up one hand and stroked my piebald hair. We had come through a long night together. Her face was very pale yet shining in the dawn light. Her hair was the bright chestnut color of a deer in summer.

She said, "I mind it mainly for your sake."

"But you deserve better, Rachel."

Straw-colored pastureland floated up to meet us. On a hilltop of Magic Acres we landed as gently as dandelion seed, and I forced my hands to release her.

I said, "You will find a young stud who can give you what you crave." I said, "I ought to go away from you and let it happen."

She put out her hand to me and said, "No, stay, Shaman. Do you love me?"

"You know I do."

"Then stay."

All of which made me her lover, in a sense of the word. I slept in her bed with her. We did things together which gave us both pleasure. I loved her.

Her mother, her friends, Wilsy, all the others, thought I was the one who had impregnated her. She let them think it. They wondered who I was, where she had met me. She let them wonder.

We had a home of our own. Only a room, really. And no jobs, only food stamps, welfare. No one wanted either of us. But we were happy. Out of the three things—a home, a lover, a life's work— we had two. Not bad. And we had memories. We spoke often of the fields of paradise, and of the mountains at the edge of the world, and of treading the clouds of sunset, and of Dark Comet.

And we had the child coming.

The burning heat of that summer gave way to a winter that was worse. Sun mother's wrath had taken another form, that was all. She turned her back, she gave us only her chilly shoulder for comfort, she let us freeze. That was a winter neck-deep in cold and snow.

On the night when Rachel felt the child coming, the streets lay three feet deep in snow. I ran down to the bar on the corner to use the phone, but the place was locked up. I pounded on people's doors—someone answered me, but after all that the phone was out, the lines were iced down somewhere. I left messages and ran back, cursing my own slowness, remembering how once on four long strong legs I had been able to race doves in flight. It is a pathetic thing being a human and not a horse. The mares foal without great pain, but Rachel lay on our bed panting and moaning between the times when she had to scream.

There was no heat, no electricity, only a puny fire in a kerosene burner. No one came to help us. Rachel's agony went on all night and through the next day, and I tried to get help again and again, but there were many who needed it, and no one came for us. Rachel was brave. She never cursed her too-narrow body or my clumsy attempts to comfort her. She never cursed the sun mother or the snow or her child or its father.

Night came again, white with snow. The child, when it slid out of her into my hands at last, shone white as the snowlight through the window, but also black with her blood. It was beautiful and misshapen, with a head too long to be quite human, a neck too long and silkily maned, legs too long and folded. It lay in my arms, and gazed at me with eyes made of white fire. They spoke to me, those eyes, as no infant's eyes ought to speak.

So many enslaved, the white fire said. *My father cannot save them. He cannot even show them his face—he burns too bright. So many enslaved. And I—I am mute.*

"Sweetheart," Rachel whispered from her bloodied bed—she heard it, too. "You are not mute to us."

But to all others I am. I cannot name them. Save them, mother, as you have saved Shaman. Give them names.

Rachel did not answer, for she fainted. I was a fool, I should have been tending her, within the next hour she very nearly died, of bleeding—I could not stop her bleeding. She lay senseless and I was weeping with despair when people finally came to help us, white-coated people with shots and oxygen who took her away to a hospital. The child they shuddered over and left with me.

It thrived, and all goodness be thanked Rachel lived, and came home to us, and we were a family.

Years passed in which we were happy together. We never forgot we were oddlings, freaks—we did not expect much. Therefore it did not matter that Rachel had only me for a lover; she had my love. It did not matter that there were no jobs for us—we had our child to tend. And it did not matter that our child was very strange, stranger than Rachel, stranger than me. To us she was beautiful, with her long pale face and her willowy neck with the chestnut hair growing wispily far down its nape.

I looked into the child's white-fire eyes sometimes and asked, "Little one, do you love me?" And always, though she held my hand as she tried to walk on her awkward legs, always the answer was *No.* For her name was Spirit, and she could not love, not any more than she could speak. Her eyes always looked far away, toward where her father wandered the dark. *But,* she would add, *my mother loves you.*

"Truly?" I could not hear this quite often enough to fully believe it.

Truly. She loves you, Shaman. I lay under her heart for eleven months. I know.

Of the three of us, Spirit was the only one who seemed not happy. Rachel and I came to understand in a wordless way that in a sense she was not ours, that someday she would fly away and we would let her go.

Often the child could not sleep, and Rachel would hold her and rock her in the shadowy night and sing to her:

> *My Spirit leaps on the mountains,*
> *My Spirit runs amid the mountains,*
> *Under a horseshoe moon.*
> *Beautiful are the farthest mountains*
> *Under a hoofprint moon.*
>
> *Where the sunrise is,*
> *There is my Spirit running on silver.*
> *Where the sunset is,*
> *There is my Spirit running on gold.*
> *Where the moonlight is,*
> *There is my Spirit shining.*
>
> *My Spirit leaps on the mountains.*
> *My Spirit runs in the far dark sky*
> *Beyond, where slowly the stars spin by*
> *Beyond, where the comets fly.*

The child was a mute starlight voice from her father's realm, and we accepted this.

Rachel did as Spirit said, becoming a namer of horses. At first she did it for nothing and no reason except that Spirit had told her to. Also, it gave her pleasure. "I name you Manito," she would call to a big old Roman-nosed rat-tailed Appalosa grazing by the road, and he would fling up his head and prance with joy at being real. "I name you Red Swan," she would whisper to a gangly lop-eared fuzz-faced foal at its mother's side, and as it grew its wild beauty would appear.

Later, Rachel began to understand that this was a huge, serious task, her life's work at last. And people began to pay her to come name their foals and the new horses they bought, to send her their pictures in the mail, because word got around: The horses she named became magnificent.

As for me, I took joy in the days, and ate greens more than most normal people do, and waited. No one wanted to hire a piebald freak. But the world might yet need a shaman.

When Spirit was five years old, she started going to a special school for wobblies, and that summer things came round full circle: with the others from her school she went to ride horseback at Magic Acres.

Wilsy welcomed Rachel with moist eyes. Dear, horrible old Wilsy. She who hoped she would go to heaven, who believed it would be a sweet-smelling orderly place with just rewards, she who thought of a horse as a thing meant to be good for humankind. I am sure she never dreamed who or what she was talking to when she greeted me.

She brought out a blue roan pony for Spirit—one thing I will say for Wilsy, she always kept glorious colors of horses. A blue roan pony with a black mane but a blazing white tail. "Her name is Magic Muffin," she chirped at Spirit, who stared straight ahead at the horizon, where a vast stallion's breath blew white across the sky. "She's a big cuddly blueberry muffin," Wilsy tried again. I had to turn away to keep from groaning. Spirit gazed. Wilsy got the child into her helmet and safety belt and onto the pony, and Spirit stared out over its small pricked ears. Its eyes were strange, I noticed, gray as slate. Walleyes, like mine.

"The most magical thing about horses," Wilsy began her speech, "is the way they give people—"

"The most magical thing about Rachel," I interrupted, "is the way she gives horses back to themselves."

And Rachel smiled a frail wisp of a smile and said to the blue roan, "Your true name is Dark Omen."

And Dark Omen bugled out a neigh fit to shake mountains, and reared up. Wilsy shrieked and grabbed at her head—and missed—but Rachel and I stood hand in hand, watching. And sitting on the pony Spirit was lovely, her thin mane flying at the back of her head, Spirit rode her mount unflinching, rapt, her gaze on the stars where they hid behind seven levels of sky. "Good-bye, little one," Rachel said, but Spirit did not look at us as Dark Omen carried her rocketing skyward, white tail streaming like fire, out of our sight within a moment.

"Gone to wander with her father a while," Rachel murmured.

But we were the only ones who seemed to see. Others were screaming and crying over the thrown body on the ground, the blue roan pony running wild. Wilsy was babbling to us over and over, "I'm sorry, I'm sorry."

"She'll be back someday," I told the Wilson woman, though not to comfort her. I was only saying what was true.

Rachel knew it, too. "Yes," she said dreamily, "She will be back. And we will live to see it, beloved. We will live long. And then when it happens, we will die."

We walked away, hand in hand. And there were tears on my pinto-spotted face, but I smiled because my beloved was brave and clear-eyed and full of poetry. She knew what I knew: that a comet, like a shaman, is one who journeys to return—even if the world should burn.

Deep in her throat Rachel began to murmur a song.

> *The sorrel horse of sunset*
> *And the silver horse of dawn,*
> *Neither of them is mine. . . .*

DREAM'S QUARRY

by Elizabeth Moon

She had eaten her last child's meal the day before; today they had feasted her with blood and ironmeal and stonedust for strength and endurance, with stolen southern wine for courage. Sitting cross-legged on the fine diamond-patterned carpet, Sekkin wore the new clothes that proclaimed her status. An outer tunic and matching pants of softest leather, supple as cloth, instead of coarse wool. Knee-high boots, embroidered all over the soles with expensive scarlet thread and tiny chips of iridescent shell from river clams, replaced the low rawhide boots of a child. She would not walk the ground until her trial was over, lest the embroidery break.

On the carpet before her lay her clan's gifts: an unnamed sword, a short bow backed with sinew, a light lance with a point of dwarf-wrought steel, a drinking horn on its thong, a leather foodsack. They had painted her face with luck charms: Stormwind Clan's spirals and Guthlac's horns and the hoofprints of the Windsteed and the Mare of Plenty. They had sung over her, dancing around her carpet throne until the dust turned the sun orange. Now she waited, while her father and uncles brought her horses, horses she had never mounted, horses they'd traded for this purpose from another clan. And the clan wizard knelt before her, asking of her dreams.

Everyone waited for her answer. "Will you name the blood you bring?" the wizard asked, three times in the ritual, with the hoof-chimes ringing after each. And then, when she did not answer, the final question: "Will you seek a dream's quarry?"

"I will," she said, eyes focused somewhere beyond the crowd. She felt that answer as they did, a cold tremor inside. A wavering cry, then silence, fell across them.

"You followed a true dream?" asked the wizard.

"I did. I followed a dun mare's hoofprints, and the hoofprints filled with water." That was a great omen, as she knew. No one spoke; even the horses were silent.

"Will you name the blood?" asked the wizard. She could refuse, a last chance at a less rigorous trial, but what she named she must do, or be exiled forever. It was a way to test the truth of dreams, or of dreamers.

Those who named the blood, and fulfilled their claim, won honor in the clan, great honor. She waited, remembering her dream, savoring their attention, then dipped her head slightly. "I will name the blood," she said. She felt pride that her voice did not shake. "I will ride with Guthlac, and claim a Huntsman of that Hunt."

At that the wizard fell back, and touched his charms: brow, throat, and wrist, mane-hair, tail-hair, hoof, and tooth. She watched through slitted eyes the crowd's response. Fear, first, for themselves, and then astonishment and even anger. She dared much; she risked more than herself, to challenge Guthlac's Huntsmen. Her quarry might bring the Hunt down on Stormwind Clan itself. But their Horsebreeder stood, sealing the ceremony: As the mare flirts, so the breeding goes. She had the right to make that choice, and the duty to abide by it.

"So it shall be for Sekkin," said the wizard loudly. "She shall not walk the earth, her foot shall not touch the ground, until she brings the blood of Guthlac's Huntsman to Stormwind's tents. By the luck of the Windsteed's foals, by hoof and mane, may this woman prove herself Clan-kin of Stormwind."

Through the crowd's busy murmur she heard the hoofbeats of the horses her male kin brought. She did not turn to see; custom forbade such curiosity. A Stormwind child who could not mount and ride any horse, known or unknown, deserved no chance at adulthood. The sound of the stride told her much. Two were nomad-bred, and perfectly sound: the same quick four-beat gait she had heard all her life. One had a longer stride, a lighter cadence, like dancing; she imagined a slender racer from far away summerward.

They stopped behind her. A leadrope dropped into her hand; her father's hand opened for her if she chose. She tucked the leadrope into her belt, and gathered her gifts without moving from her seat. Bow over the shoulder, sword through the other side of the belt, lance to brace her turn. Drinking horn tucked into her tunic, along with the empty foodsack. Now she looked. She sat before the front hooves of a dun mare, best of omens; on the saddle she could see a quiver of arrows, a rolled storm cloak. Behind was a bay, with a second saddle and a roll of blanket. Behind that was a black, a tall black horse of the summerlands, Finthan perhaps or even Tsaian, unsaddled but bearing a long coil of rope around the neck as well as a halter.

She ignored her father's hand, and rolled to her knees. She had seen nothing amiss, but she must check the girth herself. It was tight; her father had not tricked her. She reached up and slid the lance into the loops on the saddle, then checked the bridle carefully. Ready.

She could mount in several ways. Her boots might withstand a single step, though for every broken strand of thread her rank would fall. Or she could use her father's hand, and half-vault upward from her knees to the saddle. Or she could hope the dun mare had been trained to lift a rider from the ground—most Stormwind mounts would do so. But if she tried that and failed—if the mare spooked, and dumped her on the ground, that would end her trial of adulthood before it began.

Slowly, resisting the pressure of the crowd's curiosity, she scratched the mare under the chin, gently coaxing her head down. The mare did not resist. On her knees, Sekkin edged nearer, into position. No one spoke. With a last brief prayer to the Windsteed, and a touch of the piece of hoof on its thong around her neck, Sekkin threw herself up and sideways, flinging her leg over the mare's lowered neck. The mare jerked her head up; Sekkin clung, off-balance an instant, but did not fall. She slid back to the saddle, then, and settled herself, enjoying the dry, tongue-clicking applause of the clan.

"Ride with the Windsteed, Sekkin," her father shouted. "Hunt the distance and find blood." The crowd broke into a chant, her name and the clan's together, good luck, good hunting. The dun mare shied, but Sekkin caught her with legs and hands, turned her away, and booted her into a quick jog away from camp. The bay lined out smoothly behind them, and the black swung wide, snorting, to the right of the bay.

Already it was past noon, and as warm as it would be so early in spring. Sekkin jogged on, heading winterward, for the next water lay some hours' ride away, and she did not want to sleep dry. As she rode, she checked her equipment, shifting the sword to its own saddle loops, and tying the bow to a knot of mane with the Stormwind secret knot. At least, she thought, it was her own saddle, the saddle she had made two years before and broken in on her favorite mount. Rising high before and behind, padded with tailhair and sheep's wool, it made easy riding for the miles she must cover. Her legs swung free above the early grass. Horsefolk did not use stirrups as the lowlanders did, and Sekkin was glad of it. Stirrups marked bootsoles: only the horsefolk could prove they never walked any distance. Despite the lack of sleep, the strange food, the stinging burns on her feet inside her padded boots—a reminder not to walk, even barefoot—she felt elated. She had challenged Guthlac—she had named a great blood—she would be the first of her father's children to seek a dream's quarry, and bring it home.

By sunfall, she was far out of sight of the clan, and even its dustcloud had sunk to a smudge on the summerward way. The dun mare had shown a smooth, distance-eating stride, and all three horses had calmed. She had found the slough she'd hoped for, a shallow wing-shaped band of water, fresh enough for her and the horses. As they drank, she lowered her drinking horn on its cord, emptied it, and refilled it. She rode slowly along the margin, letting the horses crop tender grass almost at will, while she emptied that horn slowly. Then she halted them, and reeled in the other two horses. Leaning over, she checked the girth of the bay's saddle, and tightened it. She transferred her weapons to the bay, and the blankets from that saddle to the dun, trusting the mare now not to shy or jerk away. Finally, she vaulted to the bay, and took up the reins. When she was satisfied that all was well, she unbridled the dun, looping the bridle around her neck, and fastened her leadrope

to the bay's saddle, tying the black's lead to her.
Then she rode back to the water, and refilled her
drinking horn a final time.

Now she must decide where to spend the night.
The horses might graze here peacefully, but so any
wandering wolfpack might come. In the last light
she rode splashing through the water, noting the
black horse's high-stepping reluctance. Then she
aimed the bay's nose winterward, and let herself
sink into the light doze of her training.

She passed several days that way, riding always
winterward as the Clan reckoned it, into the face
of winter's wind, with the summer wind at her
back. She ate lightly, of what she could hunt from
horseback, or berries from the rare clumps of
bushes around some spring. And she talked to the
three horses, the foundation of her future herd
when she came home in triumph, naming them
with names no one else would know. Soon they
all came to her, eager for her gentle hands on head
and body, responsive to her and to each other.

So had all the Clans begun, by the old songs: a
woman with three horses, riding alone in the
empty lands, had called the Windsteed in a dream,
and the Windsteed had brought foals to her mares.
Then a wicked man tricked the Windsteed into
bondage, but the woman killed the man and freed
the Windsteed, and she herself bore a child as a
gift of the Mare of Plenty . . . so it was sung. Alone
on the grasslands, with the wind and her horses,
Sekkin felt happy, whole of soul and body, as she
never had before. She had no need to walk herself,
with twelve black hooves to serve her. Those func-
tions for which the summerlands folk preferred a
private bit of ground, the horsefolk managed without dismounting, when on trial or raiding. She
had done so from childhood.

But on a day it occurred to her that although
she was happy, she was no nearer her dream, and

the blood she must bring. Guthlac's wild Hunt, in tales and in her dream, rode the winter wind. She had gone winterward now so far that a blue haze grew along the line of the setting sun, and that must be the mountains she had heard of, far sun-setting and winterward of Stormwind's usual yearly migrations. But where was Guthlac? Where was the Huntsman? Had the summerwind driven them away, and must she wander until winter brought them back?

That day she rode upright, looking winterward as hard as she could, hoping for some sign that Guthlac's hunt lay not too far away. And that night, when Torre's Necklace shone above the last-ing sunglow, she sent a prayer to Torre—for all that Torre was no horsefolk deity, whatever the summerlands farmfolk thought her. Not for the deeds the farmfolk knew, but because the Horse-breeder sang that Torre's black horse was the Windsteed's foal, and not the spawn of the Black Wind of Gitres Undoer—for that, and not for her deeds, Sekkin honored her, and asked her aid. And that night's dark center, when the Necklace had been under the world's rim for two spans of star-moving, Sekkin first heard Guthlac's horn, far away.

It sent chills down her back, but she legged the dun mare toward the sound. The Hunt would have passed; still, she might find trace of its passing. Her luck held; by dawn she found trampled grass, the tracks of great horses running at full stretch, and a tangle of dark cloth in the grass that fur-rowed her brow.

She had heard of the blackrobe followers of Ach-rya, but never seen one. Among the horsefolk they were called simply blackrobes, or less commonly falkur-ste: "false-beauty," which recognized their kinship with the falkur, the beautiful, the elder singers. The dead body Sekkin found tangled in its own black robe was clearly such, its face of surpassing beauty but even in death showing the cold, perilous arrogance of its kind. So this was what Guthlac Hunted—at least here, and in this time. On such a Hunt she would prefer to ride, but she was sworn to bring back Huntsman's blood, for the clan's honor and her life.

She turned the dun onto that track, and rode sunrising, with day brightening in her face. Her tracker's eyes built the size of Guthlac's horses from the length of stride, the size of hoofprint, seen here and there between the thick grasses. And by midmorning, she had found another black-robe dead, silver-sparked blood streaking the dark cloak. She kept on, switching mounts from bay to dun and back again. So far she had rested the black, but now she measured its strides against those of the Hunt, and decided to saddle the black before dark.

She came to water, a slow stream moving summerward; the Hunt's tracks showed plain in its muddy banks. One set was cloven—Guthlac himself, or his mount. She didn't know which; the stories went both ways. Her horses drank, and she refilled her drinking horn over and over, filling herself with water for the coming dry afternoon. She had seen that even the Hunt drank here, the horses spread along the bank, standing with forefeet in the water, and bootmarks as well, from some of the riders.

As the sun sank behind her, throwing her shadow ahead, she noticed how it grew taller. She had seen that before, but never thought about it. Now it seemed both ominous and hopeful: she rode toward danger and death, but became larger thereby.

Then the trail she followed disappeared, shortly before sunfall. She looked around, ahead, as best she could, standing on the saddle with a blanket over it to protect her bootsoles, and shading her eyes. No trace of the Hunt's passage lay beyond. The grass blew unmarked between her and the edges of the world. For the first time since hearing Guthlac's horn, she felt a tremor of fear. The Hunt was not mortal—or not wholly so—but as long as she had hoofprints to follow, she had felt herself at home. But for the Hunt to disappear, leap—as it seemed it must have leapt—into the air, here in the middle of the grass, that was uncanny, frightening. She stooped again to the mare's back, stretching her legs first to one side, then the other. She would wait here. Whatever happened this night, she expected no sleep.

The sun dropped under the world's rim, and her shadow melted into a soft haze of dusk. Quickly, Sekkin transferred to the bay, shifted her favorite saddle to the black. Despite her hurry, it was nearly dark when she had made her gear fast to that saddle, and arranged the leadlines as she wished. Stars pricked the dull blue sky, brightened as day faded, and merged into the patterns she knew. All she could see of the land was starlight on the grass, and the shapes of her horses, dark against it. A light movement of cold winterward air stirred the grass, bringing the smell of ice and rock and distant forested mountains. It strengthened. She turned to face it, cupping one ear at a time out of its hum to listen for whatever might be coming.

The dun mare threw up her head. That was all the warning Sekkin got before a blackrobe sword stabbed at her, starlight flowing down the blade. She jerked the bay back; it reared, snorting. Another blackrobe had the dun, had cut the leadrope. The mare squealed and bucked, but the blackrobe held tight, and whipped her away sunrising. Sekkin tried to shift the bay near the black, dancing on the end of its lead, but the first blackrobe was still coming at her, sword moving in patterns she did not know. She had left her lance on the black's harness; with her own short sword she could not fight in front of her mount. She wheeled the bay, swung, and heard the bitter snap of her blade as the blackrobe's sword broke it like a dry stick. At that she wheeled again, kicked the bay into a flat run, and tossed the black's lead free. It would follow the bay, and her, and would run better loose.

In the dark she could see nothing of the ground; she had to trust the bay's sense. Ahead she heard the uneven hoofbeats of the dun, still fighting her rider. The black ran alongside, a bowshot off. Behind came the harsh, high calls of more blackrobes, voices as cold and alien as their faces, but less beautiful. Sekkin felt for her bow, strung it, and set an arrow to the string. The bay was catching the dun, and if she could get a shot—

Over her head shrill horns rang out, and the night was full of horses, before, behind, all around, racing flat out over the grass. The bay shied, nearly throwing her, as something twice its size pounded past. Sekkin's breath caught. They shone in starlight as if edged with pale flame: Guthlac's followers, the Huntsmen, the tireless. Ahead of them, visible in his own glow, Guthlac. The branching tines of his antlers caught the starlight in a silver web, his eyes glowed, his cloven hooves tossed the grass behind him as he ran. All around, above, the horns blew, music that caught her heart, bound her in the Hunt. She glanced aside, and saw other glowing eyes watching her, hands raised in salute, weapons gleaming.

But the bay had no speed for this chase. They fell back, little by little. She heard the cries as the Hunt closed on the dun mare and her burden. She kicked the bay frantically. Perhaps she could catch up with the dun, at least, but the little mare raced on, free now of the blackrobe's weight. Then one of the trailing Huntsmen turned and saw her, slowed his own mount to her speed. In the starlight his face was very fair: she almost named him falkur.

"You chose an ill mount for this," he said over the noise of the hooves.

"I had a better," Sekkin said, "But the blackrobes attacked—my sword broke—"

"Is the loose black yours?" When she nodded, he sped away, returning shortly with the black horse, running easily on its long lead. He tossed her the cut end, and she reeled the black in, letting the bay slow to a laboring canter. Then she swung over to the black, and left the bay free.

Ahead, the horns still sang, calling. She had no need to urge the black horse; it wanted nothing more than to run with that herd. She checked her gear as it ran, making sure of lance and bow, arrows and dagger. Hard to think, with that wild music in her ears. Hard to remember what she was there for, to Hunt the Hunt itself. The black horse ran smoothly, long strides that brought the rear of the Hunt back to them. Sekkin turned to the Huntsman who had helped her, only to see a black shadow rise from the starlit grass ahead and throw itself at his horse.

The Huntsman's horse swerved, staggered, and rolled neck over croup. With a shriek the blackrobe leapt forward. Sekkin hauled her horse down, and swerved across its path, jabbing with her lance. She felt it hang in the blackrobe's cloak, thrust harder, and found herself holding a dead weight on her shaft. Before she could free it, the Hunt had turned. Sekkin let go her lance, and turned the black away—but too late. She was caught in their circle. Two spears pierced the blackrobe besides her lance, and Guthlac strode to the dead enemy. The Huntsman who had fallen lay still. She could not see if he lived.

Now the horns blared even louder. Guthlac's eyes glowed like wind-fired coals as he looked around at the circle of horses and riders. His voice, when he spoke, surprised her—it was cool and sweet, like a young boy's.

"Another Achryan servant—good hunting, lords and ladies." He went on. "And whose kill is this? I have not seen this lance before."

Sekkin froze. Until then she'd hardly realized that she *had* killed. She had made her first kill, the kill that made her adult, Clan-kin—or would have done so, had she not named a Huntsman as her dream's quarry. Before she could answer, that burning gaze turned on her.

"Ah—a new member of our Company . . . and who may you be, Lady?"

She had to answer, dry mouth or no. "Sekkin, Lord—" she said. "Of Stormwind Clan—"

"Horsefolk," he interrupted. He was near enough now that she could see details of his face. Short tangled hair around his face, no beard of manhood, a pointed chin. Out of that tangle of hair on his head rose the twin antlers; Sekkin stared at them, fascinated. "The horsefolk," he was saying now, to the others, "have always understood hunting. Is it not so, Lady?"

She could not answer. She could not say anything, faced with Guthlac, the Hunter of Souls, in the midst of his Hunt. He took a long breath, blew it into the black horse's nostrils. The black reached out, bumped Guthlac with its nose, and rumbled a horse greeting.

"Did you choose to hunt with us, Lady of Stormwind, or were you traveling somewhere?" A mocking tone had entered his voice; it reminded her of all the tales. Sekkin sat up straighter.

"I dreamed this hunt, Lord," she said. "I followed your trail yesterday, and sought you by darkness."

A low murmur from the crowd. Guthlac turned, his cloven hooves treading a pattern she almost recognized. He reached to the blackrobe, and twitched her lance free, touched the tip to his mouth, then handed it to her. "You have sought blackrobe blood; you have chosen to hunt with me. Are you Clan-kin, Lady?"

"No, Lord. This hunt is my trial."

"This blood will free you, then, will it not?" She saw his hand reach out, silvered by starlight and darkened by blackrobe blood. And she went cold to the bone, knowing herself trapped. Hunter he might be, but Guthlac hunted more than one way; he was Lord of traps and tricks as well as the running hunt. But she had brought this on herself; she dared not lie.

"No, Lord," she said. "This blood will not free me, because I dreamed a different quarry."

"Oh—you wish to hunt longer with us, eh? Bold folk the horsebreeders have become, Lady, since last I visited your tents, if blackrobe blood will not suffice for Clan-kinship. What quarry did you name, then?"

"A Huntsman of Guthlac," she said, forcing herself to meet those glowing eyes. At her words they brightened from red to gold, and she heard the shocked whispers all around her. Then he laughed, the wild laugh of a careless boy.

"Bold indeed, daughter of Stormwind, and bolder to tell me so. Indeed, Lady, we have not had such a wild boast for many seasons. And *which* Huntsman of mine did you have in mind, Lady, and why did you seek such prey?"

Well, she would die, and leave her bones to the hunters of the air, but she would die bravely, as she had been taught. Still meeting his eyes, she settled her lance in her grip. "Lord, I followed the

ritual dream, the steps of a dun mare, and named
my prey as the law requires. I saw no face, only
a shape in the dark. In that dream, the Hunt rode
on, laughing, and let me go."

Then they laughed, all but Guthlac, wild voices
around her of many kinds. Even the horses neighed,
and it seemed mockery. But Guthlac did not
laugh, only looked at her coolly and turned away.
Sekkin braced herself for an attack, but no one
else moved; the laughter died of its own weight.
Guthlac moved lightly to the fallen Huntsman and
his horse, and knelt beside them. Then he called.

"Lady of Stormwind—"

"Yes, Lord."

"Come." She could not disobey that command;
even had she wanted to, the black horse was
already moving. It stepped carefully past the dead
blackrobe, stopped at Guthlac's signal, beside the
fallen horse. Somehow—she could not tell how,
and did not wonder at the time—Guthlac brought
a little light, silver as starlight but brighter, to
that place, and she saw the fallen Huntsman. He
lay twisted, partly beneath his dead mount and
partly free, but his arms were slack, his hands
motionless on the grass, his sword fallen away out
of his grasp. She saw his chest move, and realized
he was alive and yet could not live; she had seen
men crushed by horses, or with broken necks,
before this.

"Here is one," said Guthlac, "who cannot live.
Kill him, Lady, and fulfill your vow." The light in
his eyes flickered.

Sekkin stared at him. "Lord—he helped me! He
caught my horse—"

"He was of my Hunt. He is dying, in pain. I give
him to you, Lady, in exchange for this night's
hunt. Give the deathstroke, Lady, and be free."

"But I—but he—" In her mind he had become
almost a friend, the voice in the dark who caught

her horse, made it possible for her to catch up with the Hunt. How could she kill a friend? She had thought to kill in battle, as she killed the blackrobe, in anger or defiance, not in pity. These thoughts tangled in her mind, and Guthlac watched her with fire-red eyes, and the man at her horse's feet struggled for breath, groaning a little.

Guthlac laughed then, mocking her confusion. "You were his death anyway, Lady. But for you he would not lie thus. You have taken a Huntsman; be glad you have taken a blackrobe to pay for him."

And the Hunt gathered around her, closer and closer. Wildness filled the air, tightened her belly, made every breath a struggle. The black horse flattened its ears; she felt its back hump beneath her.

"Is it a Stormwind way to kill a shadow in the dark, and flinch from a face clearly seen? So the blackrobes kill, and all Achrya's servants. If you don't take this blood, Lady," said Guthlac, in a voice so low she could hardly hear it, "the Hunt may have a new quarry. Could you get back to your Clan, Lady, running ahead of the Hunt?" Sekkin could not control the shudder that ran down her back, as much revulsion as fear.

"But it's cruel," she said, still struggling. "He helped me—"

"And does Stormwind leave lame horses to die, and injured warriors to be torn by hunters of the sky?" No, she knew better, but she had planned to kill her quarry fairly. Later was time enough to learn that harder lesson. "You wanted to ride with the Wild Hunt," Guthlac went on, "and you wanted to take one of my Huntsmen. Lady, you had best be swift with your weapons, lest we decide you are no hunter after all, but a child afraid of blood or the shades of the dead. You made your choice; abide by it."

In the silence that followed that, she heard the injured man draw a rasping breath. "Lord—" came his voice, very faint, pleading. Guthlac stamped once, shaking the ground.

"Yes!" Sekkin hardly knew what she meant by that, as her lance went down, a clean blow to the throat, and ended that torment. At once the tension eased; the other Huntsmen drew away a little. Guthlac reached for her lance and withdrew it from the deathwound. She didn't notice when the shaft left her grasp; she was crying, her tears hot against her night-cold face. She had not believed, until then, that she herself must bear all the endings of her designs, as a mare must carry and foal what she deigns to accept from a stallion. Colt or filly, large or small, easy or hard: she was grown, and she must endure. Slower than she wanted, she regained control, gulping her sobs back. Guthlac stood before her still, holding her lance, its bloody point facing her.

"Do you fear me, Lady of Stormwind?" he asked.

Fear, sorrow, anger, and a strange peace mingled in her mind, along with the remnant of that earlier excitement. She could not say it, but he nodded as if he understood, the great antlers throwing sparks of starlight at her.

"Lady, your time will come to ride with us for long and long. For now—" He touched the lance's point to her face, tracing a design on her forehead, on her cheeks. She felt a line of fire where the point touched, but she could not move. "For now, Lady, you are free of your vows, and Stormwind should count you Clan-kin. Let this be proof of the blood you shed: if any questions your scars or deeds, let that one seek answer from Guthlac." He handed back the lance, and gave a strange snort. Two nomad-bred ponies jogged up; Sekkin was not surprised to recognize her dun and bay. Guthlac breathed on both of them, and handed her their leads. "Ride summerward, Lady: winter is mine, and I will hunt this land closely." She wheeled her horse, and the horns cried a warning note that sent all three beasts away at a good pace. Behind her the Hunt's wild laughter rose.

So it was that Sekkin passed into the tent of warriors, she who became Horsebreeder for Stormwind in later years, of whom many songs were sung, and by whose wisdom the Stormwind clan has continued in the blessing of the Mare of Plenty, riding the Windsteed's grandchildren across the endless grass.

SILVERDOWN'S GOLD

by Janny Wurts

Trionn the scullion could never pause anywhere for more than a minute without attracting a heap of cats. It did not matter whether his clothes reeked of the midden on those days when he raked out the garbage, or if he was simply sitting, huddled against the wind, awaiting his turn at the privy. The cats always found him. They settled, arranged comfortably in his lap, or stretched across his feet in sprawls like dropped knitting. All too often they betrayed him by leading those very people to him that he fervently wished to avoid.

That was how he came to be lying prone in high grass on an afternoon when he should have been helping to butcher a pig.

The blood and the smell of the slaughter pen made him sick; the cook knew as much, and cursed him for a puling ninny. There had been too many pigs killed for the table since the new Lord had inherited the rule of Silverdown; as if a feast must grace the tables each night until every pasture was emptied. The squalling as helpless animals were dragged out for the knife made Trionn sweat and turn pale. The heave of his stomach always followed, until lately, no meat sat well in his gut. Discomfort held him prone, though he knew today's victim was by now far beyond feel-

273

ing; the tripes would be boiled and the last ham set up in the smokehouse. Pots left over from the rendering waited in the scullery for washing, stuck with grease, and crusty with charred rings of gravy. He would earn another beating for his shirking.

Trionn did not care. With one cat curled between his shoulder-blades, two more nestled against his flank, and the white female who was heavy with kittens flopped over the backs of his knees, he sucked at a grass stem and stroked the ears of the tom who gnawed at his thumb. He was safe enough here, where the cook would never venture, in the neglected field that was the demesne of the blue dun stud.

The stallion that was a killer, that hated everything alive.

Mad creature that he was, the horse disdained to step on cats. Trionn basked, protected, under a warmth of beasts and autumn sunlight. No one would look for anyone here, far less the most tongue-tied of Silverdown's kitchen staff.

"There he is!" someone shouted.

Trionn started in alarm. The cat on his back was dislodged onto the turf where, with arched spine and crooked tail it glared at him in feline displeasure. Had apprehension not held Trionn rooted, he might have laughed at its injured dignity. But the voice that had raised the outcry was the new Lord's own, and for any man of highborn stature to go beating the fields for a scullion bespoke worse than a cook's irritation.

Trionn levered himself up on one elbow and peered over the grass tips. He dared not spring to his feet, whatever the Lord's displeasure; did he rise, the cats might leave, and the vicious dun would take note that a man had invaded his turf. His ears would flatten, and his nostrils flare warning, just before he thundered into a charge.

Fear of the stud saved Trionn an embarrassment,
since the Lord intended a different errand altogether. He was leaning on the fence in his velvets.
Combed blond hair tousled in the wind as he con-
ferred with a balding companion, less finely
dressed, a leathery appearance to him that
bespoke hard living. Both men watched the horse,
which spied them and bowed up his neck. He blew
a snort in challenge, his nostrils a flash of scarlet
linings against the seal black of his muzzle. Then
he flagged his tangled tail, struck once at the air,
and galloped.

Trionn flattened himself against ground that
shook to the impact of hooves. His peril promptly
compounded as the stud's rampage upset the cats,
who bounded away through the grass. Caught in
the open, he risked getting trampled to a pulp.
The sick fear inside him no longer for the pig, he
crawled on his belly toward the fence. He escaped
under the bottom rail, just barely, but his troubles
did not end outside the pasture. Silverdown had
never been kept like a manor, until now, when
even the weeds that flowered in the hedgerows
were unwelcome. The new Lord had ranted and
waved his whip and found fault until servants set
to with sickle and scythe. Trionn cowered down
in the razed-back scrub that edged the meadow,
and prayed the two men were given no cause to
glance aside. Did they so much as turn his way,
they could not help but catch him skulking.

Escape was impossible. Trionn dared not risk
the noise of movement, even to cover his ears.
Despite the spirited charge of the stud, neither
could he help but overhear every word that passed
between Lord and crony.

"Will you look at his stride!" the bald man
exclaimed in boyish excitement. "He can cover
ground, for a marvel."

The stud reached the fence, dropped his hindquarters underneath himself with a grace that could stop the breath, and whirled in pirouette. Trotting now in taut-muscled extension, he resumed his patrol against invaders. His neck was high set, and curved like a bow, capped with a mane whipped to elflocks that no groom dared to unravel. The last one to try had suffered a broken wrist. Trionn had been assigned the clearing of the supper boards at the time the late Lord, who had been young and a cripple, had gently made disposition.

"Cordiar was never bred to be gentled, but to ride to the fields of war." The Lord raised shaky hands and worried at the shawl that covered frail shoulders. His flesh was pale with ill health, the skin nearly transparent against the blankets piled in layers over his lap; his smile seemed the grimace of a death's head. "My father might have mastered him, had the fighting not sent him to the grave. Leave the horse to his field. Nail the gate closed and let him live as his nature allows. He is wild and filled with hate, but beautiful. He will run free, as I cannot, and give me simple pleasure by watching him."

And so the dun stallion had matured, handled by no man, left to gallop and kick up his heels as he pleased for the two years before Silverdown's master had succumbed to his wasting disease. Unmarried at the hour of his death, leaving not one bastard as issue, his inheritance had fallen to a cousin who was also young, but thick-set and muscled, and vigorous.

"You were right to have me come," the bald man was saying to the new master. "Everyone brags on the virtues of their horses, but this one— he's more than magnificent."

"A treasure," the Lord allowed with an offhand cuff at his cloak. Grass chaff ripped up by the stud had clung and sullied his velvet, and he fussed until the last damp stems had whirled away on the wind. Eyes narrowed against lowering sunlight, he watched the stallion reach the corner and whirl. "A good thing, too. Silverdown's treasury is empty."

Surrounded by a wealth of bearing fields, the bald man raised eyebrows in disbelief.

"Oh, yes," the Lord affirmed with a bitten-off snap of contempt. "Spent out to pay the King's levies, until war took the old man's life. The cripple who survived him had too soft a heart. Left the tenants their harvests, and ran the household on profits from the orchards. Apples and pears!" The Lord gave a laugh not meant to be pleasant. "What a fool's game! The manor house might not leak, through a miracle, but the tenants are sullen and spoiled. They'll have to be taught better manners, if I'm to win Tanemar's daughter. This stallion is all of Silverdown's gold, can we break him. If his bloodline is any judge, his get should look as fine. As a gift he will be unmatched. Duke Tanemar will take notice of my suit, and the hand of his daughter will be mine."

The bald man stroked his chin, while Trionn cowered. "Large plans," he mused, the direction of his gaze never shifting. In the pasture, unaware his wildness was at risk, or that he was being discussed as an item for barter, the stallion kicked up his heels. Hooves sliced across wind with a force that whistled the air. "He's fast enough for a fact, and made well as any man must envy. I'll start on his breaking tomorrow, right enough, but tonight, we'll settle on a fee."

The Lord banged the fence with such force that the planking rebounded with a rattle. The stallion flung up in a rear at the noise, his shadow scything across his admirers. Hooves struck out in a dancer's grace that masked blows as murderous as assassin's cudgels. "No fee," came back the clipped answer. "As I told you, the treasury's empty. Break the great brute so he can be caught and stabled. Then send in three of your broodmares. There's fee enough. While my war captain rides the beast fit so he can be shown off under saddle, the foals will be yours to increase the dun's reputation."

The horsebreaker slapped thighs clad in worn and dusty leather. "I break other peoples' stock," he declaimed. "I don't keep any for myself." As the Lord beside him left the fence, the horsebreaker remained riveted by the stud, who pranced and stamped in tight circles. The longing on even that man's jaded face was fresh and bright and transparent as at last he turned to catch up. "Still, we'll see. Would you consider a split? Payment in silver, and one foal?"

The Lord snatched his cuff from the clutch of a briar the mowers had missed. His mouth turned down. "Certainly not. Duke Tanemar's enough man to please, for setting such store by a daughter who's nobody's beauty. It's the foals or nothing, for you. Press too hard, and I'll send for a gypsy."

"What, and see your treasure stolen the moment it's tamed enough to halter?" The voices of the two men dwindled, amiably contentious as they hammered out terms for their bargain. Trionn sat up in the brush, feeling whitely shaken. He wished all the cats had not left. In balled up, tongue-tied frustration, he watched the stallion storm out one last gust of air, then settle his head down to graze.

A sadness near to pain ached in his chest at the thought that such a beast should ever be trapped or taken.

Distressed beyond concern for the slaughtered pig, Trionn saw the sun gone, and the sky turned silver at twilight before he trudged back to resume his neglected chores. The first thing he noticed as he approached the haphazard cluster of frame buildings that made up Silverdown's manor was that lights burned in nearly every window. Reflections of a hundred flames danced in the boggy, sediment choked ditch that fronted the tumbledown breastworks. Trionn might have a clumsy tongue, but he was exceptionally quick at balancing. He crossed the ditch by footing across a slime-caked log, last remains of the decrepit palisade. He reached what the servants called the yard, a narrow, irregular court whose cobbles were furred in moss; or had been. A fresh, dirt-colored scar sliced one corner, where a drudge labored by torchlight to scrape the paving bare.

More of the new Lord's fussiness, Trionn concluded. Stones could not grow clothes of moss, and wax lights and tallow dips could be burned without care, as the animals were slaughtered for the table; as a great dun stallion could be torn from his freedom and used as a bribe to court a girl. Wrapped in unhappiness, Trionn failed to notice the cat that had found him already. It trotted up and shouldered between his shins, joined at a run by two more.

The alley past the stables bustled with activity. Horseboys jogged between stalls with buckets and grain to tend a half dozen strange mounts. Notes spilled in haphazard arpeggios from the gallery window as a minstrel tuned up to entertain. A woman laughed and a hound howled, while guards who normally would have argued over dice stood up straight and silent at their posts. Their weapons had never been less than sharp, and they had stayed alert enough to challenge intruders; yet their past rows had enlivened their duty watch, ending always in companionable laughter. The change in Silverdown's rule had seen new uniforms with badges at the shoulder. Trailing streamers adorned each man's polearm, as if they were bedecked for a tournament.

But the occasion was no holiday. The servants had little cause to celebrate. All of Silverdown had been swept into change, until Trionn no longer felt at home. He hurried between a drudge with a basket of soiled linens, and the fowler, who carried the cranky old goshawk hooded, and muttered that his dearie should be mewed up and asleep to keep her health.

Trionn threaded a practiced path through the turmoil, until the orange tabby streaked across a patch of torchlight to join his impromptu escort. The cat's arrival drew the eye of the cook, enroute from root cellar to bakehouse to chastise the Lord's page for dawdling.

"You! Trionn! Where've you been all afternoon, and the pots all stacked up for washing? You're a wastrel, boy, and due for whipping. Get inside and back to work, or it's the Lord's own war captain'll be the one who stripes your back."

Trionn ducked his towhead between his shoulders and ran. The cats obligingly followed. Clumsy all of a sudden, he tripped over the door stoop and crashed into a servant with a basket.

"Boy! There's good bread you've close to spilled and wasted, and the new Lord with a hall full of guests to feed! Say you're sorry now!"

Trionn bobbed his head. He did not answer, though he was capable; speech did not always tie his tongue up in knots. His silence had long since branded him half-wit, and shy to the point of cold sweats, Trionn did not argue the misconception. Let Silverdown's staff think him stupid. The sting of their scorn was less than his dread of using words to correct them. He talked to the cats well enough when he wished, and had held very halting conversations with the old Lord, before his illness had brought physicians who would bar the master's door rather than admit a scullion presumed to be a simpleton.

With the cats, now four, trailing on his heels, Trionn left the bread girl to her curses. He zigzagged past the spits into the pantry to avoid the butcher's notice, lest his absence at the slaughter pen cause contention.

For all his care, he was spotted.

"The pigs take the knife better when you're there, Trionn," the butcher reproached gruffly. "You want them not to suffer. Well, if they're held still, the cut is fast and clean."

But it was not at all the matter of the pig's dying; had Trionn been asked his own wish, he would have let the animals stay alive. His oversensitivity was no simple affectation. Where others in Silverdown's service might lament upon the waste, and curse the Lord's lavish feasting that saw a surfeit of scraps thrown to the hounds, Trionn woke up each night in cold sweats, apologizing in half-smothered whispers to the dead beasts needlessly sacrificed.

Today's pig would haunt his dreams no less for the fact he had not bloodied his own hands.

Left at last to his duties, Trionn hauled water to the washtub and started to work the dirtied pots. Cats curled around his feet, knotted together in contentment, while the speculative gossip of the servants came and went through the rattle of plates and crockery.

Enith, as always, was most outspoken. She did not sigh over her new romance with the war captain, but turned sharp-tongued invective against the master. "Chased the linen maid as if she wasn't married, and never mind the tart he worships in his next breath is this highborn daughter of a duke."

"She may well be Silverdown's next Lady," interrupted the page. "You should be careful what you say of her."

His comment was ignored.

"She's small, and no beauty, it's said. All dark hair and wide eyes, and hips too narrow to bear a child." This from the cook, who had a brood of eight, and his wife once again near term.

"Never mind looks," the butcher ventured his opinion. "It's the lass' dowry that's at issue. She'll bring three chests of gold to her bridegroom, and if we're to have candles for the dark nights this winter, better all of us pray Silverdown wins her."

Trionn reached for another pot, and a gob of wet sand for scouring. Behind him, watched by the lazy eyes of his cats, the Lord's steward hurried in, looking harried. "Another five bottles of the red wine, and quickly, before there's trouble."

"Man's brought his horsebreaker to table," the cook grumbled. "Those kind always drink." He wiped greasy hands on his sleeves. "Enith, take down the lantern and go for more red!"

"Been to the cellar twice already tonight," she howled back. "More big spiders than bottles left, that's certain."

"No help for that." Still mournful, the cook added, "Do you suppose the horsebreaker's here to handle that murdering dun stud? If so, he'll want the wine. It's the last drunk he'll have before he's dead."

The pageboy took umbrage at this. "Khaim's better than that. I once saw him break the neck of a colt who tossed him. Hit it a blow that knocked it sideways, and it couldn't stand up afterward."

"No man's that strong," the cook objected over the creak of the hearth chain as he dragged a kettle off the fire.

"Horse had to be a weak, spindly thing, maybe," ventured the butcher.

The page insisted not.

Trionn let his scouring sand sink to the bottom of the wash water, sickened all over again. Though

he strove over the noise and the chat to picture
the stallion at his flat, free run across the meadow,
instead he was poisoned by visions: of blood in
the grass and the air split by a scream that might
have been a woman's. Except that a horse in
agony will make the same shrill sound. Trionn
doubled over and shivered.

A hard hand cuffed him back upright. "Get back
to washing, boy," snapped the cook. "There's
barely a clean pot in the rack yet."

Half dizzied, Trionn groped for a ladle. His hand
stopped still in midair. He could not touch the
gravy that seemed suddenly the same color and
sheen as congealed blood, nor could he look at the
wash water clinging to his skin, so much did it
shine like salt tears. The cook saw his stupefied
pallor, and cuffed him all the harder.

"Oh, no, lazy boy. Though you're sick clean
down to your boot tops, you'll stay and scour,
until all this stack of washing is done and dry."

Trionn nodded dully. Midnight came. The lanterns and candles all burned down, leaving darkness cut only by the struggling wick of a tallow
dip. Alone in the cavernous kitchen, he finished
his appointed chores. When he stumbled out at
last to find his cot, the mists had hidden even the
moon.

Banners snapped, and dust blew. The new Lord
had invited two friends and all of his companions
at arms to watch the dun stallion's breaking. Once
again Trionn had shirked his part in the slaughter
pen, since a calf roast was to finish the occasion.
Hidden in the crowd of Silverdown's servants, he
stood in cap and apron, only one cat by his shins;
the commotion had driven all but the boldest and
most determined tom away.

The stallion on whom all this interest centered
galloped the far fence line, ears tripping backward

and forward, and nostrils distended in deep-chested snorts of alarm. Trionn could not watch him. He could not be as the others, and admire the glossy silver coat, nor the high, black tail that cracked like a flag in the wake of his thundering run. Trionn could not bear the sight of the creature's eye, rolling white, nor could he forget the dreams that had repeatedly broken his sleep: of blood in the grass, and the stallion's ringing neigh of distress.

And yet, unlike the dragging of animals to the butcher's knife, here, he could not be absent. Tormented by a sickness of fear that ate at his spirit from within, he could not run, but only stare down at the worn-through leather of his boot toes, his shoulders as hunched as though he expected a beating; as if he carried upon them a burden that could bend and break, as finally and carelessly as grass stems were trampled under the feet of today's thrill seekers.

The scullion knew when the horsebreaker climbed the fence by the scream of the dun stallion's challenge; second and without importance came realization that the onlookers had ceased conversation, even the cordwainer's apprentice, who was said to jabber in his sleep. The slap of a rope shaken out of its coil reached Trionn's ears, eerily and evilly distinct over the drumroll of the stallion's charge. The scullion bit his lip. He felt through his feet the shake of the ground, and his sensitized nerves seemed to shudder at the step of the man who paced the greensward, eyes narrowed and line poised to toss.

The stallion came on like thunder, like storm. The crowd sucked in a taut breath. The horsebreaker poised with slightly bent knees, admiring, though his life stood endangered. He was confident when the dun snapped up short from his run and towered into a rear. The man's hand on the rope did not tremble as black forelegs raked out to strike. He tossed his loop then, supremely, recklessly sure that his lifetime of skill would not fail him.

The throw missed.

Too fast for the eye to follow, the loop collapsed in a whipping slide off the stallion's knee as his head snaked down, and he whirled.

Not off his guard, nor yet shaken, the horse-breaker shouted and snapped the rope. This horse, like a thousand others, would be bound to shy from any movement, half-seen where equine vision was obscured by the length of his muzzle. Stallions could be predicted. Their forehooves came down, then their head, with ears pricked to assess the threat to their footing; the shy ones would often whirl and run.

The dun stud twisted instead. He landed, still spinning, his ears pinned flat. The horsebreaker shouted to drive him back to a gallop, his hands swiftly reeling in rope. But the stud had done with running. His silver-blue quarters bunched, and one hoof flashed back in deadly perfect accuracy to hammer the man where he stood.

Bright blood flecked the green grass. The horse-breaker lay unmoving, while a woman screamed, and men on all sides started shouting, most jostling back from the fence, but others pressing forward. The stud danced a half pirouette, some swore, in celebration of his unholy victory. The grooms and the stable hands disagreed; the horse was a killer, but not so driven by rage that he ever once stopped thinking. The blue dun was far too crafty to mire his pasterns in a corpse or a tangle of rope.

Solitary, unmoved to any human commiseration, Trionn crouched with his hands laced over his face. He alone had not exclaimed in shocked sympathy as the Lord's men reached beneath the lower rails, and dragged the horsebreaker's body beyond reach of further mauling. The victim was wounded beyond solace, if not immediately dead, and the tears of Silverdown's scullion were shed only and completely for the horse.

His terror-inspired visions did not leave him. There was blood on the grass, but a man's, and the beast's, for a surety, must follow.

The talk in the kitchens after sundown encompassed nothing else. Trionn scrubbed his pots in his corner, and took no solace from the cats, who were thicker than usual about his feet. They might not have speech, but as he did, they could sense when trouble was afoot.

Enith was shrill in her complaints, as she tapped chilled butter from the molds. "What if the Lord sends his captain to do the killing? Waste of a fine piece of manhood, did that happen, and our champion took a kick like that horsebreaker."

"Won't," grunted the butcher, who recalled just short of a mistake that the cook would run him out for spitting in contempt on the floorboards. "The captain's a bastard for pride. He'd scarce soil his sword on a job better suited for my flensing knife. Though, mark, if I'm asked to cut that devil creature's throat, I won't, unless he's tied down."

"Who's to tie him," Enith snipped back. "No man but my captain has the courage."

"Your captain?" muttered a stable hand, in to grab dinner between seeing the guests' horses harnessed. "Man's owned by nobody, least of all any one lass. He tumbles anything in skirts, every chance he gets."

His muttering tangled with the voice of the cook, who offered, "T'were mine to say, I'd use poison. Why take chances, when a bit of tainted feed dumped over the fence could do the job just as well?"

The Lord's page overheard, as he entered with an emptied platter. "The horse won't be killed," he called clearly. "He's much too valuable for that." Heads turned, all wearing hostile expressions, except Trionn's; he stared fixedly at his hands, immersed to the wrists in grease-scummed water, while the cats butted heads against his ankles.

"The Lord has already decided," announced the page in crisp arrogance. "He's sent for a gypsy horse caller. It's broken for saddle he wants that stud, not dead."

The cook slammed his cleaver upon the cutting board. "Magic," he said in contempt. "Where's the coin to pay for such? Gypsies with the caller's gift come dear." His thick, sure hands did their task slowly as he heaped steaming meat on the platter the Lord's page held ready.

"It's the girl he wants to impress." Enith sniffed. "Silverdown will be beggared ere his Lordship wins her."

"That's not your trouble," the Lord's page sniped back, out of sorts because he was no longer entrusted to wait upon his master's table. With Duke Tanemar's daughter expected to accompany her father when the stallion was presented as a gift, the Lord had borrowed a page of higher station, and presumably more refined manners, from his brother's household in Tanley. Appointed to serve the lower hall until a gypsy could be found to tame the stud, the displaced page made his resentment felt at every opportunity. Only Enith was exempt, since the boy yet held out hope he might win her favors from the captain; to any who would listen, he bragged that soon it might be he who tumbled her in the hayloft over the barn.

Crouched over the washtub until his hands shriveled and his cuticles chapped and split from the unending mess of dirtied kettles, Trionn reflected sourly that he lost nothing from his disinclination to speak. What were words after all, but winds that blew here and there to no purpose? The cats had better sense, to express their contentment through purring. They yowled only for misery, and met daily disaffection in dignified, unblinking silence.

The slaughtering continued the next afternoon, yet Trionn was excused. The master commanded, and for fear of his Lordly displeasure, every servant not required for other duties set to work in the sun, pulling out briars by hand. Trionn was given the noisome task of raking dirty rushes from the hall. The wooden boards underneath were to be sanded and cleaned. Enith, between frequent sniffs, claimed carpets were sure to follow. When the last wheelbarrow filled with beetle infested straw was carted out, Trionn set to with sand bucket and rags. As cats scattered back from the spatter of his scrubbing, he reflected that Enith was spiteful. The rushes had been spread at the bequest of a lazy house servant, and only after sickness had confined Silverdown's doomed cripple to his bedchamber. The floors before then, back to the old Lord's rule, had been shiningly kept oiled.

Trionn was still at his work, mopping up sand in the shadows of a back corner, when the gypsy horse-caller arrived. She proved to be a woman, to the surprise of all; tiny, raven-haired, and wearing a patched mantle of greens and browns that might have been pilfered from a minstrel. The tassels at the hem were worn to a ragged motley of threads, and though her hair was braided and clean, her skin was the ocher of mud baked dry in the sun.

Trionn recognized her gift when the cats at his heels fled her presence. Silent as shadow, they stalked off in stiff-backed irritation. The scullion watched their retreat. A chill brushed his skin; as if he, too, sensed the power over beasts that this gypsy sorceress could command, and his spirit raised hackles in protest. The hounds did not run. Fickle creatures that they were, bred over generations to subservience, they converged in a pack of wagging tails, tongues lolling in canine enthusiasm. They reacted as if the strange woman in her dusty, faded finery had been the mistress they had obeyed since their whelping; as indeed she could be, if she chose. No dumb beasts, and few men, were proof against a gypsy caller's craft. But unlike humans and cats, dogs set small value on independence. Like whores, they flocked in unabashed eagerness around the woman's boots, begging and whining to be dominated.

Trionn threw down his rags, oblivious to the fuss as servants and guests, and at last the Lord himself took loud-voiced notice of the intruder. The scullion unseen in his corner did not follow the woman's words as she announced herself, but heard only the silvery timber of her voice. The pitch set up echoes inside him that no amount of clamor could still. He saw courtiers eagerly joining the circle of dogs, who were now belly down and begging. Yet Trionn's senses gave back false sight. In place of hounds and gentlefolk, his mind could not throw off the vision of the silver-dun stud with his grand neck bowed in submission.

Sudden tears stung Trionn's eyes. His stomach heaved. The blood on the grass had not been the horse's; better by far that it had been. The Lord who had died a cripple had insisted many times that death held the keys to final freedom.

Moonlight washed over the meadow. It limned soft silver over the stallion who grazed content in tall grass. Trionn sat outside the fence, his lap encumbered by sleeping cats. His hand caressed the bone handle of the butcher's flensing knife, stolen after dark from the closet. Over and over,

Trionn stroked the blade's edge, checking its razor keenness. He turned the weighty steel in his hands, and remembered the kick of a pig held pinned in his arms as it died. He licked dry lips, and sighed as he tested the resolve he had made in desperation, and found himself wanting. He lacked any kind of brash courage. The fate of the horsebreaker did not haunt him, nor fear for his own life and limbs. He simply knew. When the dun stallion bent his knees and laid down to rest, Trionn had no will to creep through the fence and cut the creature's throat to forestall its misery. Whatever freedom death might offer could not compensate for the pound of wild hooves, or the ripple and play of muscles burnished like shining silk under sunlight. The stallion would live to be broken, for Trionn did not have in him the requisite hardness for murder.

He sat in the calm of the night, surrounded by cats and the chirp of crickets, and miserably wished he were bold enough to run away. Yet far as a lifetime of travel, though he crossed the rocks of the mountains beyond the sands, the memories and the visions would follow him, locked inescapably in his mind. The gypsy caller's powers would sting him, no matter where, and he would ache for the stallion's lost spirit. Like the cling of the cats, the persistence of his dreams could not be shed.

The deepest and worst of his misery was that he could not even turn the steel upon himself. The pain did not deter him, nor the dying, but the strange, insistent surety that the cats would be left bereft. Wise as the creatures could be, they would not understand why he should desert them for the sake of one horse's lost liberty.

The butcher recovered the purloined knife after Enith, returning from her nightly tryst in the hayloft, caught Trionn in the yard by the kitchens. Particular to a fault when it came to his cutlery, the butcher's shouted obscenties progressed to extra work as punishment. Trionn was assigned the task of sharpening every tool left dull in the course of shearing Silverdown's weeds and grass.

Left wary after the slaughtering that Trionn was practiced at haring off, the butcher took no chances. He locked the scullion in the tool shed with a half filled bucket and a whetstone. The cats could find no way in, however hopefully they sniffed and circled. In time they were compelled to settle in disgruntled bundles on the door stoop.

Inside, the shed was suffocatingly hot. Hedged by darkness inadequately beaten back by a bark spill soaked in resin, Trionn set to with the whetstone. He braced the bucket between his knees, and worked the marred edge of a sickle, his mind consumed by awareness of the cats' balked desires. He was powerless to ease their unhappiness.

The butcher jammed a wedge under the sill outside. Until he chose to return, or someone else happened by to fetch a tool, Trionn's imprisonment was complete. The likelihood nobody would visit the shed before the spill burned out did not matter. Silverdown's servants had left for the meadow, the reason for their gathering a distress that already fretted the scullion raw. He dipped the stone and resumed honing, relentless in his determination. He would not think upon what must inevitably happen when the gypsy raised her powers to subdue the stud.

And yet the moment touched him, all the same. The tones of the gypsy witch's call clamored through him like the struck chime of a bell. The whetstone slipped from Trionn's fingers and splashed into the bucket. Droplets warm as blood trickled down his shins. He did not feel their wetness. Nor did he notice as the spill flickered out, leaving him kneeling in darkness. His eyes were vision-bound to a sunlit meadow, and the form of the slate dun stud shaking his back his mane, his ears snapped forward to listen.

The gypsy sorceress repeated her call, lower now, almost wheedling.

Trionn felt the resonance of her tone play through the marrow of his bones. He remained oblivious to the ribbon of true blood that laced his wrist, from the knuckle laid open on the sickle.

His eyesight remained locked as his mind: on the horse, who twitched glossy skin, as if to drive off flies. But it was no insect that stung him. From her perch half on, half over the fence, the gypsy crooned out a binding. The stud's ears flattened and he stamped, where once he would have thundered into a run with his teeth bared in fury.

The call came again, compelling. As if whipped, the stallion started. He edged one step forward, then two, while in the soundless isolation of the shed, Trionn winced. Sweat rinsed his cheeks and his nails gouged his palms as his fingers clenched to fists in the throes of unasked for empathy.

Now the gypsy began a sing-song rhythm that raised the hair at Trionn's neck. He shivered and jerked in concert with the stud as need swelled into compulsion. The horse lowered his proud crest. His hooves raised no dust as he advanced. To Trionn, the gypsy's magic squeezed and confined, as if the leaping flame of a bonfire were compressed down into one spark. His breath jerked in gasps from his chest.

"No," he whispered, "No." He closed eyes that had long since stopped seeing. "No!"

Yet his physical cry could not alter the spell. The stallion moved inexorably onward. He had crossed half the distance to the fence, and the woman, tasting victory, climbed down with her hand outstretched.

The murmurs of the servants, and the Lord's triumphant laugh rang brittle as breaking ice against the deeper vibration of the summoning that continued to draw its victim in.

One touch from the witch would seal the stallion's submission. Trionn understood this in a gut ache of intuition, and something inside of him snapped.

He bit his lip, knees clasped, as his body spasmed with the same wrenching sickness he felt at the slaughtering of the pigs. Only this time, the cramping and the agony were a thousand times more severe. He fought to breathe, fought to think, while the sweat mingled unnoticed with his blood and pattered on the dusty floor.

The stallion was a half-stride away from defeat. His lowered muzzle brushed the grass tips. His eyes were dull, unfocused, and his tail, as lackluster as any gelding's.

Trionn knew a spearing agony that threatened to rip away his reason. He clamped his hands over his sweat-slicked face and forced a half strangled breath. "No."

Before his heart could burst, before the great dun could nuzzle the woman's outstretched brown fingers, he imagined the horse as he had been, a creature of terrible beauty that no man in his right mind dared touch.

Trionn pictured the stallion with his head upflung, and his eyes rolling white rings in hatred.

There followed a moment of torment, as if the inner fiber of his being was seared by a whirlwind and torn apart. He had no voice to cry out, and no thought beyond a pinpoint awareness that centered on the slate-blue stud.

For a second he seemed to *be* that horse, his senses overwhelmed by the scent of summer grass, and a second, sourer odor left by a trespassing human. Trionn saw through the stallion's eyes the

vista of the fence, and the crowd that lined the
rails in maddening noise. He felt the unleashed
tension that whipped through the horse as the
gypsy's near-finished binding snapped like so much
spun thread.

Ever mindful of the horse's speed and power,
the woman was faster than her predecessor. She
dropped and rolled, even as the stallion screamed
in rage. He reared. His shadow raked over the
onlookers, driving them back in a panic as his
forehooves slashed through air. The woman was
no longer there, but already through the fence in
a whirl of motley robes. The stallion spun, and
from his hind legs launched himself into a gallop.
A bolt of silver fury, he ran. His mane flew, and
his tail whipped behind like the curl and twist of
a war banner.

The shouts of the irate Lord of Silverdown
seemed insignificant before the racing tattoo of
hooves.

In the tool shed, Trionn woke to himself, sob-
bing beyond all control. The finger unwittingly
sliced on the sickle was stinging in the salt of his
sweat. He splashed water from the bucket over the
cut, and found his limbs heavy with weariness.
His lungs hurt, as if he had been racing on foot
alongside the galloping horse. The fact he had not
been seemed unreal. Still weeping, he lay back
against the rolled burlap used to save seedlings
from the last blighting touch of spring frost. His
soaked hair plastered to his forehead, he fell into
a dreamless oblivion nearer to unconsciousness
than sleep.

The day waned. Trionn wakened to a slap. He
gasped, started upright, and, dazzled by the glare
of low sunlight, saw the butcher standing over
him.

"Lazy lout!" the man was shouting. "All day

you were in here, and nothing to show for your time. I should have guessed you'd pass the hours sleeping if you could!"

Trionn propped himself up on one arm. He blinked, rubbed his aching cheek, and glanced around to locate the cats, who should have stolen their chance to bolt inside the instant the door was cracked open.

No cats were in evidence.

For the first time in life that he could think of, his feline friends were not there. The stone stoop was empty of their presence, and the butcher was still howling nonsense.

If Trionn was grudging with his speech, he was equally adept at not listening. He rubbed his arms to ease the chill that swept his skin. If the cats had left due to the butcher's ranting, the troubling fact remained: none of them lurked in the shadows behind the seed sacks, or crouched with flattened ears beneath the shovels.

Above anything else, Trionn dreaded to know what awaited when he ventured out of the shed.

"I should be throwing cold water at your head, boy, to snap you out of your stupor!" The butcher raised the handle of the bucket, prepared to act on his threat, when a second voice cut him off.

"There you are, Trionn!" hollered the cook, his fat bulk damming the small band of light that made its way through the doorway. "Been following cats into crannies all afternoon, and it's here you've been skulking all along!" Oblivious to the butcher's prior grievance, the cook barged past and grabbed his errant scullion by the wrist. "Get moving, you lunk. There's a stack of pots need scrubbing, and his Lordship in a temper since that cheating snip of a gypsy disappeared and can't be found."

Distracted from his ire over scythe blades, the

butcher thumped down his bucket. "It's true, then? The woman was a charlatan?"

"The fact she ran off makes you think so." The cook jerked Trionn after as he plowed a path toward the door. "The Lord's set his riders to find her. When she's caught, I'd guess there'll be a hanging."

"And the horse?" Turned thoughtful, the butcher fished his whetstone from the water, and reached for an unsharpened sickle. "What's to become of the stallion?"

"Dogmeat," the cook affirmed, his head cocked over Trionn's shoulders. "The captain at arms was told to down the rogue with an arrow, next time the kennelman needs a carcass." Then, bothered back to priorities by his scullion's dragging feet, the cook turned his invective upon Trionn. "You heat sick, boy? Pick yourself up and walk, else I'll pack your bones for the knackerman along with that devil of a stallion's."

Engrossed in miseries far removed from the cook's irritation, Trionn stumbled through the wicket gate into the courtyard. No cats came flying to greet him. Not even the mackerel striped tabby sunning herself on the wall. Dread left him the appearance of listlessness. He responded mechanically to the cook's yanks and prods, not wanting to test what change might have touched him while he had been locked in a tool shed, and a gypsy had signally failed in the taming of a man-killing stallion.

The entry to the scullery loomed ahead. On the stoop lolled two white-muzzled hounds, skinny and scarred, but not too old or too proud to disdain begging for scraps. Enith leaned against the doorlintel, sampling a slice of sausage, while the hounds tipped their heads at her and rolled their moist brown eyes.

Trionn stiffened, half-wild with trepidation.

"Are you daft, boy?" exploded the cook. He gave an abusive yank. The scullion gripped in his meaty fist stumbled forward with a breathless cry.

The dogs immediately stiffened and turned their heads. They saw Trionn. Enith and her sausage were forgotten as they shuffled into a lope, tails wagging, and eagerness in their cloudy old eyes.

Trionn flung back from their rush, appalled to a burst of speech. "No," he croaked, "Not this," as the dogs rushed to him and leapt for joy around his knees. They whined and nosed at his fingers, as if greeting a long-sought friend.

"What's happening?" yelped the cook, put out afresh by confusion. He threw off the scullion and the dogs, hands raised in nervous trepidation. "Always before it was cats." His tone held a bite of accusation as he added, "Or have the Lord's bitches gone crazy?"

Enith shifted a lump of sausage into the back of her cheek. Around chewing, she said, "Looks uncanny to me, as if that gypsy witched the dogs instead of the stallion." Then she fixed hard eyes on Trionn. "You never said you could talk."

"Oh, he can," supplied the cook, "He just hates to. When he was little, his parents beat him for stubbornness. Didn't do any living good." He raised a booted foot and kicked the nearest dog, which yelped and bounded back, to shelter behind Trionn's knees. The scullion flinched from its touch, hunched and unaware as the discussion continued around him.

"Enough foolishness now, Trionn," berated the cook. "The pots aren't getting any cleaner while you stand out here acting foolish."

"If he fakes being dumb, maybe he's not so stupid," Enith suggested, while the cook pushed the scullion reluctantly toward the kitchen doorway.

She stepped disdainfully aside to let them past, adding, "Are you stupid?"

He gave no answer.

When the dogs sought to barge through on Trionn's heels, both she and the cook howled in chorus. Ousting the dogs required all their attention, and until the door to the kitchen was secured, neither one noticed that Trionn had not retired to his corner to silently, doggedly, scrub pots.

"He slipped out the side way," snitched the Lord's page, idle at the table chewing sausage. He gave a hopeful smile toward Enith, who responded with a flounce, cut short as the cook had a fit.

"I'll have the both of you washing pots!" he roared in fist-waving fury.

The page snickered, as if the threat was a joke. An instant later, he found himself installed at Trionn's washtub, cursing the stink of tankards and plates left awash in skins of rancid grease.

Well beyond earshot of the fracas in the kitchen, Trionn ran as a man might when driven by whips. Wherever he went, the cats in their turn fled his presence. Uncannily choosy by habit, they recognized precisely what the gypsy caller's gift had wakened in him. A horse had been wrested from her spell by his bidding, and of humans with such powers, they were chary. Trionn knew pain beyond words. The dependable warmth of the cats' companionship was lost to him, reft away by an afternoon's longing that in ignorance, he had never known to fear.

In his passionate wish to keep the stallion wild, he had never guessed that desire by itself could afflict him. He raged to admit what the cats knew, and the dogs by their mindless fawning: that the caller's talents had been somehow thrown awry by his meddling. The taint of her mystery had touched him. He did not know if the fluke could be reversed. Though his lungs ached and his muscles burned, he pressed on in useless exertion. For the inevitable outcome had not altered. The kennelman was promised a carcass, and the huntsman's arrow must fly. However far Silverdown's scullion drove his body, the vision pursued and harrowed him. Still, he saw blood in the grass, the scream of the stallion's dying an echo that resounded through his mind.

Dusk found him crouched on the rise above the meadow, his forehead cradled on crossed wrists. He had decided to break down the gate, a desperate act that would ultimately not solve anything. Loose, the dun stallion was a liability. He would steal mares from all but the sturdiest paddocks, and kill any fool who interfered. In the end, he would be chased down. The archer's shot would take him, but in the open, as he ran in all his pride and splendor.

If Silverdown's scullion escaped the fury of the horse he resolved to set loose, what should befall him at the Lord's hand for presuming such interference defied imagination. In his misery over the desertion of the cats, Trionn did not care. His fretting over the stallion's fate had long since destroyed his peace; the pain of spirit he already suffered could hardly be made any worse. All that remained was to endure until the darkest hour before moonrise.

The birds quieted, and the crickets began their chorus. Above the small sounds of the night, Trionn heard the bell that summoned the field hands to supper. Past the bog he saw the glimmer of candles wastefully alight in the Lord's hall. The feast went on regardless, the gypsy's failure with the stallion no impediment to the pleasure of those highborn guests still in residence. Yet the thriftlessness of Silverdown's Lord was of little

concern to Trionn. Now that he had firmed his
course of action, the stillness as the stars brightened lent him a measure of peace. The Lord's riders were fanned out across the countryside in
search of the vanished gypsy; patrols on the estate
would be light, and widely spaced.

The gloom deepened. The breeze carried snatches
of Enith's laughter. The Lord's page could be
heard shouting curses at the cook, while in the
gatehouse, the captain berated a dozing sentry.
The cobbled yard between lay empty, most of the
household settled inside at their supper. Trionn
chose his moment. Sweat chilled on his body as
he rose and crept downhill through mown grass
toward the stallion's pasture. From a pile of cut
brush left by the laborers who cleared the fields,
he selected a stout branch of oak. He stripped off
the bark and twigs, then hastened on toward the
gate, nailed shut ever since the forgotten procla-
mation that the stallion might live undisturbed.

No one stopped him; no rider emerged to cry
challenge. Trionn moved in fixed purpose, too
numb to acknowledge his trepidation. The gate
loomed ahead, a barred silhouette against a starlit
expanse of open grass. He shot his branch home
between the heavy planks and the post, snatched a
quick breath, and threw his shoulder into prying.

The nails were well rusted. The ones nearest the
oak branch groaned and loosened, while the others stubbornly stuck fast. Dry, weathered wood
resisted the strain with a crack. The stallion could
not help but be drawn by the noise. Horses were
curious by nature, Trionn knew; he desperately
shoved all the harder, digging his toes into dew
drenched grass to keep his stance from slipping.
At best he had a space of seconds before the stud
cried challenge. His neigh would draw the Lord's
riders. Did they catch the scullion at his meddling,

they would kill him, cut him down without trial as a horse thief.

Never mind that the stud was a rogue, and the only one wronged might be the kennelman. Luck might sour for him, since as a runaway, the dun was as likely to be slain on some other noble's demesne, with the carcass claimed as spoils in compensation. The kennelman would beat any scullion till he bled, when he learned who had cheated him of fare for his hounds.

Trionn jammed his hip into the prybar until sweat stung his eyes like tears. "Go," he grunted to the groaning, giving nails. "Go!"

The rusted steel proved oblivious to pleading; heavy oak might split, but resisted breakage. Trionn thumped his fist on the gate in frustration, then set his branch to the base of the panel and hurled himself into fresh effort.

He shoved, his sinews straining in agony. The lower boards gave way in a shower of jagged splinters. Trionn shifted his prybar, any moment anticipating the rapid-fire pounding of hooves, followed up by the bone-cracking punishment of an angry stallion's teeth. He was taking far too long. Every second his struggle lasted wound his nerves to the edge of snapping. Dizzy before he realized he was inadvertently holding his breath, Trionn jerked, dragging the next nails from the post with a force fueled by terror. He needed a rest but dared not pause as he confronted the final plank.

Something bumped his shoulder. Startled, Trionn emitted a yelp that silenced the crickets. His pry branch dropped, thudding into the ground. The stud shied back on his haunches with a snort.

Horse and boy regarded one another, each one poised to run.

Trionn licked his lips. Panic held him rooted

before the gapped boards of the gate. His thoughts raced with his heartbeat. Should he bend to retrieve his branch, the stud would strike and kill him; turn and flee, and he risked a ripping bite that would cripple him for life. Should he escape with the gate just half broken, his resolve would end in bleak failure.

The dun stud stamped in the starlight. His ears flicked and he shook his neck, his mane spattered like ink down his crest. He snorted again and took a tentative, interested step forward.

Trionn watched, paralyzed, as the horse shoved the loose boards with his head.

"Dear God," the scullion mouthed, astonished. Then his startlement faded as he noticed the horse's manner held no fury. A charged, unnatural shudder left him trembling to the soles of his feet.

The stallion shouldered his neck between the gap and snuffled the sleeve of Trionn's shirt. He lipped the cloth, and snorted again, messily wet in his inquisitveness.

"Dear God," Trionn repeated, this time in a choked off whisper. His every assumption had been wrong. After all, he had not bidden the stud to assert his own savage nature; not a bit. In his colossal, scullion's ignorance, he had done worse, in fact overturned the gypsy woman's spell with a binding entirely his own.

The dun stallion that had been a killer now answered only to him.

Blindly Trionn bent, groping through dew-drench-ed grass for the branch he had dropped in his ter-ror. Shaken to cold sweats, he loosened the final boards of the gate, while the stallion lipped at his hair, and blew gusty breaths in his ear. The huge creature eyed him through tangled strands of fore-lock as the last few nails gave way. Trionn yanked down the battered boards. "Go!" he urged, his face averted, that he need not be tormented by the

absolute trust the powerful stallion placed in him.
"Get out of here!"

The stud obliged by standing still.

"They'll kill you!" He waved his hands. "Run!"

A bony head banged his elbow.

"Oh, be off," Trionn cried. He stumbled back in
a flummoxed fit of frustration. Never in his ugliest
nightmare had he thought to guard against an
assault by the mad stallion's friendliness.

Unfazed by human foibles, the horse followed,
his nostrils widened in a companionable snuffle
that stopped just short of a nicker. As briskly as
the boy whose unwitting call had touched him
could back away, the stallion strode after, unhurried, but unshakable in equine determination. Trionn belatedly understood that short of outright
shouting, or a blow to the nose with a stick, nothing would drive the stud from him. The noise of
his outcry would certainly bring investigation
from the riders; and any blow he might strike
would now be an unthinkable betrayal. The horse
was no longer wild, nor tamed to any touch but
Trionn's own. His dilemma over the stallion was
compounded.

Bonded as he was to the horse, it was inconceiv-
able to leave him loose to be hunted and butch-
ered for dogmeat.

Trionn sat in the meadowgrass, glaring morose-
ly at his boots. They were worn at the toes,
unsuited for the miles of wear he was now going
to have to require of them. The already tired
leather would rot off his feet by wintertime, and
where could he steal or beg enough coin to pay
for the stallion's upkeep? Such worries were moot
if he failed to hide such a distinctive and costly
animal from discovery by the Lord's patrols.

The rising moon already glimmered through the
trees. No time remained to restore the gate and
formulate a reasonable escape. Shoved again by

a warm nose, then tickled about the ears by the inquisitive stallion's lips, Trionn cursed. The horse raised his head as if puzzled.

"Well, I don't know what to do," Trionn said aloud, more words than he had used in one breath for the better part of a month.

In the end, he settled for walking. The great dun paced at his heels with no more shame than a dog might show, adoring a master who had kicked him.

"You were wild," Trionn accused bitterly. "You liked it that way, remember?"

The horse only snorted, wetting the back of his neck.

The path beyond Silverdown's back thickets stretched away through an expanse of tenant farmland. It was dusty, left rutted from the passage of the costermonger's carts that would rattle to the market before dawn. Now, when the field-hands were sleeping, and most nobles sipped wine in the comfort of candle lit halls, the way was empty, a silvered ribbon twisting away toward lands that Trionn had never dreamed of seeing. He was hungry, tired, and lost outside his corner in the kitchen where the pots and the washtub waited. He brooded as he walked, while the stallion grazed the verges, then trotted between mouthfuls of snatched grass to keep up.

At intervals he would nudge Trionn, or playfully nip at the boy's sleeves. To turn around, even once, was to acknowledge the creature's magnificence. The full impact of what had gone wrong at the moment of the gypsy witch's call left an ache of unconsolable frustration.

"I'm the last person you should trust to look after your fate," Trionn cried, exasperated.

He crossed a plank bridge, the boom of the stallion's hooves at his back a disturbance that shattered the stillness.

A rustle from behind the span, and a half-seen, fitful movement, caused the stallion to a shy back. He arched his neck, ears flattened, then feinted with bared teeth toward what he saw as a threat. Startled silly, Trionn gaped as what looked like a bundle of rags extricated itself from the undergrowth.

The moonlight revealed a small woman, her manner decidedly vexed. "By my mother's blood! It was you who turned my call!" The fury on her oval face was justified. "Why in hell's name did you do it, boy? My reputation's thoroughly ruined."

The stallion screamed and struck. Quicker than he by a hairsbreadth, the gypsy hopped the rails of the bridge, still carping. "Call him off, idiot. Before we're noticed, and find ourselves cut down for stealing."

Mistrustful of words, Trionn gave a shrug, palms up.

The woman snapped back an obscenity in the gypsy language of the hills. "You've got uncommonly strong talent, for a boy who doesn't have the faintest idea what he's doing." Her acid commentary cut off as she ducked beneath the bridge to avoid the enraged stallion's strike. As teeth lunged for her wrist, she dropped out of reach and landed mid-stream with a splash.

"Lay your hand on him," she instructed, annoyed as if she had just turned her ankle on a stone. "The horse will feel your touch, and sense through you that I mean no harm."

Trionn feared to approach the whirling mass of equine nerve and muscle that could, and had, killed men outright. But the clatter as the horse rampaged across the bridge span demanded immediate reaction. He steeled his nerve, reached out, and was startled yet again as the stallion anticipated his movement, and seemed at one with his intent. The creature settled back on all fours, curved his neck, and lipped at Trionn's fingers.

From the far side of the bridge, bedraggled and wringing wet, the gypsy woman shouldered out of the briars on the river bank. She regarded the mismatched tableau presented by the awkward, diffident boy and a stallion bred to carry princes. Her eyes turned absorbed and thoughtful, while the moonlight glinted off the water that dripped from her rags like a fall of thrown diamonds.

"You're exceptionally gifted with animals," she mused. "I expect you also know how to ride?"

Trionn cast her a look of mortified affront, and the stallion snorted warning in concert.

The gypsy witch shook her head, and busied herself wringing muddy water from her skirts. She sighed at last and straightened. Trionn received a long look that chilled his flesh, and set his knees to trembling.

A gypsy horse-caller's spells could be used on more than a beast; her voice when she finally spoke held a whetted edge of threat. "If you never dreamed of owning this horse, of riding him, why in the name of the mysteries did you wrest him from my control?"

Trionn swallowed. There would be no running away from her; he must force his throat to loosen, and his tongue to shape coherent speech. "I didn't," he blurted clumsily. "I wanted the stallion to stay wild." And unbidden, the tears started, born of shame, that he, and the last person living to crave dominion, had been the one to spoil the stallion's fiery independence.

"My mother's blood!" the gypsy swore in a voice that cracked into laughter. "You've a gift to out-match mine, and you thought to stay a simple scullion? I suppose the cats jumped into your cradle since the moment of your birth, and nobody knew what that meant?"

Trionn nodded. He swallowed again, painfully. "I hate myself. For breaking the stallion's spirit."

The gypsy gave another breathless laugh. "You didn't. Not at all." Her brusqueness was intended to reassure, but caused Trionn a start of alarm. Dropping handfuls of wet hems, she sat down in the dust by the roadside, and rested her pointed chin in delicate, almost elfin hands. "Boy, listen to me carefully. You did not harm that horse. What you did was bond with him. He is now your best friend, and more. He is twinned to your thoughts. I will teach you what that means, but for now you must understand. You called, and he answered entirely of his own will. His wildness was won over by your depth of compassion, and that was no mean feat. Believe me in this, for I know. I also touched that horse, and the distrust in his heart was buried deep. You bested my skills through no mistake. That stud was listening for your voice to command him from the moment he was first foaled."

"But I don't understand how that happened!" Trionn cried in rising unhappiness. "And I felt your call! It was painful!"

The gypsy shouted back, "Hurtful to you, boy, because it was not pitched for your spirit!" Her manner suddenly gentled. "I know you're confused. But what counts this minute, is that the Lord of Silverdown will not pardon either of us if we're caught. He will find his rogue stallion gone, and believe that I accomplished the task I was bidden to. The dun's attack upon me in the meadow will be taken for a witch's trick, arranged to cover my escape. You must understand what you've caused, boy. I'll be blamed for the stud you called, and be hunted and hanged as a horse thief."

She did not exaggerate. Too well Trionn recalled the horsebreaker's warning to Silverdown's

Lord, that were he to summon a gypsy, the stallion he desired to break would be stolen the first night after gentling. Awkwardly the scullion locked his fingers in the warmth of the horse's mane. "What's to be done? I know nothing at all beyond pot washing."

The gypsy caller sighed. "I'll become accomplice to a horse thief, after all." She shrugged, rose, and gave another of her silvery laughs. "The hangman might as well find me guilty. Still, my skills should be enough to turn the Lord's riders awry. With luck, I can hide all three of us. But I have a condition to set." She regarded the scullion and his unlikely companion, a horse so nobly proportioned, that men might try murder to possess him.

Trionn looked warily back, never before conscious of how tiny she was, and how determined. Even clad in drenched rags, she had the poised tension of a wild thing, or an owl in the moment before flight. For the first time he could recall, words came easily in the presence of another human being. "What do you ask?"

"That you learn to ride, because we're going to need to travel faster and farther than either of us can go on foot." At Trionn's scowl, she bore unmercifully on. "And you must swear to stay with me until such time as you can marshal the talent you were born to."

"That's two things," Trionn pointed out.

At his shoulder the stallion stamped.

The gypsy woman caught his eyes and compelled him to hold her gaze. "Is it yes?"

And the boy who was destined to be other than Silverdown's scullion bit his lip. Haltingly he gave his oath. When he finished, he added vehemently. "I am *not* a horse thief!"

To which the gypsy witch laughed as she hurried

him on down the road. "As you wish, boy, but face fact. That's what your gifts make you best at."

The stallion's disappearance was years in the past, and forgotten by all but a few when the stranger arrived at Silverdown. He came to the gates just past dusk, clad in a dark dusty cloak. To the watchman who called him challenge, he gave no name. He insisted, quietly firm, that he had business with Silverdown's Lord.

"Lady," corrected the guardsman, his chin out-thrust over the pole of his halberd. "Have you no news of the folk you've traveled to visit? The Lord's been dead these five years, and his wife and one son survive him."

The stranger bowed in apology. He did not appear to be a brigand. Nor could he be mistaken for a beggar out to win a meal. He waited in the twilight with his head cocked, as if the palisade and stone gate keep were a surprise he had not expected. The buttons on his cloak were silver. He journeyed on foot by choice: at his shoulder stood a magnificent silver-dun stallion, bridless, halterless, saddleless. Muscled and shining like high-gloss silver, the creature had the fire of a warhorse, but with significant difference. He followed the man without restraint, apparently of his own free will. Dark, equine eyes regarded the gatekeeper, who studied the horse-master in turn with searching distrust. Yet the man carried no war gear. He was, in point of fact, unarmed.

"Let me speak with the Lady, then," the stranger insisted. The timber of his voice was persuasive, if not impossible to deny. "I will take but a minute of her time, and need not ask lodging for the night."

Much against his orders and inclination, the guard grudgingly opened the gate. The stranger strode inside. Without any visible signal, the horse flanked him stride for stride.

The pair reached the courtyard, where a tabby cat leapt up from cleaning itself. One glance at the stranger, and it fled with flattened ears and streaming tail. The stable boy who came to tend the horse was waved back.

"He will stand," insisted the man in the same voice that had placated the gate guard.

The stallion remained at liberty in the courtyard, obedient to the letter of command while his master pursued his business inside the keep. Beyond the occasional switch of his black tail, the creature might have been a statue. He raised no hoof, but laid back warning ears at the stableboys who ventured too close in admiration, and the old, half-blind master at arms whispered behind his scarred hand that despite the silver buttons on his cloak, the visitor must have a taint of gypsy blood. "At least, that stallion shows a witch's touch for a surety."

"But he had light hair," objected Enith, grown blowsy through the years since she had claimed distinction as the captain's latest conquest. "The man didn't look to me like any gypsy!"

Still regarding the horse, as if he were pricked by a memory just beyond grasp of his awareness, the armsmaster gestured in contempt. "You would see as much or as little as that man allowed, for such is the nature of his sorcery."

The discussion heated into argument, as darkness deepened over a yard left sadly gloomy by the utter absence of torchlight.

Upstairs in the hall, before trestles more scarred than he remembered, the stranger paused in the flickering firelight that spilled across the floor before the hearth. On boards scraped bare of wax or polish, he bowed in respect to the Lady. The dimness, or maybe his economy of movement made him seem at one with the shadows as he lifted a pouch from the crook of his elbow. This he placed with a clink on the table beside the embroidery she had abandoned since the last daylight had fled. He did not comment on the dearth of candles as he said, "This belongs to you."

The Lady's silk-dark eyebrows arched up. "I beg your pardon, sir? My Lord left debts, not debtors, or none that he mentioned at his death."

"This one he must have forgotten," the strange man corrected most gently. "Let me offer my condolences on your husband's passing, though we were never friends. His heir is the proper recipient. The coin in that purse is Silverdown's gold."

"Might I know what service was rendered to require such generous payment?" Piqued to curiosity, the Lady leaned forward enough that the firelight touched her. She locked trembling hands in her lap, though the gesture failed to conceal the calluses that marred her fine skin. Silverdown had fallen on hard times and yet, even as her straits were exposed to the eyes of her visitor, she did not snatch up the pouch. As if need did not demand that she count the money inside, though the fringes of her shawl were dark with tarnish, and her dress had been embroidered at the bodice to hide its past history as a cast off. Poor as Silverdown's Lady might be, her bearing never deserted her.

She carried herself regally as a queen.

Her presence was forceful enough that the stranger stood as if tongue-tied, betraying awkwardness before high-born grace. Or perhaps his diffidence stemmed from reluctance to reveal an unpleasantness between himself and the late Lord, whom very few folk had cause to love. In a musical softness that somehow did not convey the impression of grudging character, he said, "Mark the entry in your ledger as stud fees, and back payment for the purchase of a horse."

"I don't understand," said the Lady. "My Lord never stood any stallions."

Something about her smallness stirred recognition, or maybe her careworn, homely face made him ask, "Are you the Earl of Tanemar's daughter?"

Startled to an intake of breath, she admitted, "I am." Since her father had fallen out of favor with the King, not many cared to mention his name with kindness.

"Then," said the stranger in sweet courtesy, "Ask his grace the Duke of the blue-dun stud he was promised as a gift when your late Lord aspired to become your bridegroom."

The Lady glanced aside too quickly. "I can't," she admitted after a difficult pause. "My father has been imprisoned. The fine to secure his freedom is more than my brother or I have in our powers to pay."

But politics and the feuding of the highborn lay outside this stranger's concern. His silence grew prolonged. When the Lady at last sought to prompt him, she discovered the chamber left empty. Her elusive visitor had departed. Only the pouch on the table remained as proof of his presence.

The coins inside were heavy gold, and the full count of them, a miracle. When the Silverdown's ancient steward checked on his mistress hours later, he found the Lady silently weeping. A shining spill of coins lay in her lap, and in sparkling piles around her feet.

Months later, Silverdown's Lady did the stranger's bidding for more reason than to ease her curiosity. She did not inquire of her father, for the Duke became irritable at reminder that Silverdown's gold had bought his reprieve from the King. The tale was recounted by the butcher, of a man-killing stallion that had been stolen on the same night as a scullion, mistakenly called dumb, and a half-wit, had disappeared without trace from the estate.

"He was a shirker, a sneak, and a liar, too," the butcher vehemently summed up.

The Lady frowned. "I thought you said he could not speak?"

"Well, not entirely," the butcher allowed. He stroked his unshaven chin. "Trionn never talked to anybody, a queer enough habit to have. He wasn't the sort to care about repayment of a debt. He stole my best blade, you know, the same day he took off with the stallion."

The Lady tucked a fallen strand of hair underneath the edge of her hood. "You got the knife back?" she asked outright.

The butcher shrugged, then nodded. "One of the servants caught him crossing the open yard. He never said what he'd intended to do with it," this last, on a note of self-defense.

Silverdown's lady gave back no reproach beyond a sigh. "From the look on your face, I'd expect that nobody ever asked him." She reflected a moment on the gold, the value of which added up to a surprising fortune. The man who had repaid the coin, and then gone his way after scarcely a dozen words, had left wealth enough to buy out the estate and its lands, twice over; the irony of that raised a mystery. As if the fortune itself had been the pittance, and the principle behind, the tie to conscience. "If I were to guess," the Lady ventured, "I should say that none of you knew the boy."

The butcher's only answer was a mutter that may have masked contempt.

Alone in the cut of the wind through the yard, the Lady huddled into her cloak. Fiercely, and for the rest of her days, she regretted her well-bred restraint. Too late she wished she had asked the strange visitor to stay, or at least to take a light supper. He may not have been comfortable telling about himself, but perhaps she might have learned more about the horse that had restored her to fortune and future.

DAW

Now in HARDCOVER

WINDS OF FATE
Book One of The Mage Winds
by Mercedes Lackey

The kingdom of Valdemar: a land protected by the Heralds—men and women gifted with extraordinary mind powers and paired with wondrous Companions, horselike beings who know of the many perils and possibilities of magic. Only the Companions truly remember the long-ago age when high magic was lost to Valdemar as the last Herald-Mage gave his life to save the kingdom from destruction by dark sorceries. Yet now the realm is once again at risk, for Ancar of Hardorn will use every weapon at his command to conquer Valdemar. And it is Elspeth, Herald and heir to the throne, who must take up Ancar's challenge, abandoning her home to find a mentor who can awaken her untrained mage abilities. But even as Elspeth sets out in search of the forgotten magic that could prove to be Valdemar's best hope, others, too, are being caught up in a war against sorcerous evil. The Tayledras scout Darkwind is the first to stumble across a menace that is creeping forth from the uncleansed lands. And as sorcery begins to take its toll among his comrades, Darkwind may find himself forced to call upon powers he has sworn never to use again if he and his people are to survive the onslaught of an enemy able to wreak greater devastation with spells of destruction than with swords. . . .

☐ **Hardcover Edition** (UE2489—$18.95)
